Joe pulled her close again and they crossed the street to her house.

She handed him the key to her door. "You know, I think it's safer for you if I stay at your house until we find Bailey Heath."

He slid her jacket off her shoulders and Laura turned to look at him, smiling. "Oh, yeah? And is some psychopath stalker the only reason you're interested in staying here?"

He hung her jacket on the back of the dining room chair and soon his followed suit. He turned his gaze on her. It could be called nothing less than predatory.

Everything inside her heated at the look in his eyes.

"Are you saying you might be interested in something other than me being your bodyguard?" He took a step closer.

"I'm pretty sure there's something I'd like you to do with my body, but guard it isn't what I had in mind." She gripped the waistband of his jeans and pulled him closer. She took a step back until her spine was fully up against the door.

He was everythin̶ ̶ ̶ ̶ ̶ ̶ ̶ ̶s
every

OVERWHELMING FORCE

BY
JANIE CROUCH

First Published in Great Britain 2016
By Mills & Boon, an imprint of HarperCollins*Publishers*
1 London Bridge Street, London, SE1 9GF

© 2016 Janie Crouch

ISBN: 978-0-263-91926-4

46-1216

Our policy is to use papers that are natural, renewable and recyclable products and made from wood grown in sustainable forests. The logging and manufacturing processes conform to the legal environmental regulations of the country of origin.

Printed and bound in Spain
by CPI, Barcelona

LONDON BOROUGH OF WANDSWORTH	
9030 00005 3017 3	
Askews & Holts	14-Nov-2016
AF ROM	£5.99
	WW16011506

Janie Crouch has loved to read romance her whole life. She cut her teeth on Mills & Boon Romance novels as a preteen, then moved on to a passion for romantic suspense as an adult. Janie lives with her husband and four children overseas. She enjoys traveling, long-distance running, movie watching, knitting and adventure/obstacle racing. You can find out more about her at www.janiecrouch.com.

To Allison, my editor. You gave me my first shot and I'll forever be grateful. Here we are, ten books later, and you still haven't gotten a restraining order against me yet. I'll consider that a win.
Thank you for all you do.

Chapter One

She'd watched him for a year.

She'd traveled all over the country going wherever he went. Others might call it pathetic, but she didn't think so. Besides, what else did she have to do since he'd taken everything from her?

Joe Matarazzo had cost her the man she'd loved. Losing everything after that—her job, her friends, her home—had been his fault, too. Joe Matarazzo had cost her the future.

So now she journeyed around and watched him. Or when she couldn't travel she scoured the internet for information about him.

Whenever she heard his name on a police scanner she prepared to rush to the scene. She had no doubt he would save the day once again.

Why couldn't he have saved the day when it had mattered the most?

Fire had taken the man she loved. Joe Matarazzo could have stopped it, but he hadn't. Hadn't tried hard enough, not like he would today. Not like how hard she'd seen him try in all his other successful situations. He had the most important job: rescuing those who couldn't rescue themselves. Leading them to safety. Putting their lives before his own.

But he hadn't done his job a year ago. Almost exactly a year ago now. On that day he hadn't tried hard enough. Hadn't cared enough about those he tried to help.

Since that time she had observed him, followed him, studied him. She knew everything about him. Because of that, she could say with a clear conscience that he was guilty.

The time had come for Joe Matarazzo to atone for his wrongdoings. To suffer for the lives he'd lost.

He'd paid no price for what he'd done. Instead, he had women, he had money, he had everything. But soon that would change. She would see to it.

First, Joe would fall. And as he did, he would know the pain of losing what he cared about most.

Then he would burn.

Just like the fire that had taken her love.

"CASANOVA HAS STRUCK AGAIN. I know it's hard, fellas— don't be jealous just because Joe Matarazzo looks better on your girl than her outfit."

Joe rolled his eyes and tried to snatch the newspaper clipping out of Derek Waterman's—Joe's Omega Sector Critical Response Division colleague—hands. Derek shifted slightly, holding the paper just beyond Joe's reach since they were both strapped into the bench seat of the twin-engine helicopter.

Who even read a physical newspaper anymore? Joe hadn't looked at a news report that wasn't on his smartphone or computer for years. Not that his dating life was *news*, print version or otherwise.

Joe had no idea why so many people would want to read about his love life. Yeah, his family had money—a lot of it—and yeah, he'd grown up with some Hollywood A-listers and ended up photographed a lot.

And yeah—he grinned just a little, glancing out the helicopter's window as Derek continued to read and the seventy miles between Colorado Springs and Denver whirled past—Joe tended to be a bit of a bad boy. Had a reputation with the ladies.

So what? He liked women.

"The lady du jour was Natasha Suzanne Bleat, daughter of British diplomat Marcus Bleat..."

Joe tuned out as Derek read Natasha's impressive list of family credentials through the headphones that allowed all of them to communicate with each other. Jon Hatton and Lillian Muir—the first an Omega profiler and the second Omega SWAT like Derek—listened raptly from the pilot and copilot seats where Lillian controlled the aircraft.

Seriously, Joe's colleagues loved this stuff, ridiculous as it may be. They had a whole scrapbook full of Joe's clippings.

Joe had grown up with press and had learned to pretty much ignore it. The press had their own agenda and nobody's best interests in mind but theirs. He learned that lesson a little too late, but learned it.

And it wasn't like paparazzi followed him around. Yet for whatever reason, gossip sites and society pages loved to report on his dating life. A dating life he had to admit was pretty extensive. Everyone called him Casanova. The press and even his colleagues at Omega.

Joe wasn't offended. It took a hell of a lot more to offend him.

"...the redhead beauty was last seen entering the Los Angeles Four Seasons with Joe, arm in arm."

Joe raised his gaze heavenward with a long-suffering sigh and waited for the rest, but that was it.

"Last seen?" Joe finally succeeded in snatching the

paper away from Derek. "They make it sound like I killed her and hid her body."

"Oh, it sounds like you did something to her body, but I don't think anyone figures you killed her. At least not literally." Lillian snickered from her pilot's seat.

"I have no idea how you get so lucky, dude." Derek closed his eyes and leaned farther back on the bench seat next to Joe. "No matter what city we're in, the women throw themselves at you."

Joe could've pointed out that speeding their way to a hostage negotiation scene was probably not the time to discuss the press version of his love life. But he knew this sort of distraction helped keep the team loose and relaxed.

There would be plenty of time for tension and focus when they landed and assessed the scene.

Joe shrugged. "What can I say? I'm #blessed, man." He made the hashtag symbol with his hands, tapping his fingers together.

Everyone groaned.

"Don't make me shoot you. I'd catch flack for shooting an unarmed man." Derek didn't open his eyes as he said it.

Joe was the only unarmed person in the helicopter. Although he was trained in the use of a number of weapons, he almost always went into situations unarmed.

He was Omega Sector's top hostage negotiator. And he was damn good at his job.

Joseph Gregory Terrance Matarazzo III didn't need a career. At least, didn't need one for a salary. He'd been born with money, had known its benefits his entire life. Had used those benefits for a carefree, fun-loving existence until about six years ago when he'd turned twenty-five and decided maybe he'd like to do something with his time besides sit around and look good.

The laid-back, playboy, slacker and media darling had decided to become a better man.

Joe had skills. Not the same skills Derek had in his ability to formulate the best tactical advantage in any given hostile situation. Or the ones Lillian had with the many ways she could kill someone not only through the use of weapons, but just her scary, tiny, bare hands. Or Hatton with whatever he did, which was pretty much overthink everything and come up with scenarios and means of handling crises.

Joe's skills rested with people. He had a charming way with others. He knew it. Everybody knew it. Joe excelled at talking to people, listening to them, making them feel comfortable. He was likable, a cool kid. The type of person people wanted to be around.

It wasn't an act. Joe honestly cared about people, even the hostage-takers he was sent to talk to. So he tried his damnedest to connect with the people in these situations, to listen to them and see what he could do so everyone could leave the situation alive. If Joe did his job right, nobody had to get hurt.

If he didn't do his job right, the Dereks and Lillians with the guns came in with a different solution.

Most of the time Joe successfully completed his mission and nobody was harmed. Sometimes there was no other way and the bad guys got wounded or worse. Joe was trained—and wasn't hesitant—to make the hard call when he knew he wasn't going to be able to neutralize the situation and SWAT needed to step in and take the tangos out. That situation wasn't Joe's preference, but he didn't lose sleep when it happened.

Every once in a while something went terribly wrong and innocent people got hurt. Joe touched a burn scar at the base of his neck, one that continued over his shoulder and partway down his back. Innocent people had been hurt that day a year ago. Innocent people had died.

Joe planned to use his skills today to make sure another situation like that didn't happen again.

Derek and Jon began arguing over the name of the woman the press had spotted Joe with a few days before Natasha during an Omega case in Austin, Texas.

"Her name was Kerri. I'm telling you." Jon's voice came crisply through the headphones. "Kerri with an *i*. I remember it clear as day."

"No," Derek said. "That was the one before. Austin was Kelli. But also with an *i*."

Joe wondered what Derek's brilliant wife, Molly, the crime lab director at Omega, and Jon's fiancée, Sherry Mitchell, a hugely talented forensic artist, would have to say about their men's topic of conversation.

No doubt they would find it as ridiculous as Joe did.

Joe remembered both Kerri and Kelli. He'd had dinner with one, a drink at a bar with the other. Nothing more. Just like the night at the hotel with Natasha when Joe had walked her, admittedly arm in arm, to her room. And left her there.

Because, hell, nobody could be as much of a Casanova as the press wanted to label him. God knew he wasn't a monk, but sometimes the women he was with were just pleasant company—clothes *on*—and nothing more.

But Joe hated to deny his colleagues their fun.

"Would you like me to settle this, boys?" he asked, sighing.

"For the love of all that is holy, please yes, Matarazzo, settle this." Lillian's higher voice cut through the baritone of the three men.

"You're both wrong. It was Kerri *and* Kelli. Both of them in Austin. *Together*." Joe smiled as he told the lie.

If they wanted Casanova he would give it to them. He knew he probably shouldn't since it reinforced what his colleagues already thought to be the truth about him: that he was less part of the Omega team and more like a novelty. But Joe was great at figuring out what people needed and becoming that, at least for a little while. A distraction en route to a troublesome situation? No problem.

Hatton and Derek both groaned, neither knowing whether to believe him.

"I'm going to check some of the gossip sites when I get back to HQ," Hatton threatened.

"You do that," Joe responded. "Because you know everything they publish can be taken as gospel."

Silence fell as they flew the last few miles and Lillian landed the helicopter on the roof helipad of a building that had been cleared two blocks from First National Bank of South Denver. Temporary home of two bad guys and a dozen or so hostages.

Lillian landed and switched off the rotors. "Time to go to work, boys."

Joe slid the door open and he and Derek both ducked their heads and briskly made their way down the stairs, out of the building and over to the bank. Jon quickly joined them as they found the officer in charge. Lillian would be there after she took care of the helicopter. Jokes and talk about Joe's exploits ceased. Omega now had a job to do.

The older man shook everyone's hand. "I'm Sheriff Richardson. We appreciate you coming out so quickly."

"We need the most up-to-date intel you have," Derek told the sheriff. Joe was glad the locals had called Omega and egos hadn't come into play. Situations like this tended to be delicate enough without law enforcement working against each other.

Richardson nodded. "We have two men in their midtwenties holding, as best as we can tell, sixteen people hostage inside the bank. Two of those hostages are children. They've been inside for two hours and we haven't been able to speak with them, despite trying multiple times."

Richardson turned from Derek to Joe. "You're the negotiator, right? The city has a good one of our own, but she had a baby a couple of days ago. She was still going to come in but I put a stop to that immediately."

Joe nodded. "That was the right decision. I won't let you down, Sheriff. I'll do my very best to get everyone out safely."

"Do you have building plans for the bank, Sheriff?" Derek asked.

"Yes." He gestured over to a younger man who brought them over. Lillian joined them, and she, Derek and Hatton were soon poring over the plans.

Joe took a deep breath, looking out at the small bank. He couldn't see anything happening inside. The Denver County police didn't have a sizable SWAT team, but it did appear like they had a couple of marksmen. He knew Derek and Lillian were both expert sharpshooters also.

He hoped it wouldn't come to that.

Why were the hostage-takers here at this particular bank? Had they tried to rob it then got stuck so took hostages? Robbing a bank wasn't a very smart move and didn't have a high success rate, but people did desperate things sometimes.

There were kids inside. That upped the ante a lot. Joe's natural inclination was to march up to the door right now, even without backup. But he knew to set wheels in motion before Derek and the team were ready could spell disaster for everyone.

"Derek, there are kids, man," Joe said softly. He knew he didn't have to remind his friend of that—with his pregnant wife, it would be in the forefront of Derek's mind, too—but couldn't help himself. "They've already been in there a long time. Let me know which direction you'll be coming from if it goes south and I'll get started. At least get the kids out."

"There's not a lot of good options with a bank this old that was built in the fifties," Derek muttered, studying the plans more intently. "It looks like the roof will be our best bet. Probably a ventilation shaft. We might have to send Lillian through alone if it's too small."

Lillian alone would be plenty enough to put down two tangos. Joe nodded at her; she winked at him. Despite her beauty, he had never tried to make a move on her. He knew better than to hit on a woman who made a living shooting people.

"Okay," Joe said. "What's today's go-signal?"

The team always had a phrase and action, both meant only to be used as a last resort, that Joe could use to signal SWAT that the situation inside was out of hand and they needed to use deadly force.

"Word is *sunglasses*." Derek glanced up from the plans. "Action is putting your sunglasses on your head."

Joe's shades were in the pocket of his shirt. Unlike the other Omega members, all wearing full combat gear and bulletproof vests, Joe was wearing a black T-shirt, jeans and casual brown boots. It was important that he seem as normal and nonthreatening as possible when he approached the hostage-takers.

"Be careful in there, Joe." It was Jon who looked up from the building plans this time. "We've got a lot of blinds here. I know you're good on the fly, but watch your six."

Joe nodded, already beginning to walk toward the building. "Those kids and their mother will be coming out first. Be ready for them."

He blew out a breath through gritted teeth, forcing his shoulders then jaw to relax. Coming in tense—or at least looking overly tense—never helped. There were two guys in there who needed to be heard. Joe wanted to do that. But even more he wanted to get the hostages out safely. Every one of them.

Joe walked up to the glass door of the bank and knocked, then held his hands up in a position of surrender so they could see he wasn't armed. And he waited.

He was about to become best buddies with two potentially dangerous guys.

Just another day at the office for Joe Matarazzo.

Chapter Two

Laura Birchwood should've sent her assistant to the bank to get these stupid papers signed.

But *no*, Laura had wanted to get out of the office, get some nice fresh air on this relatively warm, sunny April day in Colorado. It had been a long, cold winter and it had snowed even as late as a week and a half ago.

So when it had been in the upper 60s on a late Friday afternoon and her Colorado Springs law office—Coach, Birchwood and Winchley, LLP—had needed the signature of a bank manger here on the outskirts of Denver, Laura had offered to make the trip herself. Her assistant had Friday night plans; Laura didn't. Laura decided she would have dinner in Denver while she was here. She'd be by herself, but that wasn't anything unusual.

The two guys pacing frantically with big guns, stopping every once in a while to wave them around and scare the people sitting on the bank floor, were going to ruin her dinner plans.

As pathetic as the plans were.

Laura refused to let herself panic, even when the guys glanced over in her direction. Hysteria wasn't going to help anything in this situation; as a matter of fact, she was pretty sure the hostage-takers would just feed off it and become more aggravated.

"I have to get them out of here," Brooke, the young mother sitting next to Laura, whispered. "They're going to get hungry soon. Get upset."

She referred to the two girls the mom had with her, a baby maybe eight or nine months, not old enough yet to be crawling, thank goodness, and a five-year-old. Both had done remarkably well so far. Brooke herself had done great. She'd fed the baby a bottle and given the older girl, Samantha, a box of crayons and a coloring book she'd had in her diaper bag.

Most of all she'd stayed calm. Her daughters had picked up on their mother's cues and had also stayed calm. Laura wasn't even sure Samantha really understood what was happening.

"Police will be coming, Brooke," Laura whispered to her. "I have a packet of peanut butter crackers in my purse for Samantha. That will buy us some time."

"I need to make another bottle." Brooke gestured to the baby currently sitting in her lap, playing with some teething toys. "And I know her diaper is wet. I'm going to have to talk to them."

"No, I'll talk to them—"

Laura flinched as one of the two men, the loud one, let out a loud string of obscenities. "Shut up over there!" he yelled, pacing more wildly.

Samantha looked up from her coloring. "He said a bad word," she whispered to Laura.

He'd said a bunch of them. Laura wasn't sure which one the girl meant.

"You're not supposed to say *shut up*," Samantha stated primly, then went back to her coloring.

Laura couldn't help but smile. It was nice to meet a kid whose definition of foul language revolved around the words *shut up*.

She had to get Brooke and her two beautiful daughters out of here. She knew drawing the men's attention to her by asking them to release Brooke and the girls could be dangerous. Laura had no idea what the men wanted. To be honest she wasn't even sure these men knew exactly what they wanted.

The local police had tried calling the bank. The men had made the employees unplug all the phones and then had hit the assistant manager on the head with their gun. The man was conscious but still had blood oozing down the side of his face. They'd forced everyone to put their cell phones in a trash can and placed it in the middle of the room.

If the robbers decided to start killing hostages, Laura didn't want to put herself at the front of the line. But she sure as hell wasn't going to let Brooke do it. And now that there was no way the police could contact the men to see what they wanted, Laura didn't know how the police could help.

She reached over and squeezed Brooke's hand.

"Laura, wait, don't—"

Laura was standing up when a knock on the bank's front door suddenly drew everyone's attention. She didn't have a good angle to take in the whole scene but could see the upheld arms of a man standing there. She quickly sat back down.

The robbers went ballistic.

"Who are you? What do you want?" one screamed at the person at the door, voice shrill.

"We'll kill everyone in here. Every last one of them. Get away!"

The man outside didn't move except to gesture to them to unlock the door.

The two men began frantically talking between themselves. Laura couldn't hear all of it, but knew one of the men at least understood that the man at the door was a hostage negotiator.

Hopefully the guy was a good one.

Finally the two men broke apart from their huddle. The negotiator was still standing arms upstretched by the entrance. Laura still couldn't see his face.

"You." One of the hostage-takers pointed over to the bank manager. "Get over here and open the door."

The manager got shakily to his feet and walked to the door gathering a large ring of keys from his pocket. The robber got behind him, using the man as a human shield, and put the gun directly to the manager's temple.

The baby started fussing and Laura reached over to hold her so Brooke could get out another bottle. Plus, if bullets started flying Brooke could grab Samantha and Laura could try to protect the baby.

"You better pray that this guy doesn't try anything. Because you'll be dead before you hit the floor if he does. Open it just a crack," the man holding the manager said.

The manager nodded as he put the key in the door. Rivers of sweat rolled down his face. The room remained silent.

"P-please don't do anything," the manager said to the man outside. "He'll kill me if you do anything."

"Nah, no plans to do anything to make anybody nervous." The negotiator's voice was clear and friendly. And oddly familiar to Laura. "I swear to you all, I am unarmed and just here to talk. To see what we can work out. To find a solution where all of us get out of here without getting hurt."

"How do I know you're not armed?" the robber yelled from behind the manager, keeping his head down.

"I'm going to reach down now and lift up my shirt

and turn around. You'll see. No weapon at all. No earpiece. Nothing."

She still couldn't see his face, but Laura and the rest of the bank were treated to the sight of rock-solid abs as the man lifted his shirt and turned around slowly. Under any other circumstances Laura would've just enjoyed the view.

"You could have a gun in your pants," the other man said. "An ankle holster or something. We're not stupid."

"No, you're right. You're smart to think of that. Most people wouldn't."

The negotiator was good. He'd already tuned in to what the robbers needed to hear: that they were smart, in control. The man ripped off his shirt and dropped it to the ground.

"I'm going to take off my jeans, okay? Not trying to give anyone a show, but you're smart to check and make sure I really don't have any weapons."

Strong muscular legs came into view as the man kicked off his boots and socks and then took off his jeans. Black boxer briefs were all that was left on the negotiator. Laura sort of hoped the robbers would let him in, not only so he could negotiate them out of this mess, but so she could see his face. Would it be as impressive as the rest of him?

"Miss Laura—" Samantha giggled "—that man only has his underwear on."

Laura smiled. "I know, sweetie. He's silly." She bounced the baby on her legs, thankful she wasn't crying anymore.

"So as you can see," the negotiator continued, "no weapons. Well, *one*, if you know what I mean. But I generally only bring that one out for the ladies." Laura could hear the smile in his voice. "Do you mind if I come in and talk? It's a nice day but still a little chilly out here in just my drawers."

"Fine," the guy behind the bank manager finally said. "Get in here. But if you do anything suspicious at all, I'll start killing people."

The guy grabbed his pile of clothes and quickly squeezed through the door. The manager relocked it and the bad guy got away from the danger of the door and pointed his gun at the negotiator.

Laura could feel her jaw literally drop when she got her first full look at him.

Standing there in his boxer briefs was Joe Matarazzo.

She never thought she would see him again. Had *hoped* she would never see him again. And now it looked like her life was in his hands.

Just went to prove that behind every worst-case scenario, there was a *worse* worst-case scenario.

JOE KNEW HE would never hear the end of this little strip-tease from his Omega colleagues. But he'd been certain he couldn't get into the bank any other way. These two guys were paranoid, frantic. Joe knew immediately he needed to put himself in a position of seeming to be the beta. Let them feel like they were alpha.

Joe's pride, his true feelings, his personality, didn't matter. All that mattered was getting everyone out of the bank safely.

If they had asked him to take off his boxers, he would've done that, too. But he was glad they hadn't.

Joe quickly assessed one half of the bank as he put his jeans back on. The bank manager seemed scared to death and had some bruising on the side of his face—probably took a punch—but otherwise appeared fine. An injured man, also a bank employee, sat propped up against the wall. Looked like he also had received a blow to the side of the face. Bloody, but not life-threatening.

All the bank employees being alive was a good sign. It meant these two guys probably didn't want to hurt anyone. Probably had planned to rob the bank and things had escalated.

No one was dead yet, so that meant there was a very good chance that Joe could get everyone out unharmed.

"I'm Joe, by the way," he told the two men as he pulled his shirt back over his head.

"You expect us to tell you our names so you can get a bunch of information on us? No way, man." Both men had their weapons aimed directly at Joe.

Joe wanted to point out the flaws in their logic: how was he supposed to get any information? He'd just gotten almost naked in front of them so they knew he didn't have any communication devices. And even if he did, what would a bunch of information do versus two very real guns?

But pointing out the logic flaws would only put them more on the defensive.

"No, nothing like that. I was just wondering what to call you."

"You can call me Ricky and him Bobby," the older of the two men said, sneering.

Joe recognized Ricky Bobby. "Yeah, I saw that movie." Joe smiled. "The kids, Walker and Texas Ranger. Hilarious. *Anchorman* was my favorite though."

The men's weapons lowered just the slightest bit. Good. Just keep them thinking about Will Ferrell and movies. Based on their coloring and size, Joe guessed Ricky and Bobby to be brothers.

He turned casually in the opposite direction so he

could see the other half of the bank as he crouched down to put his shoes back on.

There were the kids. Good. A little girl alternating between coloring and watching what was going on and a baby in her mom's lap. Joe glanced at the mom's face to see how she was holding up.

And found the angry eyes of Laura Birchwood.

Joe felt the air leave his lungs.

Man, she hadn't changed at all in the six years since he'd seen her, well, except for the two kids part. She still had wavy brown hair and a face more interesting than it was traditionally pretty. But it was still the face he'd never been able to ever get out of his mind.

The pain that assaulted him at the knowledge that Laura had moved on so completely from him took him by surprise. She obviously had found herself a husband and had a couple of kids, given the cute little baby who bounced on her knees.

After what he'd said to her when their relationship ended, Joe couldn't blame her for moving on. It still hurt like hell though.

Joe stood from putting on his boots and looked at the two men. He needed to focus.

"Ricky, Bobby, I want to help you guys. They sent me in here to figure out what we can do to work this out peaceful-like." He carefully didn't use the word *cops* in case that was some sort of trigger word for the two men "There's nothing that has been done here yet that makes the situation terrible. You guys and I can walk out of here right now and everything can be made right."

That wasn't totally accurate. Ricky and Bobby would be doing some jail time for this little stunt. But it would be much worse if they killed someone. Joe didn't really think they were just going to walk out with him, but it was worth a shot.

"No," Ricky said. "They'll shoot us as soon as we come out. Or at least arrest us."

"Nobody wants to shoot you. I promise you that," Joe quickly interjected. He needed to keep the level of paranoia as low as possible.

"Well, we're not going out there. Not until we have what we need." Bobby looked over at the bank manager.

Okay, so they did want something. Probably money. That was good, something Joe could work with, something he could talk to them about.

Something that provided him leverage.

"That sounds reasonable. Is what you need going to hurt anybody?"

If what they needed was to blow up a bank full of people while the press was watching to make some sort of political or religious statement, then it was going to be time for Joe to pull out the sunglasses to signal SWAT awfully quick. But Ricky and Bobby didn't seem to be the political statement types.

"No," Bobby said. "What we want is ours. We just want it back."

To the side, Joe heard Laura's baby start to cry. He needed to get her and the children out of here. Right now. He couldn't stand the thought of Laura being hurt again. Or especially her innocent children.

Joe had hurt her enough once. Maybe he could begin to make that right by getting her and her family out of danger.

"Alright, I can do that. That's why I was sent in here. To see what it is you need and help find a way to get it for you. That's my only job here, figuring out a way this can end okay for everyone."

Again, that wasn't actually true, but the baby's cries were getting louder. Ricky and Bobby both turned to glare at the child and Joe briefly thought of trying to take both of them down physically himself, but he decided not to risk it. Somebody might get hurt. Plus, it was too early in the negotiation process. If Joe broke their trust now, he would not get it back.

"She's got to shut that kid up," Bobby told Ricky.

"Listen, guys…" Joe took a small step closer so they would turn their attention—and weapons—back on him and away from Laura's side of the room. "I think we can solve a couple of problems here with one action."

"What are you talking about?" Bobby's eyes narrowed.

"Like you said, that baby is a huge headache. Plus the people outside—" Joe again was careful not to call them *law enforcement* or *police* "—would take it as a sign of good faith if you let the kids and their mom go. Works for everyone. You get rid of a screaming baby, and the people outside know you're reasonable. Win/win. You've still got plenty of people left in here for whatever you need to do."

Bobby looked over at his older brother and Ricky finally nodded. Joe felt like a hundred-pound weight had been lifted off his chest. Now, no matter what happened, at least Laura and her kids would be safe.

Keeping his eyes on Ricky and Bobby, Joe motioned for Laura and the kids to come over.

"Get the manager to open the door again," Ricky told him, so Joe turned to the man. The heavyset manager got to his feet and moved to the door.

Joe turned back to reassure Laura as best he could but found another woman taking the baby from her. Clutching the infant in one arm and holding the hand of the little girl in the other, she made her way to Joe.

"You're their mom?" Joe asked. "I thought the other lady was holding the baby."

"She was just helping me," the woman whispered. "Thank you for getting us out."

Joe squeezed her shoulder. "When the door opens, walk straight across the street. Don't stop for anything."

The woman nodded.

"Okay, are we ready?" he asked.

Joe turned to Ricky and Bobby and fought back a shudder when he saw that Bobby now had Laura held right in front of him in a choke hold, gun pointed at her temple.

"If anyone does anything I don't like, I'll put a bullet in her," Bobby said.

Joe ground his teeth. It took quite a lot to get him to lose his cool, but he was finding that a gun to Laura's temple did it very quickly. He forced the anger down. He needed to stay calm.

The manager opened the door and Joe watched as the woman sprinted across the street, the little girl doing her best to keep up. They were safe. He squeezed the shoulder of the bank manager as he relocked the door.

"Thank you for not trying to run," Joe said in a low voice. The man could've taken off when the door was open. Could've saved himself at the cost of other lives. Joe had seen it happen before.

"I couldn't let them kill someone else because of me." The manager rubbed his hands down his pant legs. "But I can't give them what they want. I don't have what they need."

Joe's smile suggested a calm he didn't really feel. "We'll work it out."

Joe finally felt like he could breathe again when Bobby had released Laura and she had sat back down against the wall. She didn't seem to be hurt in any way or even too scared.

As a matter of fact her hazel eyes were all but spitting daggers at Joe. She looked like she might grab Bobby's gun and shoot Joe herself.

Joe winced. Guess she hadn't forgiven him for what he'd said to her six years ago.

He didn't blame her. And he had to admit, as much as he wanted Laura safely out of harm's way, his heart had actually leaped in his chest—seriously, he'd *felt* the adrenaline rush through him—when he realized those children belonged to another woman. Not Laura.

It was time to get this situation resolved so he could move on to more important things. Like talking Laura into dinner with him.

He had a feeling that might take more negotiation skills than even he possessed.

Chapter Three

Joe Matarazzo working in law enforcement. Who would've *ever* figured that would happen? Certainly not Laura.

But she had to admit, he had quite deftly handled the situation in the bank with Ricky and Bobby. They had come there to steal the last remaining copy of their father's will.

Evidently dear old dad had realized what jerks his sons had become and had decided to leave his "fortune" as Ricky and Bobby called it, a sum of just over twelve thousand dollars, to the local 4-H club.

Two grown men had broken into a bank, held sixteen people—including *children*—hostage, and had threatened to kill them all to get a will. A will that ultimately would only get them twelve thousand dollars if they were successful.

The perfect storm of idiocy.

The bank manger hadn't had the other key. Every safe-deposit box needed two keys and the manager only had one. That's when the problem had escalated. Ricky and Bobby thought they could just come in, show some ID and have the box opened. But not without the second key.

Demanding the manager open it by pointing a gun at his head hadn't changed the situation. He still couldn't open it with only his one key.

Somehow Bobby and Ricky just hadn't understood that. They got loud. Someone called the cops and next thing they knew they had a hostage situation on their hands.

Laura had no idea what would've happened if Joe hadn't shown up and defused the situation.

He'd sat down with the two men and the bank manager. The manager swore he would open the safe-deposit box if he could, but that the bank had put security measures in place long ago that required two keys. It's what kept managers from being able to walk in at any time and take anything they wanted from the boxes.

Finally Joe was able to make Ricky and Bobby understand that. He'd then helped them figure out where their dead father's key might be. Explained they needed to surrender so they could come back to the bank another time.

That time was going to be after years in prison, and by then the 4-H club was going to have some pretty nice 4-Hing equipment, or whatever a 4-H club used money for, but Joe had left that part out.

Both men had exited with Joe and had been immediately taken into custody. Everyone inside could hear Ricky and Bobby screaming at Joe, claiming he'd lied about being arrested. Joe hadn't lied, he just hadn't announced all the particulars of the truth. As a lawyer, Laura could appreciate the difference.

Cops and medical workers then rushed into the bank to see who needed help. As they tended to people, Laura watched with a sort of amazed detachment as one of the large air-conditioning grates on a wall about ten feet off the ground moved and a small woman, in full combat gear and rifle, eased her way out, hung as far as her arms would allow her, then dropped to the ground.

She'd been there, probably since not long after Joe

arrived, silently ready to move in if things had gotten desperate.

But they hadn't, thanks to Joe.

The woman had just made a quiet sweep of the area with her eyes then walked out the front door. Most of the people inside didn't even notice her.

A uniformed police officer entered and made an announcement. "People, I'm Sheriff Richardson. Right now we're just trying to ascertain who is injured. If you have any wounds at all, or feel like you're having any chest pains or anything like that, please let us know so we can get a medic to attend to you immediately."

Laura's chest hurt a little bit, but she was pretty sure that was indigestion caused from seeing Joe again.

"Otherwise we ask that you stay in the immediate area of the bank so we can take your statement. Certainly you are free to go outside and get some fresh air. Also to call anyone you need to let them know you're okay. This event will make the supper-time news, for sure, and you won't want any family worrying about you."

Laura doubted her parents or brother would hear about this back in Huntsville, Alabama, but she would text them anyway and let them know she was okay. She would not mention the fact that Joe Matarazzo had gotten her out of the situation safely. Her dad and brother might catch the first flight to Denver and take Joe out themselves.

They'd have to get in line behind her.

The image of Joe stripped down to his boxers and smiling charmingly at the two hostage-taking morons popped into her head unbidden.

Damn, he still looked good. Nothing about that had changed, not that she would've expected it to. His tall, lithe body was absolutely drool-worthy: broad shoulders, hard abs that all but begged you to run your fingers over them, trim hips that eased down into long, strong legs.

And that face. Crystal blue eyes and strong, sharp cheekbones and a chin that gave strength to a face that would've otherwise been too pretty. Brown hair with natural sandy highlights, straight, a little long with a half curl that always fell over his forehead.

And his smile. Joe Matarazzo had a quick, easy smile for everyone. The man loved to smile, and had gorgeous sensuous lips and perfect teeth to back up his propensity.

His cheeks were clean-shaven now, but Laura knew firsthand how quickly the stubble would grow and exactly how the roughness of his cheeks would feel as he kissed her all over her body.

She stopped the thought immediately. For six years she'd been stopping those types of thoughts immediately. Instead she fast-forwarded to the last memory she'd had of Joe. Him standing outside her apartment and telling her their relationship wasn't going to work anymore.

That he'd liked her and all, and the last couple of months had been great, but that, let's face it, she just wasn't the *caliber* of woman someone like Joe—with his money and connections and good looks and charm—would be in a long-term relationship with.

Mic drop. Matarazzo out.

Laura could make those little jokes now, almost without wincing. Six years ago she'd just wanted to crawl under a rock and die. Joe may not have used those actual words, but basically said she wasn't attractive enough for him. Silly her, she'd thought the fact that they'd always had a delightful time together, had the same quirky sense of humor and wonderful conversations had meant something. For the six months they had dated, Joe had led her to believe that he thought it was true, too. Until he just changed his mind out of the blue and ended it.

Not the caliber of woman...

So no, she was not going to let the sight of Joe Matarazzo in just his skivvies get her hot and bothered.

"Um, ma'am?"

Laura looked over at the young police officer who had evidently been trying to get her attention for a few moments.

"Yes?"

"Were you hurt in any way? Perhaps a head injury?" The young officer looked confused.

The only damage to Laura's head was in her thoughts about Joe. "No, I'm fine. Just reliving the situation. It's a little painful." She didn't state which situation.

"Do you feel up to giving me your statement? Otherwise we can have you come down to the station tomorrow."

Laura shook her head. No, she didn't want to have to come back. She gave the officer her statement, telling how Ricky and Bobby entered while she was finishing a meeting with the bank manager to get his signature on some financial paperwork for a client.

If Laura had just beelined it for the door she wouldn't have gotten caught in the hostage mess at all. But then she thought of Brooke and little Samantha and the baby. Laura had been glad she'd been able to help them.

The officer took down Laura's information and told her they'd be in touch if they needed anything else, and that she shouldn't hesitate to contact them if she thought of something more she remembered. She was free to go.

Now all she had to do was make it to her car and get away without having to talk to Joe at all. Not that he'd try to talk to her. After all, what was there left to say?

She supposed she could thank him for doing a good job today and getting them all out alive. She'd been especially impressed at how he'd immediately gotten Brooke and her girls out.

Laura was thankful, but she wasn't willing to actually talk to Joe to tell him that. Maybe she could send the sheriff's office a letter with official thanks. Better. More professional.

She stepped out into the brisk April air of Colorado, closing her eyes and breathing it deep into her lungs. She was alive. She was unhurt. She even had the signature she'd originally come to this bank for. Everything was good.

She opened her eyes and found herself staring directly into the gaze of Joe Matarazzo.

The Rockies in all their stark majesty framed the area behind him. The bright cobalt sky made the perfect matching backdrop for the overwhelming force of his gorgeous blue eyes.

It was ridiculous. Like he was something out of a John Denver song or Bob Ross painting.

"Hey, Laura."

And must the deep timbre of his voice match the sexiness of every other part of his being? Of course. Had God realized he'd given an abnormally large chunk of good genes all to one person? Height, charm, good looks and wealth all wrapped up in one sexy package. Seemed unfair.

"Joe." It was all she could manage.

"It's good to see you. I was thrown off guard for a minute when I spotted you in there."

Laura took a slight step back. He was too close. Anything under a mile was probably too close.

"Well, thanks for getting us out." She waved her arm

like she held a wand. "For doing whatever magic you did and working out the situation so no one got hurt."

Joe shrugged. "Just doing my job."

"Wow, a job?" She tried for light laughter, but it came out tense and brittle. "That's new, right? I didn't think you would ever need a job."

Joe looked over to the side of the bank where the press and bystanders had been roped off. Laura hadn't even realized they were there, but saw dozens of smartphones recording them. Recording everyone coming out of the bank.

"Let's go around to the side, so everything we say doesn't end up online." Joe walked away from the crowd, around a corner, leading Laura with a gentle hand at the small of her back.

She could feel his hand through her blouse as if it seared her. That small touch stole her breath.

And pissed her off.

She didn't want to react this way, didn't want to feel anything when he touched her except maybe disgust. She stepped away from his hand, glad there was now no one else around to witness any of this.

"How have you been? It's been a long time," he said when they were out of earshot of everyone else.

She just stared at him. She wasn't sure what to say. If this was some sort of police follow-up to make sure she was okay, then that was fine. Otherwise she didn't want to make small talk with him as if they were old friends who had just lost touch.

"Seeing you here, like I said, it sort of threw me," he continued. He shifted a little nervously, but his friendly smile never wavered.

"Well, you did great. You were amazing with Ricky and Bobby."

He rolled his eyes. "Wasn't up against mastermind criminals there, that's for sure."

"They still had guns and could've hurt a lot of people. So I'm glad you were able to get them to surrender. Although they seem pretty mad at you for it."

They stared at each other for long moments. Laura felt the flare of attraction she knew was only one-sided and realized she had to get out of here. All the damage repair she'd done over the last six years was crumbling down in mere minutes in Joe's presence.

She took another step back. "I've got to go. I gave my statement to one of the policemen inside the bank, so he cleared me to leave."

His blue eyes seemed to bore into her. She looked away.

"Laura—"

"It was nice talking to you. Glad you seem to have a job you like. Take care, Joe." There. A reasonable, polite statement.

Now get out.

She took another step back and to the side. Her car was around the other corner, but she'd walk around the entire block out of her way if it meant she could make a clean getaway from Joe.

"Laura, let me take you out to dinner tonight."

"No." She knew she was too abrupt, but reasonable, polite statements seemed beyond her now.

Joe put his large hands out, palms up, in an endearing, entreating manner. "Just to catch up. It's been what, six years? It's great to see you."

She shook her head. "I can't."

"Why?" He took a step closer and she immediately took a step back. She had to keep some sort of physical distance from him. "Are you married? In a relationship?"

"No."

The attraction was still there for her. She didn't want it to be, but it was. Laura had done her best not to think about him for the last six years while also having to admit that the man had shaped her life like no one else. Because of him the whole course of her career and even her thought patterns had changed.

One brief, cruel conversation with him six years ago had made her into the woman she was today.

"Then why?"

Was he really asking this? Couldn't figure it out on his own? "I just can't. There's too much…" She almost said *ugliness*, but that reminded her too much of what he'd said to her that night. "There's too much time and distance between us."

Faster than she would've thought possible his hands whipped out and grabbed both of her wrists. He held them gently but firmly. "There's still a spark between us."

Laura's laugh was bitter, unrecognizable to her. She wasn't a bitter person. Even though Joe's words six years ago had shredded her she'd never let herself become bitter, even toward him.

"Spark was never the problem, at least not on my end." She wrenched her arms out of his hands. "The fact that you thought I wasn't attractive enough to be in a relationship with you, *that* was the problem."

Chapter Four

Joe watched Laura hurry down the corridor between the bank and the coffee shop next door then round a corner. He wanted to run after her, to stop her, to explain.

To explain what, exactly? That he'd been a jerk six years ago?

Seemed evident she already understood that pretty clearly.

How about that he'd been a fool? That he'd realized long ago how stupid he'd been to let her go? That Laura's honesty, authenticity and love for life had been something he'd missed day in and day out for six years?

Perhaps he could tell her that he'd nearly called her dozens of times. Had stood outside her house in Colorado Springs like a stalker more times than would make anyone comfortable. That every time he got a little tipsy out with friends it was her number he wanted to drunk-text.

That he'd never stopped dreaming about her even when he'd forced his mind not to think of her while awake.

When he'd seen her holding that baby today, an icy panic had gripped his heart. Because she'd been in danger, but more because he'd thought he'd been too late to right his wrongs. She'd met someone else and fallen in love and made sweet beautiful babies.

When Brooke had stood up and taken the baby from

Laura and he'd realized they weren't Laura's children, something had snapped into place for him. He hadn't realized it at that moment but he sure as hell realized it now.

He wasn't waiting any longer. He had to make things right with Laura. He didn't know why he'd waited until now to start trying.

By her own admission Laura wasn't married or seeing anyone. Joe planned to change that. If he could convince her to forgive him. That was a huge if.

But he planned to try. Fate, in the form of two moronic bank robbers, had brought them back together. It gave him the perfect opening to ease back into her life, to apologize in every way he knew how. And think of a few new creative ways if needed.

That would be his pleasure.

And if he couldn't talk her into giving their relationship a try, he could at least prove himself a friend to her. To erase from his mind forever that haunted, shattered look that had taken over her features when he'd let the press and gossip columns get the best of him and convince him he could do better than Laura Birchwood.

News flash: he couldn't.

He wouldn't blame her if she would never become romantically involved with him again, but he was going to try to convince her.

Starting tonight. He'd take a note from his get-whatever-I-want past playbook and follow her home. He'd charm her into going out with him.

He began walking back toward the bank. As soon as he cleared the building he could feel eyes on him. Press and bystanders were all taking pictures and recording the scene and him. Most weren't looking at him, just knew something exciting had happened at the bank.

But a few people in the crowd knew who he was. He

could feel eyes following him in particular. It never failed to make him a little uncomfortable when people seemed to be hostage "groupies."

Derek, Lillian and Jon were talking to the sheriff when Joe walked up to them.

"We'll get the rest of the statements and proceed from there. It looks like the manager and assistant manager of the bank were the only ones injured and neither of them seriously." Jon nodded at Joe in greeting.

That was good. Hopefully the judge would take that into consideration when sentencing Ricky and Bobby, aka Mitchell and Michael Goldman.

"Lillian, Joe and I are going to head back to Omega HQ since you seem to have everything under control," Derek said, shaking the sheriff's hand.

"I'm going to stay around for the rest of the evening, if that's okay," Jon told the sheriff. "I work crisis management in a lot of cases for Omega and may be able to help you with press or any questions you have."

"We appreciate Omega sending you so quickly." Sheriff Richardson turned to Joe. "And we especially appreciate what you did in there. That you kept it from becoming bloody."

Joe shook the man's outstretched hand. "The Goldman brothers didn't really want to harm anybody in my opinion. They just made some bad decisions, which led to panicking and more bad decisions."

"Either way, me and my men are thankful for how the situation got handled today. I'm sure the hostages are, too."

Jon and Sheriff Richardson turned back toward the bank while Lillian, Derek and Joe began walking the blocks to where the helicopter had been landed.

"Alright, mission completed. Let's get home," Derek said.

Lillian nodded as they began to make their way up to the roof. Joe wanted to move quicker, to rush them, so he could get back to HQ and back to Laura. But he knew it wouldn't accomplish anything but cause them to dig into why he was in such a hurry. Joe was rarely in a hurry.

But getting to Laura, seeing her again? Touching her again in any way she would allow...

His urgency continued to grow.

He wanted to give her as little time as possible to fortify walls against him. That was why he was going to see her tonight.

Derek rode in the copilot seat next to Lillian, leaving Joe in the back by himself. That was fine. He felt some of the pressure inside him start to loosen as the overhead blades began to whirl and they became airborne.

"Hey, did anyone get video footage of Matarazzo in just his undies?" Lillian asked. "I didn't have a great view from where I was in the elevator shaft."

"Oh, you better believe it, sister." Derek's amusement was obvious. "I wouldn't want anyone at Omega to miss that."

Joe didn't even care.

LAURA WALKED INTO her small house in Fountain, Colorado, just south of Colorado Springs, an hour and a half after leaving Joe standing by the side of the bank building.

What a day. She didn't know which shook her more, two idiots running around with guns or facing Joe again.

She was a liar; she knew which shook her more. But she had kept it together, talked to him reasonably, calmly, like an adult.

And then turned and ran away like a five-year-old.

Laura sighed. She could've handled the situation with

more aplomb, more pride, more professionalism—all of which seemed to have evacuated her presence when Joe entered her personal space. Thank goodness that only happened every six years so far.

She changed out of her business suit of a black pencil skirt and blazer coupled with a white blouse and slipped on brown leggings and a chunky-knit, cream-colored sweater. She looked at herself in the mirror. The person she saw looking back at her didn't cause her to cringe or turn away. Laura knew who she was. Not gorgeous by any stretch of the imagination, but she was reasonably attractive—brown hair, hazel eyes, a nose just a touch too small, lips a touch too big. Her five-foot-four-inch frame was just average. As a matter of fact everything about her looks was just sort of average.

Nobody was going to stop and follow her down the streets whistling and catcalling because of her looks, but no one was ever going to run away screaming either.

It was only when you placed her against the backdrop of someone as gorgeous as, say, Joe Matarazzo, that anyone looked at Laura and used words like plain Jane, doleful, or *reverse beauty and the beast*.

All of those had been said about her when she'd dated Joe. Mostly by people in gossip blogs. Joe had told her to ignore all press, so she had. She thought he had, too. Until he'd proved otherwise by ending their relationship so suddenly.

That had hurt, mostly because the blow had been so unexpected.

When they'd first met she'd expected it. She'd worked nights waiting tables so she could go to law school during the day. He'd come in with a couple of buddies and flirted outrageously. She'd laughed him off, not taking him even the least bit seriously.

After all, how could someone who looked like Joe Matarazzo be interested in someone like her?

But he'd pursued her. Her twenty-three-year-old, slightly socially awkward self hadn't had a chance against Joe when he'd set his sights on her.

And she would admit, he didn't have to pursue her long. She gave in. When else would she get the opportunity to have a fling with someone like Joe? He'd been handsome and charming and popular, and the sparks had flown.

She'd been expecting the blow then, too. Once he'd gotten what he'd wanted physically, she thought he'd be gone. But he'd stayed.

Laura knew she had her perks: she was focused and driven when it came to her career, but also cared about people. She tried to be honest and live by the golden rule. But she definitely wasn't someone who would be labeled as witty, or the life of the party, or a breathtaking beauty.

She didn't think she'd keep Joe's attention for long. But when weeks had turned into months and he was still always around, she'd started to believe their relationship was going somewhere.

She'd let her guard down. Let herself believe he was falling for her the way she was falling for him.

That had made the unexpected blow so much harder to take when it finally came. When he'd called off the relationship after they'd been together just over six months, with no warning at all.

Laura straightened as she focused on her reflection in the mirror, smoothing her sweater down. That was all in the past. No more thinking about Joe Matarazzo. Fate had dumped them together today, but that didn't mean anything.

The doorbell rang and Laura checked the clock. It must

be little Brad next door. The seven-year-old sometimes came over to play video games on the weekends. His father was deployed in the military and his mom had her hands full with his three-year-old twin sisters.

Good. An hour's worth of Mario Kart would cure whatever ailed her.

She bounded down the stairs and swung by and opened the door, not stopping to look at Brad on her way to the kitchen. She needed some fortification if she was going to take on the neighbor boy. He was a fiend at the driving game.

"Brad, come on in. I'm going to throw a frozen pizza in the oven. It's all over for you tonight, kiddo. No amount of coins or stunt boosts are going to save you this time."

"I'm not sure what stunt boosts are, but I guess I better learn if they're needed to save me."

Not Brad's voice. Joe's voice. Laura dropped the pizza on the counter and walked back to her foyer.

"What are you doing here?"

"You don't sound as excited to see me as you did about seeing Brad." Joe's smile was charming, gorgeous. Laura had to force herself not to give in to the appeal, to keep her expression cool.

"That may be because the most hurtful thing Brad has ever done to me was launch a red koopa shell at my Mario Kart vehicle." She turned back toward the kitchen. "And even then he felt pretty bad about it."

"Laura…"

Turning her back to him had been a mistake. His long legs had closed the distance between them quickly and silently and now he was right behind her.

"What do you want, Joe?"

He touched her gently on the arm. It was totally unfair that she could still feel sparks of attraction where his skin touched hers. She didn't turn around.

"Seeing you today… I just wanted to say I'm sorry. I—"

"Apology accepted. You can go."

It hurt Laura to say the words. But it was better this way.

Joe was quiet for a long time before coming around to stand in front of her. "You have every right not to ever talk to me again. But let me just take you out one time. Let the person I've become in the last six years talk to the person you've become."

He reached down and grasped her hands; she could feel his thumbs stroking the back of her palms. "We're not the same people we were then, Laura. I don't expect you to get involved with me, but I would appreciate it a great deal if you would just let me take you out one time to apologize for my stupidity then."

His clear blue eyes were sincere. His face pleading, engaging. A curl of sandy brown hair fell over his forehead as he gazed down at her, and hope lit his features. Laura couldn't resist him when he was like this. Nobody could resist him when he was like this.

Like you were the center of his world.

But she'd been here before. She couldn't forget that. This time she'd take some control. She thought about just cooking the pizza she'd gotten out and feeding them both that. Letting him say what he had to say. But being trapped inside a house with him where there was a bed, or a bathtub, or the couch or the kitchen floor nearby was probably not a good idea.

"Fine," she told him, her breath escaping her body when his worried look turned into one of joy, lighting up his eyes. "I'll go out with you. But no place fancy.

No romance and candles. As a matter of fact, I'll pick the place."

His suppressed half smile only added to his charm. Damn him. "Yes, ma'am."

She poked him in his chest. "And you keep your hands to yourself. You got that?"

His smile turned downright wicked.

She was in trouble.

Chapter Five

Joe seemed different. An hour later, sitting in the restaurant where they'd first met when she'd been a waitress and he'd come in with his friends after a night of partying, she had to admit he wasn't the same man she'd known six years ago.

He'd grown up.

Although he was two years older, in their previous relationship Laura had always been the more mature one. Now Joe seemed more balanced, more focused. She had no doubt of the cause for that.

"So Omega Sector, huh?" She leaned back against the booth across from him, having finished her meal, and took a sip of her wine. "I never would've pegged you for law enforcement."

"I didn't have much education, but I had a pretty developed skill set. I decided to see if I could put that to use."

Laura raised her eyebrow. She definitely remembered certain skills Joe had, but was pretty sure that wasn't what he meant. She tugged at her sweater feeling a little overheated. "Oh yeah?"

"I had a very observant, honest friend who pointed out to me that I had more potential than to just be a trust fund baby. That I had skills in observation, listening, adaptability. That I was calm under pressure and that people genuinely seemed to like me."

Laura's eyes snapped to his face. *She* had said that to him. Had truly believed it. But she hadn't dreamed he would take her words and change his whole life.

"Wow," she whispered.

"Yeah, wow." He took a sip of his wine. "I repaid the favor by saying some of the cruelest, most ridiculous words that have ever left my mouth. Ever left *anybody's* mouth."

"Joe…"

He reached over and grasped her hand. "I want to make sure you know I'm sorry. That a day has not gone by where I haven't regretted those words. I've nearly called you or come to your house dozens of times, but—"

"Joe." She stopped him, shaking her head. "You were right. About us. About me not being the right type of woman for you. You were right."

"No." The hand not holding hers hit the table just loud enough to cause her to jump. "I was not right. Whatever the opposite of right is, that's what I was."

Laura couldn't help but smile. "Wrong?"

Joe laughed and sat back, releasing her hand, the tension easing from his face. "Yeah, wrong. Wrong to let myself be convinced of it, wrong to say it, wrong not to have apologized for it before now."

Laura was not one to hold a grudge. She'd learned long ago that bitterness against him only hurt herself and had let it go.

"Well, I accept your apology and even appreciate it. What you said, what those gossip sites said, helped me turn a corner. I realized I was never going to be beautiful, but that I could at least make more of an effort. Style my hair, wear more makeup, make more attractive clothing choices."

Joe's jaw got tight as he studied her. "You look great now, but you were fine just like you were."

"I was…comfortable just like I was. But I realized when I started my own law firm how important a professional image was. Like it or not, studies show that attractiveness affects your level of trustworthiness and credibility with people. I needed to change my image."

His expression grew pained. "Laura—"

She smiled at him. She wasn't trying to make him feel bad—the opposite in fact. She wanted him to know that what had happened between them had helped her. "I'm just trying to say that I grew from the situation, like you did."

"But—"

"No more talk about the past. Okay? Or at least that part. We were young. We were stupid. Let's just agree and move on."

He looked like he was going to say something more but stopped and nodded.

Joe told her about some of the training he'd had to do to become an Omega Sector agent and some of his exploits since joining them. Laura told him about her law firm and how it had grown over the last year.

The words flowed easily. Lightly. This was how it had always been between the two of them: comfortable, relaxed. Only when other people had entered the equation had it gotten difficult and complicated.

Laura became aware of eyes on them partway through their conversation but tried to ignore it. Someone like Joe always had eyes on him. How could women not stare, even if they didn't know who he was? But Laura didn't like it. Didn't like the thoughts that began to enter her head. Were they wondering what Joe was doing with someone like her?

Amazing how the blackness could creep in unbidden. No one had said anything; maybe no one was even thinking anything, but Laura could already feel her confidence plummet. She picked at the food she'd ordered, no longer able to enjoy the meal.

She couldn't do this again.

She wasn't mad at Joe, the opposite, in fact. Spending time with him just made her remember why she had fallen for him six years ago.

Which was also adding to her panic.

She'd been around him a little over an hour and she was already back to the person she'd been. Worried about her looks, about what people thought. How many different ways did she have to be told that she and Joe were from two different realms before she accepted it as the truth?

Somebody clicked their picture. The flash made Laura wince.

Joe turned calmly to the man. "Hi, we're having dinner if you don't mind." His voice was friendly but firm. Laura saw the manager heading toward their table to ward off any problems, but the man with the camera left.

It could've just been anyone who recognized Joe and wanted to snap his picture.

It could've been someone from a major gossip rag.

Either way Laura knew she couldn't stay. She put her napkin down beside her plate; she felt like she had a knot in her stomach that wouldn't ease. Joe studied her with concern.

"I'm sorry, but I can't do this. I can't be here with you, can't do this again. Thank you for dinner, thank you for the apology. I wish you the best, Joe."

She started to stand, but he grasped her hand before she could.

"Laura, you're panicking. Don't. Please." She felt his thumb brush over the back of her palm. "It was just a photograph and doesn't mean anything."

"No, what it was was a reminder. You are you and I am me. Our worlds aren't compatible. You would've thought I learned that lesson well six years ago."

"It doesn't have to be that way. I wasn't prepared tonight, but I can take measures to protect you from the press. From the gossip."

She tilted her head to the side. "Who's going to protect me against you, Joe?"

He gripped her hand more firmly. "I don't want you to protect yourself from me. You don't need to, because I'm not going to do anything that will cause you harm. I give you my word."

Laura shook her head. She believed that he meant it, but that didn't change anything. "I can't be the person who opened up to you so completely before. That person got crushed in the fray. I don't think she exists anymore."

"Then open up the woman who does exist." A moment of pain crossed his features. "I'm sorry. I know I hurt you badly. I wish I could take it all back."

Laura let out a sigh. "I'm not trying to make you feel bad, truly. It's just I don't know if I can open up to you. If I even want to." Didn't know if the price would be too high. "All I know right now is that it's been a long day. I need some space. Some time."

Joe stared at her for long moments. She knew he wanted to say more, wanted to plead his case. Part of her wanted him to, but she knew it could just lead to disaster.

He nodded and let go of her hand, leaning back in his seat. "Okay, you're right. I'm trying to rush this. To force it. And that's not what I meant to do at all. So we'll take it slow."

"Joe…" She wanted to tell him to just leave her alone for good, that she didn't want him around her, but couldn't do it. She couldn't force herself to say the words.

Because she knew they would be a lie.

He leaned forward pinning her with his blue eyes. "I'm not giving up, Laura. I'll let you go now, but I want you to know I'm not giving up."

LAURA THOUGHT ABOUT his words the entire way home, thankful she'd had the foresight to insist they drive separate cars to the restaurant. She thought about the intensity of his blue eyes and the way his entire body had leaned toward her as he told her he wasn't giving up.

She had no doubt he meant what he said.

But despite the attraction fairly simmering in her blood for him, Laura knew she couldn't go through it again. Joe Matarazzo might be the most handsome, charming, wealthy man she'd ever met, but he was no good for her.

She would have to make him understand. Make him see that she wasn't just playing hard-to-get. That her very survival depended on him choosing to leave her, and the life she'd built, alone.

But was that really what she wanted? Deep down did she hope for something different? For him to pursue her again as he once had?

She had pushed those types of thoughts immediately out of her head for so long that she could no longer even answer them honestly. Even to herself.

She wished the universe would send her some sort of sign.

It did, with a vengeance.

One moment she was driving down a relatively deserted patch of Highway 87, the next another car had slammed into the back driver's side of Laura's vehicle.

She screamed as her head struck the side window and struggled to hold on to consciousness, her vision immediately blurry. Her car flew out of control, spinning in a sideways direction almost off the road. She jerked the steering wheel but it didn't seem to do any good. She looked over her shoulder and found the vehicle that had hit her still pushed up against her Toyota.

Was the other car trying to ram her toward the safety rail on the side of the road?

Laura glanced in that direction for just a second. She knew this part of Highway 87 pretty well. The drop past that safety rail was steep. She would definitely flip if she went over the edge.

Looking back again at the car still locked against hers, Laura slammed on the brakes with both feet, causing her car to stop and the other one to separate from it and speed past. Once her car wasn't trapped by the other, Laura had control of the steering again and overcorrected, causing her to swing around backward and land hard up against the rail. Her head flew back the other way from the force of the hit.

Her breath sawed in and out of her chest. That driver had to be drunk. Idiot had almost killed them both.

In the rearview mirror Laura noticed the other driver tap the brakes and wondered if the close call with death had sobered the person up enough to realize what they had done. But the car sped farther away. Laura tried to get a glimpse of the license plate but her vision was too blurry.

She sat for long minutes trying to take inventory of herself. Nothing seemed to be broken. She definitely had a knot on her head where she'd cracked it against the window and her hands were shaking. But it all seemed to be pretty minor bumps and bruises, considering she'd almost been run off the road. Overall, she considered herself lucky.

An older couple pulled up behind her—well, in front of her since her car was facing backward—and immediately got out to help. They opened the passenger side door and assisted her across the front seats and out of the car. The police were called and at the scene soon enough.

Laura was tempted to call Joe. He would still be nearby and she knew he would come immediately.

She also knew there was no way he wasn't going to end up in her bed if she did that.

She would attend to her bumps and bruises herself. At least right now they were just on her body; if she called Joe she was sure he'd soothe all her physical aches. But the ones he'd leave on her heart wouldn't be so easily healed.

Chapter Six

Convincing Laura to let him back into her life wasn't going to be as easy as Joe had hoped. Not that he had really expected it was going to be easy. As a matter of fact, he would've sworn before Friday there was no way in hell she was ever going to let him back into her life. That she would punch him if he ever dared show his face around her again.

Although he had known she was a better person than that. She had even accepted his apology. But he knew when she left the restaurant she had no intention of ever seeing him again. The person who had snapped their picture had spooked her. Maybe she could agree that Joe wouldn't be cruel, wouldn't say unkind things to or about her, but the press?

Joe tended to be the press's darling, but he knew they could often be harsh and callous. They certainly had been to Laura.

What Joe said to her when they broke up had been unkind, but what the gossip sites had published about her while they had dated had been downright brutal.

Once he and Laura had been seen together multiple times over a few weeks, one blog had gone so far as to print a picture of her and point out her top ten flaws. Publicly and without mercy. He hoped she had never seen that, but wouldn't have been surprised if she had.

Joe had been stupid enough to begin to believe some of what was printed. The digs against her that pointed out her flaws. He would never be so idiotic as to pay any attention to gossip sites now—particularly since he knew how much those sites got wrong—but had let it get the better of him then. Let the sites, and some stupid friends who had his ear, convince him that Laura just wasn't the right one for him.

Because it was much easier to dwell on that than to face the real scenario: he'd been falling for Laura.

Complete and utter panic because he had been falling so hard and so quickly for her. She'd been real, so full of life, and honest and passionate about helping people. She'd had a smile that lit up an entire room.

She still did. Still was. All of those things.

Had he really ever thought Laura unattractive six years ago?

No, never. No matter what the gossip sites had said about her physical appearance, Joe had always found himself overwhelmingly attracted to her. The passion between them had sizzled. Looking at other women had been unappealing.

And honestly, another reason why he'd panicked. Because for the first time he was in a relationship where he wasn't thinking about who his next conquest would be. Wasn't feeling trapped or penned in, when he knew he should be.

He was too young for love. So when his friends and random websites who didn't give a damn about Joe or his happiness had told him Laura wasn't good enough, he'd latched onto that idea.

He shook his head now at the idiot he'd been then.

Getting back into Laura's life wasn't going to be easy, not that he blamed her one bit. But like he'd told her Friday at the restaurant: he wasn't giving up.

He'd sent flowers Saturday, stargazer lilies, her favorite. On Sunday he'd had four pints of Ben & Jerry's ice cream delivered to her house, picking out the ones he remembered she'd always loved when they'd sat on her couch watching football games together.

He didn't expect either of these gestures to make a difference; Laura would see straight through them. But they were a start.

It was Monday morning now and he was walking into the room that held his desk at Omega, an open area where most of the Critical Response Division team members' desks were arranged. The team wasn't at them a lot, but it was the home base. The floor-to-ceiling windows of the room provided a gorgeous view of the Rocky Mountains to the west.

At least they normally did. Today they were covered—completely, top to bottom—with photocopied images of Joe in his well-fitting, black boxer briefs. Hundreds of them, all different shots from the scene at the bank when he'd been proving to Ricky and Bobby he was unarmed.

And—*oh joy*—they all had comments. Most of them read something asinine like "he's unarmed but his weapon works just fine."

The audible snickers from the nearby desks surrounded Joe as he walked over to the pictures, studying all the different shots.

He knew everyone was waiting to see if he was going to get angry or embarrassed. He wasn't.

He took one down and turned to face his colleagues. "Hey, I'm going to use these to re-cover my bathroom if that's okay with everyone. Most gorgeous wallpaper I've ever seen."

The laughs burst out then.

"Yeah, you guys are a riot." But he smiled, beginning to take the sheets down. "I should leave these up here. It would serve you all right."

Lillian, along with Ashton Fitzgerald, another SWAT member, jumped up to help him. "It was just such a memorable occasion." Lillian smiled at him. "We wanted to make sure everyone at Omega had the pleasure of experiencing it."

Steve Drackett, head of the Critical Response Division, walked out of his office and looked around. He rolled his eyes. "I don't even want to know what this is all about. I need SWAT members in my office. We've got a situation."

Ashton, Lillian and a few others turned to follow Steve. "By the way, Joe, nice skivvies." Steve winked at him.

Joe watched as they left, glad, not for the first time, that he wasn't a part of the SWAT team. Let them go shoot all the bad people. Joe had to write up the report from Friday anyway.

He hadn't gotten very far in the paperwork when his phone chirped with an incoming email.

Sarah Conner, an old girlfriend.

Wow, that was a blast from the past. He and Sarah had dated briefly not quite a year ago. Nothing serious, just a few weeks of a good time. She hadn't expected anything from him nor had he expected anything from her. She'd ended it because she desired to have someone around more often and Joe couldn't be since he traveled so much for his job. Everything had been on good terms although they hadn't really spoken since.

He opened the email, not sure exactly what he was expecting. Maybe her telling him that she'd found someone and planned to get married. Instead, the email contained a brief, cryptic message.

I need to talk to you. It's important. Come to my place ASAP.

Joe wasn't sure what to do with the email. On one hand he wasn't at all interested in seeing Sarah, not romantically at least. But it sounded like maybe she needed some sort of help.

He called Sarah's number but didn't get an answer. He'd been to her place enough times to know where it was in south Colorado Springs.

Not quite as far south as Fountain, where Laura lived, but definitely in that general direction. He would go to Sarah's house, then after he took care of whatever she needed, he would stop by and say hello to Laura in person.

Maybe offer her one of his colleagues' pieces of art. She'd love that. He could use it to prove he didn't take himself so seriously anymore.

That would probably go further than flowers or ice cream.

Regardless he'd be able to see Laura. Even if it was only for a few minutes, he'd take it.

Joe let one of Steve Drackett's secretaries—all beautiful, intelligent women—know that he was going out to deal with some residual issues with Friday's case and would be back later in the afternoon. They knew how to contact him if there was a hostage situation for which he was needed. But it sounded like SWAT was going to be busy somewhere else.

Joe's Jaguar F-TYPE sports car made short work of the miles to Sarah's house. Although he was curious about what Sarah had to say, he was anxious to see Laura.

He pulled up to Sarah's house, a nice chalet-style place off on its own. It didn't look like anyone was home, which only made Joe happier. But he'd driven all the way here; he might as well at least try to see what Sarah wanted.

Joe parked and bounded up to the steps leading to Sarah's front door. He rang the doorbell and waited. Nothing. He rang it again, but received no response.

Well, he could at least tell Sarah he tried.

He knocked just in case the doorbell wasn't working and was surprised when the door pushed open under his knuckles. It hadn't been completely closed.

He knocked again, still staying outside, but stuck his head in slightly and called out.

"Sarah, you around? It's Joe."

Nothing.

Something wasn't right here. Joe took the slightest step inside.

"Hey, Sarah? You emailed me to come over. I just wanted to see what's going on."

Still no answer.

Joe went back to his car and got his Glock from the glove compartment. Although he didn't use it often, it was still his official Omega weapon. He was licensed to use it. Trained to use it.

He prayed he didn't need to use it now.

He ran back to the door. "Sarah, I'm coming inside. I'm armed. Let me know if you're in there so no one gets hurt."

Still nothing. Joe went from being afraid he might be

walking in on Sarah in the shower to hoping it. Embarrassing, but at least she would be alive to be embarrassed.

He checked all the ground floor rooms first. When he found nothing in the kitchen or living room he slowly made his way upstairs.

He saw her immediately when he entered the master bedroom. Sarah laid sprawled facedown on the bed, naked, arm over her face as if she was sleeping off a hangover.

Except for the blood that had pooled all around her.

He rushed over to check for her pulse, just in case, but knew as soon as he felt the coolness of her skin that she was definitely dead, probably had been for hours.

Joe took a few deep breaths to center himself, focus on what had happened. He was an Omega agent, had seen dead bodies before, but never someone he'd known so personally.

Training took over. This was now a crime scene, and that definitely wasn't Joe's area of expertise. He needed to call in the specialists. Both local law enforcement and Omega.

He speed-dialed Steve Drackett's direct number.

"Joe, what's going on?" Steve said in way of greeting. Joe didn't call his direct line very often and only when there was a problem.

But there'd never been one like this before.

"Steve, I've got an issue. Dead woman, an ex-girlfriend of mine. I got a message from her earlier asking me to come by but when I got here she was dead. Murdered."

"You sure it was a murder?"

"Unmistakable."

He heard Steve's muttered expletive. "Okay, call the locals and get them there. I'll send Brandon and Andrea to see if they pick up on anything the locals might miss."

Brandon Han was the most brilliant profiler Omega had. Joe knew both him and Andrea Gordon, a talented behavioral analyst who was now Brandon's partner on most cases. Having them here would help, or at the very least help Joe's peace of mind.

"Thanks, Steve."

"Don't touch anything, okay? You should probably walk back out the way you came and wait for the locals outside."

Joe nodded, still looking at Sarah, then realized his boss couldn't see him. "Yeah, okay."

Steve sighed. "I'm sorry, Joe. It's always hard when it's someone you know. Even an ex."

Joe said his goodbyes and then called 911, reporting the death. Then he stood staring at Sarah for a long time.

He hadn't really felt much for the woman, besides a physical attraction. He wished he knew more about her, who he should call, family or whatever, but he didn't. The police would have to handle that.

Who would've wanted to kill Sarah? She was an accountant, or in public relations or something like that. Not a job that tended to develop enemies.

Had she known about the danger? Is that why she had emailed Joe? The cryptic message she'd sent didn't provide many clues.

Finally he did what Steve had suggested and moved outside to wait for the locals. He would need to identify himself as law enforcement and let them know why he was here. Otherwise an armed man at a murder scene tended to make cops pretty nervous.

Joe stood leaning against his car, still trying to wrap his head around this entire situation, when the locals came speeding in, sirens blaring. Four separate squad cars and an ambulance. Must be a slow day around town.

Joe had his Omega credentials out in his hand, extended so the officers could see that he clearly did not mean them any harm. The men stopped to talk to him and he explained the situation, gave them Sarah's info, then waited as three of them rushed in. The other two stayed with Joe, hands noticeably near their sidearms.

When the three men exited Sarah's house they were moving much less quickly. There was no hurry; nothing could be done to help her now. The officer in charge nodded at the two men who'd been tasked with babysitting Joe while the others were inside.

"Is the coroner on his way?"

"Yeah."

"Okay, let's rope this area off. Neighbors are going to start wondering what's going on."

The man in charge turned to Joe. "I'm Detective Jack Thompson. So you work for Omega Sector. Were you here on official business? Something to do with a case?"

"No. I used to date the victim, about a year ago. She emailed me this morning, asked me to come by."

One of Thompson's eyebrows lifted suspiciously. "Is that so? Did things end badly between you two when you broke up?"

"No, we were never very serious. Neither of us was upset when we decided it wasn't working out."

"I see." Officer Thompson jotted a couple sentences down in his notebook. "And did you and Ms. Conner talk to each other much since the breakup?"

"No, maybe once or twice, but not really that I remember."

"But she just happened to email you this morning and asked you to come by?" Disbelief clearly tinted the man's tone.

Joe didn't take offense to the question. He could admit

it was a little weird that he hadn't spoken with Sarah for months then the day she contacted him, she winded up dead.

"Yes."

Thompson studied Joe's car for a moment before turning back to Joe. The nice vehicle obviously wasn't winning Joe any points with the detective. "What exactly do you do for Omega Sector, Mr. Matarazzo?"

"Joe is one of the finest hostage negotiators we have." The sentence came from behind him. Joe turned to find Brandon Han and Andrea Gordon.

Brandon showed his credentials to Officer Thompson. "We'll need to get inside, if that's possible."

Thompson's lips pursed and his eyes narrowed at Joe. "Fine. But I'm going in to supervise, make sure everything is handled correctly. Please stick around Agent Matarazzo, in case we have any more questions." He left to enter the house.

"Sorry about your friend, Joe," Andrea said, touching him on the arm.

"Thanks," he told the striking blonde. "And thanks for coming, you guys."

Brandon shook his hand. "No problem. We're going to go inside, see if we spot anything the locals might miss. Will you be okay out here?"

"Yeah, I'm fine. You guys do whatever you need to do to help with the case." He watched as Brandon led Andrea toward the front door, a protective hand on the small of her back.

Joe leaned back against his car and got comfortable. This was going to take most of the day; Officer Thompson had just started with his questions, and didn't seem interested in making this easy or comfortable for him.

Joe wasn't going to be able to see Laura as he'd hoped. That was probably for the best; he didn't want to drag her into this anyway.

Chapter Seven

By Wednesday afternoon Laura was cursing Joe Mata-razzo's name. Damn the man. Damn him because for just a split second she thought he had really changed. That he wasn't the selfish playboy he once had been.

After the accident on Friday, her aches had made her want to forget all about Joe. But then the flowers—or more importantly the fact that he'd remembered her favorite type of flowers were stargazer lilies—had caused her to think maybe Joe really had changed. Then Sunday the ice cream had arrived.

She had to admit the frozen stuff—again, all her favorite flavors—had melted her heart a little bit. Brought back memories of their time together.

She had fully expected him to show up or call on Monday. When he hadn't, she'd been okay with it, and even wondered if she should call him and tell him thanks, but decided not to. When she didn't hear from Joe all day Tuesday, she'd gotten a little miffed.

By Wednesday at lunch, Laura was disgusted with herself and Joe. If he didn't want to see her again, that was fine. But he shouldn't act like he wanted to then not follow through.

And her? How many times was she going to fall for his sexy-boy appeal and wit?

There was nothing more dangerous than a man with charm. And Joe Matarazzo had it in spades.

And Laura was just an idiot to keep trusting his not-really promises. *I'm not giving up.* It had at least been true for two days.

So she could admit she was a little short-tempered when her law office phone rang at 4:00 p.m. Her assistant was gone for the day so Laura answered the phone herself, unable to keep her irritation out of her voice.

"Law Offices of Coach, Birchwood and Winchley."

"Wow, do you always answer the phone like you're considering strangling the entire neighborhood?"

Joe. It figured that he would know she was about to write him off for good and call now. The man's timing was impeccable.

"No, I'm just considering strangling one person."

That quieted him.

"I'm sorry I haven't been able to get in touch before now," he finally said. "Things have been complicated."

"Things tend to always be complicated with you, Joe."

He gave a short bark of laughter, but there didn't seem to be very much humor in it. "Well, believe it or not, I'm about to make things more complicated."

Laura rolled her eyes. "Why don't I just save you the trouble and stop you right there. I've been thinking over the last couple of days and realize I need to stand firm on what I told you at the restaurant on Friday. You and I are better off away from each other."

"Laura—"

"This isn't about the not calling." Damn it, why had she said that? Now it sounded like she was pissy because he hadn't called. Which, of course, she was. "I just think you and I should leave the past where it was."

"Laura—"

She didn't want to hear what he had to say, knowing if he gave her an excuse, she'd believe him. "Joe, I just can't go through the back-and-forth and you changing your mind."

"Laura, *stop*." She'd never heard that particular air of forcefulness in his tone. Joe tended to always be so laid-back most people forgot how strong he could be when needed. It was enough to stop her midthought. "I am willing to discuss this all with you at a later time, because there's no way I'm going to let you run away from us. But I'm not calling about that."

"Then what are you calling about?"

"Have you had a chance to watch the news or get online to read the news over the last couple of days?"

No. She'd been forcing herself to stay too busy to even allow herself to do anything as stupid as Google Joe Matarazzo. "I haven't, sorry. I've been too busy at work. Why?"

"I'm calling because I need you as a lawyer. A woman I used to know was murdered on Monday."

And now didn't she feel like an ass? "Oh my gosh, Joe, that's terrible. But you shouldn't need a lawyer just because someone you knew was murdered. Unless they caught you in the act."

"It wasn't quite that bad, but it wasn't good either."

Okay, that didn't sound promising. "Still—"

"And then it happened again this morning."

"What?"

"Another one of my ex-girlfriends was killed this morning."

As far as excuses went for not calling, two dead ex-girlfriends in two and a half days was a pretty good one. Laura heard noise in the background.

"Joe, where are you right now? Were you arrested?"

"They haven't brought any formal charges against me, but they're holding me for questioning. I'm at the Colorado Springs downtown station."

Laura had already grabbed her purse and blazer. "Don't say anything to anyone. I'll be right there."

"Laura, there's more. Both women contacted me just before they died. And I found both bodies."

That really didn't look good. "I'm coming, Joe. Just don't answer any questions until I get there. Okay?"

"Don't you need to ask me if I did it?"

"No. Just don't talk to anyone." Laura hung up the phone and rushed out of her office.

She didn't need to ask if Joe was guilty; she knew he wasn't. Joe might be a lot of things Laura didn't like, but he wasn't a killer.

IF JOE HAD been the police, he would've brought himself in for questioning too.

When he'd received a message this morning from Jessica Johannsen, another one of his ex-girlfriends, asking him to come to her town house in the north part of Colorado Springs, Joe hadn't thought anything bad about it. He figured she'd just heard about Sarah's death, read a newspaper or saw a news report, and wanted to talk to him. To make this about her instead of Sarah.

Jessica had always been sort of clingy, not someone capable of handling much emotional stress. And she loved drama. Joe had never really been interested in her, although that hadn't stopped him from dating her for a few weeks about two years ago.

Jessica had had delicate features with long black hair and icy blue eyes. The press had delighted at what a lovely pair they'd made.

She'd bored him silly.

But he hadn't been surprised to receive a message from her after Sarah's death. Jessica would want to be held, patted, to be the center of attention even though Sarah's death had nothing to do with her.

She'd asked him to meet her this morning in her text message. He'd texted her back and told her he was busy.

He hadn't wanted to take the time to see Jessica. He'd wanted to see Laura. After Monday's incident with Sarah, he hadn't been able to call or go see her as he'd planned. He'd spent all day on Tuesday cleaning up from Sarah's death: he'd talked to her parents since he'd been the one who'd found her body, he'd worked with Brandon and Andrea to see if they could gather any leads in figuring out who the killer might be.

He hadn't wanted to drag Laura into this whole sordid mess, so he hadn't contacted her at all.

But by Wednesday, all he'd wanted to do was see Laura. To just breathe in her smile and banter with her. It didn't need to be sexual; he just wanted to be with her.

So Jessica's text asking him to meet had just irritated Joe. When he told her no, and Jessica had sent another message telling him how scared she was, he'd decided to go see her. She'd just keep bugging him until he did.

As soon as Jessica's door floated open like Sarah's, Joe should've known there was a problem. He should've stopped right then, backed out and called the local police.

But he hadn't. Instead, just like with Sarah, he'd rushed inside to see what was going on because he didn't want to be there in the first place. He just wanted to talk to Jessica and leave.

He'd honestly thought Jessica would step out in some sort of outrageous negligee at any moment. Or even be completely naked wanting to seduce him. To get him to hold her while she cried fake tears about something that had nothing to do with her.

Jessica had been naked. But she'd been dead. Stabbed, just like Sarah.

All the lousy things he'd thought about her had rattled in his head as guilt swamped him. No one would ever hold Jessica Johannsen again as she cried fake or real tears.

Joe had called the locals immediately. He'd thought about calling Omega, too, but had stopped. Steve had helped him once but that's when it was just a random murder that happened to be Joe's ex.

Joe had no idea what it meant now that two of his exes were dead. But it wasn't a problem he was going to drag the Omega team into. He'd have to deal with this on his own.

Detective Thompson and the other local Colorado Springs police hadn't been nearly as friendly this time, not that Thompson had liked Joe much on Monday. They hadn't hauled him off in cuffs, but Thompson had left someone with Joe at the scene to watch him every minute. And once they were done with the crime scene, they'd asked to escort him to the station.

Escort, as in have him ride in the back of their squad car.

Then he'd sat in the interrogation room for two hours. He wasn't sure if they were trying to intimidate him, didn't know what to do with him, or what.

All he knew was that this looked bad. Really, really bad.

They hadn't arrested him, which was good. They did read him his rights, which was bad. They hadn't taken his phone—although that probably only happened if he was officially arrested—so he'd used his cell to call Laura.

They hadn't told him he couldn't use it, so he'd figured he would. He had no idea how long he would be sitting in this room by himself, although he was sure someone was watching him, waiting to see what he would do.

Joe could've had a team of lawyers here, and would have if Laura had refused, but he wanted *her*. Other lawyers may be more vicious, more predatory in their methods of keeping their clients out of jail, but Laura believed in him.

Had always believed in him, even if she hadn't liked him.

And with all her intensity and intelligence he had no doubt she was a damn fine lawyer.

Detective Thompson entered the room. "Sorry to have kept you waiting, Matarazzo."

Joe highly doubted it.

"I heard you made a call. Got a lawyer."

Joe sat back. "It's my understanding that I'm allowed to have a lawyer if I'm being charged with something."

Thompson mirrored Joe's gesture, head tilting away, mouth downturned. "And it's my general experience that only people who are guilty need a lawyer. Besides, we haven't charged you with anything. You're free to go at any time."

Joe just wanted this to be over with. "I didn't kill Jessica Johannsen or Sarah Conner. I haven't had any contact with either of them for months."

"Interesting isn't it, though, that both women just happened to contact you right before they died?"

What could Joe say to that?

He shrugged. "*Interesting* isn't the word I would use, but yes, it's strange."

"And you happened to find both bodies. Another interesting factor."

"I'm law enforcement, Thompson. One of the good guys."

Thompson moved in closer, leaning his elbows on the table that sat between them. "I know you're law enforcement, Joe. Is it okay if I call you Joe?" Thompson didn't wait for an answer. "You're part of Omega Sector, one of the top law enforcement agencies in the country."

"That's right."

"How does a guy like you end up working for Omega?"

"What do you mean, 'a guy like me'?"

"You don't need a job, right? You've got plenty of money. So working for Omega as a negotiator is more like a hobby for you."

Joe pursed his lips. No, it wasn't a hobby for him. But he could admit, most of the people in the Critical Response Division probably thought of him that way.

Seeing Joe's face, Thompson continued. "I'm just saying, you're on the Omega roster, but you're not really a member of the team, are you? I don't notice any of them beating down the door to get you out of here."

Joe forced himself not to show any emotion. "I thought I wasn't under arrest, so why would there be a need for them to come get me out?"

But Thompson's remark had hit home. Joe wasn't part of the team at Omega. He got along well with everyone, joked with them, did his job. But none of them would call him a true member of the team.

The other man smirked. "Okay, I'll just take you at your word that they'll be here if you're arrested." But he obviously didn't believe that was true. "So you're a part of Omega. There's a lot of stress in law enforcement. Has been known to make strong men snap. Do something stupid. Add that stress to trying to balance two women and it could get a little crazy."

"I wasn't dating either of those women. And I definitely wasn't dating both of them." Joe shook his head.

"C'mon, Joe. I see some of the gossip sites. Dating more than one woman at a time is definitely not out of your realm of possibility."

"Barking up the wrong tree, Thompson."

"Alright, so you weren't dating them both. I can buy that. But did date them separately at one time. Maybe they got together and decided that you owed them something. A man could be forgiven for a lot of things when women decide to start blackmailing him. Especially someone who has as much as you do."

Joe had talked through enough hostage situations to recognize what was happening here. Thompson was trying to lull him into a false sense of security.

Joe hoped he wasn't this bad when he was doing his job. Because Thompson's contempt for him was just one step below obvious.

Joe gritted his teeth. "No. As far as I know, both Sarah and Jessica were wealthy in their own right, or at least they were last time I saw either of them."

"There's wealthy and then there's *Matarazzo* wealthy. I'm sure they don't have as much money as you do, and felt like maybe they deserved some of your wealth."

"If they did, they never mentioned it to me or implied it in any way."

"Women can just get it in their heads, you know, that a man owes them something, even when a guy doesn't make any promises. Them working together to try to bring you down, that would have to make you angry."

Joe was beginning to genuinely not like this guy. "Neither Jessica nor Sarah had anything against me. They weren't working together to blackmail me, or anything else as far as I know. They didn't even run in the same circles so I can't imagine they even knew each other."

"You're right. The only thing that links Sarah Conner and Jessica Johannsen to each other is their relationship with you." The detective sat back and stared.

Joe realized that had been Thompson's point the whole time. And Joe had walked him right to it. He should've listened to Laura when she said not to answer any questions.

"Why don't you give me a rundown on where you were on both Sunday and Tuesday nights between 3:00 and 6:00 a.m.?" Thompson asked.

He'd been completely alone. No one would be able to validate his whereabouts. Now he knew he definitely should've listened to Laura.

But damn it, he didn't kill those women. He had nothing to hide.

But the police clearly thought otherwise.

The door to the room opened. "My client won't be answering that, or any other questions, Detective Thompson. Either charge him or he's leaving."

Chapter Eight

"I need to go talk to my boss at Omega Sector." Joe gave Laura the address and she entered it into the GPS system on her phone.

He looked out the window while she drove, tension evident in his jaw and posture. Laura had never seen him so shaken. He tried to play it off, make it seem like it didn't really matter, but obviously it did.

He wasn't inhuman; two women he had known—intimately, no doubt—were dead. Just because he hadn't killed them didn't mean he didn't grieve.

Knowing he was the only link between the two women just added stress.

"What would you have answered Detective Thompson about your whereabouts?" she asked Joe as she took the interstate exit toward Omega Sector's headquarters in the northern section of Colorado Springs.

He shrugged. "I was home alone. Both nights. No alibi."

"That probably would have gotten you arrested, you know. That's why I told you not to answer any questions."

Joe turned to study her. "I didn't do it. That's why I thought I was safe answering questions."

"Yeah, well, the legal system doesn't always work that way. Especially when there are two dead young women and law enforcement is probably getting pressure to make an arrest."

"Not to mention the lead detective having a personal dislike and possible vendetta for me," Joe murmured. He shrugged. "Doesn't matter. I didn't do it. And if they had arrested me there would still be a killer out on the loose."

"Let's give the cops a chance to do their job. They'll find something that clears you, I'm sure."

She hoped so.

It wasn't long before they pulled up to the large office complex that housed Omega Sector's Critical Response Division. It was a pretty unassuming set of buildings on the outside. She noticed construction was in process on another section of the complex.

"You guys expanding?"

"No, the forensic lab is being replaced after an explosion a few months ago."

"Oh my gosh. An accident?"

"No, deliberate. The people responsible for the Chicago bombing last May were trying to get rid of some evidence we had held there."

It suddenly hit home just exactly how dangerous Joe's job was. Somehow she hadn't thought of that last Friday when she saw him in action. He'd talked to Ricky and Bobby like she'd seen him talk to dozens of other people: as though they were long-lost buddies and Joe had nothing in the world better to do than chat with them.

But he'd put his life on the line. Did that all the time. And all the money in the world wouldn't save him if some crazy hostage-taker just decided to shoot him.

She pulled into the parking garage where Joe directed her.

"Do you want to come inside with me?"

"Do you want me to?"

"Sure. Nothing is going to be said you aren't already aware of anyway."

They got out of the car and he led her through the main entrance where a security team checked her in. They walked through a maze of offices, most of them empty since it was nearly seven o'clock.

Joe pushed the door open to a room with four desks. Three were empty but at the fourth sat one of the most gorgeous women Laura had ever seen. Long, auburn hair with creamy smooth skin. Her posture impeccable in the black dress that seemed to both fit her like a second skin and be perfectly professional at the same time.

"Hey, Joe." She smiled at him, lips with a red gloss that looked as if it had just been applied moments before, revealing, of course, perfectly straight teeth. She stood up and walked over—in three-inch heels—to hug him. "I heard about your friends. I'm so sorry."

Joe hugged her back. Of course he would hug her back. What man in his right mind would not hug this woman back?

Laura stood there feeling more frumpy and dumpy by the nanosecond.

...*Not the caliber of woman*...

"Thanks, Cynthia." The detached and perfect Cynthia moved back to her desk. "I need to talk to Steve. I know he's still here since, well, he's always here. You're working late tonight."

She shrugged one delicate shoulder. "I'll let him know you're here. And..." She gestured toward Laura.

"Laura Birchwood. Lawyer and friend," Joe said.

Cynthia turned her smile on Laura. "Nice to meet you."

Laura did her best to smile back naturally although it probably came out looking more like a wounded animal in the throes of death. "Thanks."

Cynthia spoke on the phone for just a moment before standing and opening the door to her boss's inner office, leading them inside.

"Let me know if you need anything, Joe." Perfect smile again. Laura managed not to ask how she managed to look so perfect after working so late, especially in those heels. She glanced down at her own functionally comfortable flats.

The man behind the desk stood up and came around to shake Joe's hand. "I heard about the second victim. I'm sorry. I was worried when you didn't come in today."

"I've been a guest of the Colorado Springs PD for most of the day. This is Laura Birchwood, my friend and, as of earlier today, my lawyer."

"Steve Drackett." Laura shook the man's hand. He was older than Joe by at least a decade, but the slight blend of silver around his temples did nothing to detract from his handsomeness.

Was everyone who worked here gorgeous? At least it wasn't just the women.

Steve turned to Joe. "I'm sure Ms. Birchwood is an excellent attorney, but I would've sent Brandon Han in if you'd just called."

Joe shrugged, leading her to a seat and taking the one next to her as Steve went back behind his desk. "I didn't want to take up Omega resources for something that's personal. Plus, like you said, Laura is an excellent lawyer."

Steve looked at Joe for a long moment. "Is it okay if you and I talk for a few minutes privately?"

"If it's about Sarah's and Jessica's deaths, then just go ahead and say it in front of Laura. I don't have any secrets from her."

"Colorado Springs PD of course called asking about you and your record here."

Laura nodded. She wasn't surprised.

"I want to help out with the investigation, Joe," Steve continued. "We have resources and personnel they don't have."

"Thanks, Steve."

Steve grimaced. "Don't thank me too soon. I think it's better if you take a leave of absence while the investigation takes place. That way no one can accuse anyone here of favoritism."

If Laura hadn't been looking right at Joe she would've missed it. The tiny crack under his easy smile.

Steve's request had hurt him.

But Joe certainly didn't show it to Steve. "Yeah, sure. I understand."

The older man looked like he felt bad. "I'm sorry, Joe. And I know you just donate your salary here to charity, but I'll have to suspend that, too. Officially you can't have anything to do with Omega while you're being investigated."

Joe stood, easy smile firmly in place, even the slightest crack Laura had noticed now gone. "I totally understand. You've got to do what's right for everyone overall."

"This will blow over in a week or two. They'll catch the real killer and everything will be back to normal. You'll be back in your rightful place here."

"Sure. Absolutely."

Steve grimaced again. "But right now I'll just have to ask you for your badge and sidearm."

LAURA TOOK JOE back to her house.

She wouldn't have done it if he had asked her to. Or

tried to put a move on her. Or even turned his charming smile on her.

He hadn't done any of those things. After turning his badge and gun over to Steve Drackett, he shook the man's hand and even made a joke.

Steve had looked relieved. Glad Joe had understood what needed to be done.

And Joe did understand. But he also had pushed his own feelings aside and given Steve what he needed.

That's what Joe did, Laura realized, for his job and also in his life. Read what people needed and gave them that. It was probably why he was such a good hostage negotiator.

After they'd left he'd told her the address of where his car was parked, still at Jessica Johannsen's house. He wanted Laura to drop him off there so he could make his way back home.

Despite everything that had happened between them, all the hurt he'd caused her six years ago, despite the fact that he'd probably slept with the gorgeous, perfect Cynthia and that his exes were dropping like flies, Laura could not send him home alone.

"We're at your house," Joe said as she pulled into her driveway. "I thought you were taking me to get my car."

"Change of plans. No one should have to be alone after the day you've had."

His gorgeous blue eyes became hooded. Laura could feel heat spreading through her at his look.

"Whoa, boy. This offer extends to my couch only. You need a friend. I can be that."

He stuck his bottom lip out in the most adorable pout she'd ever seen. She groaned inwardly. Having him spend the night here was such a bad idea.

"It's couch or nothing, Matarazzo."

He held his hands up in mock surrender. "Okay, couch."

She got him in, got them both fed and listened while he'd called someone and had them pick up his car from the crime scene. Then she gave him a pillow and blanket and the unopened toothbrush she had from her last dentist visit. She showed him the couch and said good-night.

She did it all trying her damnedest not to really look at him. Not to really notice the way his eyes followed her wherever she went. To definitely not think about how good the lovemaking had been between them six years ago.

She went into her bedroom, locking the door behind her. She knew that if Joe wanted in, that flimsy lock wouldn't keep him out.

She wondered if she even wanted it to.

JOE TOSSED AND turned most of the night.

His foot hung over the edge of Laura's couch, which was obviously not meant for someone of his height to sleep on. He was also thinking of Jessica and Sarah and their deaths. Of why someone would kill them.

He was thinking about how much it had sucked when Steve had asked for his badge. How important working at Omega had become to him, even if—and it was clear by how easily Steve had suspended him today—Joe wasn't really part of the inner team.

But mostly he was thinking of Laura sleeping in her room right up the stairs.

There wasn't anything Joe wanted more than to go in there. To make love to Laura until he could forget about death and evil and blood.

But she deserved more than that. He had no doubt he could get past that small click of a lock he'd heard. He had no doubt he could seduce her into letting him stay in her bed tonight.

But as much as he wanted that, he didn't want that. Didn't want to use her in that way. At one time he would've thought about nothing except the pleasure both of them would gain if he ignored that tiny lock. Now he didn't want to risk what could possibly be a future between them for one night of sex. No matter how mind-blowing it might be.

Each moment seemed to drag into the next as Joe lay on the couch. He realized he needed Laura. Not for love-making, just to hold.

He needed to put his arms around her and thank the heavens that Laura was safe and sound and alive.

Suddenly, having distance between them, a wall—metaphorically and literally—separating them, seemed totally unacceptable. Joe wouldn't try to talk Laura into sex, but he'd be damned if he was going to stay out here when everything inside him demanded having her in his arms right now.

He was crossing the room before he finished the complete thought. His hand reaching for the doorknob was stopped by his phone buzzing from where it sat on the end table near the couch.

Joe almost ignored it. Wanted to ignore it. But after everything that had happened in the last few days, he couldn't.

Olivia Knightley's name lit his screen when he picked it up. Another ex—a small-time actress he had dated for a few weeks about six months ago. He didn't know why she was calling in the middle of the night, but at least she was calling. That meant she was alive.

"Olivia?"

No response. Joe could tell someone else was on the line, but no one was talking.

"Olivia? It's Joe. Are you okay?"

Still silence. A few moments later the call ended.

Joe immediately redialed but it went straight to voice mail.

Damn it. Was Olivia in trouble? Should he call the police? Send them to her house just in case?

He was about to do just that when a text came through.

Sorry. I thought I could talk, but I couldn't.

Joe immediately texted back. Are you okay?

Yes, I'm fine. I have some info about the two women who died that I think you should see.

Why would Olivia have information about Jessica and Sarah?

Okay, fine. Can you send it? Or can we meet tomorrow?

It can't be sent. I have to show you in person. I'm leaving at dawn for a film shoot. It really needs to be tonight. Can you come now? I'm at my Colorado Springs house.

Joe didn't like anything about this, but was willing to do whatever it took to stop this killer.

Fine. He texted back. I'll be there in thirty minutes.

Chapter Nine

Olivia Knightley owned multiple houses. Two of them in Colorado, since she loved to ski. Her chalet in Vail was one of the loveliest Joe had ever seen. You could ski right in and out of it.

Her other house, her personal home, was in Colorado Springs, just north of Laura's. It was small, in an unassuming neighborhood, and Joe knew Olivia rarely invited people there. It was her hideout. Somewhere the press didn't know about.

Telling him to come to that house assured Joe she was still alive. Very few people knew about that house.

He and Olivia hadn't ended their relationship on very good terms. Mostly because of the woman sitting next to him in the car as he drove.

It hadn't taken long for the observant actress to realize the man in her bed had feelings for someone else. When Olivia had finally figured out it wasn't anyone current, anyone she could fight, but the memory of Laura that held Joe's heart, she'd cut him loose.

She'd been right to do that. Olivia deserved someone who could give her his full attention and heart. Joe's had already been partially taken.

Joe hadn't wanted Laura to come with him to Olivia's house for a couple of different reasons. First, it could be dangerous. Whatever information Olivia had, Joe knew the killer wouldn't be happy about it. Might go to great lengths to stop Joe from getting it. He didn't want to take the chance of putting Laura in harm's way.

Second, he didn't want to introduce her to an ex-girlfriend. That could be just as ugly.

If Laura hadn't had the keys to the car in her bedroom, Joe would've sneaked out without her being any wiser. But they had been in her room and she'd immediately awakened when he'd come in her bedroom door.

She hadn't thought he was looking for keys and would've been correct if he hadn't received Olivia's call and text. He'd quickly explained the situation.

"Are you sure we shouldn't call the cops?" she said now.

"We will if things look suspicious, I promise. Olivia values her privacy, especially at this house. She won't want anyone knowing about it."

Olivia would be happy to see Laura. To see that she'd been right all along about there being another woman in Joe's mind and heart. She'd spot Laura for what she was immediately.

Joe's.

For privacy's sake, Olivia's house was away from others in the neighborhood, surrounded by trees and at the end of a dead-end street. But beyond that it looked just like many of the other houses: upper-middle class, two stories, normal. Olivia loved to feel normal.

Joe parked on the side of the street. "I don't suppose I can talk you into staying in the car. Let me go see what Olivia knows and I'll·be right out."

Laura was already opening her door. "Nope." She popped the *p* sound.

Joe wished he had the sidearm he'd been asked to turn

in to Steve, or at least had made it home to get one of his other weapons. Walking up to Olivia's door he prayed it wouldn't be cracked open like Jessica's and Sarah's doors had been.

Thankfully it was closed. On it rested a note.

Joe, I'm up in my bedroom working on a script. Headphones. Just come on in.

"That's pretty stupid," Laura said. "What if it wasn't you coming to the door?"

Joe agreed but shrugged. "It's a pretty nice neighborhood, plus nobody knows she owns this house. She's pretty fanatic about her privacy when she's here. Her place to unwind, she calls it."

And at least the note meant Olivia was still alive. That's what mattered most.

"Sounds like you know a lot about her."

"We dated six months ago."

"Of course you did." Laura cocked her head sideways and studied him. "Are you still seeing each other now?"

"No."

"Does Olivia know that?"

"C'mon, Laura. You know I'm not as bad as the gossip rags make me out to be. I liked Olivia. We went out for a few weeks. But then it ended."

"Why?"

The same reason all of Joe's relationships had ended. Olivia hadn't been Laura.

"Irreconcilable differences, I guess. We weren't what the other one wanted."

Laura didn't respond to that.

"Is she going to mind that I'm here? She's not going to be waiting for you naked or anything, is she?"

Joe remembered having the same thoughts about Jessica and Sarah.

He opened the door. "No, she won't be." He entered the house, Laura right behind him. "But if she is, cover my eyes and fight for my honor, okay?"

"How about if I cover my eyes and hit you in the head with a baseball bat?"

"That works, too." Joe wasn't totally sure she was joking and prayed Olivia would be fully clothed.

Various lights were on throughout the house as Joe led them to the stairs. He wondered if he should yell for Olivia so they didn't startle her.

"Where's her bedroom?"

"Up the stairs on the left."

Olivia's bedroom door was closed so Joe knocked, loudly.

Nothing.

His stomach clenched before remembering the note downstairs. Olivia had on headphones. He cracked open the bedroom door. "Olivia? It's Joe. I'm here with a friend of mine, Laura."

Still no answer. Joe flung the door open expecting the worst. He let out a sigh of relief when no one was dead in the bedroom. He walked fully inside, Laura right behind him.

"You okay?" She touched him on the back.

He blew out a breath in a shudder. "Yeah. It's just…" His words ran out.

"This situation was like the other two women's."

"Yeah. With both Sarah and Jessica I walked into the room and found them dead on the bed."

But Olivia wasn't. So where was she? Joe gave up on keeping quiet and began yelling for her. Laura did the same. Joe searched in the bathroom and closet while Laura turned to look in the guest bedroom.

Laura's frightened cry had Joe running to her at the guest bedroom's door.

"What?"

She put out an arm to keep him from going any farther inside. "Joe, you've got to get out of here right now."

Joe felt sadness crash over him. "Oh no, not Olivia. She's dead?"

"Yes, definitely. I'm sorry."

Joe tried to enter the room but Laura pulled him back to her. "The best thing you can do for yourself is not get your DNA in this room."

Joe was looking at Olivia on the bed. Blood pooled around her naked form. Just like the other two women.

Laura's words barely registered, but her pull on him did. "What?"

She reached up and cupped his cheeks with both hands, bringing her face close to his. His eyes finally focused on hers. "Someone is framing you, Joe. Two dead women who both knew you could possibly be a coincidence. But you finding the body of three of your ex-lovers? The police will arrest you for sure."

"But I didn't kill her. I didn't kill anyone." Joe felt like ramming his fist through a wall.

"I know. But someone has done an excellent job making it look like it was you."

"We can't just leave her here. We have to call the police."

Laura nodded. "We will but—"

She stopped her sentence as every light in the house switched off.

They reached for each other in the darkness.

"What just happened?" they both asked at the same time.

"Fuse blew?" Laura asked.

"Very convenient timing. Especially for us to have just discovered a dead body." Joe half expected to look out the window and see squad cars pulling up. It was like someone was trying to keep them here until the cops arrived and Joe could be blamed once again.

"I'm your witness this time. You were with me when we found Olivia. That will count for something."

"Let's go try to figure out the fuse situation."

"You go check it out. I'm going to stay here. I feel like something's going on, Joe. I don't want to leave the body."

Joe knew what she meant. He used the flashlight on his phone to hurry out to the garage, finding the fuse box and ripping it open. The box had all but exploded.

Someone had definitely messed with the fuse box, and recently.

Joe ran back to the door leading to the house but found it locked. He pushed against it with his shoulder, but it didn't budge.

Damn it. It must have automatically locked when he came through. He jogged to the door leading to the outside and ran back around to the front of the house. As he stood in the driveway, a light in the upper window caught his attention. How could there be lights back on if the fuse box had been completely burned out?

It only took a slight flicker for him to realize it wasn't a light. The house was on fire.

Very close to where Laura had been standing.

Joe barreled through the front door. "Laura!" He ran toward the stairs then stopped as he saw fire swallowing the entire right side of the stairs.

Joe felt the tightness of the scar that covered part of his neck and back. He knew the agonizing sting of fire from his wounds last year.

"Laura!" He yelled again, but there was no response. The flames were becoming more intense now.

A fear like he'd never before experienced grasped Joe. Laura was somewhere in that fire.

Grabbing a blanket off the back of Olivia's couch, he doused it under water in the sink and threw it around himself running past the flames on the stairs.

The smoke was thick on the second floor. Joe dropped low and belly-crawled toward the front of the house where he'd left Laura. Breathing was difficult, seeing even more so. He was almost crawling on top of her before he saw her lying totally still in the hallway.

"Laura." He shook her shoulder, coughing. "Laura, wake up."

She didn't move.

Joe knew he had to get her out of here, and he prayed she was just unconscious. He couldn't even think about anything further. He wrapped the blanket around her and began dragging her down the hall. He realized after a few moments she was helping him.

"Laura, are you okay?"

"Somebody hit me."

"What?" Had she said someone hit her?

"I was watching Olivia's body and someone hit me on the head from behind."

Someone was in the house with them.

Joe pulled Laura closer. "The house is on fire. We have to get out."

"Okay, I can crawl."

The fire was worse at the top of the stairs. Joe could feel the painful singe on the back of his neck.

They needed to get out right now.

Laura wrapped the damp blanket around them both as they half stumbled half ran down the stairs and through the hall. Fire licked toward them on all sides, but they kept moving so neither of them suffered burns as they made it out the front door.

Once outside, they both collapsed on the front lawn.

"Are you okay?" His voice came out as more of a hiss than anything else. He rolled over and touched her on the shoulder.

"Yes." Laura began to sit up. "Joe, someone was in the house with us. I thought you were coming up the stairs, and someone clocked me from behind."

"The fuse box had been almost completely destroyed. That's why all the lights had gone out. Then the door locked behind me so I had to run outside to get back in. That's when they got to you."

She gripped his hand. "Someone's going beyond just trying to frame you. It looks like someone wants to kill you. Maybe make it look like you killed Olivia, me and then yourself."

Terror gripped Joe at the thought that Laura could be right.

She began to stand. "We've got to get out of here. It won't take long before someone sees the fire and calls it in."

"You don't think I should stay and talk to the cops?"

"As your friend, I suggest you get as far away from this crime scene as possible. As your lawyer, honestly, I would probably suggest the same. Nothing can be done for Olivia now, Joe." Her voice softened. "I'm sorry you lost another friend."

Another woman had died, and now there was no denying it was because of her connection with him. He looked at Laura. She could've been a target also. Could've easily died along with Olivia.

It wasn't in Joe's nature to run from a fight or from

solving a crime. Especially since he had taken an oath to uphold the law when he'd joined Omega. But Laura was right. Staying here now wasn't going to do anything but get him arrested.

Sometimes you had to break the rules if it was the right thing to do.

He gripped Laura's hand and helped her up and to the car. They needed to get out of here.

He couldn't stop whoever was doing this if he was behind bars.

SHE WATCHED THE house go up in flames, the beauty of the fire bewitching her. It had not taken Joe the way it was supposed to, but she could forgive it because of its loveliness.

He brought the woman from the bank. Laura Birchwood, the lawyer. She thought Laura and Joe had just met last weekend but realized now that was incorrect. Joe had obviously known this woman much longer. Trusted this woman.

She'd made a mistake in thinking Joe would be distraught at the loss of his ex-lovers. Killing them—watching Joe find them—had not brought out in him the emotional response she had hoped for.

But today, watching as he realized Laura was trapped in the burning house? That had been the reaction she'd been hoping to see with the others.

Laura was the key.

And to think she'd almost killed her last weekend when she ran Laura off the road. That would've been too quick, too painless.

Laura would play an important role in the revenge on Joe. Now she knew Laura's safety and well-being were the most important things to him.

Laura would die, but she would die in a way that would cause Joe the most pain. She would burn right in front of him.

But first Joe would fall.

Chapter Ten

After stopping at a twenty-four hour medical care clinic to make sure Laura's head wound and their smoke inhalation didn't require more serious attention, they'd returned to Laura's house. They'd both stripped naked in her garage, leaving their clothes—ruined by smoke—in there, and gone to separate showers. Laura didn't have anything that would fit Joe except a giant bathrobe belonging to her father. That would have to do until they could get him something else.

The pounding at her front door scared them both.

"You expecting anyone?" Joe whispered.

"Knocking on my door at seven o'clock in the morning? Um, no." She looked out her window and grimaced. "It's the police."

Joe muttered a curse.

"I knew they'd be looking for you, but had no idea it would be this soon." If they'd shown up fifteen minutes earlier, she would've had the smell of smoke still in her hair, a dead giveaway.

She turned to him. "Quick, go up in my room, stay out of sight."

"What are you going to do?"

"Talk to them. If they have a warrant to search my house, I won't be able to do anything. Otherwise, unless they see something suspicious, they can't come in. Don't come out." She pushed him toward her bedroom.

Pounding on the door resumed. Laura opened it. There stood Detective Thompson and two uniformed officers.

"Gentlemen, I have neighbors, if you don't mind. It's early."

"Ms. Birchwood, we're looking for Joe Matarazzo," Thompson said. "May we come in?"

"Do you have a warrant?"

Thompson's eyes narrowed. "No, ma'am."

Relief coursed through Laura. "Then no, gentlemen, you can't come in."

She began shutting the door, but Thompson held out a hand to stop it. Laura didn't want to add to their suspicions so she opened the door again. "Something else I can help you with?"

"Do you know where Matarazzo is?"

"Have you tried his house?" Laura sidestepped the question. "I'm his lawyer, Detective, not his girlfriend."

"Are you sure that's the case, Ms. Birchwood? We found these pictures online of the two of you together."

Thompson pulled out a half-dozen pictures he'd printed from the internet, passing them along to the other two officers to hold up as well as keeping two in his own hands.

She and Joe, six years ago, in full, unforgiving color. She found it difficult to look at the woman she'd been then. How much in love with him she'd been. The camera had captured it so perfectly.

She had to admit Joe looked pretty enthralled with her too in the photos. But she knew that had been a lie. Joe had never been captivated by her.

"Ancient history, gentlemen. Those photos were all taken half a dozen years ago."

Thompson collected the photos and got out another couple of prints. "How about these? They were taken last weekend if I'm not mistaken."

The photos someone had taken of them at dinner on Friday. The same ones that had reminded Laura why it was a bad idea to get involved again with Joe.

Glancing away from the pictures and back at Thompson, Laura realized she didn't need to lie. The truth would work best for her.

"It was dinner between two old acquaintances. I'm sure you heard about the hostage situation at the bank in Denver on Friday. Joe Matarazzo got everyone out safely and we went out to celebrate a job well done. You might want to take that into consideration during your search for him. Joe is one of the good guys."

Thompson ignored the last part. "This picture doesn't look like dinner between two acquaintances."

He was right. Damned if Laura didn't have that same look in her eyes she'd had six years ago. And Joe looked just as enthralled.

Laura crossed her arms and leaned against her door. "Detective, I'm sure if you dig just a little deeper into our past relationship you'll see why I would have to be an absolute idiot to be harboring him now or not cooperating with you if I knew anything about his whereabouts."

That was the honest truth. She *was* an idiot.

"And why is that?"

"The gossip sites hated Joe and I together. Said I wasn't attractive enough, polished enough, *sparkling* enough for someone like Joe. I'd be foolish to set myself up for that again."

Thompson shook his head. "Gossip reporters are vicious. No one takes them seriously."

"Joe Matarazzo took them seriously. Told me himself

after a few months of dating that I wasn't the caliber of woman someone like him should be with. Why would I want to be around someone who doesn't think I am good enough for him?"

Thompson's eyes narrowed. Evidently Laura had just confirmed the detective's poor opinion of Joe. "I knew Matarazzo was an idiot. Has to be to say something like that. But you're still his lawyer?"

"He has no problem with my caliber as a lawyer. Plus, Joe is very wealthy. He made it worth my while to forget about past—" she shrugged "—misjudgments. On both our parts. So I helped him out yesterday. I imagine he'll get a full team of lawyers if all this continues. But there's nothing romantic between us and definitely nothing that would have him at my house at the crack of dawn."

"I see." Thompson nodded, but still didn't look completely convinced.

"Why are you looking for him so early? Something else must have happened or you would've charged him yesterday."

Laura knew it was risky bringing up the new murder, but it would be more suspicious if she didn't ask.

Thompson nodded. "There's been another murder. Someone else Matarazzo dated. Killer tried to cover it with a fire, but we got an anonymous tip-off that someone matching Joe Matarazzo's description was seen around the victim's house."

Laura's lips pursed. Anonymous tip-off could've been a neighbor. But it also could've been the true killer trying to make sure Joe was arrested since he'd made it out of the house alive. Especially since no one mentioned her being there with him.

Thompson held up a picture of Olivia Knightley. "This was the lady who was murdered. Know her?"

Laura had to be careful here. "Not personally. She's an actress, right? Olivia something."

Thompson nodded. "Olivia Knightley. Matarazzo and Ms. Knightley dated six months ago."

"I wouldn't know anything about that. Now if you'll excuse me, I'm late for work."

"If Matarazzo does get in touch with you—since you're his lawyer and all—please call us. As his counsel I'm sure you would do the right, legal thing and tell him to turn himself in since there is a warrant out for his arrest."

"Of course."

"You should be aware that as an ex-lover of his, you are in danger, too. The only connection we've found between the three women so far is Matarazzo."

"I'll keep that in mind, Detective."

Thompson shot out his hand to keep her from shutting the door. "Matarazzo is a womanizer at best, Ms. Birchwood. I'm afraid he might also be a killer. Either way, women he's been intimate with keep winding up dead."

"Joe may be a jerk, but he isn't a killer, Detective. You need to keep searching for the real person committing these murders, not spend all your time looking for Joe."

Thompson's eyes narrowed and Laura feared she'd said too much. "Even if he isn't the killer, someone is targeting women he cares about, so that puts you in danger."

"Joe doesn't care about me. I'm just his lawyer and someone he knew a long time ago."

"I'm not so sure about that."

"Look at the women he dates and look at me, Detective. Olivia Knightley. Jessica Johannsen. They're stunningly gorgeous." Laura gestured to herself. She wasn't wearing any makeup, had her hair wrapped in a towel. "And look at me. No one could possibly think Joe and I belong in the same social realm together, much less that we could be a serious couple."

Thompson and the two other officers looked uncomfortable. She didn't blame them. They all knew what she said was the truth, even if they didn't want to admit it.

"Six years ago, I thought I had something special with Joe, then out of the blue he ended it with me because he figured out he could do better. He could find women superior in beauty, grace, wit and spark."

"Ms. Birchwood—"

"Well, three of those superior women are now dead. So I suppose I should be glad Joe found me so lacking then, or it might be me lying in the morgue right now."

Laura grabbed the door and pulled it partway shut.

"Joe and I aren't a good fit. That's what Matarazzo discovered years ago, and I agree wholeheartedly. I'm pretty sure I'm safe from whoever is killing the beautiful women Joe cares about."

Thompson nodded. "Again, I'm not so sure about that. Just be careful."

She murmured her thanks and shut the door, leaning her forehead against it.

Nothing like reliving all the painful details of your past to make a bad morning even worse.

JOE ALMOST SURRENDERED himself a half-dozen times while Laura spoke to Detective Thompson. It would've been easier than listening to all of that.

She was so wrong about how he'd felt six years ago. None of what she'd said to Thompson had been accurate. Not that Laura would know that.

Joe had been scared. He could admit that now. He'd been twenty-five and scared that he'd found the woman he wanted to spend the rest of his life with. Her looks, her *caliber*, had nothing to do with why he'd truly broken off their relationship.

Not that it made it any easier for her. To Laura he'd just been cruel.

Moving around the corner and seeing Laura leaning against the door destroyed Joe further. Before he could think better of it he walked over and wrapped his arms around her, pulling her back against his chest.

For just a moment she lay against him, her head resting back on his shoulder. A perfect fit, just like they'd always been. Then she stiffened and stepped away.

"I can't," she whispered. "Not right now. I don't want to touch you. To touch anyone. I just saw a dead woman lying five feet from me. Just washed smoke out of my hair from a fire that almost killed both of us. And my head is killing me."

"Laura—"

"Talking about the past, about what a fool I was? That was the last straw."

He had to try to make her understand. "That stuff I said six years ago, I didn't mean it."

She walked past Joe, careful not to touch him in any way. "You know what? It doesn't matter. You've got so many more important issues going on right now than our past."

She was right, but the pinched look on her face was still hard to swallow.

Laura walked into the kitchen. "You've got to get out of town. If Thompson doesn't have a warrant to search my house yet, he will soon. I'm not sure he believed me."

Laura's words about how she'd be a fool to get involved with Joe again had been pretty damn convincing, but he didn't point that out. "I don't want to run. I want to find out who's doing this and stop it."

"That's fine, but getting arrested isn't going to help with that plan." She rubbed a hand over her face. "I have a cabin in Park County about an hour west of here. It's in my mother's maiden name. No one would even tie it to me, much less you."

Joe shook his head. "No. I don't want to run."

"You're not running. You're retreating and regrouping. Let me finish up work today and tomorrow, then I'll join you. We can try to get a handle on this."

He didn't want to go. Didn't want to take himself out of where the action was. What good could he do at her cabin?

"What good will you do sitting in a cell?" It was as if Laura could hear his inner monologue.

He gripped the kitchen counter. "I feel useless."

Her face softened. Laura couldn't stand to see other people in pain, even someone like him, who had caused her so much of it. "You're not useless. But we have to be strategic. And getting you out of Dodge is the best move right now."

She was right. But he still didn't like it.

"Okay. I'll go. But only if you promise to meet me at the cabin right after work tomorrow."

"I will. Hopefully, me going to work just like everything is normal will convince Thompson that we're not together. I'm sure he'll be watching me. They're probably watching my house, too, by the way. Just because they couldn't get inside doesn't mean they won't wait to snatch you as soon as you walk out."

"I'll use stealth—don't worry."

She smiled. "That robe is not going to get you any points in the nonconspicuous category."

"I'll handle clothes. Have something delivered." It was one of the perks of not having to worry about money.

All the money in the world couldn't bring back the women who had died. Joe planned to make sure it didn't happen to anyone else.

Chapter Eleven

Laura tried to act as normally as possible at work. That proved to be more difficult than she thought.

She shouldn't have been surprised. In the last twelve hours she'd seen a dead woman lying in a pool of her own blood, been knocked unconscious by an unknown assailant and had almost been killed in a fire. After that she'd lied, or at least intentionally misled, law enforcement officers, and harbored a fugitive.

That had all been before 8:00 a.m.

But all of that, as difficult to deal with as it might be, wasn't what had her utterly unfocused today. Joe was what had her unfocused.

More specifically Joe looking so lost this morning and yesterday at Omega. His whole world was bottoming out beneath him and he didn't know what to do.

Laura wanted to help him. Wanted to wipe that look off his face. She was sure most of the world would agree that Joe Matarazzo's face needed to be plastered with an easygoing smile, not lines of worried exhaustion. A quick and charming wit was what the world expected of Joe.

He wanted to fix this, stop this killer. She knew if he could he would give his entire fortune to have the three women back safely. But neither his money nor his charm could mend this.

Joe had become a man of action. Wanting to do. Wanting to help. These women dying had hit him hard.

Omega Sector suspending him, despite it being the best thing for the organization overall, also had him reeling.

Laura had to face the fact that Joe was no longer the man she'd known six years ago. He'd grown, matured. Had begun to put others' needs—even those of people he didn't know—before his own. Working in law enforcement had changed him.

It both pissed her off and caused her heart to flutter.

She had no idea what the hell she felt for Joe. For a woman used to knowing her own mind, it was frustrating.

She had to help Joe clear his name. The thought of Joe sitting in a cell, even temporarily, made her feel sick to her stomach. And she knew if Thompson found Joe he would definitely be detained, probably arrested and charged.

But right now Joe was safe at her cabin. She had planned to join him tomorrow, but she would go tonight instead. They needed to figure out the pattern behind the killings so they could get a lead on who was committing them.

Laura spent the last couple of hours of her day clearing her calendar and rescheduling meetings she'd had for the next day.

Yes, going to meet Joe tonight was better. He needed a friend. Laura could be that for him.

Just a friend.

She rolled her eyes. Yeah, right. She must be a glutton for punishment or something, but she couldn't stay away from him.

It was after seven when she finally finished everything she needed in order to clear her calendar for tomorrow.

Everyone else was gone from the building. Laura would go home, grab a couple changes of clothes and meet Joe at the cabin.

And her changes of clothes would involve no sexy underwear whatsoever. Definitely not the red thong and matching bra she'd purchased a few weeks ago on a whim.

Because she definitely did not remember how partial he was to that color on her.

She walked into the parking garage her office shared with other offices on the block, taking the stairs down to the bowels where she was parked because she'd been so late getting here this morning.

A woman stood over in the corner, looking out at the lot. She smiled oddly at Laura so Laura gave her a little wave. Maybe she'd forgotten where she had parked. That had happened to Laura before, after a particularly long day.

Laura turned the corner toward her car. Besides the red lingerie, she would need her laptop so they could try to figure out the pattern the killer was using.

The brutal shove into a car caught her completely off guard. Laura was usually much more diligent when walking into the garage alone, but she'd been so caught up in getting to Joe she'd let her guard down.

She turned and saw a masked man. Laura tried to dive to the side, away from him, but he grabbed her arm.

"Where are you going, bitch?"

Remembering the other woman, Laura let out a scream, hoping she would call the police. Although by the time they got here it would be too late.

"So he cares about you, huh? We'll see how much," he muttered, wrapping his hand around her upper arm with bruising strength.

Was this guy talking about Joe? Was he the one who had killed the other women?

Laura began fighting with a renewed frenzy. She would not let this man kill her and frame Joe for it.

She threw her arms and legs around wishing she had more background in self-defense. Her captor grunted as some of her frantic blows connected with sensitive places. He cursed and backhanded her. She fell against another vehicle.

"Let's go, Max. Hurry up!" Another masked man in an SUV parked toward the exit yelled.

Laura tasted blood in her mouth as she got up from the hood of the car where she'd fallen. Out of the corner of her eye she saw the woman again, just watching, too afraid to get involved.

The large man grabbed her by the hair and began dragging her toward the other van. She punched at him but it wasn't enough to stop him. She dropped all her weight to the ground crying out at the stinging pain in her scalp when he didn't let go. She couldn't let him get her in the vehicle.

"Help me with her," he called out to the other guy.

A few seconds later she felt the other guy grab her legs. Laura screamed, trying to draw any attention to herself, until a meaty fist covered her mouth.

She bit it.

The man yelled and she saw fury burn in the eyes visible through the black ski mask. She braced herself for the fist flying toward her face.

Instead she and her two captors went flying to the ground as a huge force knocked into them.

Joe.

He kicked the guy who had been holding her legs in the jaw and sent him flying back. Laura scurried out of the way as the first man rolled with Joe on the cement, both of them giving and receiving bone-crunching blows.

Joe obviously knew what he was doing. These weren't just lucky punches he was getting in. And even with both of them rolling on the ground he effectively blocked many of the attacker's—a man much bigger and meatier—blows.

Laura scrambled to her feet and saw the second man rushing back at Joe with a knife in his hand.

"Joe, behind you. A knife!"

Her words gave him just enough time to spin around, the blade catching him in his shoulder rather than the middle of his back. Laura heard a sickening snap and a high-pitched scream from the attacker as Joe made short work of the knife in the other man's hand, breaking his wrist and recovering the weapon himself.

This was a Joe she had never seen before. Had never known existed. Would've sworn didn't exist if she couldn't see him with her own eyes.

There was no carefree in him now, no charm. Just deadly intent and overwhelming force.

Both men began backing away now that Joe had not only proved himself capable of handling them, but had a weapon. Within moments they were fleeing to their vehicle and speeding out of the parking garage.

Joe rushed to her, touching her lip gently where the guy had hit her. "Are you okay?"

Laura's short laugh had a bark of hysteria. "Me?" She looked at his arm where blood was dripping through the sleeve of his blue shirt. "You're the one bleeding. We need to get you to a hospital."

"No, I'm fine. Plus a hospital might ask too many questions. We've got to go."

She let him lead her to her car. "Why are you even here? I thought you went to the cabin."

"I couldn't do it. Couldn't run, leaving you alone. What if one of Olivia's neighbors had reported that they remembered seeing us *both* outside her house? The cops could've come back and arrested you. There was no way I would let that happen."

She nodded.

"Not to mention someone killing people linked to me." He gestured vaguely toward where the masked guys had driven off.

Joe opened the passenger door of the car for her, but she stopped, leaning against the side of the vehicle, closing her eyes, needing a minute. Trying to stop the spinning in her head, not just from the blows.

Joe's hand softly cupped her cheek. "Are you sure you're okay?"

"Those were the guys trying to frame you."

"I know."

"They were going to take me and kill me like the others. You would've found me dead at my house."

Joe didn't say anything, just pulled her closer to him. She breathed in his scent, feeling his lips at her temple.

"We need to leave," Joe finally said.

Laura nodded. The guys might come back, or the police. Either way, staying here was dangerous.

"We'll both go to the cabin."

THEY DROVE STRAIGHT out of town. Joe ripped a strip off one of the shirts he'd purchased and had delivered to Laura's house this morning. It stemmed the bleeding from the cut on his shoulder. Not getting stitches would probably leave a scar, but a hospital wasn't worth the risk.

They stopped only once on the way to the cabin, at a

super center to get a first aid kit, some clothes for Laura and enough food for while they holed up and tried to figure out who was trying to frame Joe. The cashier had given the two of them quite a look, for once not because she recognized Joe, but because she was worried he was some backwoods husband beating on his wife.

Joe couldn't blame the cashier. Laura looked exhausted. Her lip was swollen from the punch she'd taken, her hair and makeup were a mess. Her eyes dull and unfocused.

So unlike Laura.

He paid in cash and put the bags in the cart, grabbing Laura's hand. It was icy. He rubbed her arms up and down, feeling her coldness even through her blouse. He bent down so his eyes were right in front of hers. "You okay?"

She blinked and focused on him. "Yeah, I just…" She shrugged. "I'm sorry."

"Let's get you to the cabin." He wanted to take off his jacket and give it to her, but his blood-soaked sleeve would be too memorable. They had already drawn enough attention. He tucked Laura to his side and pushed the cart out with one hand.

Laura's cabin on Lake George, fifty miles west of Colorado Springs stood private and simple. She was right; no one would look for them here. Joe led her into the cabin, checking it thoroughly himself first, and sat her on the couch. When he came back in from carrying the bags she was still sitting exactly where he'd placed her.

This wasn't good.

He knew she was exhausted, in pain—she'd taken two hits to the head in the last twenty-four hours—probably hungry and definitely in shock. If it wasn't for his training with Omega, Joe would probably be all those things too.

He saw bottles of alcohol on an antique tray by the kitchen table. A good shot of quality scotch would probably do them both good. Hell, a finger of *any* scotch would do them good. He poured two glasses and sat down next to Laura.

"Here, drink this."

She did without comment, which just confirmed how far gone she was.

The strong burn pulled her back. "What *is* that?" she sputtered.

Joe grinned. "Whiskey."

"I think enough people have tried to kill me today without you joining the club, thank you very much." Coughs racked her body.

"Just call it liquid fortification. You were looking a little hollow there for a second."

She nodded. "I was feeling a little hollow."

He slipped off his jacket and grabbed the first aid kit. Laura helped him clean and wrap the cut on his shoulder that thankfully wasn't too deep and had long since stopped bleeding. It hurt now, but it wasn't going to cause him any permanent issues.

Joe put the first aid supplies on the side table then leaned all the way back against the couch next to Laura. "Hell of a day, hasn't it been?"

"Where did you learn to fight like that?"

"Not everybody liked rich kids as I was growing up. It was either have full-time security following me around middle school or learn how to protect myself."

"Did your middle school moves include learning to break someone's wrist?"

Joe was glad to see the liquor was working. Laura

didn't seem nearly as brittle as she had before. He pulled her so she was resting next to him, back against the couch.

"When I started working at Omega Sector I ended up learning a lot more defensive and offensive tactics. Weapons training, close-quarter fighting. The whole works."

"Well, it showed today."

"Thank God for that."

She let out a huge yawn and he slid to the side of the couch, pulling her with him, until they were both lying flat, her tucked against him. He felt her stiffen.

"You're okay. I'm okay. Let's just rest," he murmured. "I don't need anything you're not willing to give me. I just want to hold you and know you're alive."

Because she very easily might not have been. Listening to his instincts—staying in town rather than going to the cabin—had never served him better than it had today.

He felt her relax and drift off to sleep. Good, she needed it. He would just hold her here while she slept.

It was more than he'd ever thought he'd get again, anyway. He'd take it.

He slept also. He knew he did because when he woke Laura's soft sweet lips were on his.

"We didn't die," she murmured against his mouth. "When that guy came at you with the knife I thought he would kill you."

Joe reached down and grabbed Laura's hips, pulling her more fully on top of him. There. Touching him from head to toe. That's how he wanted her.

"When I came around the corner and saw those two guys trying to carry you off—" he broke away and whispered "—my heart stopped."

"Make love to me, Joe." Her fingers were already loosing the top button of her shirt.

"Laura." He brought his lips back to hers, rubbing his hands up and down her spine. "I want to make sure this is what you really want. This has been a crazy day. We don't have to do this."

She rolled her hips against his. "Are you suggesting you don't want to?"

He half groaned, half laughed. "That is obviously not the case."

"Then what's the problem? I've crawled on top of you. I'm unbuttoning my blouse. I'm feeling pretty confident about what I want. And I'm definitely not drunk if that's your concern."

What was his problem? Why was he not helping her with said blouse and moving things right along? He definitely wanted to.

He cupped both sides of her head and brought her face up so he could see her. Hazel eyes, clear and focused, stared back at him. Her little chin jutted out as if she was daring him.

To stop or go further, he didn't know.

He realized the problem. He didn't want this to just be let's-celebrate-we're-alive sex. He wanted it to mean something to her. An emotional connection between the two of them. Because as much as he wanted her—which was pretty much more than his next breath—he didn't want to jeopardize a possible future with her for a few hours of passion.

Oh, how the mighty Casanova had fallen.

He could feel Laura start to stiffen, true doubt entering her eyes. It gutted him, the thought that she doubted his desire for her. Laura wanted him. He would take her any way he could get her.

And pray it would be enough to tie her to him more completely.

He wrapped his arms around her, sitting up so quickly a little squeak escaped her. He swiveled and sat back against the couch so she was straddling his hips. He tilted his head and took her mouth.

He stopped thinking, and just allowed himself to feel. To sink into that soft, wet mouth. To trace it with his tongue, tease her warm lips apart and explore.

He kept the pace slow and easy, wanting to enjoy, to savor. Laura unbuttoned and peeled his shirt off him, careful of the wound on his shoulder. He made short work of her blouse before bringing her back in for a kiss.

The pace was much more frantic now. She gripped his waist, tugging him to her.

He couldn't breathe for the pleasure of it. All he could do was get closer. Her body was too far away even though they were plastered to each other.

He wrapped his arms around her hips and stood, still holding her to him.

"Where's the bedroom?" His words came out as a growl against her lips.

"Two rooms, both have the same size beds. Take your pick. But be quick about it."

He smiled, carrying her across the room to the first door he came to.

"This better not be a closet, or I'm not going to make it to a bed."

She giggled and he reached down and gently bit the juncture of where her neck met her shoulder. Her laugh turned into a sigh. She wrapped herself more tightly around him.

It was a bedroom. Within moments he had her on the bed, both of them naked. And he proceeded to lose himself in the woman he'd never been able to fully get out of his heart.

Chapter Twelve

The next morning Laura awoke to the smell of coffee and an indentation in the mattress where Joe had recently lain.

What had she done?

Besides having had the best night of lovemaking since…

Since she and Joe had broken up six years before.

She groaned into her pillow.

The physical side of their relationship had never been a problem. As a matter of fact, no side of their relationship had been a problem. Or at least Laura had thought as much.

Until the day Joe dumped her out of the blue.

"I can almost see your brain working at a million miles an hour." Joe walked into the room holding coffee.

He was so sexy, so rumpled and casual. Handing her a perfect cup of coffee.

Laura could see so easily why she had fallen in love with him before. She would be a fool to let herself make the same mistake twice. She should not forget that Joe—despite all the ways he seemed to have grown—could change his mind and decide out of the blue again that he didn't want her anymore.

She couldn't survive her heart shattering twice.

"Just trying to figure out how we're going to get out of this mess unscathed."

Joe's eyes narrowed slightly and Laura knew he wasn't sure if she was referring to the bedroom situation, the police situation or both.

Good. Let him wonder. She was wondering, too.

"We've got to figure out who's setting me up."

"Okay." Laura took a sip of her coffee then set it on the nightstand. She ran out into the living room, aware she was only wearing one of his T-shirts. It was too big on her, but she was still conscious of how much of her legs was exposed.

She grabbed her legal pad and pen from her bag and came back to the bedroom. "We need a list. 'Who would want to hurt Joe?'"

"I don't think I like this list."

"We can call it 'people who think Joe is an ass.' Is that better?" She smiled innocently.

He rolled his eyes, shaking his head. "I think the first one will suffice."

They worked on the list for the next couple of hours, and while they fixed and ate breakfast, forming two basic categories: people he'd helped put in jail and his ex-lovers. She didn't make him name all his ex-lovers—because seriously her heart couldn't take it—just people with whom he'd had relationships that ended badly. They'd both realized quickly that Laura would be at the top of that list so they'd moved on to the people he'd put in jail.

"Sometimes people feel like I fed them untruths. I try not to lie to hostage-takers, but my first priority is always getting everyone out alive. If I suggest no jail time will be involved and they believe me and surrender..." He shrugged.

"It can't be anyone from inside jail. It has to be someone who's out."

"It could be someone connected to someone I put in jail, but I can't remember all those names on my own. We're going to need my case files from Omega."

Laura put down her notepad. "Will they give them to you?"

Joe shrugged. "I don't know. I'm not going to ask. We'll need to sneak them out."

Why wouldn't he ask? Asking seemed much simpler than sneaking. "Steve Drackett seemed pretty reasonable. If you tell him we think—"

"No."

Laura waited for the rest of the explanation but none came.

Good thing she was a lawyer and talking sense into people was sometimes part of her job. "Joe, from everything I know and have seen of Omega Sector, it's a pretty tight-knit group. You are part of the team. Steve will help if you ask him."

"Things aren't always as they seem. There is a team, but I'm more of an outsider. Trust me—they don't want to be a part of this problem, especially now that a third woman connected to me is dead. I'm sure Steve would rather I just use my money to help get myself out of this mess."

She reached for his arm but he slid away.

"Joe—"

He reached forward and kissed her on the forehead before standing and walking across the room. "It's not a big deal, seriously. It's not like they dislike me or anything. I'm just not part of the inner core."

"That's not how it looked to me."

"Like I said, sometimes things aren't always the way they look."

She wanted to argue but didn't have the facts to back up her case. "Okay, so we have to sneak them out. Great, breaking more laws. How will we get in?"

"My ID probably won't work right now. Or will at least alert security if I enter the building since I'm on suspension. The files are in a relatively unsecured section in a different building, but getting in the front door is the problem."

"Do you have a plan?"

"Yeah." He grimaced. "But you're not going to like it."

JOE WAS RIGHT; she didn't like his plan.

They were back in Colorado Springs, at a bar not far from Omega Sector headquarters. It was actually called Barcade—as in, bar and arcade mixed—and it was chock full o' geeks. The group of particular interest to Joe were the geeks who worked at Omega Sector. Data-entry people, if Laura understood correctly.

They all knew Joe and had fallen over themselves when he'd shown up at "their" bar. Evidently he'd been invited a few times but this was the first time he'd shown up. They'd either not heard the news about him being suspended or totally didn't care.

Joe was talking to them like they were the bestest buddies he'd ever had. Not that he was being insincere—no, Joe genuinely liked people. Liked listening to them, liked talking to them. He liked *these* people.

But he had an agenda. He was using them to get what he wanted. The fact they would've given it to him willingly was irrelevant.

Three rounds of drinks and an untold number of jokes,

laughs and stories later, Joe and Laura walked out of Bar-cade, two "borrowed" Omega IDs in Joe's back pocket.

The data-entry gang was going to see a movie. Joe told them he and Laura already had plans, but insisted they wanted to meet up with them afterward for a nightcap.

So he could slip their IDs back in their pockets, although Joe didn't tell them that.

Admiration and disgust warred within Laura as she and Joe walked the blocks to Omega after seeing the gang off to their movie.

"You're mad," Joe said, not slowing their brisk pace.

"*Mad* isn't the right word."

"Those guys are low clearance. No one could get into any highly secured part of Omega Sector with their IDs. So there's no real security breach here. But it will get us what we need."

"I'm not mad about security clearance."

"Your eyes tell a different story."

Laura took a deep breath. "I'm not mad. It's just… those people trusted you. Really thought you were interested in them."

Joe stopped walking and turned to face Laura, grabbing her arm. "Wait a second, I *was* interested in them. They're an interesting group. A little geeky, but not bad overall."

"You were only talking to them because you wanted to shoplift their IDs. Only laughing and pretending to like them because you needed something from them."

He looked affronted. "That's not true. I walked into that bar because of needing their IDs, but talking to them, listening, laughing—that wasn't fake. They're good people."

"Have you ever hung out with them before?"

Now he looked a little sheepish. "Not here, outside of work. But I've talked to them inside Omega."

Laura shrugged. It was a fine line. But she realized it was a line he walked all the time in his job as a hostage negotiator. He got people to trust him for a living. Got them to talk, listened to them, made them feel special.

"Laura, this was the quickest, least painful way to get us into Omega. None of them are hurt in the process and you and I are able to get the info we need to stop another woman from getting killed."

"You used them, Joe. Plain and simple."

Joe's face fell, became shuttered. Obviously he hadn't seen it that way.

She wasn't trying to hurt his feelings, but damn it, it sucked to be used. She knew.

And when had this become about her?

"You know what?" Laura started walking again. "Forget I brought it up. You're right—getting the info, saving women's lives is more important than how we get the info."

"Laura—"

"Let's go. We've got to be back at the bar by the time they're done with the movie."

Laura caught Joe's gaze out of the corner of her eye. He had more he wanted to say, but just nodded. They walked in silence the rest of the way to Omega. Joe turned toward a side entrance rather than the front door.

"Records are held in this section. It's not connected to the regular building. No security guards, but you need an active ID to enter." Joe's voice was no-nonsense.

"Okay."

"Try to look down as we enter because there are security cameras. I took IDs from one guy and one woman, the two whose features are most similar to ours, but we still don't want to be looking at the camera as we walk in."

"Do you even know the names of the people you took the IDs from?" Were they just two more people Joe used and discarded?

Joe stopped again. He held the cards out to Laura without looking at them. "Cory Gimbert and Carolyn Flannigan. She's pretty new, so I have to be honest, I don't know how long she's worked here. Cory's been here two years. We both love *Star Wars* and he emails me whenever new rumors or trailers or anything hit the web. We're buds."

His eyes were hard when he handed Laura Carolyn's card. "Ready?"

Laura nodded. She'd hurt his feelings. She hadn't even been aware of the level of buried hostility she'd felt for Joe. But evidently it was high.

Now wasn't the time to deal with it. "Yes."

Joe walked up to an unassuming back door, nothing like the front door with its guards and weapon scanners. He scanned his ID then walked through. Laura did the same.

He waited for her inside the door, body held at a slightly odd angle. She realized he was protecting them both from the eye of the camera.

"Do the cameras have sound?"

"Not that I know of. I have a buddy in security I chat with from time to time—that's how I know about the security camera. But he didn't mention sound."

Another buddy. Laura was beginning to see a pattern. A lot of buddies. No real friends.

They kept walking down the hallway. "Hard copies of closed case files will be down here in written records storage." He led them quickly to a door.

"Okay, you take the top half of the list, I'll take the

bottom. I wish we had time to scan the files and leave them, but to be honest, I'm not sure how long we have."

"So we'll just take the files?"

Joe shrugged. "Sometimes it's better to ask forgiveness than permission. If we use these to stop the real killer, I don't think anyone is going to question our methods. Besides, they're all cases I worked. Technically I have access to them whenever I need them."

If he wasn't suspended.

"Okay, let's get started." There were nearly twenty cases on the list Joe had texted her. Joe used Cory's ID to enter the written records room, which was exactly what it sounded like: rows of filing cabinets holding printed records of cases Omega had been involved with.

"I don't have any friends who work here," Joe said almost apologetically. "I don't know how their filing system works."

"Let me see if I can figure it out." Laura used Carolyn's ID card to log in to the computer at the front of the room. It seemed to be a closed system, low-level clearance like everything else in this section of Omega, but it got them the info they needed.

"I can run a search with your name and the last three years." She printed the paper listing where the files were held.

Joe took half. "Okay, let's get them and get out of here."

Finding the files wasn't difficult once they understood the system, but it became obvious they were going to have quite a lot to go through back at the cabin. After, of course, they met Cory and Carolyn and the gang for one more drink so Joe could slip their IDs back from wherever he'd gotten them.

"Ready?"

Laura handed him the files she had collected and he slipped them all into his backpack. It was full. "We've got a lot to go through."

"I just hope it will get us the answers we need. Or at least somewhere to start looking."

Joe turned and opened the door to the hallway so they could exit.

There stood Steve Drackett, Joe's boss, waiting for them.

Chapter Thirteen

Damn it.

Steve had a reputation for never leaving Omega, but it was ten-thirty on a Friday night. What the hell was he doing here?

"Hey, Steve." Joe had no idea how he was going to talk himself out of this one. He was about to go to jail.

"Joe." Steve nodded. "Ms. Birchwood."

"Director Drackett. Good to see you again." Laura gave Steve a professional smile as if they hadn't just been caught sneaking into a law enforcement building, while on the run from law enforcement, to steal law enforcement files.

Steve leaned against the door frame. "I'm sure you're aware that another woman—Olivia Knightley—was killed yesterday. Another ex-girlfriend of yours if I'm not mistaken."

Damn it. "Steve, I—"

"And with that third girlfriend being killed, there is officially a warrant out for your arrest."

"I didn't kill them, Steve. I swear."

Steve continued as if he hadn't heard Joe. "Of course, as a law enforcement entity, I set our Omega computers to ping me if something with your name came up in any computer. Credit card use, someone spotting you and posting on their blog, arrest reports. So it struck me as weird when someone was searching your name here in my very own Omega Critical Response Division building."

Joe saw Laura wince from the corner of his eye. If she hadn't been so logical and efficient at getting them the files, Steve wouldn't know they were here.

Joe tried to sort the options out in his head. He could fight his boss, try to get himself and Laura out of the building. But Steve was no old man—forty or forty-one at the most—and despite not taking part in active missions anymore, still kept himself in top shape. He'd probably forgotten more fighting tricks than Joe had ever learned.

Joe would have to talk his way out of this. "Steve—"

Steve held up his hand. "I'm going to assume those are case files in your backpack."

"They are." Joe nodded.

"I will therefore assume that you are not the person killing these women and that you're looking at past cases for suspects."

Steve actually believed him? "Yes, that was our plan."

"I'd like to assume that this elaborate plan to sneak into the building and take these files was due to some misguided thinking on your part to protect me and Omega from ramifications with other law enforcement agencies."

"Well, yes, actually. I didn't want to—"

Steve didn't let him finish. "But what I really think is the issue is that you didn't think we would have your back."

Joe sighed. "I didn't want to drag you or anybody else into this mess. *My* mess."

"Looks like you were willing to drag Laura into the mess, as you call it."

That was true. But not because he'd wanted to. But because… Hell, Joe didn't know why he'd been willing to drag Laura into it.

"You trust her." Steve finished the thought for him. "And you don't trust your colleagues at Omega."

"That's not true. I put my life in their hands all the time."

"Because that's their job, and your job, and everyone is damn good at it. But you don't trust them to really see you as part of the team and to have your back when the going gets tough."

Because he *wasn't* really part of the team. Joe had always known that. Everyone was friendly; everyone joked with him, and even invited him out when they were getting together. But inside, Joe had always known that they thought of him as different. That his money, his pseudo-celebrity status, made him different in their eyes.

That they thought of him as a great guy, laid-back, fun. But not as a member of the team.

"I got suspended, Steve. Remember that?"

Steve's eyes narrowed. "That is standard procedure when someone is being investigated for something as serious as murder. For your protection and Omega's."

Joe knew that. Logically, he knew that. But it had still stung.

Steve shifted. "Let me ask you something. How long do you think it took me to find that cabin of Ms. Birchwood's?"

Joe heard Laura's sharp intake of breath.

"Once there was a warrant out for your arrest, Omega was legally compelled to help find you. Detective Thompson was the first person here demanding info. It was a damn shame a virus ate all the information we had about you and Laura."

Steve was protecting him.

"How long do you think you could hide if I was using all Omega's resources to find you? Maybe if you took your money and got out of the country you'd be safe. But you didn't do that."

"Because I didn't kill those women." Joe felt Laura's hand slip into his. It meant everything to him.

"Hell, Joe, I never for a single second considered that you killed those women. It's my job to look at every possibility when it comes to a crime and I never considered you a viable option. Nobody here did."

Joe wasn't sure what to say. He'd obviously misjudged his boss. "Steve—"

"Take your files and get out of here. Find out who's doing this and let's stop him. I need my team back together."

Joe nodded and put his hand at Laura's back leading her down the hall.

"And give those kids back their IDs," Steve called out after them. "Tell them to be more careful or I'm going to fire their asses."

LAURA WAS, IN JOE'S humble opinion, having way too much fun with her legal pad and the list of "who thinks Joe is an ass." She'd brought up the ex-lovers again, although given that those were the people who were dying, that wasn't likely. Plus, Laura pointed out it made the list too long, so they were better off just dealing with something more manageable.

Joe responded to that by backing Laura up against the wall and kissing her until neither of them could breathe. At first she'd been stiff, but had turned soft and compliant after just a few moments.

She was still mad, Joe knew, about Cory's and Car-

olyn's IDs. Laura's practicality had won out overall—
she had to admit it had worked and returning the IDs
had been even easier than taking them—but she hadn't
liked it.

She thought Joe was using the techs. And in that case,
yes, Joe could admit he was. But it wasn't his normal
practice. He normally didn't need people to get what
he wanted. Hell, if he wanted something he could usually buy it.

He wanted Laura's trust, but money couldn't buy that.
Tonight's stunt had just pushed him a couple steps backward from winning her trust.

First he'd take care of a maniac, then he'd concentrate
on showing Laura she could trust him.

Now they were looking at the case files, studying the
people Joe had a hand in putting behind bars.

There were a lot.

Joe grimaced, looking up from a case three years old.
"Some of these people are still in prison. We can rule
them out."

"Unless it's a member of their family trying to get revenge. We know there are two men involved, from the
guys who tried to take me from the parking garage."

"Well, there's Ricky and Bobby, aka, the Goldman
brothers, Mitchell and Michael. But they're definitely still
in lockup. Although I suppose they could be out on bail."

"One guy in the parking garage called the other guy
Max. So it can't be the Goldman brothers."

"He said Max? Are you sure?" Joe found the Ricky/
Bobby file and opened it.

"Pretty positive, why?"

"Well, there are actually four Goldman brothers.
Mitchell and Michael were the ones from last Friday,

and were evidently pretty irritated at me that they were arrested."

"Why? They were the ones who took sixteen people hostage and assaulted the manager and assistant manager."

Joe shrugged. "Evidently they thought that having a good reason for taking people hostage gave them a free pass."

Laura shook her head. "Wow."

"So yeah, they're threatening revenge and all that stuff. I thought I would worry about that when they got out of jail in three to five years. But, interestingly, they have two other brothers."

Laura rolled her eyes. "Great. Just what the world needs."

"Brothers' names are Melvin and Max."

That got her attention. "Max?"

"Interesting, isn't it, that the murders started a couple days after the Goldman brothers were arrested and that someone named Max tried to kidnap you, presumably to kill you?"

"Do you really think it's them?"

Joe got out his phone and made a call. Sometimes having a lot of money at your disposal helped. During his past few years in law enforcement Joe had made a lot of contacts, some that worked inside the law and some who worked outside it.

Deacon Crandall did both.

"Deacon, this is Joe Matarazzo."

"Joe." He heard Deacon yawn. "It's seven o'clock on a Saturday morning. And, btw, you're wanted by law enforcement."

"Yeah, well, that's because my exes keep showing up dead."

"Lucky bastard. I wish some of my exes would do the same. What can I do for you?"

Deacon didn't ask Joe if he'd murdered the women. Joe didn't know if that was because he trusted Joe was innocent or he just didn't care.

"I need you to find a Melvin Goldman in the Colorado Springs area. Shouldn't be hard. He would be brother of Max, Michael and Mitchell Goldman."

"Okay. What do you want me to do with Mr. Goldman, whose parents didn't know the alphabet contained other letters besides *m*?"

"I need you to find out if he has a broken arm. If you happen to see Max Goldman, he probably will have a pretty bruised face."

"Okay. Do I need to pick them up?"

"Nope, just let me know if they have those wounds and their whereabouts. If so, I'll want to talk to them myself. And Deacon, I'll pay you triple your normal rate if you can get me the info in the next hour."

"You can expect my call."

An hour later Joe and Laura had already received Deacon's call. Not just a call but photos of both Max and Melvin. Sure enough Melvin's arm rested in a sling and Max's face still held bruises from Joe's fists. Deacon sent them an address where the brothers were lying low.

"I'm going to talk to them." Joe grabbed his coat.

"I'm going with you."

Joe was torn. He didn't want to leave Laura alone, but he also didn't want to bring her into a potentially dangerous situation.

"I'm not staying here in the cabin, Joe. Not when something could happen to you while you're in town. You might need me as your lawyer."

He needed her as so much more than that.

"Fine."

"Do you want to call any of your Omega people? For backup, or whatever?"

Joe hesitated. He knew what Steve had said last night about being part of the team. But it was one thing for his boss to believe him, another thing for all his colleagues to just trust Joe was telling the truth when all the evidence said otherwise. He was better off not even asking.

"No. I'm going in alone."

"What about what Steve said?"

"Steve is one thing. My actual colleagues? I can't be sure they're not going to choose the job over me. I wouldn't blame them for choosing the job over me."

Laura shook her head. "I think you're wrong."

Joe shrugged. He couldn't chance it. He shook his head. "Alone. I took the Goldman brothers once. I can deal with them again."

Chapter Fourteen

Laura didn't like the thought of Joe going in alone to question the Goldman brothers, but he seemed adamant about not calling any of his colleagues.

She realized for all of his money, his nice cars, vacation houses and gadgets, Joe Matarazzo was essentially alone. He'd be the first one to laugh off her words with a joke about poor little rich boys. But that didn't make it any less true.

It wasn't that Joe didn't trust other people, it was that he just didn't want to put them in a position where they had to state outright that they trusted him.

His easygoing nature and charm were what made him such a critical part of the Omega team, but it was also why he thought no one took him seriously. That no one would take his side in this situation.

That no one trusted him. When they all would, Laura knew.

Of course, she felt a little hypocritical because Laura didn't trust him, at least personally. She was still afraid he would turn around at any moment and say that now that he'd thought about things again, his initial inclinations had been correct and they really weren't from the same worlds.

Truly, it was only a matter of time before he said that again. Laura knew it had to be true.

"Laura, I've been thinking." Joe's eyes were on the road. His voice somber.

She felt her heart catch. Was this it already? The last two nights had been amazing, but sex had always been amazing for them. Was Joe already coming to his senses?

This time she wasn't going to let it destroy her.

"It's okay, Joe. Just say it."

Now he glanced over at her, brows furrowed. "Just say what?"

Laura cleared her throat. "You know, whatever it is you're thinking."

She could take it. Yeah, her heart would crack, but it wouldn't shatter like last time.

"I was thinking there should probably be a third group on the 'who thinks Joe is an ass' list."

Okay, that wasn't what she had been expecting. She struggled to regroup mentally. "Okay. Who?"

"Families of people I've killed."

She could feel the shock rock through her. "*What? You killed someone? Who did you kill?*"

"There have been innocent people who have been killed because I couldn't make enough headway with the hostage-takers who had them." She could hear the pain in his voice. The guilt. The doubt.

"But that doesn't mean you killed them."

He shrugged. "It might be considered close enough by some grieving family members."

"Have many people been killed in hostage situations?"

"No. The SWAT team at Omega and I have a great record. Almost anyone I haven't been able to talk down they've been able to take out."

"But not always."

Joe shook his head. "Last year around this time was a particularly bad situation. Guy had a hand grenade. Killed four people. Almost killed me."

"Are those the burn scars on your neck and back?"

His hands tightened noticeably on the steering wheel. "Yeah. A much smaller price to pay than what the four hostages did. They all died."

"You know that wasn't your fault, right? The man with the grenade, the one who took the people in the first place. He was at fault."

"It was a guy who'd gotten fired. Came back into his office and walked into the conference room. I got him to release six people. But he wouldn't let his bosses or office mate leave. He said they were the ones directly responsible."

"Joe—"

"I should've known he wanted blood. He let the other people go too easily and I thought I could handle him. The SWAT team thought they could take him out in time if needed, but none of us saw the hand grenade."

Laura knew there were no words that could make this any better for Joe. She reached over and touched his knee.

He glanced at her briefly before looking back to the road. "Anyway, that should probably be another list of people who hate me. People who lost loved ones because of my mistakes."

"I'm sure they don't hate you."

"I think I might if I was them. I met with the families after last year's incident. Tried to give them as much closure as I could, explain what happened as best as I was able."

"None of them blamed you, Joe. I know it."

He reached down and grabbed her hand. "One of the men who died—the office mate—was about to become a father for the first time. His wife was three months pregnant when he was killed."

The anguish was clear in his voice.

"That kid—it was a little girl—is never going to know her father."

"Because a madman walked into a building with the intent to hurt people. To kill people. And he would've hurt and killed even more if it wasn't for you."

He tried to ease his hand away from hers but she wouldn't let him.

"A kid will still be growing up never knowing her own father."

"And that's a tragedy. But she won't blame you for it. She'll blame the man who walked into her father's offices with weapons of death in his hands."

It was plain to see Joe wasn't convinced. That he carried more than just physical scars from that particular attack.

Laura held on to his hand tighter. All law enforcement workers were heroes in her opinion, but for some reason she hadn't really included Joe in that group.

Why?

Because she'd convinced herself that his money, his charm and his charisma somehow kept him sheltered, separated from the most painful aspects of his job.

She realized with no small sense of shame that her line of thinking was the same reason Joe felt like he wasn't truly part of the Omega team. Because people thought his job as hostage negotiator was just a hobby for him. That he was doing it as some sort of charity work he could walk away from at any time.

That he wasn't invested.

Everything about the conversation they'd just had—from the words he'd said to the way he'd held himself as he'd said them—told her otherwise.

Joe was every bit as much of a hero as other law enforcement personnel. Just because he didn't need the money they paid him didn't make him any less of one. Although he'd never admit it, probably even to himself, it hurt Joe to think that other people assumed he didn't care as much as they did.

Joe did.

Laura was still pondering the man she realized she didn't really know, still holding his hand tightly in her lap when they pulled up to the address Joe's contact had provided.

"What do we do now?" She turned to look at the apartment complex where the Goldman brothers were staying.

"It's early on a Saturday morning. I'm going to assume neither of the Goldmans is leaving for a job anytime soon. So I'm going in there and you're staying out here."

She watched as he reached into the glove compartment of the car and pulled out two guns.

"I thought you had to turn in your gun at Omega when you gave Steve your badge."

Joe gave an innocent shrug then winked at her. "I had to turn in my official weapon, but it certainly wasn't my only weapon. These are both Glock 42s. Are you familiar with handguns?"

"I've been to the shooting range a few times, but not with this particular pistol."

Joe showed her the basics and left one of them with her.

"I don't like leaving you here alone, but I like even less the thought of taking you in there with Max and Melvin. Just stay here and keep your eyes open for any trouble."

"Like what?"

"Like the police, who will gladly arrest both me and them and sort it out later."

Laura grimaced. She couldn't pull a gun on the police and expect it to end well for anyone.

Joe took out his phone and showed her the info his guy Deacon had sent. It was surprisingly thorough given the man had only had an hour to put it together. Pictures of Max and Melvin without their masks—looking remarkably like Ricky and Bobby in the bank, a photo of their apartment, stats on their life—unemployed, unmarried, both in their 20s, neither with a college education.

"Do you think they're just going to confess?"

"No. But we're not dealing with rocket scientists here. All I need to do is get them to let it slip that they know anything about any of the women and then we can start hunting down details in earnest."

"Joe, questioning people is what I do for a living. I'm a lawyer. Let me come in with you."

Joe stared at her for a long time.

"You know I'm right. Having two of us there is much better than just one."

He grimaced, not liking it but having to accept the truth of her statement. "Fine. But I'm going in there first. Once I have them secured then I will call you and you can come up. You don't come up without a message from me, no matter what. Got it?"

Laura rolled her eyes. "Yeah, got it. Little woman will just sit in the car waiting for the big strong man to face all the danger."

Joe reached over and grabbed her chin, pulling her to him. He gave her a hard kiss, almost bruising in its intensity.

"I'm not taking any chances with your life. You're too valuable to me. Wait for my message."

He was out of the door before she'd even caught her breath.

WHAT THE HELL was he doing? Joe walked silently up the stairs to the second floor apartment the Goldman brothers lived in. Laura had been right in the cabin when she'd suggested he call in some Omega backup.

Going in here alone seemed like a fine plan when it had just been him. But now that he was bringing in Laura, having more good guys in the room seemed like a much better plan.

But his arguments still applied. He couldn't drag his colleagues into this. Or, more honestly, couldn't trust they would choose to take his word over what seemed like pretty damning evidence.

Either way, it was too late now. Joe needed answers from the Goldman brothers and he needed them directly.

He knocked on the door, keeping his face averted in case they were smart enough to use the peephole in their door.

"Doughnut delivery. We have your order ready."

Joe didn't know of any places that delivered doughnuts, but it seemed less suspicious than pizza this early in the morning. All he needed was for them to open the door just the slightest bit.

He pulled his gun out from where he'd tucked it into the waistband of his jeans.

The door cracked open. "Look, we didn't order no—"

Joe flew into the door with his uninjured shoulder, sending it slamming open and the man—it looked like Melvin by his picture and arm in a sling—flying back to the ground. Joe immediately trained his weapon on him.

"Where's your brother?" Joe asked, looking around the small place without taking his gun off Melvin.

"You!"

"Yeah, me. You guys should've finished the job when you had the chance." He used his foot to push the door back.

"How did you find us?"

"Believe it or not, Einstein, finding out details about other people is not difficult in this day and age." Particularly when you had a Deacon Crandall on your side. "Especially when you know what you're looking for. Where's Max?"

Melvin looked back and forth from one bedroom to the other.

He cocked his head to the side. "He's sleeping."

Joe eased his way toward the room Melvin gestured to and opened the door.

There was no one in the bed, sleeping or otherwise.

He caught Melvin's grin out of the corner of his eye and realized he'd made a mistake underestimating the man. Joe wasn't going to be able to stop whoever he could feel flying toward him.

Chapter Fifteen

Joe's gun slid out of his hand as Max tackled him. He must've come through the front door. Joe would've seen him come out either of the bedrooms.

He grunted as Max's fist found his face and realized Melvin would soon have Joe's gun. Things were getting out of hand quickly and the only saving grace was that Laura waited safely in the car.

"If you touch that weapon, I'm going to be forced to shoot you."

Maybe Laura wasn't safely in the car.

"And you." She turned her Glock toward Max and Joe. "Get off of him. Joe, are you alright?"

Joe pushed Max to the side and onto the floor by his brother. He picked up his own weapon.

"You suck at following directions, you know that? What part of 'stay in the car until you hear from me' didn't you understand?"

Laura rolled her eyes. "The part where I saw Max arrive after you and thought maybe I should come in and see if you needed help. Which it looks like you did."

She kept her gun trained at the Goldman brothers and damn if that wasn't one of the sexiest things he'd ever seen. He wrapped an arm around her waist and kissed her forehead.

"Thanks."

She smiled. "No problem."

Joe shut and locked the front door and checked the rest of the rooms to make sure there wouldn't be any more surprises. He found some plastic zip-ties and used them to restrain Max's arms behind his back. He swore Melvin would get the same treatment also, regardless of his broken wrist, if he gave them any problems.

"You going to arrest us like you did Michael and Mitchell?"

Joe shook his head. "Your brothers took sixteen people hostage in a bank. Hurt two of them. They deserved whatever they got. But I wasn't the one who arrested them."

"That's not what they said," Mitchell muttered.

"I was the one in there making sure the SWAT team didn't kill them outright. So the next time your brothers want to talk trash about me, you remind them that I am the reason they aren't sitting in the morgue right now, rather than in a cell."

Max and Melvin glanced at each other. Evidently the facts Joe provided didn't jibe with what their brothers had told them.

"But no, I don't plan to arrest you." Mostly because Joe was wanted by the law himself, although he wouldn't be telling them that. "I just need answers to some questions."

"You were trying to kidnap me in the parking garage on Thursday," Laura interjected. "Why? To kill me like the rest and frame Joe for it?"

"What?" Mitchell's eyes flew to her. "No. We weren't going to kill you. We were just going to hold you hostage until they let our brothers out."

Laura pointed at Melvin. "You had a knife."

The man shrugged. "I always have a knife. You never

know when you're going to need it. But I wasn't planning to kill you with it." He turned to Joe. "I wasn't even planning to kill you with it. I just got a little carried away in the moment."

"What about Olivia? Or Jessica or Sarah? Did you kill them with your knife?"

Melvin looked over at his brother then back at Joe. His face had lost all color. "Dude. I swear I didn't kill nobody. Not with a knife, not with anything. I don't even know who you're talking about."

Joe grabbed Melvin by the shirt. "I think you do know what I'm talking about. I think you killed those three women because you were mad at me for bringing down your brothers, and you were planning to kill Laura, too."

Melvin was sweating now. "No. I swear, man. I have no idea who those other girls are. We were just taking her—" he gestured to Laura "—to get the police to let Mitchell and Michael go."

Joe resisted the urge to ram his fist into the other man's face. He wasn't a violent man by nature, but the thought of his exes' pointless deaths filled him with rage. A rage that had nothing on what he felt about Laura being their next victim.

It was Laura who brought him back, touching him on the arm. She kept her back to the Goldman brothers and leaned her face close to his. "Look at them. I think they might be telling the truth. Let me ask them some questions."

He didn't want to. He just wanted to pound on them until their blood covered his hands.

Laura reached up and touched his jaw. "Joe, you're not in this alone. Trust me to help you with this."

Joe nodded and released Melvin, who fell back, still sweating.

Laura turned to them.

"You boys been watching the news over the last week?"

"Nah. Our cable got cut off since we didn't pay the bill," Melvin said.

"You heard anything about three women in the greater Denver/Colorado Springs area being murdered over the last few days?"

Both men shook their heads. "No. We didn't know nothing about that," Max told her. "We've been busy trying to figure out how to get our brothers out of jail."

"And that's why you came after me."

The brothers looked at each other then nodded. But they were hiding something. Joe wanted to stop Laura, demand the men tell them what it was they were hiding. But Laura touched his arm so Joe kept quiet. She'd asked him to trust her.

A team meant trust on both sides.

"Tell me your plan once you had me," Laura demanded.

Melvin sat up a little straighter, obviously happy they weren't accusing him of murder anymore. "We were going to put a call in to the police telling them we had a hostage. Demand that Joe Matarazzo meet with us. Once he saw it was you we had hostage he would do whatever it took to get our brothers out. Since they were innocent."

Joe barely restrained from rolling his eyes.

Laura continued questioning. "Did your brothers tell you how much Joe cared about me from when they saw us in the bank together?"

Max and Melvin looked at each other again. "Not exactly," Max responded.

Laura nodded. "That's what I thought. Because Joe and I didn't even talk to each other in front of your brothers. So there was no way they would've known he cared for me any more than he cared for anyone else. Who told you that, Max?" She turned and looked at the other brother. "You didn't come up with the plan to kidnap me yourself, right, Melvin? You boys didn't really want to hurt me. You're not kidnappers. You're not murderers. Who gave you the idea?"

Joe just sat back and watched Laura work. He had no doubt she was this formidable in the courtroom also. Melvin and Max had no chance against her.

"Some lady," Max blubbered. "She came up to us on Wednesday. Said she had seen the whole bank thing on Friday and had a way we could get our brothers out of jail."

"Yeah, like you said, we didn't want to hurt anybody," Melvin chimed in. "We just wanted to help them. She told us where you worked. Where you would be coming out and when. Told us that Joe would do anything for you, even get our brothers out of jail."

Joe stepped up and grabbed Max's shirt. "Who? Who told you all this?"

"We don't know her name. I swear."

Melvin nodded. "She knew everything about you, man. Loved talking about you and all the details she knew. All the women you dated and all the money you had. Talked about some burn scars."

"She was kind of scary." Max's voice lowered. "Wild look in her eyes, you know? Said you deserved to be punished." Max looked at Joe. "Said you deserved to burn."

"But she said first you would help us get our brothers out. If we took Laura and held her ransom, you would get our brothers out."

"More likely she would've killed all three of us and

framed Joe for the murder." Laura dropped her gun to her side.

Both men's eyes bugged out.

"What did she look like?" Joe asked.

"Long black hair," Max said. "Really pretty."

"Yeah, sort of tall for a woman. Maybe five foot nine. Curvy. Nice rack."

Trust these two idiots to remember her breast measurements.

"How old was she?" Joe demanded, trying to think of women from his past who fit the description.

Max shrugged. "I don't know. Our age. Midtwenties."

"Had her hair pulled back in a tight bun."

"Joe." Laura pulled him closer to her so the brothers couldn't hear. "I know who they're talking about."

"Who?"

"I don't know her name, but she was at the garage the day they tried to grab me. I saw her. She was sort of staring at me. I thought she had just forgotten where her car was parked. But now I know she was definitely watching."

"Do you remember what she looks like? Do you think you could identify her again?"

"Absolutely."

It was a start. The Goldman brothers weren't the ones trying to frame Joe. But at least they now had something on the person who was.

They just had to find her.

Chapter Sixteen

They went back to Laura's house in Fountain, rather than the cabin. It was time to stop running, stop hiding. Joe would always have fond memories of the cabin, but the next time he took Laura there, it wouldn't be to escape police trying to arrest him.

Her house was a risk since the cops were still looking for him, but Joe was going to stay and fight.

And he'd called in for reinforcements. Laura was right—he'd be stupid to try to fight this battle alone. Upon leaving Max and Melvin's apartment, Joe had called Steve. He'd let Steve know what the Goldman brothers had told him: their suspect was a woman.

And she seemed to know a great deal about Joe's professional and private life.

The first thing they needed to do was search through any footage they had of crowds surrounding Joe's hostage cases. Omega routinely recorded the crowds that gathered at cases and investigations. Often the perpetrator couldn't resist coming back to inspect his or her handiwork.

Joe knew that woman was in the footage somewhere. But as evidenced by the number of case files they'd had to steal, Joe had worked on dozens of hostage cases in his career. It was going to take a long time to go through that footage.

Time they didn't have.

Steve agreed to send someone to pick up the Goldman brothers, keeping them out of the hands of the Colorado Springs PD for a little while, and to send someone with the digitized footage to Laura's house.

At least they didn't have to break into Omega to get the footage. Joe hadn't liked asking for anything, but Steve hadn't even hesitated when Joe made his request.

It was sort of a weird feeling, trusting someone to help him.

Laura was taking a shower and changing into her own clothes when the doorbell rang. Joe checked to make sure it wasn't the police and was surprised to find that instead of some low-level courier Joe had been expecting from Omega, it was Jon Hatton.

Joe opened the door. "Hey, wasn't expecting you."

"I have some footage Steve insisted I bring over. Not only am I one of Omega's top profilers and crisis management experts, I am now a pack mule."

Sherry Mitchell, Jon's fiancée and forensic artist, stepped out from behind him. "Don't listen to his lies, Joe. He volunteered. Plus I have doughnuts."

Joe let them through and introduced them both to Laura when she came down from her shower. Within just a few minutes Joe and Jon were getting the footage set up on multiple computers as Sherry worked with Laura to create a drawing of the woman she'd seen in the parking lot.

Sherry labored patiently with Laura for the next two hours, asking her questions and helping her remember seeing details about the woman. She was truly a gifted forensic artist.

"My gal is something else, isn't she?" Jon asked.

"Unbelievably talented." Joe couldn't doubt it.

Jon smiled. "It's nice to see Sherry working with

someone who isn't traumatized. Normally she works with rape or battery victims. Kidnappings. It's not easy for her." He walked over and kissed her on the head. Sherry just smiled up at him and kept working.

Finally they had a drawing. A clear image of a woman.

"That's definitely the lady I saw in the parking garage." Laura handed the picture to Joe. "Do you recognize her?"

She didn't look familiar at all. "She's definitely not someone I've ever dated." He rolled his eyes at Jon. "Despite what you and the rest of the gang think, I do actually remember the people I've gone out with. I would remember this woman's face if I knew her."

Jon took the picture. "I'm going to send this to Steve, see if the Goldman brothers recognize her." He snapped a picture with his phone.

"Alright. We've got a face. Let's start studying footage at crime scenes I've been involved with." Too bad facial recognition software wouldn't work from a drawing. Plus, if the woman wasn't in their database it wouldn't help anyway.

"It's going to be slow going with all the cases," Jon pointed out.

"Then we better get started."

They each had a computer or laptop and split the cases. Then began the grueling process of pausing each video and comparing the drawing to the people in the crowds. Crowds that were sometimes hundreds of people thick.

"Steve just texted me back. Confirmed that is the woman who approached the Goldman brothers."

At least they knew they were looking for the right person. Even if it was going to take forever to find her.

The doorbell rang again and Laura's eyes flew to Joe's. They both worried it was the police.

But it wasn't. More of Joe's Omega colleagues had arrived. SWAT members Derek Waterman, Lillian Muir and Liam Goetz, Derek's wife Molly who worked at the Omega lab, even Brandon Han and Andrea Gordon, who had helped him at the first crime scene when Sarah had been found.

They were all here, on their day off, laptops in hand.

"Heard you needed more eyes." Derek slapped him on the back on his way in.

"Yes, Joe, we want to help." Molly waddled through. "Especially when this big buffoon won't let me do almost anything else. I'm pregnant, not terminally ill." She smacked Derek on the arm.

Never had Joe expected to see his colleagues here. Especially not en masse. Not to help him.

"You guys, I…" Joe shrugged not sure how to even finish the sentence.

Andrea, who he had gotten to know a little better last month when they'd watched over Brandon Han in the hospital smiled at him. "Joe, we want to help. All of us."

Of everyone here, Andrea probably most understood how Joe felt. Until recently she'd kept herself, and the fact that she used to be a stripper, far away from all her colleagues, afraid to ever make attachments.

Joe wasn't ashamed of his past, but he'd sort of done the same thing: kept himself apart, thinking they didn't really include him in their inner circle.

Although with Laura's house almost full to overflowing with people here to help him—here because they wanted to be, not because it was part of a case or an order from Steve—he could no longer use that reasoning.

He was part of the team.

As everyone settled in at a computer, Jon divvying up

the cases, Laura made her way over to Joe. He could see the smile she tried to keep tamped down.

"You going to say I told you so?" he asked as she sat next to him, laptop in hand.

"I would never stoop so low." She grinned. "But maybe nanny-nanny-boo-boo."

Joe lowered his voice so no one else could hear. "I can't believe they're all here."

"You'd do the same for any of them, right? If they were in danger and needed your help? Even if it was off-the-record and might get you in trouble?"

"Sure."

"Same thing. You're part of the team, Matarazzo. Money, no money. Gossip sites or not. They have your back. Just like you would have theirs."

Joe didn't tend to be at a loss for words very often, but looking around the room, watching his friends stare at screens, doughnuts in most of their hands, he was.

"I don't know what to say to them."

Laura reached over and cupped his cheeks. "You don't have to say anything. That's the great thing about family. They just do what needs to be done, no words necessary."

Joe had grown up with a lot of money, a lot of privilege, trips, gadgets…but he'd never really had family. The best boarding schools money could buy, but no one close.

"Family." The word seemed awkward on his tongue.

"Family isn't always blood, and blood isn't always family." She smiled. "Now get to work."

Joe looked back down at his screen realizing Laura was right. These people were his family. In every way that counted.

"I'VE GOT HER." Liam Goetz's voice called out.

"Are you sure?" Joe asked.

Liam grinned. "One hundred percent. Check her out."
The laptop got passed around. No one could doubt that
was the woman Laura had described and Sherry had
drawn.

"You're spooky good," Laura said to Sherry, who just
shrugged.

"What about me?" Liam said. "I found her. Isn't anyone going to tell me how awesome I am?"

Somebody threw a pillow at him.

"What case is that?" Jon asked.

Liam put the pillow behind his back. "Jewelry store
hostage situation in Palm Springs. Ten months ago."

Everyone looked at Joe. He shrugged. "I remember it,
but there wasn't much out of the ordinary. No casualties.
Hostage-takers stepped down without the use of force."

"Okay, let's branch out from that case, see if we can
find her," Jon said. "I'm going to send the picture to
Omega, see if she blips on any of our facial recognition
software. Maybe we'll get lucky."

Laura began looking through the case file for the jewelry store while everyone began searching footage with
a renewed sense of purpose.

"You're right," Laura agreed after reading through the
file. "I don't see anything in this case that would make
someone angry at you."

"I've got her again," Lillian said a few minutes later.
"Six months ago. She's in the crowd when that guy was
threatening to blow himself up at the home improvement
store. I remember that."

SWAT had to take the guy out. Joe couldn't help him.
That had been clear early on.

"Yep, I've got her in Austin last month," Derek said.
"Right at the very front of the crowd."

"Wow. Looks like Joe has got himself a stalker." Liam smirked. "Some guys have all the luck."

"I'm afraid Liam's right, Joe," Derek's wife, Molly, cut in before Joe could make a sarcastic comment to Liam. "I have her in the crowd at last weekend's bank heist."

Joe looked over at Laura. Her expression was as worried as he knew his had to be. This woman had been following him for months.

"Okay." Jon took charge. "Everybody get a screen shot of when you have her, as well as the date and location. We need to find out when she first started showing up."

Laura ordered pizzas for lunch as they continued to look. The woman was everywhere. She had been at every case Joe had worked on for at least the past year. Had traveled all over the country to watch him.

Downright scary.

"Okay, I don't have her," Brandon Han said. "I'm one hundred percent positive she's not in this crowd."

Nobody asked to double-check Brandon. The man was a certifiable genius. If he said the mystery woman wasn't in the crowd, then she wasn't.

"Okay," Joe said. "Let's check the case immediately before that. Maybe she was sick that day or something."

They didn't find her on the footage of the previous case either. Or the one before that.

"It looks like she first made an appearance at the Castlehill Offices case," Lillian said, voice grim. "I've got her there."

Silence fell over the room.

"Which case is that?" Laura asked, coming to stand by Joe.

He wrapped an arm around her. "The one we were talking about this morning. Where I lost four hostages to the guy with the grenade."

"Joe, none of us knew that guy had such a death wish and need for revenge," Lillian said. "Or that he had the grenade. I was watching through my rifle sights from the other building and didn't see it."

Derek stood. "Yeah, Joe. We were all there, and have all reviewed the footage. There was no way you could've known. Sometimes people are just crazy."

Joe shrugged. Regardless of whether the guy was crazy or not, four people had died.

"Joe," Andrea's soft voice cut in. She didn't say much, didn't waste words, so when she did talk, everyone listened. "Look at these pictures of the woman."

Andrea brought her laptop over to stand with Joe and Laura. "Look at her at the Castlehill Offices. She's distraught, terrified." She flicked the screen to show other pictures from other crime scenes. "Now look at her as time progresses. She's becoming filled with rage. Resolve."

Andrea had a wonderful gift as a behavioral analyst. Her ability to read people's nonverbal communication and emotion was uncanny.

"On cases where you were successful and no one was hurt she's most angry. On cases where SWAT had to be used, she's less so," Andrea continued. "Regardless, she is connected to someone—probably one of the victims who died—at Castlehill. I can almost guarantee that."

Joe had thought he was on good terms with the victims' families—as good as someone who had caused the death of their loved ones could be. But evidently he'd been wrong. It was time to talk to the families again. See if any of them knew this woman.

SHE HAD WATCHED them all come in this morning, and watched them all leave a few at a time.

She thought of setting a fire while they all gathered inside. Of barring the doors so no one could escape. But she didn't have what she needed in her van.

She pulled at her hair and rocked back and forth. She'd missed a perfect opportunity because she was unprepared.

But no. That plan would've killed innocent people. People who had no part in Tyler's death.

She had to stay focused. Punish only Joe and anyone he loved or who loved him. These people he worked with did not love him. He kept himself separate from them almost always.

She'd been surprised to see them here at all.

She counted them as they left to make sure they were all gone. Then watched, rage boiling through her veins as Joe left hand in hand with the lawyer woman, Laura.

Why should Joe Matarazzo find love when he'd killed her Tyler?

Tyler had loved her. Would've eventually made a life with her.

She forced herself to remain calm until Joe and the woman were far away, then made her way to the house.

Inside the house.

All she needed now was patience. That she had.

Joe Matarazzo would burn like Tyler did. And the woman would burn with him.

Chapter Seventeen

"I talked to all the families after the victims died, but have remained closest with Summer Worrall," Joe said as they drove toward the woman's house.

Laura didn't know exactly what her feelings were on the fact that Joe had remained close with the young widow of one of the men who had been killed under his watch.

She knew even less when Summer opened the door and invited them in.

The woman was beautiful. Slender, despite having just had a baby in the last few months, petite with auburn hair and big green eyes. She had a fragile, tragic air about her. It made Laura want to take the woman in her arms.

She could imagine that Joe felt the exact same way.

Summer took Joe in her arms instead.

"Joe! What are you doing here?" She hugged him hard. Joe looked over at Laura with an apologetic smile as he hugged Summer back.

As if Laura would begrudge him hugging someone who had gone through so much tragedy.

Laura just wished the woman wasn't quite so *beautifully* tragic. Shouldn't someone with a newborn look frazzled and sleep-deprived?

"Please, both of you, come in." She turned to Laura. "I'm Summer Worrall."

"I'm Laura Birchwood, Joe's lawyer."

"She's my girlfriend, too, Summer."

Laura expected a laugh or raised eyebrow at that announcement, but the other woman just grinned. "Good. He needs someone to keep him in line." She opened the door wider so they could come in.

"How's Chloe?" Joe asked, walking toward the living room. He'd obviously been here before.

"She's beautiful. Sleeps like an angel, thank God. It makes a huge difference that I can stay home. Joe. Again, I wanted to say thank—"

Joe put a finger over the woman's lips. "You've already said it multiple times. No need to say it again. It's no trouble."

Laura almost felt like she was intruding on an intimate moment. Joe and Summer obviously knew each other and had a rapport that needed more than what a single "I'm sorry your husband was killed" visit would provide. There didn't seem to be anything romantic between the two of them, but definitely a closeness.

But Joe grabbed Laura's hand as he sat down on the sofa across from Summer, so Laura let it all go.

"We're here on business, Summer," Joe said.

The other woman looked a little surprised. Obviously Joe didn't usually come over to her house for business.

"Does it have to do with your ex-girlfriends who died?"

"Yes." Joe nodded. "But I didn't have anything to do with their deaths."

Summer stared at him as if he had lost his mind. "It never occurred to me that you'd had anything to do with it."

Anybody who knew Joe would never think he had

anything to do with it. Laura had been trying to tell him that all week.

Joe brought out his phone and pulled up a picture of the woman from the crime scenes. He showed it to Summer.

"Do you know who this woman is?"

She startled them both by flying out of her chair and snatching the phone out of Joe's hand. Tears immediately began streaming down her face.

Laura and Joe both stood at the sudden movement. Laura was closest to the woman and put an arm around her. "Are you okay? What's wrong?"

"Where did you get that picture?"

"She's a woman who has been hanging around a lot of crime scenes. Particularly hostage situations where I've been involved."

Summer looked at Laura then at Joe. "You have to stay away from her. She's dangerous. Crazy."

"Do you know who she is?" Laura asked. Summer was visibly shaking. Laura led her to the sofa so she could sit down.

"Her name is Bailey Heath." Summer looked at the picture again. "She's emotionally unstable."

"Have you met her, Summer?" Joe asked. He was probably thinking along the same lines as Laura was: Summer and her daughter might need protection from this woman.

"Not recently. Tyler and I had a restraining order against her before he died."

"Why?"

"Tyler and Bailey worked together at Castlehill for a few months. She became obsessed with him. He talked to their bosses and they transferred her to another building after looking into it."

Laura squeezed her hand. "But that didn't keep her away?"

Summer shook her head. "Then she just started showing up at the house. She would follow me around and tell me that Tyler loved her and would be leaving me soon."

"Do you think there was any truth at all to the statements?" Joe asked gently.

"No. None. I trusted him completely." Her eyes filled with tears again. "Tyler and I spent hours talking about what he might have done that gave her any impression he was interested at all, much less intending to break up his marriage for her. He hated that he had somehow allowed her into our lives."

Summer took a shuddery breath. "She's unbalanced. Would sit outside our house and watch it for days on end. That's when we got a restraining order."

Laura rubbed her back. "Definitely the right thing to do."

"You can tell she's sort of crazy after just talking to her for a few minutes. She fully believes whatever fantasy world she's living in is actual reality. There's no way to convince her otherwise."

"Has she contacted you at all since Tyler's death?"

"No. Thank God. Somebody told me she was at Tyler's funeral, but I didn't see her. And I had too much to worry about to deal with her then."

Laura's eyes met Joe's. At least it seemed that Summer and Samantha weren't on Bailey's hit list.

"Why are you asking about her?"

Joe's brows knitted. "We think she might be involved with killing my ex-girlfriends. It seems like she's got an axe to grind against me."

"She was so obsessed with Tyler," Summer whispered.

"Maybe she blames you for his death. The one-year anniversary of his death was on Sunday you know."

Joe glanced up sharply. "That's when the first woman was killed."

"That could've been what triggered her. The fact that it had been a year." Laura frowned. Bailey Heath obviously was holding on to her delusions pretty tightly.

Joe came over to crouch by Summer. "I'm sorry that I didn't come by. I should have remembered."

Summer patted him on the cheek. "Joe, Tyler's death was not your fault. I have never for one moment of one day blamed you for him dying. You have to stop blaming yourself. His death was a tragedy, but not *your* tragedy."

Joe nodded and stood. Obviously this wasn't a new topic of conversation between he and Summer.

"Now that we know who the woman in the picture is we've got to find her. Stop her before she strikes again."

Laura nodded. Summer had never blamed Joe for Tyler's death, but there was a psycho out there who did.

"WHAT WAS SUMMER about to thank you for at her house when you stopped her?"

They were on their way back to Laura's house. Joe had already put in a call to Omega. Steve had issued an APB to try to find Bailey Heath. Brandon Han was working up a profile on her based on what information they could find. Andrea Gordon was studying the footage to try to read any nonverbals she could.

The team was working overtime to try to clear Joe's name. Laura knew he appreciated it. If nothing good came of this entire situation, at least Joe would know his friends truly considered him part of the Omega family.

"No big deal. I found Summer a job."

"I'm sure there's more to it than that."

Joe rolled his eyes. "Fine. I created a job for her. She manages social media for some of the Matarazzo holdings."

"But it allows her to work at home. So she can be with baby Chloe."

He gave a self-deprecating laugh. "I tried to just give her money outright, but she wouldn't take it."

"She doesn't blame you. She would've taken the money if she blamed you."

He shrugged. "I still want to help out whatever way I can. I started a college fund for Chloe. She'll be able to go wherever she wants to go."

"The best thing we can do for both of them right now is get Bailey Heath behind bars."

"Absolutely."

He pulled up to a side road close to her house and parked. They weren't parking in her driveway in case the police came by still looking for Joe.

Laura opened the door to get out of the car but he stopped her, grabbing her arm.

"What's wrong?"

"That van over there. Do you know it? Does it belong to any of your neighbors?"

A white cargo van, pretty nondescript. "I don't think so. Somebody could be having some work done or something."

"It was parked there when everyone got here this morning. Still there ten hours later. A long time for a work van to be parked in a residential neighborhood, especially on a Saturday."

They got out of the car and Joe led them down the sidewalk away from both her house and the van. "We'll walk around the block and circle back to it."

Laura felt Joe's arm snake around her waist. She

couldn't help but lean in to him. "What you're doing for Summer is admirable, you know."

He shrugged. "The least I could do."

He kept her tugged to his side, keeping their stride casual, until they came up on the van.

"Stand to the side while I announce myself as federal law enforcement. If anything goes bad, just get out of the way, okay?" He kissed the side of her head.

"Are you expecting anything to go wrong?"

"One thing I've learned with my years at Omega is to expect anything."

Once they were on the rear side of the van he turned to her, taking his gun from his holster. He banged on the back door. "This is federal law enforcement. If anyone is in there, I need you to open the door."

Nothing happened. Joe looked over at her, without lowering his weapon. "If it's unlocked, you pull the door open and keep out of the way."

"Be careful."

He motioned a countdown with his finger and Laura pulled the handle. Finding it unlocked, she pulled the back door wide-open, stepping to the side as she did so.

In just a few moments, Joe replaced his weapon in the holster under his jacket. "It's clear. Really is a work van. Go figure."

She peeked around the door. Sure enough some paint cans and cloths lay on the floor of the van, some tools and other items strewn about.

Nothing suspicious.

They closed the door and Joe put his forehead against hers. "I'm paranoid. I'm sorry."

"Hey, I'm a lawyer. I'm all about the 'rather safe than sorry' theory. Especially when the person we're looking for has a history of sitting outside of someone's house and watching."

Joe pulled her close again and they crossed the street to her house. She handed him the key to her door. "You know, I think it's safer for you if I stay at your house until we find Bailey Heath."

He slid her jacket off her shoulders and Laura turned to look at him, smiling. "Oh yeah? And is some psychopath stalker the only reason you're interested in staying here?"

He hung her jacket on the back of a dining room chair and soon his followed suit. He turned his gaze on her. It could be called nothing less than predatory.

Everything inside her heated at the look in his eyes.

"Are you saying you might be interested in something other than me being your bodyguard?" He took a step closer.

"I'm pretty sure there's something I'd like you to do with my body, but guard isn't what I had in mind." She gripped the waistband of his jeans and pulled him closer. She took a step back until her spine was fully up against the door.

He was everything she should run from. He was everything she craved.

All she knew was if he was here, she wasn't going to waste a chance to enjoy him again. Enjoy *them* again.

She licked her lips.

He groaned and pushed his body flush against hers. "If you don't stop looking at me like that, we're not even going to make it up to the bedroom."

"Maybe I don't want to make it to the bedroom."

She felt his lips work their way up her throat to her lips. Not a gentle, searching kiss.

Hot. Demanding.

The way it had always been with them.

As Joe slipped off his shirt she saw the scar on the side of his neck more clearly now that she knew what it was from.

She had almost lost him that day and she'd never even known. The thought caused her to pull him closer, even more desperate not to have space between them. He obliged, cupping her face and licking deep into her mouth.

They both moaned and tore at the rest of the clothes between them.

Somewhere in the back of Laura's mind she knew she was letting herself fall too hard. Letting Joe mean too much to her again. The price she would pay when he finally walked away again would be too high.

But when his lips worked their way to her ear then lowered to her throat she pushed the voice of reason down where it couldn't be heard.

And let the flames engulf her.

Chapter Eighteen

Joe studied Laura as she slept beside him. It was late on Sunday morning. They'd spent the entire night laughing and talking and making love.

His heart broke at the pointless deaths of those women from his past, but part of him was grateful it had thrown Laura back into his life so completely.

She wouldn't be in this bed with him otherwise—he knew that for sure. Laura's wariness had flashed in her eyes last night when she thought he wouldn't see it. Not when they were making love—he knew for certain her guard remained down then—but other times.

Like when she had mentioned a colleague's white-water rafting trip and he'd stated they should go together this summer. She'd smiled, then smoothly changed the subject.

Laura wasn't making any future plans with him.

At first he thought it was because she didn't want to spend time with him in the future. But gradually he'd come to realize that she was waiting for him to change his mind again.

Bracing herself for the impact.

Joe would give every dime he had if he could go back and change the stupid, panicked words he'd said that night six years ago.

But all he could do was keep Laura as close to him as possible. Love her every single day until it saturated every thought she had.

Love used to be a word that scared Joe. Not anymore. Not when it had to do with Laura.

"Hey," she whispered, her eyes opening a little. "What are you growling about over there?"

He hooked an arm over her hip. "No growling. Just determination."

To have her. With him. For the rest of both their lives.

"To catch Bailey Heath?"

The temptation to tell her his complete thoughts almost overwhelmed him. Only the knowledge that she couldn't accept it, wouldn't believe him if he started declaring his true feelings for her, stopped him.

"Yeah. There's been no word on her yet."

"How long does Steve think it will take to find her?"

"She's got the full weight of Omega's resources on her shoulders. That's a lot. They've fed her image into the facial recognition program. That thing is pretty damn scary. If she drives past a traffic light, uses an ATM, walks past any security camera that uplinks to a mobile server, she'll get tagged."

"Good. She needs to be caught."

He reached over and kissed her. "She will be, don't worry. Not many people can hide from Omega for long. Particularly someone with no covert training."

"Speaking of not hiding anymore, I think you ought to consider turning yourself in to the police."

"Won't they arrest me?"

"I don't think so with the new evidence that has come to light. We'll show them what we have on Bailey Heath. The Goldman brothers are in custody and can attest to her hatred for you and that she had suggested my kidnapping. Plus, we'll have Steve call and back up everything you're saying."

A couple of days ago Joe would've been loath to ask Steve to do even that, but this situation had changed everything.

"I can't be in a cell. Not right now, not with her still out there. I won't leave you unprotected." He pulled her over to lie against his chest.

"Why don't we call Brandon Han and get his opinion? He's a great lawyer and I think he'll agree with me. Plus, walking into the station of your own accord, rather than being picked up, goes a long way toward proving you have nothing to hide."

"Alright, I'll call Brandon." The other man might be on a different case—along with being licensed to practice law, he was also one of the best profilers in Omega—but he would come if he could.

"We just need everybody in law enforcement looking for her. Not wasting any time or resources looking for you."

He reached in and kissed her. "I agree. And if both you and Brandon feel confident that they're not going to throw me in jail then I'll go."

"Even if they do, we could expedite a bond hearing and get you out on bail by tomorrow."

Joe would have to think about whether he was willing to risk leaving Laura even for a night. He would have to trust his friends at Omega to keep her safe.

Could he do that?

He ran a hand down Laura's cheek. He realized that he could do it. He could trust them. Trust her. Not that he'd have a good night's sleep being apart from her, but he could trust the team to guard Laura if it became a necessity.

Because what was important to Joe was important to them.

It was nice to know someone had his back. And that it had nothing to do with his money. His team wanted nothing in return.

She cupped his hand where it rested against her cheek. "Okay, as much as I'd love to lie naked in bed with you all day, that's not going to get your name cleared with the police."

She slipped out of bed and Joe leaned back against the pillows with his arms linked behind his head enjoying the view as Laura put on yoga pants and a T-shirt. "Actually, I'm pretty sure if you showed up at the precinct naked they would give you anything you wanted."

She smiled at him and he literally felt his breath being taken away. Laura might never be a beauty in the classic sense but damn if she wasn't the most gorgeous thing he'd ever seen.

"Maybe I'll try that at my next court case."

"I'll be sure to clear my calendar." And clear the courtroom so he'd be the only one able to lay eyes on a naked Laura. "I'm going to take a shower."

"I'll get coffee and breakfast going then we can call Brandon."

She bent to tie on a pair of sneakers and he patted her bottom on his way to the bathroom. The temptation to do more, to drag her back to bed and remove the clothes she'd just put on, almost overwhelmed him. But she was right, they needed to go to the police and get his name cleared.

Joe turned the shower on and stepped in before the water could even turn warm. The cold helped get his raging body under control and Joe didn't fight it, despite preferring to handle it a much more pleasurable way.

He wanted his name cleared. Wanted the women from his past—and his much more important present—to be safe. He wanted this behind him so he could court Laura properly the way he desired. The way she deserved.

The water turned warmer and Joe quickly finished his shower. Now that he had a plan in place he didn't want to waste any time putting it into action. After toweling off and getting dressed he grabbed his phone off the bathroom counter and put in a call to Brandon.

"Hey, Joe, how are you hanging in there?" Brandon answered by way of greeting. "Any news on Bailey Heath?"

"Nothing that I've heard so far."

"It won't take long with all of Omega's resources utilized in the hunt."

"That's my hope. Laura thinks I should voluntarily submit myself to the Colorado Springs PD." Joe explained what he and Laura had discussed. "She wanted to know if you could come over to review anything she might be missing."

"Well, I'm sort of in the middle of something." Joe heard Brandon whisper something to someone at his house.

Of course. It was Sunday morning. Brandon would be with Andrea.

"Brandon, I understand. Seriously, man—"

Another conversation Joe couldn't quite hear.

"Never mind. We'll be there in thirty minutes. Andrea says we'll bring brunch."

Joe smiled. "Thanks, Brandon."

"Hey, you sat with me in a hospital after a psychopath tried to turn me into Swiss cheese. This is the least I can do."

Joe laughed, saying his goodbyes and ending the call.

"Hey, Laura," he called out to the hallway as he put

on his shoes. "Brandon and Andrea are coming over and bringing food. So it's okay for you to leave your rightful place in the kitchen for a little bit."

He waited for a smart-aleck remark from her but got no response.

Joe chuckled. Obviously she hadn't heard him because there was no way Laura would let that slide.

He bounded down the stairs. "You're not waiting to clock me with a frying pan, right?"

Still nothing. He would be worried that Laura was truly irritated but knew it would take more than one silly sentence to get her mad. It was one of the things Joe liked most about her: her sense of humor.

But that didn't mean she wasn't about to jump out and pour a bucket of water over his head or something.

"Okay, I surrender." He held his arms up in front of him as he entered the kitchen. "I promise I will do all the cooking for the rest of our lives if you don't kill me now."

Actually he would do that for the rest of their lives if Laura would agree to share hers with him. Maybe he should start trying to get her to agree to those terms.

She wasn't in the kitchen.

Now things were a little weird.

"Hey, Laura?"

He poked his head around the corner to see if the bathroom door was closed, but it wasn't.

All humor fled. *Where was she?*

"Laura? Answer me, honey."

She wouldn't hide from him in jest, not now, not in the situation they were in. Joe pulled the door open to the garage, but she wasn't there. He systematically searched each room. Laura wasn't anywhere on the ground floor.

He ran back up the stairs to make sure she wasn't in

one of the rooms up there. Nothing. He entered the bedroom where they'd spent the entire night together.

His eyes flew to the nightstand.

His Glock was missing.

It had been there when he'd gone into the shower; he knew that for a fact. He'd grabbed his phone and brought it into the bathroom with him, not wanting to take a chance on missing a call from Steve if they found Bailey Heath.

Had Laura taken his gun for some reason? Why would she do that?

Joe slipped the phone from his pocket. He hit redial. Brandon answered just seconds later.

"Brandon, Laura's missing."

"What? Are you sure?"

"She's not anywhere in the house. It had to have happened in the last twenty minutes. While I was in the shower, or when I called you."

He heard Brandon murmur something.

"Joe, don't touch anything. I'll call Steve and let him know what's going on. Andrea and I will be at Laura's house in five minutes."

Joe didn't say anything, just disconnected the call. He ran back down the stairs to look at the kitchen again.

His heart plummeted when he saw the cups of coffee that had been knocked over on the table. The only signs of struggle whatsoever.

But they were definitely signs of struggle.

Laura had been taken.

A maniac who had sworn revenge on Joe now had the one person he cared about most.

Joe tried to remain calm, but rage and terror fought for dominance inside him. All he could see were visions of dead women left for him to find. Stabbed, lying in pools of their own blood.

That could not happen to Laura. Joe couldn't survive if it did.

Chapter Nineteen

After last night with Joe, Laura had decided she just wasn't going to worry so much about their relationship anymore.

She had to face the facts: she was in love with him. Had been in love with him six years ago. Was still in love with him now. Worrying about their relationship wasn't going to change that.

In the six years she and Joe were apart, Laura had dated. Had even gotten a little serious with a couple of guys. But it had never worked out.

Because they weren't Joe.

And it didn't have a single thing to do with his money. Joe could work at the local 7-Eleven and Laura would still love him. She wanted him despite his money, not because of it.

So she wasn't going to worry about it anymore. If Joe changed his mind in two months again, decided a serious relationship wasn't for him—*again*—Laura would have to deal with it.

She rubbed a hand across her chest. It would hurt—God, how it would hurt—but she would deal with it.

Right now she just wanted to concentrate on keeping him out of jail. Joe would call Brandon when he got out of the shower and get his opinion about turning himself in to the police. Brandon was a brilliant attorney; she and Joe both would be fools not to listen to his advice.

But first coffee. After the night she and Joe had shared—she smiled just a little thinking about it: her boyfriend was so dreamy—they needed the coffee. Laura made her way down the stairs.

She got the coffeepot going and stood next to it with two mugs in hand. She heard some thumping upstairs over the sound of the water and rolled her eyes. What was Joe doing, break dancing in the shower? She wouldn't put it past him.

A minute later she could breathe in the blessed caffeinated aroma and soon poured two cups, turning to set them on the small kitchen table.

Right behind it stood Bailey Heath. A gun in her hand pointed straight at Laura.

Laura jerked and knocked one cup over, vaguely feeling the burning liquid slopping onto her hand. The rest of it spilled onto the table.

"What are you doing here?"

The woman looked dirty, unkempt. Madness danced in her eyes.

"I'm here for you. I'm here to make Joe pay. He has to burn like Tyler did. Joe took Tyler away from me."

Tyler. Summer Worrall's husband. The man who had gotten a restraining order against Bailey. Joe hadn't taken Tyler away from Bailey. He'd never been hers to begin with.

Of course pointing out any of that probably wasn't a good idea.

But Laura knew she needed to stall.

"Joe's upstairs in the shower. Why don't we wait for him to come down and we can talk about it."

Bailey shook her head. "No, the time for talking is over. It's now time to burn. You need to come with me."

"What if I don't?"

"Then I'll kill you right here. Since this is Joe's own gun, I'm sure that will be enough to put him in jail for a long time, right?" Bailey brought the gun up so it was pointed right at Laura's head. "Your choice."

Laura nodded. She couldn't see any way around it. It was better to give Joe time to find her than for him to come down now and discover her dead.

Laura knocked over the other coffee cup, trying to get any signal she could to Joe that there was a problem. Bailey's eyes narrowed as she cracked Laura in the back of the head with the gun. It wasn't hard enough to make her lose consciousness, but Laura still cried out at the throbbing in her skull.

Bailey grabbed her arm. "Let's go. And if you try anything on the way out, I will kill you. Killing you in the street then watching Joe find you will be much more satisfying than watching him find those other women. He didn't care about them at all."

Pain rocketed through Laura's arm from Bailey's punishing grip as she pulled her down the hallway and out the front door. Laura tried to figure out how the woman had even gotten into her house at all. The front door they'd just gone through had been locked. She and Joe had checked all the doors.

Bailey pulled her across the street and into the very van Joe had found so suspicious the day before. He'd been right; it didn't belong there.

Bailey threw Laura in and stepped in behind her. Laura winced as Bailey bound her arms behind her back.

"Time to go."

Bailey was crazy. Being this close, Laura could smell

the woman's body odor. She obviously hadn't showered in at least a couple of days. Laura couldn't help but make a face.

"Do I smell?" Bailey asked. "Hiding in vans and attics will do that. Showers aren't easy to come by."

"You've been in my attic?" So she hadn't gotten through locked doors.

"Ever since all Joe's little friends left yesterday. It's not comfortable, but it works."

Laura just stared at the other woman. She obviously couldn't be reasoned with.

"The Goldman brothers were supposed to snatch you and lure Joe out. I would've been able to kill you both then and blame it on them, but they couldn't even get you out of the parking garage." She rolled her eyes in disgust.

Bailey pulled a piece of cloth from a shelf and wrapped it around Laura's mouth as a gag.

"I lost you for a couple of days, but then picked you back up again when you showed up at the Goldmans' apartment. I've been watching you both ever since, waiting for a time to plant myself in your house."

Bailey shoved Laura to the side. Without her hands free to catch herself she fell hard onto the van's floor.

"It's time for Joe to pay for what he did to Tyler. I've been waiting a very long time for this. Your death right in front of him will just be the icing on the cake."

Bailey smiled. A bright, beautiful one, like she'd received a precious gift.

If Laura had any doubts that smile erased them all: Bailey Heath was a psychopath.

"We've got one more stop to make before I call Joe and the game begins." Bailey pulled out a canvas sack and placed it over Laura's head, cutting off her vision.

"Although I'm not sure it can be called a game. Not when there's no chance of anyone winning except me."

Laura struggled to breathe through the gag. Through the panic. The other women Bailey had killed had just been a warm-up. Killing Laura while Joe watched would be the grand finale.

And Laura had no idea how Joe could possibly stop her.

JOE WOULD NEVER doubt he was part of the Omega team again.

They showed up in minutes.

They *all* showed up to help figure out what had happened to Laura.

Steve had arrived not long after Brandon and Andrea. Joe knew investigating a crime scene wasn't his strength, so he just tried to stay out of the way.

Joe couldn't stop staring at the spilled cups of coffee. They were the only signs of struggle at all. If it wasn't for them, he might have thought Laura had just decided to get out. Get as far from the situation—and him—as she could.

He wished like hell that was the case as he attempted to keep his panic pushed down.

Joe had already called his non–law enforcement contact Deacon Crandall. Explained as briefly as possible what had happened. He promised Crandall a million dollars if he had any part whatsoever in finding Laura alive. Another million to the individual who gave Deacon the tip.

Joe would keep offering a million dollars until he ran out of money or they found Laura. Because every dollar he had meant nothing without her.

Steve and Brandon stepped over to Joe.

"We think Bailey Heath was hiding in the attic. We're not sure for how long." Brandon rested a hand on Joe's shoulder. "There's no sign of a forced entry at all. And Laura definitely would not have just opened the door to Bailey."

"We found some pieces of insulation from the attic on the floor, suggesting that the pull-down door had been opened recently," Steve continued. "And a hole had been drilled through the door. Probably so Bailey could see and hear at least part of what was going on in the house."

Joe thought his rage had capped out, but he'd been wrong. The thought of a sicko like Bailey Heath listening and watching him and Laura last night sickened him. His hands tightened into fists.

"As best we can tell she just waited." Brandon squeezed his shoulder. "Once you were in the shower and Laura was alone, Bailey made her way out and took her."

Joe's curse was low and pointed.

Steve nodded. "She probably had another weapon. Taking your gun was just a more convenient method of framing you."

For when Bailey decided to kill Laura. Steve didn't say it but they were all thinking it.

Joe could feel the panic working its way up his chest.

"Joe." Brandon stood in front of Joe, placing both hands on his shoulders. "I have every confidence that Laura is still alive. If Bailey Heath had just wanted to frame you, she would've shot Laura and left her here in the house. It would've fit the MO of the other crimes and would've almost certainly landed you in jail."

Joe could hear Brandon's logic, knew he was probably right, but still couldn't get the terror under control.

"Bailey has some sort of elaborate plan," Brandon continued. "It's the only logical reason for her taking Laura out of the house."

"We will figure out how to beat Bailey at her own game. I promise you that," Steve said, sincerity clear in the man's eyes.

Joe nodded, and Brandon dropped his hold. "I just want Laura back. I have money. I know you guys know that, but I'm talking about cash I can have available in minutes if that will help. I'm willing to use other channels if it means getting Laura back safely."

Criminal channels. Mercenary channels. Joe didn't care what side of the law they were on.

"Joe, don't. Don't turn to illegal pathways." Steve took something out of his pocket. Joe looked down and realized it was Joe's Omega badge and official weapon.

Steve handed him the items. "You're part of this team. Part of this family. Give us every opportunity to get her back before making decisions you might regret."

Joe nodded. He wouldn't rein in Deacon Crandall, mostly because he trusted the man to stay on the right side of the law if he possibly could. Joe wouldn't move into dark territory.

Yet.

More of the Omega team showed up at Laura's front door. "I'm going to handle everybody here," Steve said. "Send them to HQ. A crime lab team is coming to process the house. Everyone else needs to get to work, pressing in harder to find Bailey Heath and Laura."

Steve walked over to the rest of his team.

"You going to be able to keep it together?" Brandon asked Joe.

"As long as I know she's alive, I'll keep it together. Hell, as long as I think there is any possible chance Laura is alive, I'll keep it together." He had to. For her.

Brandon nodded.

Joe looked down at the badge in his hand. "But I can't promise not to work outside the law on this, Brandon. Not if it means getting her back safely. I don't care if I lose everything—money, job, even my freedom."

Joe saw Brandon looking at Andrea across the room.

"What would you do if a psycho had Andrea?"

A psycho had held Andrea in his grip just a month ago. Brandon had nearly died trying to save her.

"Absolutely anything," Brandon said softly. "Pay any price. Employ any measure. Become someone I don't even recognize."

Joe knew he would do exactly the same.

Chapter Twenty

Back at Omega Headquarters the Critical Response Division team worked like the well-oiled machine they were. Joe remembered the van, which was now gone, and Derek Waterman found it on a traffic camera in the area of Laura's house at a time fitting when Laura had been taken.

Joe computed the distance of that traffic light from Laura's house and the time the van sped through the light.

He rammed his fist down on the desk next to Derek.

"Damn it."

"What?" Derek took his eyes off the screen to look over at Joe.

Joe rubbed his hand over his face. "In order for them to be at that light at that time, I must have just missed them. If I had just run outside instead of checking the rest of the house…"

Derek shrugged. "Checking the house first was the right call. I would've done the same."

But the thought that he could've stopped it burned like acid in Joe's gut.

Derek and Ashton Fitzgerald, another member of Omega's specialized tactical team, continued the search for the van, splitting the work and using different cameras in different directions. They followed as long as they could but eventually lost it when cameras became more scarce as the van headed out of town.

Which meant Laura and Bailey could be anywhere west of Colorado Springs. Unless, of course, Bailey had thought they might catch her on camera and circled back.

A dead end.

Jon, Brandon and Andrea continued their profile of Bailey Heath, digging further into people Bailey had known. It would be helpful, but so far was just another dead end.

Others on the team watched the footage again from his crime scenes trying to pick out anything they might have missed watching it the last two days.

Joe was about to go out of his mind without something concrete to put his energy toward. When the crime lab team called into headquarters with some questions, Joe felt almost relieved to have to go back to Laura's house to clarify some things.

"Lillian is going to go with you," Steve told him. "We're not leaving you unprotected in case Bailey decides to make you a target also."

Joe nodded down at Lillian. The tiny woman could kick someone's ass more ways than most people could learn in a lifetime. She might not look like protection detail, but Joe trusted her.

"Okay. Let's go." He prayed the crime scene crew would have something that gave them a clue to where Laura was. Every minute Bailey had her was a minute too long.

When they got to Laura's house, Joe could see the lab workers were doing a thorough job. Every inch of the attic, where Bailey had been hiding, had been searched. They ran what they could through a portable computer system at the scene. The rest would be done back at Omega headquarters.

Getting a hair sample from Joe helped them eliminate his DNA from all possible evidence sources. A pregnant Molly Humpfries-Waterman, Derek's wife, oversaw it all.

Joe answered all her questions about when Bailey could've gotten into the house and the van he'd seen outside. The crew sent someone to gather evidence in that area also.

"We're going to find something, Joe." Molly stroked his arm. "We'll get some sort of reading from all this. Some direction to send you."

But would it be in time?

Because this was also starting to look like another dead end. Like it couldn't get much worse.

Then the doorbell rang followed by a pounding on the door.

"Colorado Springs Police Department. We need you to open the door. We have a warrant for the arrest of Joe Matarazzo."

Joe let out a bitter string of obscenities and met Molly's eyes. "They still think I'm responsible for the deaths of the other women."

"And Laura being missing isn't going to help your case."

He nodded. "I can't let them take me right now. They'll confiscate my phone. What if Bailey calls? Or Laura? I'm going out the back."

Lillian moved silently from the rear of the room to Joe and Molly. "No, you're not. They've got uniformed cops coming up the back. No way out that way."

"Damn it." Joe slammed his fist against the wall.

"Steve will make some calls. He'll have you out as

soon as possible. Hopefully in just a few hours." But Molly's eyes were worried. So were Lillian's.

The cops banged on the door again. All the Omega techs stared at Joe, unsure what to do.

"Bailey didn't kill Laura here. If she wanted just to frame me she could've killed Laura here with my own gun and it would've been the perfect setup."

Molly nodded. "I hate to admit it, but I agree."

"Everything in my gut tells me Bailey is going to contact me. Make some trade of me for Laura." Or something worse.

"You and I can try to strong-arm our way out," Lillian said. "We're outmanned and outgunned by the locals, but we might make it."

Joe considered it for just a moment. He squeezed Lillian's shoulder. "Thanks for the offer, killer. If I thought it would work, I might try."

He reached in and got his phone out of his pocket and handed it to Lillian. "Keep this. Better Omega has it than the cops, for when Bailey contacts me. Because she will."

Lillian took it. More banging on the door. A threat to enter the premises using force.

"There's a contact in there, Deacon Crandall," Joe told Lillian. "He's aware of the situation and is willing to color outside the lines if and when needed. Tell him it's probably needed. Especially if Steve can't get me out fast enough."

Lillian nodded. "We're not going to let you sit in some cell while this is going down, Joe. Believe that."

He sure as hell hoped he could. He walked quickly over to answer the door before the police decided to ram it down. He opened it, immediately met by Detective Thompson, the same man who had questioned him before.

"I'm here, Detective. No need to shoot the door down or anything."

Thompson looked a little sheepish. Perhaps they'd been about to do just that.

"Why didn't you answer?" He looked around at the crime scene investigators still working. "What's going on here?"

Joe sure as hell wasn't going to mention Laura's kidnapping if he didn't have to. He was sure Thompson would immediately add that to the list of crimes to charge Joe with.

"We're looking for possible evidence to help us find the woman who is trying to frame me for the murders of my ex-girlfriends. The real villain in this situation's name is Bailey Heath, if you happen to care."

Thompson raised an eyebrow. "You'd be surprised at how many people claim they're being framed when the police come to arrest them."

Molly joined Joe at his side. "I'm Dr. Molly Humphries-Waterman. I am the head of the crime lab at Omega Sector. I assure you that what Joe says is true. He is not the one who killed those women."

"I'm sorry, but I have a warrant for his arrest. If there is proof he didn't commit the murders, I'm sure he'll be out in no time." Thompson looked around. "Where's your lawyer?"

"She's not here at the moment."

"After the way she busted my chops at the station for questioning you, I would assume she would want to read this over before I take you in."

Joe was thankful for everyone's silence. "Doubtless. But she had business that couldn't be delayed so she's not here. I'll read the warrant myself."

Joe took the paper, well aware he was stalling. Molly

had turned to the side and immediately called Steve to see what could be done. He didn't see Lillian anywhere.

"I'll need your weapon, your badge and your cell phone."

Molly looked over from her phone call. "He needs a warrant in order to go through your phone."

"Phone is listed on the warrant." Thompson grinned, beady eyes narrowed. He obviously took a great deal of pleasure lording his power over Joe.

Joe handed his weapon and badge. "I don't have a cell phone with me."

"Quit screwing around, Matarazzo. I know you have a phone."

Joe shrugged. "You're welcome to search me. Search the entire place. I lost my cell phone."

Thompson shoved Joe toward the wall. "I was trying to be nice, but if that's the way you want to play it… Hands against the wall."

Thompson searched Joe, obviously not believing him about the phone. When he didn't find anything he pulled out a pair of handcuffs.

"Is that absolutely necessary?" Molly asked. "We're all on the same side here, Detective Thompson. It won't be long until Omega gets the evidence over to your precinct exonerating Joe."

"No offense, ma'am, but until that happens, this guy—" he jerked Joe forward "—and I are not on the same side. I work for a living. Very hard. I don't think a jerk like this truly understands that concept at all. He thinks he can do whatever he wants."

Concern flew across Molly's features, "Detective—"

"It's okay, Molly," Joe cut in. "You stay here and work. Get the info we need. And tell Steve to hurry up and get me the hell out of Colorado Springs' finest's custody."

Molly nodded and Thompson led Joe out to the squad car, putting him in the backseat. Joe didn't say what was on his mind because Thompson didn't know about Laura's kidnapping, but his thoughts were dark.

If Laura died because of the detective's refusal to see beyond his own prejudice when it came to Joe, Joe would spend the rest of his life making sure Thompson had good reason to feel prejudice against him. He wouldn't physically hurt the man, but he could make his life a living hell in many other ways.

Joe sat in the squad car a long time before they began the drive from Fountain north toward Colorado Springs. The farther away they drove Joe from the action, the larger the ball of acid grew in his gut.

Lillian had his phone. She would get it back to Steve, or whoever, at Omega. If Bailey called—*when* Bailey called—someone would be able to talk to her. What exactly they would say to an obvious psychopath, Joe had no idea. He just hoped they could reason with her, explain the situation.

He hoped Bailey would believe them and not hurt Laura because of something completely out of her control.

"How's it feel sitting back there?" Thompson gave a deep, satisfied sigh. "All your money isn't going to help you now. You're going to jail, Matarazzo. And I'm going to be known as the one who put you there."

"The only thing you're going to be known as is the jerk who couldn't see reason when it sat six inches from his face."

Thompson rolled his eyes. "Be sure to tell that to your cell mate. I'm sure he'll think it's a lovely story."

Joe ignored Thompson. Fighting with him wouldn't accomplish anything. Hopefully Lillian had gotten in

touch with Deacon and the man would have the best lawyer in the state—second to Laura, of course—waiting
for them when Joe arrived.

Or he would have some blackmail info on someone
who could get him released. Joe had learned long ago
that Deacon worked on the side of justice, not necessarily the law. Deacon knew Laura's life was in danger,
knew Joe wasn't guilty, knew his arrest might cause her
further harm.

If Steve couldn't get Joe released through proper channels, Deacon would make sure it happened other ways.

Joe just hoped it would be in time.

The detention building was in the northeast section of
town. Joe watched as they got off I-25 onto the smaller
back roads. Past the airport, in a relatively deserted section of town, they came to a red light. It turned green but
an armored car, stopped in front of them, didn't move.

Even this small delay increased Joe's frustration.
They needed to get to the station immediately so someone could get him out. Had Bailey called? Not knowing
was killing him.

Another armored truck pulled up directly beside them
and stopped, effectively blocking Thompson from being
able to go around the vehicle in front of them.

"What the hell?" Thompson murmured.

The detective honked but neither vehicle moved.

"They have engine problems, Thompson. Just reverse
and go around for God's sake."

Joe wasn't expecting a third vehicle to come up behind them and physically hit their car. The jolt rammed
him into the seat in front of him.

Thompson cursed as two masked men ran up to the
car, their guns pointed clearly at him and the uniformed
officer riding next to him.

"Out of the car. Now!" one masked man—the one pointing his weapon at Thompson—said. The other kept his gun silently pointed at the other cop.

Thompson looked back at him. "Do you have something to do with this, Matarazzo?"

"What the hell are you talking about? How could I have something to do with this?" Was it people working for Bailey Heath? Had she been watching Laura's house then sent someone to finish the job?

"Get out of the car. Right now." The man shot at the engine. Everybody in the car jumped.

Thompson was sweating. "Okay, fine, fine."

Thompson and the uniformed officer opened the door and before either man could get completely out and to their feet, both the masked guys reached over and injected them quickly with something in their necks. Thompson and the cop fell unconscious onto the street.

The guy who'd spoken to Thompson reached down and got the detective's keys, then unlocked the back door. He pulled Joe out roughly and put a sack over his head.

"Let's go, Mr. Matarazzo." His voice was clear and menacing. "I hope whoever is in charge of your bank account is willing to pay or you're a dead man. Of course, you're probably a dead man anyway."

Chapter Twenty-One

The man dragged Joe over to the armored car that had stopped behind them and threw him in the back. He hit hard, unable to catch himself. Damn Thompson for insisting on handcuffing Joe.

"Don't kill him for God's sake. That defeats the purpose."

A woman's voice. Bailey Heath's?

The door slammed in the back of the armored car and they began moving.

"You alright there, Joe? Your man Deacon is quite the prince." Joe was shocked to find Lillian at his side helping him sit up and taking the bag off his head.

He couldn't stop his gaping stare. "What in the world? I thought you guys were kidnapping me. Working for Bailey Heath. That was a pretty elaborate ruse." Lillian unlocked his handcuffs and Joe rubbed his wrists where they'd chafed against the metal.

"We had to make them believe it was an actual kidnapping, so you can't be charged with anything later." Deacon had removed his mask and was now driving the armored car away from the scene.

"I'm assuming Thompson and the cop will be okay?" Joe didn't think he'd lose much sleep over it either way.

"They'll be out another thirty minutes. I wasn't sure

if there were any recording devices in the squad car, so I kept up the act just in case."

Lillian shook her head. "Yeah, not because you enjoy breaking the law and risking your life. That would be crazy."

Deacon looked back at them and winked. "Anything worth doing is worth overdoing."

Lillian rolled her eyes and glanced over at Joe. "That's some friend you have there. Questionable moral compass."

Joe just shrugged. He didn't care about Deacon's moral compass, at least not in this case. They'd gotten Joe out without anyone getting hurt.

"Thanks you guys. I don't know how you pulled it off this fast, but you're amazing."

"Wait until you get the bill. You might not think me so amazing then."

Joe couldn't care less about the money.

"Were there any calls on my phone while you had it?"

Lillian shook her head. "No. I'm sorry."

She removed the overalls she had on over her clothes. "We've got to ditch this truck before Colorado Springs' finest wake up. We need to get you deep inside Omega where they can't look for you."

"I've already got it set up. Car ready for you." A few minutes later Deacon pulled up to a parking garage. "This is where I leave you, kids." He tossed keys to Lillian.

"Deacon—" Joe couldn't find the words to express the size of his gratitude as he got out of the back of the armored car and walked around to the driver's side.

"Another time, boss. I've still got a lot of feelers out all over about your woman. Hopefully you'll hear from me again soon. Right now I need to finish cleaning up this mess."

He winked at Lillian, who just glared at him, and drove off.

Lillian drove the most direct route to Omega headquarters. It wouldn't be long before the police either reported Joe missing or reported him as a fugitive. He didn't care which. He was just glad to be back actively participating in finding Laura again.

In the end none of their work helped them find Bailey Heath. Bailey decided she wanted to be found. Joe and Lillian had been back an hour when he received the call on his phone. The bustle of search tactics fell silent. Joe's phone had already been connected to a recording device. He turned it on speaker so everyone could hear.

"Hello."

"It's time for us to talk face-to-face, don't you think?"

Joe had never heard Bailey Heath's voice, and found it shrill and annoying.

Or maybe that was just because he wanted to kill her so badly.

"Is Laura alive?"

Bailey laughed. "I'm glad I finally found someone you actually care about, Joe. I was afraid I'd have to kill all your ex-girlfriends before I got the reaction I wanted."

Steve nodded at Joe. They were recording this. Bailey had pretty much just admitted to the murders and cleared Joe's name. At least now he wouldn't have to worry about the Colorado Springs police coming after him again.

But he noticed Bailey hadn't answered the question. "Bailey, is Laura alive? This conversation doesn't go any further until I have that information."

"Yes, she's alive. For now."

"Let me talk to her."

There were a few moments of silence. Was Laura dead and Bailey was attempting to figure out what lie to tell?

"Now, Bailey. Let me talk to her now."

He had to know.

"Fine." Bailey's voice became shriller.

He could hear murmuring and something brushing against the phone, obviously from Bailey's movements.

"Joe?"

He almost dropped to his knees in relief from hearing Laura's voice.

"Laura, has she hurt you?"

"No, I'm fine but she has—"

Joe heard the thud of flesh against flesh before Laura cried out.

"Laura?" No one answered. "Laura!"

A few moments later Bailey came back on the phone. "No more talking to her. Laura is, um, unavailable."

Joe closed his eyes and took deep breaths to remain calm. Laura was alive. That was the most important thing.

Thinking of ways to kill Bailey Heath was secondary.

"What do you want, Bailey?"

"A simple trade. You for Laura."

"Fine. Deal." He didn't even hesitate. He would give himself to this madwoman a thousand times over if it meant Laura's safety. "But only if Laura is alive. Do you understand?"

She rattled off an address. "You have thirty minutes. And no press that you love so much, Joe. No cameras. Not like when you allowed Tyler to be killed. And none of your friends either. If I see anyone but you, Laura dies."

"Fine." Joe had no problem telling the lie.

"You remember how Tyler died, don't you, Joe?"

"Yes." He had the burn scars to remind him every day.

"It would be a shame for Laura to die the same way. To burn."

Joe grimaced. "I'll come alone, Bailey. Just don't hurt her."

"See you soon."

As soon as Joe hung up, Steve reached over and grabbed Joe by his shirt collar. "Don't you say one damn word about going in there alone, you got it?"

"You heard what Bailey said."

"That woman is planning to kill you, Joe. It is obvious to every person in here. She aims to kill you and Laura, too."

Joe looked around the room. Everyone nodded.

"Trust us to do our job," Steve continued, his hands on Joe's shoulders now rather than his shirt. "You get in there with Bailey, buy us time to get in position. If she gives you Laura, great, we'll get her out immediately and then get you out. Maybe you can even talk Bailey into surrendering and nobody has to get hurt."

Joe closed his eyes. His boss was right. Bailey wasn't planning to let anyone live, least of all Joe and Laura. She wanted to hurt him in any way she could.

"I'll buy you the time with Bailey that you need." Joe opened his eyes. "But you promise to get Laura out first."

"Absolutely."

"Then let's go. We'll need almost the entire thirty minutes to get there."

"Alright, people." Steve walked as he spoke. "We're wheels up in five. Security alert red. And somebody get a copy of that recording to whoever Jack Thompson's boss is at Colorado Springs PD. Plus, tell them that Joe fought off his 'kidnappers' and is with us."

Everybody moved at Steve's words. Activity buzzed instantly.

"We've already pulled up the building plans," Lillian said. "SWAT will study en route."

"We need the best plan we can formulate before we get there," Steve said. "Give Joe the smallest earpiece we have."

Joe shook his head. "But what if Bailey sees it?"

"She won't. But we have to be able to communicate with you. To let you know when we've got Laura out."

Joe nodded. There were so many things that could go wrong with this mission it was difficult to consider them all.

LAURA LAY ON the ground, blood pooling in her mouth. Bailey had taken off the gag and sack to let Laura talk to Joe.

They were in some sort of warehouse or old factory or something. A large, dirty building with rafters in the high ceiling and dust on the ground.

She had wanted to get Joe information—what little of it she had—but all that had gotten Laura was a bruised face and a hard fall to the ground.

She'd tried to warn Joe he was about to walk into a trap. That there was someone else involved.

Bailey had stopped somewhere and picked up another person. Laura didn't know who—the person hadn't talked at all, and Bailey had turned the radio up so loud in the van that no one could hear anything.

Laura looked around. The person wasn't here now. Was he or she waiting to ambush Joe? Was it someone who would be keeping an eye out for the rest of the Omega team and notifying Bailey if anyone else came with Joe?

Laura hoped beyond all hope that Joe would accept help from his teammates. Otherwise he had no chance to survive this.

Laura watched Bailey douse some discarded piles of wood on the ground with gasoline.

She wasn't sure Joe had a chance even with the rest of the team.

"Don't worry. Everything else is already soaked with one sort of accelerant or another. I've had a year to study fire and know exactly what works best." A blissful smile lit Bailey's face. "Once fire touches anywhere in this building, it will only take minutes for flames to engulf it entirely."

Bailey planned to die today. And she planned to take Laura and Joe with her.

Laura tried to scoot back when Bailey walked over to her with her can of gas, but with her hands still bound behind her back, there was nowhere to go.

"No, don't—"

She stopped talking so she wouldn't get gas in her mouth as Bailey poured it on her.

"Trust me. It's better this way. It will be much quicker." Laura flinched as Bailey smoothed a piece of gas-soaked hair away from Laura's face. "But now it's time to get you in place. I'm sure Joe and his friends will be here early if they can manage it."

"But you told Joe to come alone."

Bailey rolled her eyes. "I've been watching that group for a year. They're not going to let Joe go into this building alone. He'll try to stall me while they look for you. It's like SWAT 101."

Laura realized that's exactly what would happen. "So you're going to take on all of Omega Sector?"

"No, although I have to admit, I wish I could've figured out what member of the SWAT team was responsible for not taking the shot at the man who killed Tyler. They must have had a sharpshooter somewhere who didn't do what he needed to do. I would like for that person to burn also." She shrugged. "But you take what you can get."

"What's to keep them from just shooting you, storming in and rescuing me?"

Bailey smiled. "They'll consider it. But they won't know where you are. They'll think they know where you are, but they won't."

Laura had no idea what Bailey was talking about. She was beginning to wonder if Bailey even knew what she was talking about.

"You'll be right here." Bailey walked a few steps past Laura and opened a hatch in the floor.

Laura tried to scoot away again as Bailey reached for her. She couldn't hold in the groan of pain from her sore arms and shoulders as Bailey dragged her across the floor. Bailey stopped just as they got to the hatch. She took the gag back out of her pocket and tied it back in Laura's mouth.

"You'll be right here where all the action is, but they'll never know it."

Laura screamed as Bailey pushed her into the hatch, tears coming to her eyes as she hit the ground hard even though it was only two feet down.

"See? It's not deep. Some sort of false floor." Bailey jumped in with Laura and tied her feet together. Then grabbed a strange-looking poncho. "This material blocks your heat signature. So when Joe's friends are trying to find you, you won't show up on their equipment."

Bailey tucked Laura's legs under it. "Plus, I've given them something else to chase. They'll be happy about that. I'm not a complete monster, you know."

Laura longed to ask Bailey what the hell she was talking about.

"Bad thing about this material is that it may smother

you if you're left under it too long." Bailey shrugged apologetically as she tucked it around Laura like a cocoon. "But honestly, I think the fire will get you before that."

Bailey pulled the material up and over Laura's head. "Don't worry. It will all be over soon."

Laura didn't even try to answer. She just focused on breathing in and out in the darkness. She heard the hatch door close, but that didn't change her focus.

She had to stay calm. Had to keep breathing. Had to stay alive until Joe got here.

And pray he could outsmart a maniac.

Chapter Twenty-Two

Joe drove Steve's SUV, which allowed Derek and Steve to sit low in the backseats and not be noticeable. Under any other circumstances Joe would've found it pretty funny to see his boss and friend twisted like pretzels to fit their large frames near the floor of the vehicle.

Joe couldn't find anything humorous right now.

Two other Omega vehicles approached the address Bailey gave Joe—an abandoned lumber house that had last been used over fifty years ago—from a different direction. Steve had on the speakerphone so they all could coordinate.

"The building has some pretty vast square footage," Ashton Fitzgerald, a SWAT team member, announced. "Terrible for us, tactically."

"So heat signatures are our best bet?" Steve asked.

"Definitely," Derek responded. "Joe, you've got to keep Bailey talking. Give us a chance to find Laura and get her out."

"I will."

Joe tuned out as the SWAT team spoke back and forth to each other. Who would be coming in from what direction. That wasn't Joe's job. He'd trust that the team would have his back when he needed them.

Joe's job was damn near impossible. To go in, look

Bailey Heath in the eye and pretend like he gave a damn about anything she had to say.

The only thing he cared about was finding Laura.

He could still hear her cry of pain as Bailey had obviously struck her. His fists gripped the steering wheel tighter.

"You okay, Joe?" Steve asked from the back.

"What if she's dead? That would've been a smart play on Bailey's part, right? Letting me talk to Laura and then killing her?"

"Don't go down that road. It leads nowhere," Steve told him. "We go into every hostage situation as if we can get everyone out alive. This is no different."

But it was different. It was Laura.

"You have to go in there with a cool head. Keep your training in place. Talk to Bailey like you would any other hostage-taker. I know it's hard but it's what you have to do."

Joe took a deep breath. "Okay."

"I've seen you walk into situations I would've sworn no one was coming out of alive. But you've gotten everyone out. You've listened to people as if you were their psychiatrist or priest or something. You've given them a chance to be heard. Give that to Bailey Heath."

"Hell, Steve. She's hurt Laura. I don't know if I can."

Derek knew what it was to have a psychopath hurt his woman and not be able to do anything about it. "Then you listen to Bailey not because you give a damn about her, but because it will give us time to get Laura out. We'll get her out, Joe."

Joe prayed that was true. "Alright. We're almost there."

"Pull to the side," Steve said. "I'll direct from here. Derek will join the rest of the SWAT team once we've figured out where Laura is."

"It will take us a while to manually scan a building this big, Joe. Buy us as much time as you can."

Joe took his weapon and waist holster off and put it in the passenger seat beside him. "See you guys on the flip side." He opened his door.

"We'll get her, Joe."

Steve's voice was the last thing he heard before closing the door. Joe didn't care about his own safety. Only getting Laura back. He was glad Steve and the team understood that.

He found the door and allowed his eyes to adjust to the dimness of the building before walking any farther inside.

"Bailey, I'm here," he called out. "Where are you?"

The place seemed even more vast from the inside. Bailey could be lying in wait any number of places. She could step out at any minute, dump Laura's dead body at his feet and shoot him between the eyes.

The only thing stopping her was her need for the theatrical. For Joe to burn. It wasn't a comforting thought.

He could smell the accelerants all around him. He had no doubt Bailey planned for this place to go up in flames.

"C'mon, Bailey. We can't talk if I don't know where you are."

He heard a disturbing cackle from deeper inside the lumber house. Joe began walking toward it.

"I don't know that I really want to talk," Bailey said. He couldn't see her, but could tell he was heading in the right direction.

"But you wanted me here."

"But not necessarily to talk. More to watch you burn. And your girlfriend, too."

Joe sucked in a breath and forced himself to remain calm. "Is Laura alive?"

The question was more to keep Bailey talking than to gather information. He knew he couldn't trust anything she said.

"I think so."

"What does that mean?" Joe kept walking toward Bailey's high-pitched voice.

"She's alive. I want to hurt you, not her."

"Unfortunately, I don't think that's true. You killed three other women I used to care about."

Bailey's voice was much closer now. She laughed. "Okay, you got me. I don't mind hurting her if it also hurts you. And you care much more about her than you did those other three. I was able to tell that easily."

Joe advanced into a room that looked like it was once an office. Bailey stepped out from behind the broken paneling of a wall. She had a gun in her hand. Probably still Joe's Glock.

"Hi, Joe." She smiled at him, but hatred burned in her eyes.

Along with a whole hell of a lot of crazy.

"Bailey. Where's Laura?"

"She's not here with me."

"I can see that." He fought to tamp down panic.

The tiny earpiece inside his left ear clicked on. Steve. *"That's an affirmative, Joe. There's only two heat signatures in the room you're in. You and Bailey. We're systematically searching the rest of the building."*

"Is Laura alive, Bailey?"

Bailey grimaced. "Yes. She's alive. For now."

"Let her go and you can do whatever you want to me."

Joe realized he meant it. He would die whatever agonizing death Bailey planned if it meant Laura would live.

"Oh, I have plans for you, Joe." Bailey smiled again. "Don't I get a striptease like the people did last week?"

"Are you worried I have weapons?"

"Not really. If you kill me you'll never find out where Laura is. And she will die. Of course, she's probably going to die anyway."

Joe had his first glimpse of hope that Laura was still alive. Bailey wanted drama. Maybe she planned to kill Laura in front of him as some big, painful gesture.

Let her have her plans. He would give the team the time they needed to find Laura and thwart them.

"Sure, I'll take off my clothes, if that's what you really want. But I thought you loved Tyler. I wouldn't have thought you would want to see another man naked."

The earpiece switched on again. *"We've detected a faint heat signature. In the southwest corner of the building—it's the only one. It's a weird signal, but it's definitely a person. We're going to get her."*

"I don't want you to get completely naked, Joe. Just take off your shirt," Bailey sneered. "I want to see the burn marks from when Tyler died."

Joe began pulling his T-shirt over his head as the earpiece clicked on again. *"Ashton and Derek are trying to work their way to her. Keep Bailey talking."*

"Is this what you want?" Joe asked, walking over to her and turning his back so she could clearly see the burn scars that stretched down his neck and back. He flinched as she touched him.

"Did it hurt?"

Joe didn't know if he should lie or not. Wasn't sure what he should say to keep Bailey in the moment and give the team the time they needed.

He turned back to look at her and there was such a sadness in Bailey's eyes, he almost felt pity for her.

Bailey was crazy. Had ruined lives. Had killed people.

But she loved Tyler, and had lost him.

Joe tried to think of what he would say to Bailey if she wasn't holding the woman he loved captive.

What he would say to do his job.

"Yes, the burns hurt. But I'm sure my physical pain wasn't nearly as bad as what you went through by losing Tyler."

"Now you're just trying to manipulate me." She pointed the gun at him.

"I'll admit that was my plan coming in here. But now I'm not. Now I'm just trying to talk to you."

Bailey began to cry. "Why, Joe? Why couldn't you get Tyler out that day? I've watched you for a year now. I've seen you go into one situation after another and almost always get everyone out safely. Why couldn't you do that for Tyler?"

"I've asked myself that same question every day. If I could go back and change the past I would. Bring Tyler back for you."

Of course, Tyler would be going back to the wife he loved and his baby daughter, not to Bailey. But Joe didn't mention that.

His earpiece clicked again. *"Derek and Ashton are on the other side of a door where Laura is. But they are going to have to make some noise to get through it, and it will definitely alert Bailey that the rest of us are here."*

Once Bailey heard the noise she would certainly shoot Joe or herself or light the place on fire.

Could he talk Bailey down? Was she determined to kill him no matter what? He had to try.

"Let's hold on for a second."

"Roger that," Steve whispered.

"What?" Bailey asked, eyes narrowing.

"Let's hold on to the memories," Joe covered. "And

I'm saying this not just for my sake, but for yours, too. Would Tyler want you to do this? To kill people?"

Bailey began pacing back and forth.

"I don't think Tyler would want you to pay that price, Bailey. To carry that weight."

She stopped pacing and looked at Joe. For the first time there was some semblance of clarity in her eyes.

"It's too late. I've already killed."

"It's not too late if you stop now. We can't do anything about the past. It's only the future we can change."

Bailey lowered her weapon and for just a moment Joe thought she might surrender. Looking at her he realized just how young she really was. Lost. Frightened. She hunched her shoulders and put her hands in her jacket pockets.

And something changed. Joe didn't know what or why, but when Bailey looked back up at him it was with complete resolve and determination.

All the crazy was back.

"No. It's too late. I'll do whatever it takes to avenge Tyler the way he would want me to."

She was going to kill Joe and herself and take Laura with them.

"Go, Steve, go," Joe said. No longer caring if the secret was out. Three seconds later a huge noise blasted through the air as the SWAT team took out the door at the other end of the building to rescue Laura.

He looked at Bailey expecting to see surprise or fear. She just smiled. Joe realized this had been her plan all along and somehow they had all just played into it perfectly.

"Sounds like your friends found her. Good. Believe it or not, my fight was never with her. With them." Bailey took a deep breath, holding her arms out slightly as if she was breathing in a beautiful dawn.

Joe smelled it, too. The building was on fire.

Bailey looked at him, tilting her head sideways. "And now we burn."

Chapter Twenty-Three

Joe realized Bailey must have doused just about everything in accelerants. The place was going up fast.

He pressed a hand to his ear. "Steve, report. Do you have Laura?"

"Yes, Ashton has her. She's hurt, but alive. They're carrying her out. Busting the door must have triggered some sort of ignition. The whole building is burning."

Ashton tried to cut in on the frequency to tell Joe something, but there was too much noise from the fire. Joe couldn't understand him.

Laura was safe. That was all that mattered.

"Laura's out, Bailey. Your plan failed. You and I need to get out too before this whole building comes down around us."

She brought the gun back up and pointed it at him. "Actually you and I and the woman you love burning was the plan all along."

"Laura's already gone, Bailey. You'll have to try your plan another day."

After she'd spent three consecutive life sentences in prison.

"You might want to check with your boss there, Joe. Make sure everything is how you think it is."

Something about Bailey's calm expression sent a chill through him. He pressed the earpiece closer to his ear.

"Steve? I need you to confirm that you have Laura."

"Hold. Derek and Ashton are coming out of the building right now."

Joe heard lots of coughing then the distinct sound of a baby crying. He pieced it together before he heard what Ashton had to tell Steve.

"This is Summer Worrall and her baby."

"Joe, we don't have Laura. I repeat, we don't have Laura."

Joe took the earpiece out of his ear and put it in his pocket. His friends couldn't help him now.

"You took Summer and the baby."

Bailey shrugged. "I didn't hurt her. Like I said, my fight was never with her. I understood why Tyler found it difficult to leave her. They'd taken vows."

"Where's Laura?" The smoke was getting thicker even though the fire wasn't near them yet.

Bailey stomped her foot and Joe looked down realizing there was a hatch door of sorts underneath her. "She's been with us all along. Wrapped in some material that made her heat signature invisible to your friends."

Joe took a step toward Bailey. She pointed the gun at his head. "You can get her out, but slowly."

Joe nodded, praying Laura was still alive in there. He opened the hatch door and saw a form wrapped in a blanket unmoving. He jumped in and gently started unwrapping Laura.

She was covered in sweat, skin red and blotchy, her breathing shallow. The stench of gasoline permeated the air.

Bailey looked down from where she stood, gun still pointed at them. "Yeah, sorry. The price for hiding a heat signature is material that has been known to smother people."

Joe unwrapped the gag from Laura's mouth, wiping sweat from her brow. "Laura, are you okay? Sweetheart?"

Her eyes blinked open but didn't focus. "Joe."

"C'mon, let's get you out of here." He reached back and untied her arms, forcing his thumbs into the joints at the front of her shoulders to relax them enough that they could move after being held at such an awkward angle for so long. He knew it had to hurt—saw tears roll down her face—but she didn't make a sound. He untied her feet and climbed out of the hole with Laura in his arms.

Bailey had the gun pointed right at them. "See? I knew you loved her. I'm sorry I killed those other women because that was just a waste. Laura was the only one I needed to kill to make you feel my pain in losing Tyler."

Joe felt desperation swamp him. He could smell the smoke getting thicker. They didn't have much time.

He had to get Laura out of here. He turned his back to Bailey so he could talk to Laura in his arms.

"Laura." He shook her slightly, trying to get her to remain conscious. "Can you stand, baby? Walk? Open your eyes for me."

She did, her beautiful hazel eyes focused on him this time. "I need you to be able to walk, okay?" He set her on her feet when she nodded again.

He was going to make a deal with the devil and pray it was enough. He turned back to Bailey, one arm behind him to help Laura find strength to stand. This would only work if she could get herself out of here.

"You want me to burn, Bailey. I know you do." Joe knew exactly what Bailey needed to hear and was willing to give it to her. "I deserve to burn."

Bailey's eyes lit. "Yes, you do."

"I will stay here and burn with you. But you have to let Laura go. She's innocent."

"No!" Bailey pointed her gun at Laura.

Joe pulled Laura more fully behind him. She was still wobbly but seemed to at least be able to walk.

"Then I fight you, Bailey. You may shoot me, and that's fine. But maybe I'll still be able to get the gun from you and get away. Then I won't burn. Or maybe you kill me, but I die quickly and painlessly. Either way, are you willing to take that chance?"

Bailey cursed foully, pacing back and forth. Her need for vengeance won out. "Fine, she can go."

Joe didn't hesitate. He turned to Laura and began pushing her toward the door. Her eyes, still fuzzy and hazy from something akin to heatstroke, looked at him without much comprehension.

"Run toward the door, baby. There might be some fire, but just keep moving forward, okay? Crawl if you have to." He handed her his T-shirt. "Use this if you need it, to hold over your mouth."

She nodded. "You?"

Joe framed her face with both hands. He would've gladly spent the rest of his life with this woman. But knowing that she would live and have a life would be enough. "I'll be right behind you," he lied.

He kissed her. The sweetest, briefest of kisses. "I love you. Now run, okay?"

He turned her and pushed. She stumbled slightly then found her footing and ran wobbling toward the other side of the room.

Joe had to believe she would make it.

He picked the comm unit out of his pocket and put it back in his ear. "Steve? Anybody? If you can hear me,

Laura is on her way out the front door. Send someone to help her. She's injured."

Joe looked up as Bailey turned her gun from him to where Laura was running.

"I've changed my mind. She can't live. If she lives you haven't suffered enough."

Joe ran toward Bailey but knew he would be too late to stop her from shooting Laura's retreating form in the back.

But out of the smoke stepped Steve Drackett. He shot Bailey before she could fire her gun. "I think you've caused quite enough people to suffer."

Bailey fell to the ground.

Steve walked forward and kicked the gun away from her hand.

At the sound of the gunshot Laura stopped and turned around. "Joe?"

"I'm here, sweetie." He ran over to her and put an arm around her. "Steve, let's go. This building is going to collapse any minute."

The smoke was already unbearable.

"She's still alive," Steve responded, gesturing to Bailey. "I'm going to carry her out."

Joe saw it at the same time Steve did. Bailey reached into her jacket pocket and pulled out a hand grenade.

Just like the one that had been used to kill Tyler. Bailey reached over with her other hand and pulled the pin.

"Grenade!" Steve yelled. "Get her out!"

Joe knew he wouldn't be able to get Laura to safety in the seconds they had. He saw Steve dive behind a wall in the other direction and dove with Laura back down into the false floor pulling the hatch closed over them. He wrapped the blanket around them and tucked Laura under him, shielding her as much as he could with his body.

A second later heat washed over them as well as an unbearably loud noise. Joe tightened his arms around Laura as everything went black.

LAURA TRIED TO figure out if she was dead.

It was the second time today she'd had to purposely use her brain, *force* it to work—something it usually did quite well on its own—to figure out if she was still alive or not.

She felt the same smothering heat she'd felt the first time. Unbearable heat that made breathing, moving, thinking, nearly impossible. Her breaths had come in short gasps, the effort forcing them further and further apart, until she'd been sure each breath had been her last.

Then she'd heard Joe's voice talking to Bailey. Laura hadn't been able to make out what they were saying, but she knew he was nearby.

She'd held on. Her shoulders and feet and lungs wailed in agony but she'd held on because Joe had come for her.

But at some point she'd stopped even being able to focus on his voice.

The heat, the fumes from the gas Bailey had poured on her, had pulled her completely under.

But the next thing she knew Joe was there. Carrying her out of the hot hole of death. Shirtless. That didn't help her figure out if she was alive or not. Why wouldn't Joe have a shirt on if she was still alive?

Maybe she was in heaven.

It was just that everything had seemed so far away. Even Joe. Especially Joe.

She'd screamed in torture when he'd cut the bindings off her wrists and moved her shoulders, but no sound had come out. His fingers had helped her survive it.

The pain had let her know for sure she was alive, not in heaven.

Joe and Bailey had talked but Laura couldn't understand. Couldn't process.

Joe had wanted her to stand so she'd tried her best. Then he'd asked her to run, so she'd done that too.

But first he'd kissed her. He told her he loved her.

She wanted to stay with him. Wanted to kiss him more, but he'd told her to run.

She'd known something was wrong, but still couldn't get her brain to work enough to know what it was.

But as she lay here in the dark now, her brain figured out what it was.

Joe had made a deal with Bailey: he would die with her, if she would let Laura go. The bitch had reneged and tried to kill them both.

Joe had protected her by throwing them back in this hole and covering her with his body.

She was suffocating again, with Joe on top of her as well as the blanket. But this time her hands weren't tied; she could do something about it.

"Joe? Are you okay?"

He didn't answer. She twisted to her side, rolling him off her, and pulled the damn stifling material off them both.

Joe groaned and coughed.

It was the most beautiful sound Laura had ever heard.

Without his weight and the blanket on her, Laura could breathe more freely. There didn't even seem to be fire burning above them any longer.

"Are you okay?" she asked him again. Longer sentences still seemed beyond her.

"Yes. I think so. Are you?"

"My brain still hurts."

"You may have had a partial heatstroke from being trapped in that heat signature blocking material. It's not meant to be used indoors, or for extended periods of time."

Laura didn't like that. "Will my brain always be this slow?"

She couldn't see it, but she could hear Joe's smile. "I hope so. Then maybe I have a chance of keeping up with you."

Joe reached up with his legs and pushed against the hatch door. It didn't move. Then he touched the door with his hand. "It feels like Bailey's hand grenade actually saved us. It probably blew up so much of the roof of the building there wasn't enough to burn or suffocate us to death. It doesn't feel hot anymore, and the air seems cleaner."

"But we're trapped here."

"The team will be in here looking for us soon. We're not in any actual danger anymore. I just hope Steve made it out alive. I saw him dive the other way before the grenade went off."

Steve had been there, too. Laura's brain began to put pieces of information together. They lay there in silence while she figured it out, both of them content to just be with one another. Alive.

"You were going to let her kill you to get me out."

"Yes." Joe's voice was soft, husky.

"Why didn't you just fight her?"

"I couldn't take a chance you might get hurt in the process."

"Well, it was a terrible plan. Giving yourself over to die rather than take a chance fighting her."

Joe chuckled, wrapping an arm around her and pulling her closer. "How about next time a raging psychopath has us in her clutches I discuss the plan with you first and get approval."

"Yes. Better." She snuggled in to him. "Thank you."

"For getting you to approve the plan next time?"

"For keeping us both alive. For trusting that your team would have your back. For risking everything to find me."

"If you weren't here to share my life, it wasn't going to have much meaning anyway."

"Joe, I'm just afraid that—" She wanted to tell him she loved him. That she'd never stopped loving him. But that she was also scared that six months from now he would decide again she wasn't enough for him.

Being trapped in an enclosed space while a building burned down around them seemed like as good a place as any for that conversation.

But damn the Omega team for being so good at their job. Moments later they heard Joe's team calling for them.

"We'll finish this conversation soon, I promise." He kissed the side of her forehead before using his legs to kick up against the door to draw the team's attention.

Moments later the hatch opened. Steve stood there looking down at them.

"Joe with no shirt on and a beautiful woman in his arms. Seems about right."

Chapter Twenty-Four

Two weeks later Joe picked Laura up to take her on what he promised would be a "special lunch date."

Considering he'd been with her almost 24/7 since the incident with Bailey Heath, and that he'd taken her on a number of luxurious dates—including a couple on a private plane carrying them to Los Angeles and New York—she couldn't imagine what "special lunch date" meant.

She got into the car as he pulled up next to her law office building. "I can't miss any more work. I have to be back in no more than an hour."

He turned, tilted his head and gave her his most charming smile. "Hello to you, too, love." He reached over and kissed her.

Between the look and the kiss, every part of her body, and certain pieces of her clothing, just about melted. She sighed leaning into him.

"Sorry," she murmured against his lips. "I just can't afford to go flying across the country today. Work has been piling up."

She'd been hospitalized for complications stemming from heatstroke and fumes inhalation, including a seizure. The doctor had released her after just two days, but strongly suggested a couple of weeks of just low stress, fun activities.

Joe had taken two weeks' vacation from Omega and

proceeded to escort Laura to all the places he loved. Places he'd always wanted to show her. Some were extravagant like the Four Seasons in Manhattan. But they also went to places like Sonny's Cafe in Galveston, Texas, a tiny hole-in-the-wall restaurant that he loved.

She had to admit, it had been fun. More. It had been lovely and peaceful and healing. Just what they both needed to put the nightmare of Bailey Heath behind them.

Joe's name had been cleared, of course. Although evidently there had been some other incident with the police involving Joe—Laura still didn't have all the details. But it had all been worked out.

The gossip sites had a field day with her and Joe's relationship. But after the story with Bailey was somehow leaked, and Laura was made out to be the heroine of the story, the sites seemed to take a different slant toward their relationship.

In every picture posted of the two of them Joe looked at her with such adoration, it was nearly impossible for the sites to say anything damaging about Laura without looking like fools. Joe's looks, his gestures, his movements toward Laura spoke volumes about his feelings.

But how long would they last? She forced herself not to think about tomorrows. Joe hadn't brought it up, so she didn't either.

"I promise to have you back in under an hour." He put the car in Drive and pulled away from her building.

"Okay, so where are we going for this 'special lunch date'?"

She'd barely gotten the question out before he pulled the car around the corner and parked it in a lot, then strode around to open her door for her.

They were at the county courthouse. Laura and her law partners had specifically chosen their office building because of its proximity to City Hall and the local courtrooms.

"What's going on? Oh my gosh, Joe, are you in trouble with the police again? You should've told me so I could be more prepared. What are the charges?"

She racked her brain trying to think of what charges could've been brought against Joe that would have him at the county courthouse rather than the criminal court downtown. This court was primarily used for real estate and marital purposes.

He gripped her elbow gently and led her up the stairs. "The general charge is being an idiot for too many years."

She couldn't help but laugh. "Well, in that case you really should've given me more time to prepare." He opened the door for her. "Seriously, what's going on?"

They went through security, Joe presenting his weapon to be held in a security box since he wasn't here on official business. "You'll figure it out in a minute. I enjoy being ahead of you for once."

They walked down the hall. "Figure what out? Joe, just tell me what's going on."

He stopped them in front of a courtroom door. "Get there faster, Laura. I know you can."

He twirled something around on the end of his pinkie as he said it.

A ring.

They were here to get married.

"Oh my God, Joe, we can't. It's too soon."

"Too soon? Hell, it's six years *too late.*"

"But what about…" She trailed off unable to find the words she wanted.

"What about what?" He put his forehead against hers. "You need this so I can prove I'm not going to wake up one morning and change my mind again. I need this so

I can have you legally bound to me while you're still slightly addled and will say yes."

"But—"

"I want you, Laura. I want you so badly I can't think straight for it. I love you so much that the thought of life without you causes me to break out in a panic."

"Are you sure?"

He cupped her face with both hands. "I have never been more sure of anything in my entire life." He kissed her. "We'll have a big wedding soon and invite everyone we know. We'll do this here today because I want you bound to me right now. Just you and me."

She nodded. He kissed her again and opened the door to the courtroom, his hand still gripping hers.

But when they walked in they realized they were not alone. Every member of the Critical Response team was already in the courtroom. She felt Joe's hand tighten around hers.

"You guys. How?" Joe basically sputtered.

Steve stepped forward. "You work for one of the most elite crime fighting agencies on the planet. Did you think we wouldn't discover the wedding of one of our own and be here to celebrate it?"

Joe wrapped his arm around Laura. "I guess not."

"Welcome to the family, Laura," Steve said.

Laura couldn't think of anywhere else in the world she'd rather be.

* * * * *

Don't miss the gripping conclusion of
Janie Crouch's series
OMEGA SECTOR: CRITICAL RESPONSE
when BATTLE TESTED goes on sale next month.

You'll find it wherever
Mills & Boon Intrigue books are sold!

Before he could activate his lightning-quick reflexes, she went up on her toes and kissed him on the cheek.

Then she turned back to the vending machine. Over her shoulder, she said, "Couldn't help it. You're cute when you get befuddled."

He was willing to concede that she was smarter than he was… and probably a better leader…and, very likely, she was more confident. But he wasn't about to let her take the lead when it came to what happened between them.

He was the bodyguard. He was in charge.

He grasped her upper arm and spun her around to face him. Holding her other arm to anchor her to one spot in the bland, empty break room, he kissed her. Not a belittling peck on the cheek, but a real kiss on the lips. His mouth pressed firmly against hers, he tasted mint and coffee. Though their bodies weren't touching, the heat that radiated between them was hotter than a furnace.

MOUNTAIN SHELTER

BY
CASSIE MILES

MILLS & BOON

First Published in Great Britain 2016
By Mills & Boon, an imprint of HarperCollins*Publishers*
1 London Bridge Street, London, SE1 9GF

© 2016 Kay Bergstorm

ISBN: 978-0-263-91926-4

46-1216

Our policy is to use papers that are natural, renewable and recyclable products and made from wood grown in sustainable forests. The logging and manufacturing processes conform to the legal environmental regulations of the country of origin.

Printed and bound in Spain
by CPI, Barcelona

Cassie Miles, a *USA TODAY* bestselling author, lives in Colorado. After raising two daughters and cooking tons of macaroni and cheese for her family, Cassie is trying to be more adventurous in her culinary efforts. She's discovered that almost anything tastes better with wine. When she's not plotting Mills & Boon Intrigue books, Cassie likes to hang out at the Denver Botanical Gardens near her high-rise home.

Hello, Gorgeous!
To my sister, Marya Hunsinger.

And, as always, to Rick.

Chapter One

With eyes wide open, Jayne Shackleford stared at the glowing numbers on her bedside clock: 9:29. Though it didn't really make a sound, she heard *tick-tick-tick*. She rolled over so she couldn't see the number switch to 9:30 p.m., which marked a sleepless half hour in bed.

She wanted a full eight to ten hours of deep, delta-wave slumber before she performed the operation tomorrow morning. Was anxiety keeping her awake? It shouldn't. Her success rate with this neurosurgical procedure was nearly 100 percent: thirty-three operations and only one partial failure. That patient hadn't died, but the surgery didn't erase the effects of his stroke. She had this procedure in the bag. There'd be no problems. Why so tense?

Possibly, she was overly eager, like a kid waiting for Christmas. About an operation? *Tick-tick-tick*. But she couldn't imagine any other pending moment of excitement.

Flinging out her arm, she reached for the wineglass on the bedside table. She didn't take sleeping pills, but she'd found that a glass of merlot before diving between the covers helped her ease into REM.

Her fingers brushed the glass. It slid off the night-stand and fell to the floor. "I'm a klutz!"

The irony annoyed her. She could perform delicate microsurgery without a slip, but when it came to regular life, she was the queen of clumsy, barely able to walk across a room without tripping over her own feet. Her nanny used to say that Jayne was so busy racing to the summit that she couldn't bother to look where she was going. Well, yeah! How else had she gotten to be a top-rated neurosurgeon by the time she was twenty-eight?

Though tempted to ignore the spill, she didn't want to ruin the pale peach Berber carpet that had taken several hours and the advice of two interior designers to select. She sat up on the bed and clapped to turn on the lights. Nothing happened. She clapped again, an undeserved ovation. No glow.

Pushing her long brown hair away from her face, she reached for the switch on the lamp and flicked it. The light didn't turn on. And the digital clock had gone dark. Her electricity must be out, which meant she'd have to go down into the creepy basement to the fuse box. *Well, damn.* This wasn't supposed to happen. After the last bout of piecemeal repairs on her two-story house, the electrician promised her that she wouldn't have problems. At least, not until the next time she did renovations.

And then, the neighbor's dog sent up a howl.

As if she needed another annoyance?

The chocolate Lab, with dark brown fur almost the same color as her long hair, wasn't usually a barker, but these occasions when he—or was it female?—dashed around woofing reminded her why she didn't have pets. Barefoot, she padded to the window and peeked through the blinds at her usually quiet neighborhood in the Washington Park area of Denver.

Peevishly, she noted that everybody else's lights were on. Looking down from the second floor, she saw the Lab dashing back and forth at the fence bordering her yard.

She should yell something down at it. What was the animal's name? Something with a *k* sound, it might be Killer or Cujo.

The light at the top of her neighbor's back steps went on and potbellied, bald-headed Brian appeared in the doorway. He called to his dog, "Cocoa, hush. Is something wrong? What's wrong, Cocoa?"

Did he expect an answer? Jayne simply couldn't abide people who spoke to their pets. Though she had high regard for the intelligence of nonhumans, she didn't like to see animals treated in an anthropomorphic manner, i.e., asking their opinion or dressing them in doll clothing. Such interactions lacked focus and functionality. In this case, however, Brian's voice had an effect. Cocoa ceased to woof, charged toward the house, crashed up the back stairs and through the door.

The neighborhood was tranquil again. Jayne looked down at the five-foot-tall chain-link fence covered with English ivy that was already starting to turn crimson in late September. As far as she could tell, there was nothing to bark at.

She opened the blinds so she could use the moonlight glow through the window to see. Going down to the basement meant she needed something on her feet. As she slipped into her moccasins, she heard noises from downstairs. Not the *tick-tick-tick* of a soundless clock, but a click and a clack and the squeak of a floor-board. The sound of a door being opened. Footsteps.

Impossible! No way could an intruder break in. She'd purchased a state-of-the-art security system that set off an alarm and called the police if a door or window was compromised. The system worked on battery even in a power outage. Jayne had specifically asked about the backup—electricity was fragile.

She crept around the edge of her bed to the night-stand where her cell phone was charging. She wanted to be able to call 911 if she heard anything else. Her thumb poked the screen to turn it on. There was no response, no perky logo, not even a welcoming beep. What was wrong with this thing? There had to be enough juice—it had been charging for the past hour. She held the phone close to her nose and pressed in various spots. The screen remained blank.

The noises from downstairs became more distinct. She was almost certain that she heard heavy footfalls crossing the bare wood kitchen floor. The amygdala in the frontal cortex of her brain sent out panic signals, causing her pulse to accelerate and her muscles to tense. If she had an intruder, what should she do? Fight or flight? Fight wasn't her forte. She didn't own a gun and knew nothing about self-defense. Maybe she could hide…under the bed…or in the closet.

Any hope that she might be imagining this nightmare vanished when the third step from the bottom of the staircase squawked. The flicker of a flashlight beam slid across the carpet onto the landing outside her bedroom. *Flight, baby, flight.*

There was only one place to run. She dove into the small adjoining bathroom and closed the door. Not exactly a fortress. The door was flimsy; the lock wouldn't hold. She had to find something to brace against the door.

The beam from the intruder's flashlight shone under the lip of the bathroom door. He was right outside, only a few feet away from her. The knob rattled as he turned it.

She tore down the stainless-steel rod that had been holding the shower curtain around the old claw-foot bathtub. Thank God, she hadn't remodeled in here yet. Thrashing and yanking, she managed to brace the pole between a cabinet and the door.

"Jayne," he whispered, "let me in. I won't hurt you."

Damn right, you won't. "I called nine-one-one."

"I don't think you did." He kept his voice low, but she detected a hint of an accent. "I don't think your phone works."

He must have done something to disrupt her cell-phone signal. And turn off her security system. And cut her electric.

He was smart.

And that was bad news for her. He'd be able to figure a way around her crude door brace in seconds. She couldn't just stand there, wringing her hands. She needed to escape.

The narrow window was her only outlet. If she could get the old paint unstuck and open the glass, she could slide down three or four feet to the slanted roof that covered the wraparound porch. From there, she could lower herself past the eaves to the porch railing.

He pounded the door. "Open up, Jayne."

Using her hairbrush as a wedge, she forced the sticky window latch to release. Frantically, she shoved the glass open. A brisk autumn breeze whooshed inside, and she shivered. Her skimpy cotton nightie wasn't going to provide much warmth. There were beach towels on the top shelf of the cabinet near the door. One of those would have to do.

She grabbed a towel, threw it around her shoulders like a shawl and leaned closer to the door to listen. It seemed quiet. Had he left? She put her ear to the door. Her panic spiked.

What was worse than an intruder who had you trapped in the bathroom? *Two intruders.*

She heard them whispering. They were plotting together, and it wouldn't take them long to determine that she was going out a window. She had to move fast.

She threw the oversize towel with an orange-and-yellow sun out the window, and then she followed, slipping through the bathroom window and down the bricks to the slanted roof over the front porch. The angle wasn't steep, but her footing felt precarious. As she wrapped the sunny-colored towel around her shoulders, she realized that she'd brought the hairbrush with her. A weapon?

The bedroom window to her right lifted. The head and shoulders of a man wearing a black ski mask emerged. He was coming for her. The synapses in her brain fired like a pinball machine. She screamed.

His buddy might already be downstairs on the porch, waiting for her to drop into his lap. She glanced up at the narrow bathroom window. No way could she climb back in there.

He spoke in his whispery voice through the mask, "Be careful, Doctor. I don't want you to get hurt."

"How do you know I'm a doctor?"

"I'd be happy to explain."

He held out his arm, beckoning her toward him. In the moonlight, she saw what he held in his hand. "You've got a stun gun."

He didn't bother with a denial. "I don't want to use it."

He sure did. His plan was to zap her into a state of helplessness and carry her away. Anger cut through her fear. Using all her strength, she pulled back her arm and fired her hairbrush at him.

She was surprised that she actually hit him. And so was he. The intruder dropped his stun gun.

In the moonlight, she could barely see the outline of his weapon against the dark gray shingles. She scampered forward, grabbed the gun and brandished it. "Don't come near me."

He swung his leg over the windowsill.

She went to the edge of the roof. Climbing over the gutter attached to the eaves looked more difficult than she had anticipated. "Help, somebody help me!"

Brian had been on his back porch only a moment ago. She continued to yell. Where was the barking dog when you needed him? "Please help me!"

Her shouts had an effect on the intruder. Instead of climbing out the window, he pulled back inside. Taking advantage of his retreat, she crept across the roof until she was right above Brian's porch, screeching like an emergency-alert siren.

His front door opened. Dumbfounded, Brian squinted up at her. In his left hand, he held his cell phone. From inside his house, Cocoa was barking.

"Nine-one-one," she yelled.

"Your house is dark," he yelled back.

"I have an intruder."

"A burglar?"

Now was not the time for a discussion. "Call the police. Please, please, call."

He gave her the thumbs-up signal and made the call while she perched above the eaves with her knees pulled up. Her long hair fell forward and curtained her face. Though she could have climbed back into one of the windows without too much difficulty, Jayne didn't trust herself to move another inch, not even to grab the towel she'd dropped. Her throat tightened as she gasped for breath. Adrenaline flooded her system.

In her subconscious mind, she must have known something was coming. *Tick-tick-tick.* But she never expected this. Shivering and sweating at the same time, she held her left hand in front of her eyes. Her fingers trembled. A sob exploded through her pinched lips.

Suffice it to say, she would not be getting a restful sleep tonight.

AN HOUR AND ten minutes later, Jayne was still scared. Her hands had stopped trembling enough to type, but her nerves were still strung tight. Wrapped in Brian's green velour bathrobe that smelled like pizza, she sat at the desk in his home office with Cocoa at her side. His house was smaller than hers, only one story, but he worked from home three days a week. The intruders should have come here. Brian's computer equipment was worth more than anything she had at her house.

From the front room and kitchen, she could hear people coming and going, voices rising and falling. It was time for her to rejoin them, but she wasn't ready.

All she really wanted was to hide until the danger had passed.

She'd behaved badly when the police officers first arrived to rescue her from the roof. She and Cocoa had both been problematic. The chocolate Lab had been barking and baring his teeth, which seemed like threatening behavior but was, more likely, an adrenal fear response. The dog was scared of all these strangers. Jayne's issues weren't that different.

Frightened, she hadn't known who to trust and didn't like taking orders from anybody. Not the police. Not the paramedic who wanted her to get into an ambulance. She was disoriented. Her neat-and-tidy world had gone spinning madly out of control, and she was so damn scared that she could hardly move.

In Brian's kitchen, a uniformed officer had pulled out a small spiral notebook and started asking questions. Jayne snapped. "Why should I give you a statement? I'll just have to repeat myself when the detective in charge of the investigation arrives."

"Calm down." The officer—a thickset woman with short blond hair—gestured to a chair at the kitchen table. "Have a seat, Ms. Shackleford. May I call you Jayne?"

"It's Dr. Shackleford," she said through tight lips.

"Any relation to Peter Shackleford?"

"My father."

The officer literally took a step backward. When hearing the name, a lot of people kowtowed. Although her father hadn't lived in Denver for ten years, he'd left an impressive legacy including a twenty-seven-story office building downtown and a small airport, both named after the man the newspapers called "Peter the Great."

Jayne hated using her parentage for leverage. She'd left home when she was really young to attend college and hadn't moved back to Colorado until her father was settled in Dallas. Trying not to sound like a brat, she confronted the policewoman.

"Here's what I'd like to do," Jayne had said. "I'd like to take some time alone to calm my nerves and to use my neighbor's computer to type up every detail I remember."

"That's not usually how we do things."

"I have a rational basis for my suggestion." She had explained that much of her work in neurosurgery focused on memory. According to some theories, it was best to write things down while adrenaline levels were high. She had colleagues who would disagree, and her words were taking on the tone of a lecture. "Without the sharp focus engendered by panic, the brain may sort details and bury those that are too terrifying to recall."

The policewoman had patted Jayne's shoulder. "Tell you what, Doc. You can take all the time you need."

Hiding out in Brian's office had given her a chance to catch her breath. She'd finished her statement for the police, printed it and sent a copy to her email. She should have emerged, but fear held her back. The tech-savvy intruders had chosen her house for a reason. She had no idea why, but she felt the pressure of danger coiling around her.

Cocoa rested his chin on her thigh and looked up at her. He truly was a handsome animal. She gazed into his gentle, empathetic brown eyes. He'd tried to warn her.

"I misjudged you," she murmured as she stroked the silky fur on the top of his head. "I thought you were a pest with all that running around and barking."

Not a good sign…she was talking to the dog.

There was a tap on the office door, and Cocoa thumped his tail twice—a signal that the person at the door was friendly, probably Brian. If a police officer had knocked, Cocoa would have growled.

Swiveling to face the door, she said, "Come in."

In a quick move, a man with glasses and a ponytail stepped inside and closed the door behind him. He confronted her directly and said, "I'm the guy."

Chapter Two

Jayne would have reacted to "the guy" with more hostility, but she'd used up her quota of snarkiness for the day. Besides, Cocoa seemed to trust this person. With much tail wagging, the chocolate Lab bounced toward the stranger, who reached down to scratch behind the dog's ears.

She cleared her throat and pushed her messy hair off her face. "What guy?"

"The one who can repair your security system."

She vaguely recalled a two-minute conversation with Brian. When she told him that her home alarm system had been compromised and her cell phone wouldn't turn on, Brian might have said something like *I know a guy who can fix that*. And she might have said that she wanted an appointment with that guy.

"I didn't expect you tonight," she said.

"Fine with me. I like being unexpected."

"How so?"

"Since I'm buds with Brian who's an IT specialist and I know how to repair your system, you might think I'm all about computers. You'd be surprised to learn that I'm also the part owner of a security firm with a license to carry a concealed Glock 17."

To prove his claim, he pivoted and flipped up the tail

of his plaid flannel shirt to show a holster attached to his belt. He turned to face her, pushed his horn-rimmed glasses up on his nose, grinned and said, "Ta-da!"

In spite of her fear, she had to grin back at him. "Did they send you in here to bring me out?"

He shrugged. "I don't have much luck at rock-paper-scissors."

Her initial impression was *NERD* in capital letters. He certainly wore the uniform: glasses, baggy plaid flannel, jeans rolled up at the cuff and a purple baseball cap on backward.

Then she took a second look—a lingering assessment from head to toe. She tilted her head, and her hair rippled all the way down her back. Though she was seated and not able to judge his height accurately, she estimated that he was well over six feet tall. The wide shoulders under that flannel shirt were impressive but he wasn't bulky. His body was long and lean. His wrists were muscular, and he wore an expensive dive watch. Behind those dorky horn-rims, his eyes were a smoldering shade of gray.

Unexpectedly, very unexpectedly, she was attracted to him. *Tickity-tick-tick-tick.* Maybe he was her early Christmas present. "Do you have a name?"

"Dylan Timmons." He held his hand toward her and then curled the fingers inward for a fist bump.

She tapped her knuckles against his. "Jayne Shackleford."

"I thought you might prefer a bump. Being a neurosurgeon, you have to take good care of those hands."

"I'm not that much of a prima donna." She frowned, thinking of the way she'd behaved with the police. "At least, I try not to be."

He placed her cell phone in her hand. "They said I could give this to you."

The screen flashed on, and she felt a glimmer of hope. "You fixed it."

"The phone fixed itself. Somebody used a signal-jamming device to disrupt your signal."

"That's just wrong," she said.

"But not illegal. I've heard that pastors are using jammers during their sermons."

Now that she had the cell phone, her mind jumped to practical concerns. "I might need to cancel my surgery for tomorrow morning. I should get a good night's sleep before I operate."

"Why so much?"

"The surgery takes five or six hours. I'm not intensely involved the whole time, but I need to be alert."

Still, she hated to cancel. Rescheduling the staff was a hassle. A guest neurosurgeon from Barcelona would be observing. Jayne had prepared and reviewed the most recent tests, neuroimaging, PET scans and MRIs. Starting over at another time was an inconvenience for the medical personnel involved. But postponement was much worse for the patient, who had already checked into the hospital, and for his family and friends.

He asked, "What kind of surgery is it?"

"It's not life threatening. Using implanted electrodes, I hope to stimulate the brain so the patient can regain the memory functions he lost after a stroke. The patient is actually awake through much of the procedure."

"Cool."

And she should be able to handle it. "I'll wait until tomorrow to make the decision whether to postpone or not."

"But you need more sleep," he said. "I can start repairs on your alarm system tonight if you're ready to go back into your house."

"No," she said quickly. "Not ready. Not tonight."

After she'd seen the police charge through the front door with guns drawn to search for intruders, she'd never again be able to think of her home as a sanctuary. She felt attacked, violated. Might as well close it up, burn it, sell it. Jayne was ready to call the real estate agent and hand over the keys.

Dylan brought her back to reality. "Where do you plan to sleep?"

With you. The words were on the tip of her tongue, but she kept from saying them out loud. She'd done enough inappropriate blurting for one evening. "I don't know."

"Is there anybody you can call?"

Her cell-phone directory was filled with colleagues and acquaintances from all around the world, ranging from the president of the American Association of Neurological Surgeons to the teenager who shoveled her sidewalks in winter. But there was no one she could call to come over and take care of her. No one she could stay with at a moment's notice.

She pushed the hair off her face and looked up at the surprisingly handsome man who stood before her. "You said you owned a security firm. Do you ever work as a bodyguard?"

"I do, TST Security."

She rose from the swivel chair and straightened the sash on the Brian's dark green bathrobe. "I'd like to hire you."

"You're on," Dylan said without the slightest hesitation. It was almost as though he'd been waiting for her to ask.

"I've never had a bodyguard before."

"Then I'm the one with experience. I've got only one rule—don't go anywhere without me. For tonight, I'll put together your suitcase and book a hotel room. Do you have a preference?"

She was so delighted to have somebody else taking care of the details that she wouldn't dream of complaining. "Anything is fine with me."

"Write down the clothes, including shoes and toiletries, that you want me to pack for you."

Her excitement dimmed when she thought of him pawing through her things, but the alternative—going back to the house and doing it herself—was too awful to contemplate. "I'll make that list right now. And there's one more thing."

"Name it."

She held out a flat palm. "Whatever you use to fasten your ponytail, I want it. My messy hair is driving me crazy."

He whipped off his baseball cap, untwined the covered-elastic band and dropped it in her hand. "For the record, I like your hair hanging long and free and shiny."

His fingers stroked through his own mane, and she realized that his hair was lighter than she'd thought. Thick, full and naturally sun-bleached, the loose strands curled around his face and down to his shoulders. Jayne wasn't usually a fan of men with long hair, but "the guy" pulled it off. She couldn't imagine him any other way.

DYLAN HADN'T COME here looking for work. His intention had been a simple response to Brian's call, helping out a friend with a crazy lady for a neighbor. But he was happy with the way things had turned out; spending time with this particular lady promised to be a challenge and a pleasure.

With that extra-large bathrobe swaddled around her, he couldn't tell much about Jayne's body. But he liked the bits he saw: her slender throat, her delicate hands and her neat ankles. Drooling over her ankles probably qualified him for the Pervert Hall of Fame, so he transferred his gaze to her long, thick, rich brown hair. A few strands escaped the ponytail and fell gracefully across her cheek. Never before had the word "tendril" seemed appropriate.

He didn't even pretend to look away. It was his duty to watch her body. He murmured, "I love my job."

"Excuse me?"

"I'll enjoy getting to know you."

Her full lips curled in a wise smile as she accepted the compliment. He'd always believed that smart women were sexier, maybe because of their intensity or creativity or strength.

Then she licked her lips.

He swallowed hard.

"Also," he said, "your break-in is the tip of the iceberg for a very cool puzzle. Your security alarm system is one of the best on the market. Disarming it took technical finesse that's above the talents of the average burglar. Not that I think the intent of your intruders was robbery. After they entered the house, they went directly to your bedroom."

"How do you know that?"

"While you were writing out the list of things you need, I read your account." He gestured to the two single-spaced sheets of paper that lay behind her on the desk.

"How could you read it? The paper is upside-down to you."

"It's a skill." He shrugged. "Do you think they wanted to rob you? Do you have some hidden treasure in your house?"

"I don't keep anything of value at the house."

Why did they break in? Since there were two of them, it didn't seem likely that they were stalkers or that the break-in was for sex. Not his problem. As a bodyguard, he wasn't expected to solve the crime. "Are you ready to talk to the police?"

She held her hand level in front of her eyes. "There's only a slight residual tremor."

"Not enough to register on the Richter scale. Let's move."

Keeping a hold on Cocoa's collar, Dylan guided her from Brian's home office to the kitchen, where a plain-clothes cop sat at the table with Brian. Dylan handed over the dog to his owner and introduced Detective Ray Cisneros, a weary-looking man with heavy-lidded eyes and a neat mustache.

After Jayne shook his hand and gave him her typed statement, she approached the uniformed lady cop. Her name, as it said on her brass nameplate, was E. Smith. Dylan had met her when he first came in.

"I need to apologize," Jayne said. "I'm sorry for the way I behaved earlier. I was rude."

E. Smith darted a suspicious glance to the left and the right as though looking for somebody or something to jump out at her and yell boo. "Um, that's okay."

"Thanks for accepting my apology." As Jayne turned away from the cop, her moccasins tangled in the overlong hem of the robe and she stumbled. Quickly recovering, she went toward Brian. "I want to thank you for being a great neighbor. If there's ever anything I can do for you, just ask."

Dylan didn't know what she'd done to make everybody mad, but he respected her for facing up to her mistakes. And she wasn't just offering phony pleas for forgiveness. Her pretty blue eyes shone with sincerity.

When she returned to the kitchen table with a glass of water, DPD Detective Cisneros looked up from the typed statement and smoothed the edges of his mustache. "You work at Roosevelt Hospital, correct?"

"Yes."

"And you're a neurosurgeon. A resident?"

"I completed my residency last year."

"Is that so?"

Dylan heard the disbelieving tone in the detective's voice and didn't blame him for being skeptical. She looked too young for such an important occupation. In the droopy bathrobe with her hair in a ponytail, she'd have a hard time passing for eighteen.

"It is, in fact, so." She took a deep breath and recited her accomplishments by rote. "I completed college at age sixteen, med school at nineteen, internship at twenty and fulfilled the requirements of an eight-year residence in neurosurgery last year. Twice, I've won the Top Gun Award from the YNC, Young Neurosurgeons Committee."

If his theory that smart women were sexier was correct, Dylan had hit the jackpot with Jayne. She was a genuine, kick-ass genius.

Cisneros took a minirecorder from the inner pocket of his brown leather jacket, verified with Jayne that it was okay to record her and launched into the standard questions.

"Do you have any enemies? Anyone who would wish you harm?"

"There's professional jealousy. Some of my colleagues wouldn't mind if I vanished off the face of the earth, but none of them are likely to hire thugs with stun guns and stage a break-in. Likewise with patients and the families of patients."

"What about in your personal life? Do you have a boyfriend?"

"Not at the moment," she said.

Dylan stifled a cheer.

"Any bad breakups?" Cisneros asked. "Is there anyone who won't take no for an answer? Or women who think you stole their boyfriends?"

"My personal life is super dull."

"In your statement," he said, referring to her typewritten account, "you quote the intruder as saying he doesn't want to hurt you. Did you believe him?"

"He had a stun gun," she pointed out.

"But he didn't use it."

Cisneros asked half-a-dozen more questions that circled the main issue, trying to get a handle on why the intruders had staged this break-in. They had to be after something.

Jayne's responses weren't real helpful. Not that she was being difficult. She just didn't know why men wearing ski masks had attacked her.

Cisneros glanced down at the account she'd written with such care. Very deliberately, he set those pages aside. His unspoken message was clear. "Maybe they don't want to hurt you, Jayne."

"No?"

"Tell me about your father."

"Please don't call him," she said quickly. "He doesn't need to know about this."

Dylan heard fear in her voice.

Cisneros picked up on it, too. "Are you afraid to tell him?"

"It's not that." Frown lines bracketed her mouth. "It's just… I haven't spoken to him on the phone for a couple of months, haven't seen him since the Christmas before last."

"Is he local?"

"Dallas, he lives in Dallas."

Dylan watched as the cool, sexy, smart woman transformed into a little girl with messy hair. She gazed down at her hands, pretending great interest as her slender fingers twisted into a knot on her lap. Her feet in their scuffed moccasins turned pigeon-toed.

Her father, Peter Shackleford, was rich enough to have an airport named after him. His fortune was tied to the oil-and-mining business, and he had a rep for being smart. Not as smart as his neurosurgeon daughter but savvy enough to surf the waves of business and avoid a wipeout.

Cisneros smoothed his mustache and said, "Could this have been a kidnapping attempt."

"I just told you that I'm not close to my dad." Without looking up, Jayne shook her head. "I can't imagine he'd pay a ransom for my release."

"Does your father have any enemies?"

"Yes."

"Any enemies who might want to hurt you."

She lifted her chin and looked directly at Dylan. "My father isn't a bad man."

He didn't believe her.

Chapter Three

Dylan excused himself to go next door and pack a suitcase for Jayne. He didn't want to listen to her heavily edited version of what a great guy her dad was, and he expected that was all Cisneros would hear from her. Though Dylan gave her points for loyalty to Peter Shackleford, he doubted that she'd score high in the honesty department. He could almost see her digging in her heels. No way would she speak ill of her father even though her mysterious intruders were very likely tied to dear old daddy.

That was Jayne's business. Not his. He was her bodyguard, not her therapist.

Before he left Brian's kitchen, Detective Cisneros ordered Officer E. Smith to accompany him to the crime scene. Cocoa escorted them to the back door and wagged goodbye. The dog needed to stay inside while the strangers on the DPD forensic team ferreted out clues at Jayne's house.

Dylan glanced down at the lady cop, whose short legs had to rush in double time to match his long-legged stride. "Does the *E* stand for Emily?" Dylan guessed. "Or is it Eva, Ellen or Eliza?"

"Eudora," she said. "That's why I go by Smith."

"Nice meeting you, Smith."

"Same here." She had a broad smile and big, strong teeth. Her orange-blond hair stood out from her head in spikes. "Did Jayne give you a list of things she needs?"

"In detail," he said as he took the list from his jeans pocket. "I'm not sure how accurate it is. She's still shaky. Her map of the upstairs of her house shows three separate bathrooms."

"That's true," Smith said. "The weird floor plan is because of the renovations she's been doing on the house since she moved in four years ago. Brian told me all about it."

Dylan had also heard a lot about Jayne and her intense renovating. Since Brian spent a lot of time working from home, his neighbors were a source of amusement. He'd told Dylan how she'd dive in and work like mad on some project, then she'd come to a complete halt while concentrating on her career. For several months, the eaves and porch in the front of her house were painted charcoal gray while the back was sky blue.

Though the electricity at her house had been re-connected, Smith pointed the beam of her Maglite at the back door. "If you look close you can see a couple of scratches from where they picked the lock and the high-security dead bolt."

Since the intruders had already turned off the alarm system, breaking out a window would have been a simpler way to gain access. The neatly picked locks showed a level of finesse that made him think these guys were professionals. In her written account, Jayne had described a whispery voice with a slight accent.

As he strolled through Jayne's house with Smith

nodding to the forensic team, he noticed an eclectic sense of decorating that seemed to mimic the pattern of off-and-on renovations. He believed you could tell a lot about a person from their living space. If that was true, Jayne had multiple personalities.

Her renovated kitchen was ultramodern, sleek and uncluttered. Directional lighting shimmered on polished granite countertops, stainless-steel appliances and a parquet floor. This room told him that a modern, classy woman lived here…not necessarily someone who cooked but someone who appreciated gourmet food.

Walking through the archway into the dining room and living room was like entering a different house. The chairs and tables lacked any sort of cohesive style. The walls were bland beige and empty, without artwork or photographs. The only notable feature was a dusted and polished baby grand piano. From these rooms, he might conclude that Jayne didn't do much entertaining at home and was passionate about her piano playing. The sheet music on the stand was for Scott Joplin's "Maple Leaf Rag."

He caught a quick glimpse of the library opposite the staircase at the front door. The big, heavy, rosewood desk and wall-to-wall bookshelves showed an old-fashioned sensibility and a reverence for tradition. Not like the kitchen at all.

Climbing the carved oak staircase, he noticed the loud creak on the third step that had alerted Jayne to the intruders. The stairs and banister had been cleaned and refinished but otherwise remained unchanged from when the house was built in the 1920s. The same held true for the carved crown molding on the upstairs landing. Again, he had the feeling that she appreciated the work of a long-ago craftsman and was perhaps old-fashioned.

Her bedroom, which had been redesigned in shades of peach and gray, looked like the sanctuary of a fairy-tale princess…a tasteful princess but super feminine with a dainty little crystal chandelier. Set aside on a chair were three stuffed animals, all cats with white fur. The kitties were worn but sparkling clean. Though he didn't see any fresh flowers, the room smelled of roses and cinnamon.

He doubted that anybody had sex in this room. There was zero hint of testosterone apart from the forensic guy who was crawling around on the carpet, peering and poking into the fibers.

Dylan noticed the wineglass on the bedside table. In her account, Jayne mentioned spilling the wine but never said that she'd picked up the glass.

"Excuse me," he said.

The CSI popped up. "Who are you?"

Smith said, "He's with me. Are you about done in here? We need to get some clothes for the owner."

"I'm wrapping it up." Like Smith, he held a Maglite with a beam that flashed wildly when he gestured. "How come we're making such a big deal about this break-in? Nobody got killed."

"A weird situation," Smith said, "what with cutting the power and disabling the alarm system and all. Have you found anything?"

"A bunch of prints, but they all belong to the lady who lives here and her employees—a maid and a cook."

"How did you get them read so fast?" Dylan asked.

"Computer identifications, plus I've got one of those

handheld fingerprint-readers." As he stood, he picked his satchel up off the floor. "Everything I need to break open a crime is right in here."

"When you arrived," Dylan said, "was this wine-glass on the floor?"

"No, sir, it was standing right where it is."

"Have you checked it for prints?"

"I'll be doing that right now." He gestured over his shoulder. "I'm done with the closet and the dresser, if you need to pack."

Dylan found Jayne's hard yellow suitcase with spin-ner wheels in the back of the closet right where she said it would be. The organization of her clothing and shoes was impeccable, and he would have thought she was obsessive-compulsive but those characteristics didn't fit with the casual messiness downstairs. He packed the three outfits that she had described precisely. One was for before the operation, then a pair of baby-blue scrubs and then another outfit for post-op.

When he opened the top drawer of her dresser, there was an outburst of colorful silk and satin. Jayne had mad, wild taste in panties and bras. He held up a black lace thong and a leopard bra. For a long moment, he stood and stared.

She baffled him. A brainy neurosurgeon who wore stripper underwear and played ragtime on her baby grand. Who was this woman? He needed to find out more about her.

The CSI made a harrumphing noise. "I've got two prints on this glass—a thumb and a forefinger. And they don't look like all the others."

"Run them," Smith ordered. "I'll step over here and help Dylan pick out the right undies."

When she rapped his knuckles, he gratefully dropped the thong and said, "I'd appreciate your help."

She lectured on why most women wouldn't want to wear a thong in the operating room and how a sports bra was most comfortable for a long day's work. Her anatomical details were too much information for Dylan.

The CSI had turned away and kept his focus on his handheld fingerprint-matching device while Dylan followed Smith across the landing to the incredible bathroom. With the marble and a fluffy white throw rug, this space was as feminine as the bedroom, but there was a difference. The bedroom was suitable for a princess. The bathroom was meant for a sensual queen.

Smith made quick work of packing the essentials on Jayne's list. They were almost ready to leave when the CSI stepped into the doorway. "I've got a match for these prints."

"And a name?" Dylan asked.

"You're not going to like it."

JAYNE APPROVED OF the downtown Denver hotel where Dylan had arranged for a suite, but she wasn't pleased that he'd called in one of his partners to drive the car to the hotel and accompany them onto the elevator and into the room.

While Dylan stood beside her with one hand clamped around her upper arm, ready to yank her out of there at the first hint of danger, his partner, Mason Steele, drew his gun. Looking like a secret agent from an espionage movie, Mason searched the attractively furnished outer room with the sofa, chairs, table, television and kitchenette. He nodded to Dylan before entering the adjoining bedroom.

Though impressed by their professionalism, Jayne didn't appreciate the show. She had a real life. No time for games. "Tell me again why all this is necessary."

"Standard procedure," he said. "When we take you to a new place, we search. It only seems overprotective because there's nobody lurking in this room. If there was a monster hiding in the closet..."

With a start, she realized that Mason hadn't yet looked in the closet by the entrance. A dart of fear stung her, and she stared at that door, remembering herself in the bathroom when the knob had jiggled. *Don't be scared. It's just a door.* Shivers trickled up and down her spinal column as Dylan helped her out of her heather-blue trench coat. When he opened the door, her jaw clenched.

And nothing happened. The boogeyman didn't jump out. There was nothing to be scared of. The sooner she remembered that, the better.

After he hung up her jacket, he returned to her side. Towering over her, he pushed his glasses up on his nose with a forefinger. "You went through a scary time tonight."

"I'm fine."

"Yeah, you are." Though she refused to meet his gaze, she knew he was watching her and had seen her fear. His voice was low and soothing. "Over the next couple days, you might have flashbacks or be jumpy or tense for no apparent reason. I'm sure you know all about post-traumatic stress. I mean, you're a brain surgeon."

"Not a behaviorist."

"What's that mean?"

"There are many theories about how the brain works, and I can only speak for my own opinion. The source of many emotions can be pinpointed on the naked brain, but it's extremely difficult to control behavior."

"Emotion isn't your thing," he said. "You're into memory."

"With my neurosurgery, I can stimulate old memories that have already formed, but I can't implant new memories without the experience."

"But you don't have to experience something to recall it. I've learned about volcanoes but never seen one erupt."

She hadn't intended to meet his gaze, but she found herself looking into his cool, gray eyes and seeing the sort of deep calm associated with yogis and gurus. At the same time, she realized that her moment of panic and flashback had passed. Dylan had distracted her by luring her into lecturing him about her work.

"Very clever," she said. "You handled me."

He directed her to a side chair upholstered in a patterned blue silk that echoed the colors of the wallpaper, while he sat on the sofa and opened a metal suitcase on the glass-topped coffee table in front of them. After removing a laptop computer, he flicked a switch on a mechanism inside the case. A small red light went on.

"What's that?" she asked.

"It means we can talk freely in here without fear of someone listening in."

The various dials and keyboards in his case were nowhere near as complicated as the equipment she

dealt with in neurosurgery. "You can be more technical, Dylan. I'm capable of understanding."

"I don't doubt your smarts," he said. "I just don't expect you to be interested in my security tools."

"Unless I say otherwise, you may talk to me in the
same depth you use with your colleagues."

"That won't be too hard." Dylan called out to his
partner. "Hey, Mason, do you want to know about the
circuitry in my white-noise machine?"

His partner stepped into the bedroom doorway. "As
long as it works, I don't care."

She glanced between the two men. Mason was
clean-cut and muscular. Dressed in a leather jacket
and khakis, he looked like a bodyguard. Dylan was a
different story. With his horn-rimmed glasses, his purple Colorado Rockies baseball cap on backward and his
long hair, he didn't appear to be a tough guy. And yet,
if given a choice, she'd pick Dylan every time. There
was something about him that connected with her.

He motioned for Mason to join them as he explained
the machine to her. "Much of my equipment is proprietary. I invented this stuff for my own use in security.
This machine emits a noise that disrupts any other listening device but is too sensitive for our ears to hear.
While we're in this room, we can speak freely."

As a neurosurgeon, she understood the concept of
blocking different frequencies of sound, but she didn't
understand why this sort of machine was needed.
"Who would want to overhear?"

"I have something important to discuss." He glanced
toward his partner. "You need to hear this, too."

"Shoot."

"There were prints found in Jayne's bedroom. They were on the wineglass that was on the bedside table."

"I didn't pick up the glass." Revulsion coiled through her as she visualized the man in the ski mask touching her things.

"The fingerprint belonged to Martin Viktor Koslov, a hired assassin from Venezuela who learned his trade with the Columbian drug cartels."

Mason growled, "What kind of trade are you talking about?"

"Think of the worst torture you heard about interrogation methods," Dylan said. "Koslov has worked for Middle Eastern emirs and superrich oil men from his home country. For the past eight years, he's been sighted in the US, including Alaska."

"Why Alaska?" She couldn't imagine why an assassin would take a side trip to Juneau.

"The pipeline," Dylan said. "He's not a bomber or a terrorist, but he's suspected in several murders, thefts and complex arms deals."

Mason looked toward her and asked, "How did you get away from this guy?"

"He said he didn't want to hurt me." She remembered his accent. It didn't sound like Spanish, but she really didn't know. Languages weren't her thing. "Detective Cisneros seems to think he wanted to kidnap me and hold me for ransom so he could get something from my dad."

"Your father is…?"

Dylan filled in the blank. "Peter Shackleford, international oilman with interests in the Middle East and in South America."

Mason nodded. "Kidnapping seems like a neat, logical working theory."

"I'm not so sure," Dylan said. "I'd like more evidence, starting with interviewing the person who disabled Jayne's home alarm system. That hack took a high level of expertise, and I can only think of three or four locals who could pull it off."

"Did you contact them?" Mason asked.

"I'm the bodyguard, not the investigator. I gave their names to Detective Cisneros."

Mason sank back in his chair and rubbed his hand across his forehead. "What do you want me to do?"

"That depends on Jayne." Dylan turned to her. "You had a surgery scheduled for tomorrow morning at eleven o'clock. My advice is for you to postpone."

Though she had been thinking the same thing, she didn't like having her plans dictated by some South American assassin. Koslov didn't rule her life. She took her cell phone from her jeans pocket and checked the time. "It's just after midnight. If I could sleep until nine in the morning, I could operate."

"We don't know what to expect from this kidnapper. He might come after you again. Are you sure you don't want to schedule the operation for another time or have someone else take over for you?"

"I'm the best surgeon for this procedure, possibly the best in the world." She wasn't bragging, just stating a fact. "Also, I have a relationship with this patient. He's a professor of philosophy in his early sixties. A stroke robbed him of his memory. I can get it back for him, and I don't want to wait."

Dylan regarded her with a measured gaze. "Is his condition life threatening?"

"No, but this is about the quality of his life. He's brilliant and wise. He needs to be able to use his memory."

"Agreed," Dylan said, "but he could wait a few days."

"I want my life to proceed as normal. That's why I hired you as a bodyguard." She rose to her feet as she played her final card. "But if you can't protect me…"

Dylan unfolded himself from the sofa and stood, towering over her. Though she was above average height at five feet nine inches, he was over six feet, maybe six-five. He was taller, broader, stronger. An archetypal male, he was everything a man should be. She felt herself melting.

Gazing down at her, he removed his horn-rimmed glasses and made direct eye contract. "I'll keep you safe, Jayne."

The effect caught her off guard. Desire twitched in her belly. Goose bumps erupted on her arms. She wanted to grab his arm and pull him into the bedroom with her. *No way, absolutely not.* She shouldn't be thinking about sex.

She pivoted, took one step and walked into the chair beside the sofa. Lurching to an upright position, she marched to the bedroom door, stepped inside and closed it with a loud slam.

Chapter Four

The aroma of fresh coffee twitched in her nostrils. Chords of harp music tickled her ears. *Where am I?* Her usual wake-up alarm was as loud and as harsh as a fire engine, the better to wake her up. Then Jayne remembered that she wasn't sleeping at home.

The harp continued as she lifted her eyelids and saw a man with long, sun-streaked brown hair sitting in the chair beside her bed. Dylan wasn't wearing his glasses…or his baggy flannel shirt…or his baseball cap. His black T-shirt outlined his wide shoulders and lean chest. A handsome man, there was nothing of the nerd about him.

Without thinking, she extended her arm toward him. He caught her hand, raised it to his lips and brushed a kiss across her knuckles before she was aware of what he was doing. The gesture seemed absurd, given that she was wearing flannel pajamas. After being caught on her rooftop in a filmy gown and feeling exposed, she'd chosen the world's unsexiest flannels on purpose.

"Nine o'clock, Jayne."

"I love the harp music."

"It's a wake-up app called *Morning Angels*." He gestured toward two china cups on a silver room service tray. "Coffee?"

"Sure."

Her usual clumsiness was even worse in the morning when she wasn't wide-awake, and she hated to risk slopping a hot beverage all over herself. But it couldn't be helped; she needed caffeine. While she arranged the pillows against the headboard, Dylan went to the windows, where he opened the shades and the filmy drapes. She couldn't tear her gaze away from him. Those jeans were the same ones he'd worn yesterday, still rolled at the cuff. But today they seemed well fitted, not tight but snug enough to outline firm glutes and muscular thighs. Long legs—he had very long legs.

He returned to her bedside and poured steaming coffee from a white room-service pot. He added two dollops of cream and gave it a quick stir before passing her the eggshell-white cup and saucer.

"I never mentioned that I took cream but no sugar."

"If you know your way around the internet, you can find almost anything."

She figured that discovering her coffee preference required a search that went deeper than a quick identification. He'd researched her. On one hand, she didn't like being spied upon. But she was complimented that he'd taken the trouble. Last night, she hadn't been sure he'd want to stick around after she'd slammed the door and thrown out an unveiled threat to fire him.

He took a sip from his cup. "How are you feeling?"

"Are you asking whether I'm alert enough to proceed with the scheduled surgery?"

"I am."

Jayne tasted the delicious coffee and considered for a long moment. "Not sure."

After he fiddled with his wristwatch, the harp music went quiet. "I'm resetting an alarm for eight minutes while you make up your mind. You've already had a bunch of phone calls and—"

"Stop!" She held up her palm to halt him. "About these calls, why didn't I hear the phone ringing?"

"I took your cell phone into the outer room."

"Are you telling me that you came into my room, uninvited, and took my phone without my permission?"

"As your bodyguard, I have to invade your personal boundaries. Coming in and out of your bedroom, even watching you sleep…" He shrugged. "It's part of my job."

"Watching me sleep?"

A warmth that had nothing to do with the hot coffee spread through her body. Though she didn't recall her dreams last night, some of her REM and delta-wave activity had to be about sex. As she lifted her cup to her mouth, she sloshed coffee into the saucer.

"I took your phone," he said, "because you wanted to sleep until nine, and I was afraid you'd get calls earlier than that."

Reaching for a napkin, she tilted her saucer, almost spilling coffee over the lip. He passed her a napkin which she used to dab at her mouth, then to swab the near spill. "I'm glad you caught those calls. I needed the sleep, and I'm surprised that I got it. After all that happened last night, I didn't think I'd be able to relax."

"Oh, yeah, you relaxed. There was some big-time snoring going on. One time, I peeked in to make sure you weren't being trampled by rhinos."

A lovely image! "Who called?"

He recited from memory. "Eloise, your assistant, needs to know something about scheduling the ER. Mrs. Cameron is worried about her husband's surgery and wants to know if he can eat chocolate-chip cookies later today. Three doctors—Lewis, Napoli and Griggs. And one more."

When he hesitated, she cast a curious glance in his direction. "Are you going to tell me who?"

His eight-minute alarm went off, blasting a noise that sounded like screaming cats in heat. He silenced it. "What's it going to be, Jayne? Are we going to the hospital or not?"

"Why won't you tell me about this person who called?"

"It was your father."

His words hit her with a jolt. She spilled her coffee, with most of the liquid being sopped up by the napkin before she shoved the whole mess onto the tray. "What does he want?"

"He didn't tell me."

Belatedly, she realized that if Dylan was answering her phone, he must be giving some kind of explanation for why she was unavailable. She didn't want wild stories about her intruder to spread all over the hospital. "What have you been telling people?"

"Not a thing. I'm saying that you're not available and you'll call back. Your assistant demanded to know if we were dating, and I told her that she'd have to ask you."

"And my dad? What did you tell him?"

"He was a different story."

She knew he would be. Peter Shackleford, her esteemed-by-everybody-else father, was a man who expected people to take his phone calls, especially his only grown daughter. She figured there would have been loud shouting, threats, demands and a hearty dose of cursing. "What happened?"

"He was at your house."

"Here? My house here in Denver?"

"That's right."

Panic exploded through her. She threw off the covers and charged toward the adjoining bathroom. In the doorway, she pivoted and faced him. "Did you tell my dad where we were staying?"

"Nobody knows we're here. It doesn't do much good to take you to a safe place if I tell everybody where it is."

"And my dad accepted that?"

"He wasn't happy about it," Dylan said. "He called about half an hour ago, and I expect he thinks he can triangulate your phone signal to get your location. But I have my own signal jammer that I attached to your cell phone."

"Another of your proprietary inventions?"

"That's right." He finished his coffee and stood. "We need a plan for the day."

"I'm going to perform the surgery. Give me fifteen minutes to get dressed, and we'll go to the hospital."

"And your father?"

"Later."

She didn't want to deal with him right now, but she had to contact him. He was at the center. If an international assassin/kidnapper had broken into her house because of something her dad had done, he should be the one to fix it.

This wasn't her fault. She'd gotten sucked into this high-stakes game, and she didn't want to play.

LAST NIGHT WHILE Jayne was sleeping, Dylan had done computer searches on her, her father, Martin Viktor Koslov and local hackers who might have helped out Koslov. After a sickening dive into the dark web where you could buy any sleazy thing for the right price, he'd found a set of digital footprints running away from Denver. Well-known cyber-ace, Tank Sherman, was erasing himself, changing to another identity, trying to escape. If Tank had worked with Koslov, the local expert might want to make himself invisible before Koslov erased him.

Martin Viktor Koslov was a ruthless killer whose land of origin was Venezuela. Reputedly, he had garroted, beheaded, shot and stabbed his targets. Never caught, never even arrested, he was known for planning down to the last precise detail. The neatly picked lock on Jayne's back door was typical of Koslov; leaving behind a fingerprint was not.

What had thrown the assassin off his game? Was it the instruction to kidnap rather than kill? Koslov avoided explosives because he'd lost several family members, including his mother, to a bomb explosion. Koslov had a brand of violence that was not inspired by any type of loyalty or ideology; rather, he committed acts of atrocity for the highest bidder. And that might make him an enemy of her father.

Dylan had also found a number of connections between Peter the Great and Koslov. They knew many of the same people, visited the same cities and were both cruel in their own way.

Jayne's dad—the man she defended so fiercely to the DPD detective—wasn't a murderer, but he hired and fired without concern for his employees and didn't hesitate to destroy his competitors. He'd made plenty of enemies. Most were businessmen and women based in the US, but there were a few Middle Eastern sheikhs and South American oil magnates who might consider kidnapping to be nothing more than leverage on the next deal.

When Dylan got the phone call from Mason, telling him that he would arrive at the side entrance in five minutes, he rapped on Jayne's bedroom door. "Time to go."

"Are we coming back here tonight?"

He wouldn't make that decision until later today. Right now there was no time for a discussion. The plan was for them to jump into the vehicle as soon as it pulled up to the curb.

Dylan shoved open her bedroom door. "Now, Jayne."

She was dressed in a pair of dark teal slacks, a matching suit jacket and a shiny black blouse. With her dark hair pulled up in a high bun, her appearance was professional and classic. "Give me a sec, I need to find my sneakers."

He grabbed her sneakers off the floor and lobbed them into the gym bag on the bed where she had packed other clothing items. He zipped the bag and tossed it toward her. "Remember when I said there was only one rule for you when I'm being a bodyguard?"

"Don't go anywhere without you," she recited.

"I lied. There's another rule."

"Which is?"

"When I say go, we have to go."

She stuck her toes into a pair of polished black loafers. "Why are we in such a big rush?"

"No questions. I'm serious." Though he wasn't trying to scare her, Dylan didn't want her to think this was a game. "Your life might depend on your ability to respond to my instructions."

The grin fell from her face as she picked up her gym bag and purse. He grasped her elbow and rushed her through the suite, out the door and into the concrete stairwell. He went first so she'd have to keep up with his pace.

As they descended, he explained, "Lots of abductions occur when the victim is in transit, moving from one location to another. That's why Mason is driving over here to pick us up. It's also why we're taking the stairs. It's too easy to trap you in the elevator."

"I'm glad it's only five floors." Their steps were loud on the concrete stairs, and their voices echoed. "I'm guessing that you aren't carrying my bag so your gun hand will be free."

"Good guess." And he didn't feel guilty about making her drag a heavy burden. All she had was a shoulder purse and her gym bag. He pointed to the bag. "Are your scrubs in there?"

"Lots of stuff—lotion, scrubs, comfortable shoes, a cap that's big enough to cover my hair, extra barrettes and more. These operations take several hours, and it's important to have clothes laundered exactly the way I like them. By the way, you did a good job choosing my undies. The sports bra is just what I need."

"That was Smith's idea. If it had been up to me, I would have picked the red satin bra and the leopard panties."

"Most men do."

Was she flirting with him? He couldn't let himself be distracted right now. Dylan had to keep his focus on getting her to the car without incident.

They rounded the last turn in the stairwell. Both he and Mason were familiar with the layout of this particular hotel. If they had their timing right, Dylan and Jayne would emerge from the stairwell, walk down a short hall and exit onto the street just as Mason pulled up to the curb.

Entering the lobby, he scanned quickly. No heads turned. No one noticed Jayne. He pushed open the exit door.

Bright sunlight hit them smack in the face. Holding her arm, he moved across the wide sidewalk adjacent to downtown's central mall. Mason was waiting in Dylan's dark green SUV.

He opened the rear door, got her seated and followed her inside. The minute he closed the door, Mason drove away. Safe!

"Seat belt," he said to her. "Mason, do you know the door we'll enter at the medical center?"

"Northeast corner."

"That's near my office." She opened her purse and started digging. "I have a key card to use on that entrance."

"It's handled," he said. "We downloaded the hospital floor plan and figured out your routes to and from the OR and your office. Detective Cisneros arranged for key cards and necessary identifications since I'm carrying a concealed weapon and can't go through scanners."

For the first time since he'd met her, Jayne seemed

to be impressed. Usually, he didn't care if the clients noticed that TST Security did a solid, professional job, but her opinion was important to him. He liked Jayne and wouldn't mind getting closer to her. After this job was over, he'd like to get close enough to pick out her wild undies.

"What are we going to tell people about you?" she asked. "If I introduce you as my bodyguard, I'll have to explain a thousand times why I need guarding."

The thought had already occurred to him. He didn't consider himself a master of disguise, but he was capable of fading into the woodwork as a computer nerd and—thanks to Mason and his bodybuilding workouts—Dylan could expand his narrow frame enough to look big and tough. Today, he was wearing a tweed sports coat, jeans and a black T-shirt. His hair was pulled back in a tight ponytail at his nape.

He adjusted his horn-rimmed glasses. "I think I can pass as a professor."

"Interesting thought," she said as she studied his look. "You do have an academic look, but you'd need a whole background story. Somebody would catch on."

"I could be a boyfriend."

Her full lips drew into a circle. "No, no, no, no, no. I don't want to start that rumor. Besides, we don't let friends and family into the OR."

"Much as I'd like pretending to be a neurosurgeon…" He actually would enjoy playing that role. The brain fascinated him. "I don't think your patient would appreciate that disguise."

"Or my insurance carrier."

"I've got it," he said. "I'll be a journalist doing an article on America's hottest neurosurgeons."

"Oh, swell, and doesn't it bother you to reduce the schooling and talent it takes to become a neurosurgeon to an article about physical attractiveness?"

"I'll be a regular old journalist. My catchphrase will be—don't pay any attention to me. I'm here to observe."

"Perfect." Glancing toward the driver's seat, where Mason sat stoically behind the wheel, she lowered her voice. "Do you really think I'm hot?"

"You sizzle, Doc."

At the medical center, a sprawling complex at the edge of Denver's suburbs, he rushed her through the side door and up one flight of stairs. From studying the floor plan, he knew exactly where her second-floor office was located. It spoke well of her status that she had her own small office space with a door that closed. Not much larger than a walk-in closet, the room had one floor-to-ceiling bookshelf, a desk with a chair and two other chairs for guests.

From his web research, Dylan recognized the man who had taken the swivel chair behind her desk.

Jayne stopped short and glared. "Hello, Dad."

Chapter Five

Inhaling through her nose and exhaling through her mouth, Jayne attempted to maintain a calm breathing pattern. Nobody wanted a jumpy brain surgeon; she had a responsibility to her patient to remain calm. The worst thing would be to let her father get her rattled.

Dramatically, Peter the Great rose from the chair and stood behind her desk. His barrel chest puffed out like a rooster. She hadn't seen him in ages, not since she'd bought her house and he came to Denver to tell her it was a dump in spite of the changes she'd made, which she took as a challenge to renovate even more. In his tailored gray pinstripe suit with his neatly barbered chocolate-brown hair, which was the same color as hers, he managed to look decades younger than the age indicated by his birth certificate.

He wore his "concerned" face—an expression that hadn't changed since she'd come home from kindergarten with a bloody nose and Dad had hired a professional boxer to teach her self-defense. There was a crease between her father's dark eyebrows; his chin jutted out and his mouth pulled into a frown.

"Last night," he said in his resonant baritone, "you

should have called me to let me know you were all right. I was worried."

It's not always about you. Anger seethed inside her. She wanted to scream and yell and tell him that she could have been hurt, could have been kidnapped *and it was his fault.* But what if it wasn't? What if their suspicions were wrong? She was furious and, at the same time, she felt an ache inside. She wanted to rest her head against his shoulder and cry away her fears and doubts.

Preventing either response—yelling or weeping— Dylan extended his hand and introduced himself as her bodyguard. "I'm the one who kept Jayne from calling you. For her safety, we moved her to a secure location and turned off her cell phone so the intruder couldn't triangulate her signal and find her."

"You're the guy I talked to on the phone this morning, the one who wouldn't tell me where you took my daughter."

"That's correct."

"You've got one hell of a nerve, son."

"Over the phone, I can't accurately verify your identity."

"You sure can. I can send you my photo. Or you can watch in real time while I'm talking on my cell phone."

"The intruder disarmed a high-tech, high-quality alarm system at the house. Hacking a cell phone and transmitting a false identification would be child's play for him."

"Jayne should have used another phone to call me."

"Dr. Shackleford requires several hours of sleep before she performs delicate neurosurgery." Dylan turned to her. "Doctor, you should speak to your assistant,

Eloise. I have a few questions for your father regarding Martin Koslov."

He practically shoved her out of the office, and she couldn't have been more grateful. She walked down a short hallway to an attractive waiting room, where two patients sat in comfortable chairs reading old magazines. The medical assistant/receptionist was feeding the gang of tropical fish in the five-foot-long aquarium. With her hair dyed a purplish red, Eloise was nearly as bright as the fish with their streaks of neon blue, yellow and mottled green. She had named her fishy friends and made up fishy stories about their lives.

"Sorry about my dad," Jayne said.

"You don't need to apologize. Meeting Peter the Great is a big deal for me. If I'd known he was going to be here, I would have brought a used plane ticket for him to autograph."

"He's not in the airport business anymore." But he probably flew one of his private planes up here from Dallas. "Maybe he could autograph a used oil can."

"You know, Jayne, I never ever pry, but my fish are totally nosy. Hedda—the black one with yellow stripes—wants to know about your cute male friend with the glasses and ponytail."

"A journalist, he's doing a story on neurosurgery."

Eloise hiked up her eyebrows in an expression of disbelief. "And why was he answering your cell phone at seven-thirty in the morning?"

"We met for breakfast." That was somewhat true. Dylan had insisted that she have a bagel and a couple of bites of bacon from his room-service order.

"Is he going to be hanging around all day?"

"For as long as I am." She went to Eloise's desk and jotted a note. If she moved fast, Jayne might be able to escape without confronting her father again. Though she shouldn't leave the office without Dylan, she felt safe in the hospital. There were guards at the doors; nobody entered without passing through a metal scanner.

"I like older men," Eloise said. "Is your father married?"

"Not at the moment." She slid the note across the desktop. "Would you mind returning these calls for me? Especially to Mrs. Cameron, she needs to be reassured about her husband's surgery. I'm going to slip out so I can review the most recent charts and blood work for Dr. Cameron."

Her dad's voice thundered through the closed door and down the hallway. "How dare that cheesy detective accuse me? I'm a law-abiding citizen."

If Eloise's eyebrows went any higher they would disappear behind a swirl of colorful hair. "Detective?"

"I don't know what they're talking about."

Eloise grasped her arm. "Jayne, what's going on?"

"Don't tell anybody."

"Of course not."

But the story would get out. There was no chance of keeping this juicy secret. It'd go viral. She knew from experience that the hospital was a swarming petri dish of gossip. "Somebody tried to break into my house last night and kidnap me. The DPD detective thinks it might be related to my dad. The guy with the ponytail and glasses is my bodyguard."

One of the other doors leading to the reception room swung open and the short, skinny Dr. Bob, the oncologist, popped his head out. He was a worse gossip than Eloise. "No joke?" He gaped. "You were almost kidnapped? Why?"

Eloise pointed down the hall toward Jayne's office. "Rich father. Peter the Great."

"Wow," Jayne said glumly. "You put it together quicker than the police investigator."

"Doesn't take a rocket scientist," Eloise said. "There's only one reason to be kidnapped—ransom. And your dad's loaded."

The door to her office flung open. Her dad and Dylan spilled into the reception area. Her father did something she never would have expected: he hugged her. His big arms wrapped around her, and she was surrounded by the pine-forest scent of an aftershave that he'd worn since she was a girl.

"I could have lost you," he whispered.

"It wasn't that bad."

"Dylan told me there were two of them, wearing ski masks and carrying stun guns. He said that you had to flee across a rooftop."

All of Dylan's description was true. She hadn't realized how dramatic her escape sounded until her dad said it out loud. She added, "And I took the stun gun away from him."

"My sweet little gal, you shouldn't have to suffer for my mistakes. If it's somebody I know…"

He shook his fist. His pupils were so dilated that his blue iris was reduced to a slender rim. Either he was in an elevated emotional state or he'd been taking advantage of Colorado's legalized marijuana. She assumed the former. Her dad didn't do pot.

He concluded, "You can be damn sure I'll find out who's responsible. And I will make them pay."

Over her father's shoulder, Jayne saw the shocked faces of Eloise and Dr. Bob. Their eyes bulged. Their jaws gaped. The patients waiting in the reception area had dropped their magazines and were watching. She gave her father one last squeeze and stepped away from his embrace.

There was moisture at the corner of her left eye that she refused to believe was a tear. Jayne cleared her throat. "I appreciate anything you can do to help the investigation."

"I'll talk to my friend Razzy." She doubted any of the other people in the room would be aware that her dad was referring to Rashid bin Calipha, one of the richest men in the world and the leader of a sheikdom. "There have been occasions when your good old Uncle Razzy might have used this Koslov character."

"I'm so sorry to hear that." Uncle Razzy? Oh, please!

"I've got plenty of contacts. I'll check in with my oil people in South America." He pulled his cell phone from his pocket. "I'll start with Javier Flores. He's got an office here in Denver."

"Is he an enemy?" she asked.

"A friend, and he's a good enough friend that he might have information about who wants to hurt me."

Before he could punch in the phone number, Dylan stopped him. "I have to take your daughter away. She needs to prep for surgery."

"Not today," her dad said in a firm, no-nonsense voice. "She needs to take the day off. Somebody else can fill in. One of the other docs can pick up the slack."

"That's not how it works." Her tenderness toward him evaporated like dewdrops under a heat lamp. "This surgery is my specialty. I have a relationship with the patient, and I want him to have the best care."

"Sweetheart, I'm sure you do a great job…"

Was he patronizing her? Her temper simmered.

"…but I need to keep you safe," her dad continued.

What did he intend to do? She'd already hired herself a bodyguard. She'd fled from her house.

Once again, Dylan came to her rescue. He pressed a cell phone into her dad's hand. "It's a burner, programmed with only one number. We'll use it to keep in touch with you."

"Unacceptable." Her dad thumped his puffed-out chest. "She's coming back home to Dallas with me."

She remembered why she avoided living in the same time zone as her dad. It was just too damned painful. To him, she would always be a sweet little girl who reminded him of her mother, his only true love, who had died when Jayne was seven. He'd gone through half-a-dozen wives since then, but the oil painting that hung over the mantel in every house he owned was her mom, Rachel Shackleford, a well-respected biochemist.

Her dad wasn't being deliberately cruel or belittling. He truly wanted to take care of her. Dragging her back to Dallas was, of course, his first solution to the threat.

But she wasn't a child. After her mom died, she'd grown up quickly. She loved her dad, but she resented his steadfast refusal to accept her as a capable, accomplished adult. He never called her "Doctor" in spite of the years of study and hard work it had taken to gain that title. He never complimented her on her achievements, couldn't be bothered to attend her graduation at the top of her class in med school when she was nineteen.

She stumbled backward a couple of steps and bumped into the fish tank. "Sorry, Dad, I'm not going to Dallas with you. This is my home, my life. And Dylan is right about my needing to prep for surgery."

Before he could respond, she swept through the door into the hallway with her bodyguard following close behind.

RECALLING THE ROUTES from the hospital blueprints, Dylan stayed at her side as she stalked through the corridors in the medical building. They passed offices, a break room and a pharmacy before climbing an open staircase to the second floor. He congratulated himself on remembering to grab her gym bag with the special scrubs and sneakers before leaving her office. In spite of her precise skills and her particular, somewhat fussy, need to have the right clothes, shoes and underwear, Jayne was absentminded. He'd also noticed her tendency toward clumsiness, an endearing trait that made him want to be close so he could catch her when she fell.

Without slowing her pace, she glanced up at him. "Thanks for helping me get away from my dad."

"You're good at handling him."

"Our conversations don't feel good. We're always battling."

"He's a tough guy."

"Yes."

"But he means well." He lightly touched her arm, thinking he'd reassure her. Instead of relaxing, she gasped and pulled away, reacting as though she'd been stabbed by a hypodermic.

He gave her space as they marched along the gray-and-blue vinyl floors. For a bodyguard, a hospital created several problems. The interior was a sanitized labyrinth. There was tension in the air. Most of the staff dressed in scrubs or lab coats that all looked alike, and many of them wore masks. When passing people in the corridor, he scanned their faces. As they walked, he frequently looked over his shoulder to make sure no one was following.

Jayne muttered under her breath. "Why won't he

accept that I'm an adult? I bought my own house. I'm renovating. I'm fully capable of taking care of myself."

He nodded. "Uh-huh."

"He has no idea what kind of work I do. I mean, he knows I work with the brain, but he thinks that means curing a headache with two aspirin and a good night's sleep."

"Uh-huh."

"Are you going to stroll along and not say anything?"

"I thought your comments were rhetorical," he said. "Do you want an opinion?"

"Of course I do, as long as you say I'm right and my dad is wrong."

"You're both right." He shrugged. "You're a grown-up and deserve respect. But he doesn't want to treat you like an adult because that means you don't need him anymore. He wants to be needed. Dads are like that."

She came to a complete stop and looked up at him. "That's a really smart explanation. Do you have kids?"

"Not yet."

"I shouldn't have asked, too personal." A pink flush crept up her throat to her cheeks. "Besides, I already knew you didn't have offspring. And I also know you've never been married."

"Internet search?"

She put her head down and proceeded with long strides into the wide second-story overpass that connected the med center with the hospital. Her blushing baffled him. Why would she be embarrassed about looking him up? That was standard procedure for a first meeting. It seemed to be the marital-status part that bothered her. Was she showing an interest that was more than that of client and bodyguard? He hoped so.

On the hospital side of the overpass, she took an unexpected left turn.

"Wait!" He pointed in the opposite direction. "The OR is that way."

"I need to go to the locker room and change."

Ignoring the double-wide chrome elevator, they descended an enclosed stairwell to the first floor. All the doors along the corridor were clearly marked except for the one nearest a side exit with a key-card lock blinking red for locked. He imagined that door was used by most of the staff when coming and going.

They entered a break room with vending machines, counters, a coffee urn, fridge, microwave and toaster oven. Three women in scrubs sat at three separate tables, reading or texting. An open door on the left led to rows and rows of lockers. There were other rooms beyond. Dylan could hear the sound of a shower.

She stopped in front of a beige locker midway down the third row. The number on top was 374. Jayne twirled the combination lock. Before she could open it, he placed his hand over hers.

"I have a few questions," he said, taking out his cell phone. "I need your full cooperation."

"Shoot."

"Last night, you saw Koslov. Would you recognize him again?"

She thought for a moment. "I'm sure there's a perfect image imprinted somewhere in my brain, but I don't think I'd know him. He was wearing a ski mask. It was dark, and I was scared."

Koslov was careful about hiding his identity. Even after all his research, Dylan had found only one partial photo of a profile. He pulled that image up on his cell phone. "This isn't much, but I want you to take a look. If you see anyone who resembles this man, tell me."

She squinted at his phone screen and shook her head. "Not exactly a clear portrait, is it?"

"It's all I've got."

"I wouldn't know his face, but I'd recognize his voice. He had an accent that I didn't recognize as Spanish but it probably was. I'll listen for him." She removed the combination lock and opened the door.

"How much of the cool equipment do I get to play with?" he asked.

"You aren't sanitized," she said, "so you aren't allowed in the OR. But you're free to observe. The neurologists use computers and electronic equipment that you'll find interesting."

"Will you saw off the top of his head?"

"Only in horror movies. But his brain will be exposed throughout surgery."

He jammed his hand deep into his pocket to keep from doing a fist pump. Watching machines that were hooked up inside somebody's brain was astounding. This was real-life, super circuitry. He'd barely tamped down his excitement about witnessing the cool technology when he realized that Jayne was preparing to change clothes right in front of him.

In a calm tone, she explained the difference between an MRI and electro-monitors that pinpointed brain activity. At the same time, she slipped off her teal jacket and hung it in her locker. Without glancing in his direction, she started to unbutton her shiny black blouse. The outline of her black sports bra emerged.

Dylan dragged his gaze away from the milky, smooth skin above her breasts. She wasn't doing a striptease for him, wasn't trying to be sexy at all. And he wasn't supposed to think of her as anything more than a client.

But he'd been a little bit turned-on by a glimpse of her ankles. Seeing the curve of her breast and her slender waist was enough to send him into overdrive. He made a desperate lurch away from her. "I'll go find... something. Bodyguard stuff."

Knowing that he shouldn't leave her sitting in the locker room alone made the situation even more complicated. He hadn't noticed anyone or anything suspicious on their way here, but that was no assurance that Koslov had given up.

Was this long enough to stay away? He didn't want to interrupt her with her pants off, so he stood at the end of the row and peeked around. Jayne sat on the bench in the middle, dressed in scrubs and tying her sneakers. At the other end of the row was a man in burgundy scrubs with a matching surgical cap and a baby-blue mask obscuring the lower half of his face. He moved toward her.

"Jayne," Dylan alerted her. "Do you know this guy?"

She bounded to her feet and took a good, hard look at the stranger. Then she shook her head and frowned. "Not sure."

When the masked man stuck his hand into the pocket of his scrubs, Dylan stepped in front of Jayne and eased his gun from the holster. "Identify yourself."

The man held up an ID and a gold badge. "Special agent Wayne Woodward, FBI."

Chapter Six

"Take off the surgical mask."

The stranger in scrubs pulled the mask below his chin, thrust out his arm and waggled his FBI badge.

Dylan estimated that the population of the Denver metro area was near three million, which meant that law enforcement personnel numbered in the thousands. As part-owner of TST Security, he'd met dozens of cops, deputies and agents. But there were only a handful he knew well. Special agent Wayne Woodward was one of them.

Reluctantly, he introduced him to Jayne. His relationship with Woody was the opposite of friendly, but they shared an interest in computer technology. Often they found themselves hacking away at the same cybercrime.

Dylan put away his gun. "I'm surprised to see you out of the office."

"I could say the same about you."

"Did Cisneros contact you?"

"Kidnapping," Woodward said. "It's FBI jurisdiction."

"Wait a minute." Jayne held up her palm. "Nobody has been kidnapped. I'm standing right here."

"She's right," Dylan said. "Kidnapping is only a theory. The only real crime that's happened is breaking and entering."

Woody sucked in his cheeks and pursed his lips, thinking. He was a careful man. "My office should have been involved from the start." Dylan was reluctant to give up control. Jayne had a tendency to be irritating, but it was his job to keep her safe. More than that, he wanted to protect her, to swaddle her sharp edges in cushioned layers of safety.

Pointing down the row of lockers toward the exit, he tried to herd her out the door and away from Woody. "Dr. Shackleford is expected in the operating room."

Jayne balked. "Agent Woodward," she said, "you can lose the surgical mask. It looks ridiculous, and you won't be getting close enough to my patient to contaminate anything. Another hint—most surgeons and surgical nurses don't wander around wearing their scrub caps, not unless the cap is extra fabulous. Like mine."

She tucked her long, heavy hair into a pastel-blue surgical cap with a design that resembled tangled branches or spiderwebs. Dylan recognized the pattern. "Neuron art."

"Yes." She gave him a quick nod of approval, and then her gaze turned cool again. "As you know, Dylan, I had hoped to avoid talking about the abduction, but after the scene with my dad, the secret is out. There's no need for you to pretend to be anything more than a bodyguard."

"Got it." He matched her curtness. "I'll try not to appear too smart."

"Not what I meant," she snapped.

"I know." He understood. She had not intended to be insulting. Her standoffish attitude was a shield that she used to hide the real Jayne—the woman who wore sexy panties and was a little bit clumsy.

"I trust that you—" she encompassed both of them in a stern gesture "—gentlemen will be discreet."

They nodded. Dylan noticed that Woodward had yanked off his cap. Not one hair on his head was out of place, no doubt a result of FBI training.

They hiked up the stairwell to the second floor and followed a yellow stripe through swinging doors at the eastern end of the corridor. Over the past couple of years, Roosevelt Hospital had undergone extensive renovation, and Operating Room 1A looked brand-new. The spacious room was sparkling clean with a circle of lights suspended above an adjustable operating table. In addition to the usual IVs and monitors, the neurological tracking and mapping equipment took up two walls.

Dylan stood and gawked like a nerd at his first Comic-Con. There were gazillions of switches, buttons, dials and tubes. One screen was a vertical light table that displayed a series of CT and MRI scans. On another screen, he saw a rotating, three-dimensional image of the brain. He wanted to ask Jayne how all these machines were used, but she was already deep in conversation with another doctor.

Special agent Woodward tugged on his sleeve. "How long before they get started?"

"The surgery was originally supposed to be at eleven."

"I know that," Woody said. "It was posted."

An official schedule meant that anybody who wanted to know where Jayne was would be able to find her easily. Dylan looked toward the corridor, half-expecting to see Koslov. "It's already ten minutes past eleven."

"I'm aware. When do we eat lunch? How long does this operation take?"

"The surgery takes five or six hours," Jayne said. "Once we get started, unauthorized personnel are not allowed in the OR. Dylan, if you'd like to come in right now, change into a pair of scrubs from the supply closet and cover up your shoes with booties."

"Yes, ma'am."

Roosevelt was a teaching hospital, and Jayne's surgery provided an experience worth studying. She was one of the only surgeons in the nation who regularly performed this procedure, and there would probably be students and other docs who wanted to watch.

Dylan pointed to the long, high window and the row of theater-style chairs on a platform looking down at the operating theater. Two young women in street clothes were already there. "That's where you're supposed to sit, Woody."

"Don't call me that." Under his breath, he muttered, "Who the hell does she think she is? Granting me her permission to observe? She doesn't call the shots."

"Yeah, she does. This is her surgery, and she's the boss."

"If I wanted to, I could pull the plug right now."

"Let the doctor do her job." He positioned himself near a nurses station, where he had a clear view of both directions in the corridor. "As long as you're here, we should talk."

"Why would I talk to you?"

"Because I know things."

"Such as?"

He sounded like he was offended, as if the FBI deserved more consideration. Dylan knew other agents who cared deeply and passionately about their work.

Woody wasn't so inspired. He worried about not having enough time for lunch. A nine-to-five kind of guy, he was a nitpicker...not that there was anything wrong with knowing the details. He'd probably done his homework on this case. If Dylan played his cards right, he might tease some useful information from Woody.

In a low, conspiratorial voice, Dylan said, "Let's start with Martin Viktor Koslov."

Woody raised his eyebrows, creating furrows across his formerly smooth forehead. "How do you know about Koslov?"

"He left his fingerprints in the doctor's bedroom last night."

"He's not in the FBI top ten, but Koslov is definitely on our Most Wanted list." Woody shuddered. "Some of the murders he's committed are horrific. Beheading is the least awful. They say that he cut a man in half with a chainsaw while he was still conscious."

"Wow, how old is he?"

"In his late forties, maybe even early fifties, he's been around for a long time, considering the dangers of his profession. He has a reputation as kind of a health nut, watches his diet and runs five miles a day."

Long-distance running might come in handy for an assassin. "Any family?"

"None are mentioned in his file, which is about this thick." Woody held up his thumb and forefinger six inches apart. "We suspect his first crimes were for the Romero cartel based in Venezuela. Somebody in that group might be family. Oh, and his mother was Russian. She was killed in a bomb blast."

Dylan hadn't known about the connection with the Romero cartel. They were so famously evil that even he had heard of them. The cartel lurked like a giant spider on the web of crime in South America, but they weren't involved in oil…and oil was the motive for the kidnapping.

"I thought his mother was Saudi," Dylan said, trying to keep his question innocuous so Woody would blab even more.

"Nope, Russian. His mother's name isn't Koslov, but she's Russian."

"He's done a lot of dirty work for the sheikhs."

"Your sources are behind the times." Woody scoffed. "He hasn't been involved in the Middle East for years."

"But he's still active, right?"

"You bet, he is. Four months ago in June, Koslov was in Dallas, and he—" Woody clenched his jaw.

"You can tell me," Dylan encouraged.

"It's FBI business."

"Come on, Woody, it's the era of the internet. Everybody knows everything and has a flash photo."

"I said too much."

"I've been doing research on my own," Dylan said. "I know that Koslov has never been arrested. He's been taken into custody a couple of times, which is how his fingerprints got into the system, but never charged with a crime."

Tight-lipped, Woody turned away.

Apparently, he was done talking. Dylan's patience was all used up. "Last night, Koslov got careless. He left a fingerprint. And he let his intended victim escape. Why?"

"That's not typical." Woody said.

"Think about it," Dylan said.

"I'd appreciate if you'd keep an eye on her while I change into these scrubs. You're armed, aren't you?"

"Always." He darted a nervous peek down the hallway. "Do you think Koslov would come after her in the hospital?"

"Would the horrific assassin take on a bunch of unarmed civilians? The only thing stopping him is you and me." Dylan pointed toward the operating theater. "If she goes anywhere, you follow. I'll be back in ten."

He would have preferred having Mason as his backup, but Woody could probably handle a short stint of Jayne-watching. Also, Dylan had other jobs for his partner. He wanted Mason to check them out of the hotel and to stop by Jayne's place and pack at least two more outfits. After the operation, he planned to take her to a safe house, where nobody could find them. This topic wasn't up for discussion. His decision was made. It was best for her to disappear for a few days.

He ducked into a supply closet and switched into the light blue scrubs, the same color as Jayne's. He positioned one of his guns, the Glock 17, under his armpit with a body harness. His second weapon was in an ankle holster.

When he returned to the OR, he found Woody standing where he was supposed to in the observation area. As soon as Dylan joined him, the FBI agent complained, "I'm hungry."

"When you go for lunch, there's something I want you to check."

"Now you're giving me orders."

While Woody launched into a monologue about how the FBI deserved more respect, Dylan peered through the window and focused on Jayne. The blue in her scrubs and in her cap brought out the color of her eyes. For a moment, she looked right at him, caught his gaze, and he felt a tug that drew him toward her.

Aware that Woody had stopped talking, Dylan shrugged. "Okay, fine. I won't tell you my lead."

"I didn't say I wouldn't help you. Go ahead."

Dylan went through the deductive reasoning that made him believe Koslov had used a hacker to disable Jayne's alarm system. "I checked some of our local computer experts and found that Tank Sherman seems to be on the move. He's trying to hide."

"Because Tank did a job for Koslov, and Koslov doesn't leave loose ends." Woody nodded. "I'm going to lunch, and I'll track down these loose ends later."

Dylan watched him go, figuring that he wouldn't see Woody for at least two hours.

Though the patient wasn't yet in the OR, there were seven people, including Jayne, in the room. All wore scrubs, caps and throwaway gloves. Nobody had on a mask. None of them looked in the least bit suspicious.

Jayne popped her head into the outer area. "Dylan, why don't you scrub up, put on some gloves and come in here."

With all the cool machines? She didn't need to ask twice. In the operating room, she waved him over and introduced him to the nurses, another surgeon and a neurologist who seemed to share his raging fascination with the equipment. The atmosphere was friendly and relaxed, but Jayne was clearly in charge. Not bossy— these people were her peers. She was genuinely more comfortable than he'd ever imagined she could be. No wonder she insisted on staying here. For Jayne, this was home.

Listening to the neurologist, Dylan picked up enough of the technical specs and data to generally comprehend how these machines worked. Some of the hospital equipment was dedicated to keeping the patient alive during the procedure. Others monitored and displayed. The shiny chrome superstars of technology were designed to mimic the interconnectivity of nerve endings. He particularly liked the brain-wave measurements on the oscilloscope.

Jayne appeared at his side. "What do you think?"

He gazed down at the neuron design on her surgical cap. Her brain, he suspected, was beautiful. "Impressive."

"And now, all we need is the patient."

"Do you bring him in here before you knock him out?"

"He's not unconscious," she said. "The anesthesiologist has to numb the physical pain while keeping the patient awake. It's a difficult procedure."

It all sounded difficult to him but also interesting. "I'd like to come here another time, when we don't have anything else to worry about."

"That can be arranged. What happened to your little fed friend?"

"Lunch break."

"That figures," she said dismissively. "He seemed like the type who would be more concerned with filling his belly than learning something."

Not like me. He waited for her to pat him on the back for taking an intelligent interest in the process, but she was already talking to the neurologist about a complex procedure involving the subthalamic nucleus. Jayne wasn't the type of person who scattered compliments like confetti.

He wanted her to notice him…in a positive way. He felt the words crawling up his throat and did his best to tamp them down. It was no use. He spoke up, "It's only a matter of time, you know, before the computer experts and the medical experts get together and invent a machine that can do neurosurgery."

Her full, pink lips flattened in a cold smile. "Then I'll be out of a job."

"Not what I meant," he said.

"I know."

They'd spoken these words before, but it was the other way around. Dylan thought he knew her deeply, that he recognized the Jayne under the facade. Surprise, surprise, he wasn't the only one with X-ray vision. She understood his need to appear cool and smart, not unusual for a nerd.

She took his arm. "Let me show you around before my patient arrives."

They went through the swinging doors and down a corridor wide enough for gurneys, and then she took a left at a short dead-end hallway that led to a break room. Just outside were bathrooms. Though Dylan's trained eyes were constantly on the lookout for any threat, he found himself focusing on the gentle touch of her hand on his arm.

Thrusting out his free arm in a disjointed gesture, he pointed to the ladies' room. "We should talk about bathroom breaks. I should enter before you and make sure nobody is hiding inside."

Not paying attention, she nodded, dropping his arm as she strode through the empty break room. Much of the color scheme in the hospital was typical Southwestern colors, like turquoise, gold and terra-cotta red. In the break room, the colors were deeper, with an added purple and a red the color of chili peppers. Not exactly soothing after a long surgery, the loud colors might be why the room was empty. She stood before the vending machine, contemplating the choices. "I should probably eat something."

He wanted to feed her a lavish gourmet meal and watch her eat, chewing slowly. All that appeared to be available were a variety of candy bars, snack cakes and chips. "I could go down to the cafeteria. Well, I wouldn't go myself because I need to stay with you, but I could get someone else to…"

She turned and faced him. Before he could activate his lightning-quick reflexes, she went up on her toes and kissed him on the cheek. Then she turned back to the vending machine. Over her shoulder, she said, "Couldn't help it. You're cute when you get befuddled."

He was willing to concede that she was smarter than he was…and probably a better leader…and, very likely, she was more confident. But he wasn't about to let her take the lead when it came to what happened between them.

He was the bodyguard. He was in charge.

He grasped her upper arm and spun her around to face him. Holding her other arm to anchor her to one spot in the empty break room, he kissed her. Not a belittling peck on the cheek, but a real kiss on the lips. His mouth pressed firmly against hers, he tasted mint and coffee. Though their bodies weren't touching, the heat that radiated between them was hotter than a furnace.

When her arms tugged to be free, he mentally prepared to be slapped. But she didn't end the kiss after he released her. Her slender arms encircled his neck. Her body joined with his, and her tongue plunged into his mouth. Entwined together, they maneuvered past chairs and tables until he had her pressed against the chili-red wall. His tongue probed her lips, and she opened her mouth, welcoming him inside.

For the first time since they'd met, Dylan and Jayne were in complete agreement.

Chapter Seven

Jayne reveled in the physical sensations that his kiss activated in her body. Every nerve ending trembled with excitement. Her limbic system was on fire, and the dopamine was flowing. She was overwhelmed by sensation.

All the intelligence sapped out of her as she wrapped her left leg around him and felt his erection pushing against her abdomen. It had probably been two months ago that she'd been on a date and been held by a man. But those caresses hadn't felt like this. That date had been the very definition of *who cares*?

Dylan's kiss was something far different. It consumed her. There was probably a solid neurological explanation for why she was swept up in tremors of ecstasy. But she didn't care.

A low moan of pleasure escaped her lips. So inappropriate, that they were doing this in the break room next to the stale chips and wretched coffee. She needed to stop. *Right now*, she told herself. *Or in a minute*.

As if reading her mind, he separated his mouth from hers and gazed down at her. When he reached up to straighten his glasses, he instead removed them. His unshielded gaze focused intently upon her. Reverting to her true identity as a neurosurgeon, she noted that his pupils were so dilated she could barely see the gray of the iris—a clear sign of attraction.

Proudly she smiled. She'd done that to him. He was so thoroughly turned-on that his eyes were solid black and his erection was rock solid. She had done it, and it felt good.

"What's funny?" he asked.

"I am." She shrugged. "And you are."

Jayne hadn't planned to kiss him. From the first time she'd seen him, she'd thought he was oddly attractive, but she wasn't looking for a mate, unlike the OR nurse who'd taken one peek at Dylan and asked if he was single. Was that why she'd kissed him? To put her mark on him and let other women know he was taken?

A silence stretched between them. Not because they were uncomfortable. They didn't need words to communicate.

She took a backward step. Without speaking, she was telling him that they needed to get moving. The time for the operation was nigh. She didn't release his hand—another silent communication. She wanted to stay connected to him.

He squeezed her fingertips, asserting his dominance.

She squeezed back lightly, letting him know that she wasn't a total pushover and deciding that she was reading far too much into minor gestures.

Returning to reality, she said, "There's someone I want you to meet."

"Sure." When he put his glasses back on, their moment was over. "Lead the way."

She made the walk down the long corridor that led to one of the waiting rooms for the friends and family of surgical patients. Though her hypothalamus was still doing a happy dance, certain memories sobered her mood. This was the walk she took to inform those waiting of the results. There were six times in the eight years when she'd been in charge of the surgeries that she'd had to deliver bad news. She remembered each of those patients and their families. Even now, their names and faces resurfaced in her mind. She and her team had tried their hardest to save them, but their best wasn't enough.

She was glad that her memory-stimulation surgery—the procedure on the agenda for today—wasn't life threatening unless some terrible accident occurred, something like a power outage or mislabeled anesthetic. She wasn't careless about the operation: all surgery was dangerous. But her outcomes on memory stimulation, except for one man who certainly wasn't made worse by her surgery, had been a parade of successes.

By the time they got to the waiting room, Jayne was smiling. The next time she made this walk, she would have good news. Seated in the corner with a very large backpack at her feet and a book in her hand was Cordelia Cameron, the wife of the professor who was Jayne's patient. The small woman with graying hair fastened in a chignon at her nape greeted the surgeon with a big hug.

When Jayne introduced Dylan, Mrs. Cameron cocked her head to one side and looked up at him. "Are you the man who answered my phone call this morning?"

"Yes, ma'am."

She went up on tiptoe to hug him, too. "I'm so glad Jayne finally has a boyfriend. Are you a doctor?"

"He's in computers," Jayne said quickly.

Mrs. Cameron returned to her chair. "My goodness, Dylan, you're a big one, aren't you?"

"I am," he said.

"And I'll bet you're hungry." She unzipped the top of her backpack and took out a round plastic container. Inside were fresh-baked goodies. "Jayne is always half-starved, and she really likes my chocolate chip cookies."

Dylan accepted a treat. "You asked about cookies this morning."

"This container is for you two. I have another for Henry." She continued to dig through the backpack.

Though Jayne hadn't expected food, she was salivating. "What else have you got there, Mrs. Cameron?"

"You told me that the operation would take five or six hours, and I've eaten in the hospital cafeteria more than once. It is not a delight. I made some sandwiches for me and some extra for you. Tuna salad, ham or peanut butter?"

"I have a few things I wanted to explain before I started to operate." In the past, Mrs. Cameron had been interested in hearing about the procedure. "Why don't we take your yummy backpack and go into one of these conference rooms?"

Jayne led the way back into the corridor and opened the door to a small room with windows along one wall. The plants and soft pastel green-and-yellow walls did their best to make this simple space with a sofa, a round table and a few chairs seem comforting to those who waited. Jayne preferred the loud purple and red in the break room, but that area was reserved for the hospital staff.

While tearing into a tuna sandwich, she ran through

the basic tests that had already been performed on Henry Cameron, professor emeritus at University of Denver. "The MRIs and CAT scans are clear. His blood work didn't show any new or unusual problems. Pressure is good. I can tell that you've been watching his diet and keeping him healthy."

"You bet I am." Her small hand clenched in a tight, determined fist. She wasn't about to let her husband go. "His cardiologist says his heart is doing fine after the bypass."

"And he's able to walk without assistance?"

"He's capable of getting out and about as much as he was before the heart attack," Mrs. Cameron said, "but he doesn't want to go anywhere. He's depressed."

"About his memory loss."

Jayne ate the sandwich, sipped water from a bottle that Mrs. Cameron produced from her ubiquitous backpack and listened as the concerned lady described her husband's frustration with being unable to recognize old friends or students. He couldn't recall lessons he'd taught for forty years, and when he started reading up on them again, he was angry with himself for forgetting such simple truths. The worst thing about being very smart was that you noticed the gaps when you forgot.

Professor Cameron was the perfect candidate for her memory-stimulation surgery. Apart from the brain issues, his health was good. And he was motivated, eager to regain what he had lost.

"As I've told you before," Jayne said, "there's very little risk with this procedure, and your husband will be awake most of the time. After attaching electrodes, we start by drilling two holes in the skull."

She noticed Dylan leaning forward in his chair and

listening, showing a real interest. "Excuse me," he said. "Why do you need two holes?"

Jayne looked toward Mrs. Cameron. "Do you want to tell him?"

"One is for the right side," she said, "and another for the left. I think I understand, Jayne. After you make the holes, you send in a probe to find exactly the right spot, and then you implant a microelectrode, which is as tiny as a human hair, to stimulate memory."

The description sounded so very simple. It seemed crazy that it had taken vast improvements in technology to provide the equipment needed and countless hours on her part to perfect her technique. "Essentially, that's all."

"When will we know if it worked?" Mrs. Cameron asked.

"Right away. Henry will be talking throughout."

Dylan asked, "What about the anesthesia? It'll take him a while to recover from that."

"It's a light dose," Jayne said. "Similar to the lidocaine used by your dentist."

His expression of disbelief was comical. "And it doesn't hurt?"

"The brain itself doesn't feel pain," she said. "There are many complicated explanations of this issue. Suffice it to say, I can cut into a naked brain, and the subject won't experience discomfort."

"How is that possible?" he asked.

"Pain is a warning system. If you touch a flame, the pain tells you to move your hand. If the brain is injured, the warning has come too late."

Jayne didn't want to get too graphic about what happens, not with the wife of her patient listening. But she'd heard of cases where an individual with an exposed brain could walk about and speak coherently.

"I have another question," Mrs. Cameron said. "When you're done with Henry, will you say something to him for me?"

"Of course."

The older woman's eyes filled with tears as she spoke, "It's a quote. 'Shall I compare thee to a summer's day?' He used to recite that sonnet to me. If he remembers, I'll feel like he has truly come back to me."

Jayne gave her hand a squeeze and went toward the OR, where Henry was being prepped.

AFTER THE FIRST two hours of the procedure, Dylan leaned back in his seat in the gallery, looked away from the OR and checked his cell phone. There were two text messages from Detective Cisneros.

The first read, PS cut back on his Mid-East biz. No current enemies. Unlikely terrorism. The initials "PS" must refer to Peter Shackleford, and "no current enemies" indicated that Jayne's father hadn't ticked off anybody in the Middle East, not lately. Cisneros had to be pleased that the threat to Jayne didn't involve terrorism...just an assassin with a ruthless sensibility.

The second message: PS talked to source in Mid-East. Koslov not working for his usual employers.

Dylan sent back a text telling the detective that the feds were on the case, and Agent Woody was looking into their hacker. He also noted the link between Koslov and the Romero cartel and suggested Cisneros question Jayne's dad to find out if he'd managed to irritate Diego Romero, the most bloodthirsty drug lord in Venezuela. Then he turned off the phone again.

He looked down the row of chairs to where Woody

was sitting. The FBI agent had returned to the hospital about an hour and a half ago with his wardrobe changed to his typical dark suit, white shirt and dark blue necktie. He didn't need to produce a badge—Woody was a walking advertisement for the feds.

Now might be a good time for a chat with him, not that Dylan was in any way bored as he sat in the gallery among students and docs. A short man with a little potbelly pushing against the front of his dark blue scrubs gave a running commentary of what was happening. It was "amygdala" this and "hypothalamus" that. One of the nurses referred to him as a "neurogroupie" who liked to pretend that someday he'd grow up and be a surgeon.

Dylan appreciated the play-by-play commentary. He was fascinated when they drilled the holes into Henry Cameron's skull. As Jayne had promised, there wasn't much blood. And there were nurses who seemed to have the sole job of suctioning away anything that might be messy.

Every person in the operating room wore a sterile gown and cap over the scrubs. Even in that shapeless outfit with a mask covering her mouth and special goggles, Jayne was hot. He remembered how her firm, slender body had molded to his torso when she'd kissed him back and wrapped her leg around him.

In the operating room, she was definitely in charge. The other docs, even a guy who was clearly her senior, deferred to her judgment and followed her orders. She had wakened Henry from his light sleep and was talking to him…while he had holes in his head. There were constant bleeps from some of the stainless-steel electronics. The screens with imaging of the brain showed precisely what happened when Jayne probed in different areas.

After two-and-a-half hours, they still hadn't finished with the left side. He signaled to Woody and they stepped away from the others for a private talk. Once again near the nurses' station, Dylan positioned himself so he was able to see every approach to Operating Room 1A.

Dylan spoke first. "What did you find out about Tank?"

"Nobody's seen the kid since yesterday afternoon." Woody shot a furtive gaze down the hallway. "My people tracked his laptop to an abandoned house in the foothills. No sign of Tank. He had removed the computer's memory and destroyed it."

"But he left the tracking system intact?" That made no sense whatsoever…unless Tank wanted them to find some kind of evidence. "What else did he leave at this house?"

"Nothing," Woody said. "Are you sure he was the one who did the hack?"

"I'm sure." He'd explained once already. He had discovered digital evidence that the kid had hacked into Jayne's security system last night and disabled it. Dylan's fingers were itching to get onto a keyboard and find answers for himself. "I hope Tank is okay."

"He's a criminal. These hackers don't deserve sympathy."

Spoken like a heartless fed. "Have your guys unearthed any news about the Romero cartel? Any reason they might want to get revenge on Jayne's father?"

"They've been quiet, lately. The old man, Diego Romero, hasn't been well. He's an evil bastard and so are his men. I don't know why they'd go outside the cartel to find an assassin."

"Kidnapping takes more finesse."

"Maybe so."

"I need to check in with my partner. I'd appreciate if you could stay here and keep an eye on Jayne for fifteen minutes."

"I owe you for the tip on Tank Sherman. Take your time. I'm going to be here until she's done."

As if on cue, Jayne stepped into the hallway. She'd already slipped out of the bundle of sterile clothes that covered her. Another doctor—the gray-haired man—joined her.

In an instant, Dylan was beside her. He kept his voice low. "Is everything all right?"

"It's great," she said. After two-and-a-half hours of meticulous surgery, he expected her to be tired or stressed. It was the opposite. Energy crackled around her. This woman loved her job. "The patient is responding beautifully. I've finished my work on the left side."

The doctor accompanying her said, "We needed a break before moving to the next phase."

"More food?" Dylan offered. "Water?"

"I've been staying hydrated," she said. "Maybe a bit too well hydrated. I'm out here for a bathroom break."

He fell into step beside her, leaving Woody and the other doctor standing in the corridor outside the OR. Escorting clients to the toilet was *not* one of Dylan's favorite things. When they got to the door, he stepped in front of her and pulled his handgun.

"This will just take a minute." He pushed open the door to the ladies' restroom and yelled, "Anybody in here?"

His voice echoed off the tiled walls. The room with three stalls seemed empty, but he wasn't taking any chance. He whisked her inside, and then he searched each stall. Avoiding her gaze, he held the door open.

"Um, thanks," she murmured.

"I'll be waiting outside."

As if he couldn't feel like more of a jerk, Dylan stepped out of the ladies' room and immediately saw Jayne's father walking toward him. Peter Shackleford was accompanied by a black-haired man with heavy-lidded eyes, stubble on his jaw and a suit that looked like it had been made for him.

"Javier Flores," Jayne's dad introduced him. "His family has been in the Venezuelan oil business for three generations."

The area outside the OR and the intensive-care unit was restricted. But Dylan had the feeling that Flores went wherever he wanted, whenever he wanted to go. He was sleek and intense. His dark eyes held un-readable secrets, and there was an edge about him. This was a mature and formidable man. Dylan needed to keep his eye on Flores.

Chapter Eight

After exchanging polite greetings with the Venezuelan, Dylan glanced toward Peter and said, "Jayne will be happy that you're here."

"Why?"

"You'll be able to watch the rest of the surgery she's performing."

Peter blinked as though he'd just awakened and found himself in a hospital corridor. "Surgery?"

"The procedure she created," Dylan said, reminding him. "She's able to stimulate memory in stroke victims."

"Fascinating," Flores said. "I did not know your daughter was a brain surgeon. Is this procedure successful?"

"Very much so," Dylan said.

Jayne emerged from the restroom and confronted them. Her gaze rested on her father. Dylan knew she was looking for a sign of acknowledgment from Peter the Great. In the medical community, she received a ton of recognition. She was a superstar. But she still wanted applause from her father.

Peter came toward her. "I hope we're not too late to watch you do your thing."

"My thing?" Her eyes narrowed suspiciously.

"Implanting the memory electrode," Flores said as he shook her hand and introduced himself to Jayne. Dylan hadn't mentioned electrodes or implants. How did Flores know?

Her father asked, "When will you be finished?"

"About another hour or hour and a half."

"Afterward," Flores said, "we must take you out for an early dinner to celebrate another success."

Dylan's protective instincts came to the forefront as he watched the handsome, perfectly tailored Venezuelan oozing charm all over Jayne. Was Flores naturally gushy around women? Drawn to Jayne in particular? Or did he have a more nefarious motive?

Dylan was glad when she turned to him and asked, "What do you think about dining out?"

The standard policy at TST Security was to allow clients to set their own agenda and then work around them. But Jayne wasn't a standard client...not after that kiss in the break room. Dylan didn't trust himself to stand by silently and observe while she was wined and dined. "We might need to take you to a safe house."

To Flores, she said, "We'll talk later. Now I need to get back to surgery."

As she returned to the area where she would wash up and don her sterile gear before entering OR 1A, Dylan took her dad and Flores to the seating area nearby. "You can observe from here."

"An hour and a half longer," her dad muttered. "You know, the procedure is already under way. We probably won't understand a thing."

"No problem," Dylan said as he introduced Jayne's father to the talkative groupie. The chatty observer in the dark blue scrubs was delighted to meet the father of the brilliant Dr. Shackleford and equally pleased to have a fresh audience.

Dylan pulled Flores to one side and asked, "What can you tell me about Martin Viktor Koslov?"

"Vermin." His lip curled in a sneer. "If you had not found a fingerprint, I would never believe this was the work of Martin Koslov. To disable the alarm is like him, but I have never known him to allow a victim to escape. Why would Koslov be hired for a kidnapping?"

"His employer might be someone he's worked for on a regular basis," Dylan suggested, "someone from his home country."

"He was born in Venezuela, but I hate to claim him as one of my countrymen." Flores clenched his fist as though he could strangle bad influences. "Koslov comes from the dark underbelly of my culture and represents the worst atrocities."

Dylan pushed for a more specific answer. "I've heard that Koslov is linked to the Romero cartel."

"More than a link," Flores said in a low voice. "Koslov is rumored to be the bastard son of Diego Romero himself."

According to the information Dylan had unearthed, Koslov lost his father when he was very young and was raised by his Russian mother in Caracas until he was eleven. Then she was killed in a street explosion, and he was taken in by another family. "My information about his parents is vague, except for the detail that his mother was Russian."

"A stunning woman, she played the violin and sang in a nightclub in Caracas. Diego Romero could not resist this exotic flower. He took her as his mistress, leaving his wife and his other three children behind in their village. When she was killed, Martin Koslov was bounced back and forth between the Russian consulate and an aunt of Diego Romero."

Quite an elaborate backstory for an assassin, and Dylan took it with a grain of salt. "Do you think Koslov is working for the cartel?"

"The old man has been unwell, certainly not strong enough to launch an attack against Peter. What would be gained by such an assault? Romero has nothing to do with the oil business."

"Are you sure he's not branching out?"

"Oil is the business of my family." His gaze was as dark and hard as anthracite. "I know nothing of a threat against Peter, surely not a tactic that involved the abduction of his daughter the doctor."

If Flores was lying, he was doing a good job of it. When he'd heard that Jane was a brain surgeon, he'd seemed honestly surprised and impressed with her skill. And he definitely wasn't the type to hold Jayne in a kidnapping.

Dylan directed him toward the seating where Peter the Great was being lectured by the chatty man in scrubs who seemed to know more about Jayne's procedure than she did. Peering through the glass, Dylan observed her delicate expertise as she continued the surgery. He wished he could gather her up, wrapped in her sterile gown and mask, and whisk her away to safety.

JAYNE GAVE HER full concentration to the procedure, posing questions to Professor Henry Cameron about lessons he'd taught many years ago and then asking what he'd had for breakfast this morning. A problem arose when Henry tried to translate his memories into language, and she dealt with that aspect, smoothing it over as best she could. The recovery of memory wasn't an exact science, not yet anyway, and she warned her patients not to expect perfection.

In the back of her mind, she was aware of her dad showing up to watch her surgery. Would he stick around for the whole thing? She hoped so. His approval was important to her. He'd never been disparaging, but his enthusiasm for her career in neurosurgery was at the same level as when his third wife's Yorkie won second prize at a kennel club show. Actually, he was more excited about the pooch. She wanted those pats on the head, wanted to be stroked and told that she was a good girl.

The wounds on Henry's head were closed when she removed the brace from his jaw and forehead, allowing him to move more freely. His wide grin filled her with hope and joy.

"Better?" she asked.

"So much better. Thank you, Jayne."

"Your wife asked if I would say something to you when the operation ended." She cleared her throat and quoted Shakespeare. "'Shall I compare thee to a summer's day?'"

"Here's what you tell her," he said. "'Thou art more lovely and more temperate.'"

Tears prickled the backs of her eyelids. Her priorities adjusted themselves. This successful procedure would help Henry and his wife have a better, more meaningful life. That success was what gave Jayne satisfaction. She hadn't become a neurosurgeon to prove anything to herself or to impress her father. She was a doctor. She was in the business of helping.

As Henry was wheeled away into ICU, she peeled off the sterile garb and got down to her scrubs. She left the OR, glanced at the observation area and didn't see her father. Had he left? Already? Dylan was down the hall, talking to Detective Cisneros.

She didn't want to lose the joy she felt at the successful operation. Waving to Dylan, she said, "I'm going down the hall to talk to Henry's wife."

"Wait," he said.

She kept going. After she delivered her sweet Shakespearean message to Mrs. Cameron, she'd hurry back to the OR and find out where her father had gone. She couldn't believe he'd left, not after his friend had offered a celebratory dinner.

Arms swinging, she passed the brightly colored break room where she and Dylan had kissed. Halfway down the hall, she went by the door to the room where she'd earlier talked to Mrs. Cameron. In the waiting room, she saw the backpack, but Henry's wife wasn't sitting beside it. There was only one other person in the waiting area, a haggard blonde woman who slouched over in a row of chairs.

Jayne approached the blonde and asked, "Excuse me, have you seen the lady who was sitting in this corner?"

"Bathroom," she mumbled. Her eyelids slammed shut.

Jayne was aware of someone coming up behind her. Dylan? Before she could turn to face him, she felt a pinch on her thigh as though she'd been given a shot. A masculine arm coiled across her waist. A low voice whispered, "Come with me, Jayne."

She recognized the accent.

It was the guy from last night. Martin Viktor Koslov had found her, caught her. His callused hand clamped over her mouth.

Frantic, she jerked her forearm back, aiming for his face and hitting nothing but air as he easily avoided her blow. She drove her elbow back sharply and hit his rock-hard rib cage. *I have to get away from him, have to run.* Hopping from one foot to the other, she tried to counterbalance and wrench herself from his grasp, but he held her arms, pinned her backside against his chest as he yanked her away from the woman whose eyes were still closed. How could that lady just sit there? She must have heard the struggle. *Open your eyes, lady, help me.*

Instead, the woman deliberately turned away and hunched her shoulder.

Help me, help me! Jayne twisted her head so she could scream. His hand stayed over her mouth, muffling her attempt to make noise. Her strength was waning. Whatever he'd given her in that shot was taking effect. She wouldn't give up. *Not without a fight.* She opened her jaw and chomped down hard on the fleshy pad of his hand.

He growled a feral curse, spun her to face him. She took note of his surgical mask and cap, keeping the lower part of his face covered like it was last night. He smacked her hard, a fierce backhand that caused her head to snap back.

She actually saw stars, pinpoints of light against a black velvet curtain that threatened to fall and blank out her mind.

Though reeling from the blow, she opened her mouth to scream. Her lips stuck to her teeth. Her throat was dry. No sound came through her lips. *Losing control, I'm losing control.* She wanted to fight, but she couldn't.

Where was Dylan? He was her bodyguard. He was

supposed to prevent this sort of thing. It felt like she'd been struggling for hours, but she knew it was only a few minutes since Koslov had plunged a hypodermic into her thigh, probably something like chloral hydrate or ketamine, knockout drops.

Her knees weakened. She braced herself against the back of a chair to keep from falling. *Which way is up? Which is down?* The room was spinning around her. Dizzy, disoriented, clumsy, she stumbled a few paces and sank into the wheelchair he held for her.

He pulled down the footrests and whispered, "Don't try to move. Don't make a sound. I'm not going to hurt you."

She didn't think she would have recognized him. Not with the mask. Not in those dark blue scrubs. Half the people in this building were in scrubs. They looked alike, all alike.

"Jayne?"

She swung her head toward the sound of her name. It was Mrs. Cameron coming out of the restroom. Far away, she was so far away. Jayne didn't want to frighten the woman. She tried to smile, tried to tell her that her husband had given the correct response. "'Thou art more lovely and more temperate.'" Jayne spoke the words, but she knew they came out garbled.

Before she could explain, Koslov whisked her away. He propelled the wheelchair toward the elevators. She tried to sit up straight, tried to move her legs and tumble from the chair. Her head felt unwieldy and heavy. With a sigh, she let her chin loll forward onto her chest.

She forced her eyes to open, saw Dylan running toward her. *Too late, he's too late.* Her last conscious thought was that she might never get to kiss him again.

And that would be a damn shame.

Chapter Nine

Even before she awakened, Jayne knew she wasn't at home in her comfy bed with the adjustable firmness and Egyptian-cotton linens. There was a strange aroma. Her nostrils flared as she inhaled a long, deep breath of freshness and nature. She sneezed and groaned. The bedsprings creaked as she burrowed deeper under the heavy pile of blankets.

Some people liked earthy smells, which she'd never been able to comprehend. The olfactory region in her brain interpreted the great outdoors as stinky, causing her to literally turn up her nose. Her favorite fragrance was sanitary nothingness. No smell at all, or maybe a hint of citrus.

Bemused, she imagined the map of the brain with an orange blossom sheltering the olfactory area. Part of the limbic system, sense of smell was connected to the amygdala and emotion, which was why particular smells helped recall events in the past. She inhaled, remembering the sharp pine scent of her father's aftershave. Unexpectedly, tears oozed through her closed eyelids.

She gave herself a mental shake. *Wake up, Jayne!* Her mind was fuzzy around the edges. She had vague memories of many things, some of which didn't make sense and others that couldn't possibly be true. She was a respected neurosurgeon who never indulged in wheelchair chases through the hospital corridors. Why was she imagining such a mad dash?

There had been explosions…fireworks or gunfire or something else? And Dylan, she definitely recalled being held in Dylan's arms, snuggled against his warmth, soothed by the steady rhythm of his heartbeat.

He had told her that they were going somewhere safe. As if she could just up and leave whenever she felt like it? Deserting her patients, dismissing consultations, altogether dropping the ball? She wouldn't do that. She was, above all, responsible.

Pursing her lips, she tried to say "responsible." She pushed out each individual syllable. Then she said the full word: responsible.

Her jaw ached. When she patted her cheek lightly, she felt a wide area of tenderness on her face. There would be a bruise. Someone had hit her. Koslov!

Adrenaline flushed through her veins. She was wide-awake. Though she wasn't alert or aware of what had led to this point, she was conscious. Sitting up on the bed with the polished brass frame, she looked around with new eyes. Morning sunlight spilled around the edges of the curtains and across the warm, knotty pine paneling on the bedroom walls. She had the sense that she was in a cabin in a forest. Yes, she was sure that she'd been driven into the mountains when it was dark.

Climbing from bed, she noticed that she was wearing her own baby-blue flannel pajamas with penguins skiing across them. She didn't remember changing clothes. Had Dylan undressed her? Probably not—a man would have chosen one of her skimpy gowns instead of long-sleeved flannel, which was so practical during the chill of a September night.

She pulled open the dark burgundy curtains and stared past a thick stand of pines toward a two-story cedar house and a big red barn. A cowboy rode toward her window. It was Dylan.

The moment she recognized him, she smiled, causing a twinge in her cheek. Dylan was wearing a dark brown flat-brimmed hat, jeans and a denim shirt rolled up at the sleeves. His long hair was tucked behind his ears. He didn't have his glasses.

He sat tall in the saddle...of a camel.

Jayne widened her eyes and blinked. *Not a hallucination.* For some reason, Dylan was perched atop a Bactrian camel with two humps and a lot of fur. She couldn't recall if the coat on a camel was referred to as fur or as wool. Her father owned an overcoat of camel hair, but she'd never thought the fabric was the hair of a camel, literally.

And why was she worrying about cowboys and camels? She had more than enough problems of her own without getting involved in Dylan's weirdness. Barefoot, she stalked from the bedroom through the cozy front room of the cabin, almost tripping over a very large gray cat, and out the front door, where she stood on the porch with her arms folded below her breasts.

Dylan tapped the camel with a riding crop. After a haughty look down its long nose, the animal batted extra long eyelashes. When the camel opened its mouth, the sound was a cross between an infant's cry and squealing brakes at a ten-car pileup. Charming!

"What on earth are you doing?"

He made an introductory gesture. "This is Loretta."

"I don't care."

He reached back to pat the camel's rump. "Don't pay any attention to her, Loretta. Jayne's a grouch, but you're lovely."

She narrowed her gaze. "Have I ever told you how I hate when people have conversations with their pets?"

Loretta let out another screech.

"Now you've upset her." Dylan poked along the animal's side, giving a signal of some sort. "Get back, Loretta."

In response to his gentle prods, the beast folded its knees, first in the front and then in the back. Dylan swung his leg over the front hump, dismounted and approached the porch. In his cowboy boots, he was even taller than usual. His hat shaded his silver-eyed gaze.

Though Jayne had never been a big fan of cowboys, with their long legs and lean torsos, Dylan looked good in that gear. He was studly enough to spark a dozen fantasies.

She was tempted to throw herself into his arms and encourage him to erase her concerns with his kisses. But she'd never been so easy to please. Jayne didn't know what was going on…and probably wasn't going to be happy about it. She held out her palm in a gesture that meant *halt*, and he obeyed.

He stood at the bottom of the four wide stairs leading to the porch. "How are you feeling?" he asked.

Not wanting to get sidetracked by symptoms, she didn't mention her aching jaw or her headache or the overall stiffness in her muscles and joints. Her body would heal. It was more important to find out what had happened.

"My last clear memory," she said, "is sitting in a

wheelchair and watching an elevator door close. You were running toward me."

"I didn't make it in time," he said. "Do you know who was pushing the wheelchair?"

"Koslov." Instead of shuddering, the muscles in her shoulders tensed and her fingers drew into fists. Her fear was turning to anger. "He came up behind me and shot a hypodermic into my thigh. He kept me from screaming by covering my mouth with his hand. Then I bit him."

"You bit him?"

"That's right." She braced herself against the handrail at the edge of the porch. She closed her eyes to stimulate her auditory and olfactory memories. "He growled. His flesh smelled filthy. He tasted like salt." Her eyes opened and she saw the upper portion of his face. His eyes were dark and angry. "That's when he slapped me."

"Bastard," Dylan muttered as he reached toward her.

"Don't touch me."

"Why not?"

"I need to cling to these shreds of memory." She concentrated. "He said he didn't want to hurt me. But he shot me full of drugs. And he slapped me."

"For somebody like Koslov, those are love taps." He climbed one step higher on the stair. "He hasn't killed you. Twice, he's chosen to let you escape."

"What happened when the elevator door closed?"

"He must have gotten off quickly with you, but he punched every button going upstairs and down. That was twelve stories, and the elevator stopped on each floor. Detective Cisneros went directly to the helipad on the roof."

She didn't have any recollection of being carried

away by a chopper, and it seemed like something so dramatic would make an impression, even if she was almost unconscious. "Was I in an aircraft?"

"Very likely, that was Koslov's original plan, but Cisneros was able to shut down air traffic over downtown. There was an unauthorized helo in the area of Roosevelt Hospital, but they zipped away."

"You came after me," she said.

"I ran the odds on several possible scenarios in my head." In spite of the cowboy outfit, his true nerd-like nature shone through. "Koslov needed to get you to a vehicle to escape. Because I had memorized the blueprints for the hospital and medical building, I knew the most likely escapes were the parking area and the main entrance, where a person in a wheelchair wouldn't be noticed. My brother, Sean, was nearby and I contacted him to watch the front."

"And where did you go?"

"Ran up the stairs to the second floor," he said as he took another step closer. "I backtracked the route we took from your office this morning, crossing the walkway into the medical building. The med building has an underground parking lot."

Of course, she knew about the underground lot. She used it in bad weather. "But he couldn't go there. That parking is restricted to hospital personnel."

"Koslov isn't exactly a model citizen when it comes to following the rules."

Dylan eased his boot onto the next stair. Only one stair down from the porch where she was standing, he paused. It occurred to her that he was being extremely cautious about approaching her. Had they argued?

Her excitement at seeing him was rampant and obvious, but she didn't know whether her adrenal surge

was because they were feuding or because of the unexpected attraction she'd felt from the first moment
they'd met. Though the effect of the drug had almost
worn off, she was still a bit off balance. Glancing at the
far end of the porch, she saw two long, furry animals
racing around in a circle. "What are those?"

"Ferrets," he said.

She wanted to know more about the camels and ferrets, but she wanted the rest of the story about Koslov
first. "What happened when you focused on the underground parking?"

"I tried like hell to catch him in the walkway or
heading toward the elevators in the building where you
have your office. But the medical complex is a maze
with twists and turns in strange, illogical patterns."
He was speaking faster and faster. "On the blueprint
in my mind, I imagined every single door that exited
the building. Koslov could have taken any of them. Or
even a window."

"Not a window." She pointed out, "I was in a wheelchair."

"Yeah, sure, but he could have picked you up, could
have carried you. I was so damn scared that he'd get
away. I kept telling myself that he needed a car. I'd
catch him when he tried to get you into his vehicle."

Dylan was on the porch, talking fast. "There are
three parking levels underground, and I had no way of
guessing which he'd use. I needed to stop him before
he exited the garage. With phone coordination from
Detective Cisneros, I arranged for cop cars to quietly
pull into place and block the exits."

As he spoke, she felt his energy building. He was a
compelling force. She hung on his every word. "You
did this while you were running through the building?"

"Cisneros did most of the contacts."

"It was your idea. You set the trap."

"But Koslov isn't a simple country mouse. This man lives for danger. He's an assassin. There were a lot of flaws in this plan."

"The wheelchair gave you an advantage," she said, getting caught up in the story. "He couldn't run, couldn't even move very fast while he was dragging me along."

"The disadvantage," Dylan said, "was also you. I didn't want to put you in danger by using my gun. And I sure as hell didn't want Koslov to get into a shoot-out with the cops outside the garage."

"If you'd been running hard on the walkway, you might have arrived at the underground parking before Koslov."

"I think, maybe, I did. There were so many variables—over twenty-seven—but only one constant," he said. "Two elevators connect the main floor with the level where you exit onto the street. Both open into the same enclosed glass area."

She added, "Don't forget the two concrete stairwells beside them."

"Actually, there are eight stairwells in different parts of the underground. Marked by Exit signs, their doors are locked, only used in emergency, which isn't an efficient use of the space if you ask me."

"Not asking." He certainly got sidetracked easily. "What happened next?"

He held her in his gaze. "Are you certain you don't remember?"

"Why do you think I might?"

"You and Koslov were talking."

She couldn't believe it. Her mouth gaped. Dylan

was close enough for her to collapse into his arms, but she needed to stand on her own two feet. Pivoting, she turned and stumbled toward a wooden porch swing. A large orange-striped cat sprawled across the seat.

She pointed to the cat and then to the floor. "Move."

"You don't know much about cats, do you?"

"I know that their job is to catch small rodents. That's their place in the food chain."

"Taffy begs to differ."

"Who?"

He approached the cat and reached out to stroke the orange fur. "Good morning, Taffy. Nice, sunny day, right? Would you mind moving off the swing?"

Instead, the cat stretched out to his full length and rolled to his back, displaying his belly for petting. She was fairly certain that Dylan could chat himself blue in the face and the cat wouldn't pay the least bit of attention. "You're aware, aren't you, that you're talking to an animal?"

With an agile display of feline grace, the orange cat coiled into a ball and then stood. After parading from one end of the swing to the other, Taffy glared at her with cold, yellow eyes. Then she hopped down.

"There you go," Dylan said.

Instead of taking the seat that had been so ceremoniously vacated, she leaned her back against the smooth log wall beside the door. "You said that I had a conversation with Koslov. Explain."

"I jammed the elevator doors so they wouldn't pop open and surprise me. Then I entered one of the stairwells, moving as silently as possible. There was no one inside. As soon as I stepped into the second well, I felt a presence. Are you sure you don't recall?"

She shook her head. This was so very unlike her.

She could count on one hand the number of times she hadn't been able to come up with the correct answer. The drug he'd given her had wiped her mind clean.

Dylan continued, "I heard a low murmur. Noise echoes and reverberates in those stairwells, but it seemed to be coming from below me. I looked down at the landing on the lower floor and saw you staring back at me. Your eyes were wide open. And your lips were moving. Do you remember what you said?"

Closing her eyes, she tried to access that portion of her memory. She came up blank. "I don't know."

"Koslov was behind you. He was talking. Then he whirled to face me and fired off three shots. I dodged. When I stepped back, he was gone. And you were still sitting there."

"I remember the noise," she said. The explosions she'd heard must have been gunfire. "Were there only three shots?"

"There were a lot more. When Koslov got went into the garage, he started shooting. The cops returned fire."

"Was anyone hurt?"

"Nope, but Koslov got away clean." He gave her a warm smile. "Back in the stairwell, you were on the floor, wedged in a corner with your hands over your ears. I knelt beside you and started looking for injuries. You frowned and said, 'I am a doctor.' Then you passed out."

"I don't get it," she grumbled. "From what my dad and his friend Javier said, I expected Koslov to be a mastermind, a genius bad guy. The idea of racing through a hospital with your hostage in a wheelchair isn't exactly brilliant."

"Keep in mind that this was plan B," Dylan said. "His preferred method of escape would have been the helo on the rooftop. If Cisneros hadn't been so quick to react, Koslov would have loaded you up and flown."

Not only had the timing been lucky, but Dylan and Cisneros had done exactly the right thing at the right time. "I should send the detective a thank-you."

"I'm guessing he wouldn't say no to a bottle of Stranahan's." He pulled open the door and tried to herd her inside. "Coffee?"

But she wasn't ready to let him off the hook. "I still have more questions. You're trying to divert my attention with the offer of caffeine, and I don't appreciate your methods."

"I'm having coffee." He shrugged and went inside. "Stay out here if you want or come inside with your questions."

"I need an explanation about Loretta. Why is she here?"

"Does it really matter?"

"Yes." She stared at the beast, who sat watching through impossibly thick, long eyelashes. "If there's one thing more obvious than an elephant in the room, it's a camel by the cabin."

Chapter Ten

Dylan seldom brought guests to the RSQ Ranch. He'd designed this place as somewhere he could go to escape. Only his brother, Sean, knew the precise location, which was lucky because he'd needed Sean for backup while he drove Jayne halfway across the state to the Upper Arkansas River Valley. A beautiful location, he'd purchased this acreage near Buena Vista in the forested land above the river when he was eighteen.

He left his hat on a hook by the door. His boot heels clunked on the hard wood floor as he crossed the front room of the cabin. He didn't use the kitchen for much more than making coffee or boiling water. Usually, he grabbed his meals at the main house, where the caretakers—Betty and Tom Burton—lived full-time and housed the other occasional part-timers they needed when the ranch got busy. Dylan kept this cabin private—it was his sanctuary.

Glancing over his shoulder at Jayne, who looked cute in her penguin pajamas, he came to a realization. "I've never brought a woman here before. You're my first."

"The camel, Dylan… Tell me why there's a camel sitting in front of the cabin."

"Loretta got sick, and her owners couldn't provide the care she needed. We took her in."

She followed him into the kitchen. "Why?"

"That's what we do. RSQ Ranch is a home for animals that are old or retired or sick or no longer wanted. RSQ stands for rescue."

"Only if you can't spell." But the heavily etched frown lines between her eyebrows smoothed, and she almost smiled.

As he filled the coffeemaker with cool spring water from the tap, he explained the philosophy of the RSQ Ranch.

"We find homes for them, and we have the facilities to handle large animals. Most of our referrals come from vets or zoos. We get a lot of exotic animals…an orangutan, a pair of ocelots, an albino python, and we even have a giraffe right now."

"Why on earth would someone get rid of a giraffe?"

"She's pregnant."

He set the coffee to brew and turned toward her. She'd taken a seat at the round wooden table between the kitchen and front room. Her dark brown hair fell loosely around her face but didn't hide the swollen bruise on her right cheek.

Her vitality was starting to return. Though he still didn't see the vivacious doctor who performed surgery in the hospital, he could tell that she was almost back to normal. The haziness that had clouded her eyes was gone as she looked up at him and said, "You keep saying 'we.' Almost as though you're a part of this rescue operation."

"I own it."

"But you're a bodyguard," she said.

"Being a bodyguard is one thing I do. RSQ Ranch is another."

"You're a hard man to figure out. When we met at my neighbor's house, you looked like a nerd. At the hospital, you pulled off the professor look. And now, you're a cowboy and maybe a zookeeper."

"Tip of the iceberg," he said. "My skill sets are many and varied."

Her blue eyes glimmered as she looked up at him through her thick lashes...not as thick as the camel's, but thick. "I had a taste of another of your skill set in the break room."

A reference to their kiss. Was she flirting with him? That seemed to be the obvious conclusion. At least, he hoped it was.

He cleared his throat. Dylan had never been good at reading signals from women. Should he come right out and ask her? Grab her and kiss her? "There are a few skills you could help me with."

His face prickled with hot embarrassment. Nerd! He just didn't have the knack.

"After I've had coffee," she purred, "we can go back into the bedroom. For now, tell me about when you were a kid."

"Like you, I was kind of a prodigy."

This story, he'd told a million times.

His genius moment had come when he got into computer games in a big way. His best friend, Mason Steele, would let him come over and play on prototypes that Mason's dad, a software designer, was developing. Long story short: Dylan created the circuitry, coding, artwork and stories for several original games. With help from Mason's dad, he sold his products and made a ton of money. The ongoing royalties were enough to keep RSQ Ranch in operation.

The fragrance of brewing coffee wafted through the kitchen. He took two ceramic mugs down from the shelf beside the sink and found a container of milk in the fridge. He held it up. "I know you prefer cream and no sugar, but all I have is milk."

"That's fine. Why aren't you wearing your glasses?"

"I lost them while I was chasing after Koslov. I've got in my contacts." He poured their coffee and placed both mugs on the table. Sitting across from her, he fought the urge to reach out and brush a wisp of hair off her face. The bruise made her features lopsided, but she was still lovely. He asked, "Are you done with the questions?"

"I've barely started." She sipped from the mug and gave a nod to indicate the coffee-to-milk ratio was all right. "Back to the story. We were in the parking garage and…"

"Koslov was on the run. I don't know how he got through all those cops, but he did."

"And you took care of me."

"I carried you into the elevator. On the main floor, I snagged a wheelchair, sat you in it and took you to the front entrance where my brother was waiting. We got into his SUV. I made the decision that you needed to be at a safe house."

"You decided." She growled. "Without consulting me, you decided?"

"You were pretty much unconscious."

"What does that mean?" she demanded. "Either I was conscious or I wasn't."

"Drooling," he said. "You didn't look like somebody I'd call in for a consultation."

"Did you even try to talk to me?"

"Actually," he said, "my number-one concern was your medical condition. Lucky for us, you're best buddies with the top brain surgeons in the world. I put in a call to Dr. Napoli, and he arranged to check you out."

"Napoli is acceptable," she said. "Not brilliant, but not bad. What did he say?"

"I recorded it."

He took his cell phone from his pocket and played back the doctor's examination. It didn't take a genius to figure out that she'd been drugged. While Napoli had her blood tested to make sure the drug wasn't lethal, he applied a cold compress to her cheek. Napoli had a lot to say about how the bruise probably didn't indicate concussion. Dylan skipped to the lab results about the drug that was used.

As soon as she heard the multisyllable name, she shrugged and said, "Not life threatening."

"Napoli gave permission allowing you to travel. I promised to keep you quiet, loaded you into the passenger seat, put on the seat belt and reclined it so you could nap."

"And we came here," she said.

"After some evasive driving to make sure Koslov wasn't on our tail."

She touched the collar of her pajamas. "How did my clothes get here?"

"My brother, Sean, went to your house and packed up a ton of stuff. Sean discovered that Koslov or his men were watching your house, and he led them on a crazy chase all over town. He made damn sure that he lost them before he came here."

"And how did I get changed?"

A memory of silk and satin undies flashed across his mind.

"Betty and Tom Burton live here full-time. Betty unpacked your clothes and got you ready for bed. She whipped up some kind of lotion for your bruise that smelled like weeds and grease."

"And then?"

"You drifted off to la-la land. I went to bed in the other room in this cabin so I could keep an eye on you."

Last night, he'd watched her sleep, synchronized his breathing with the slow rise and fall of her chest. The cool temperature in the cabin made him think of a quiet morning under the covers with fresh sunlight pouring through the windows. "Are you about done with that coffee?"

"Are you sure we're safe?"

"Nobody knows about this place."

"Clearly, that's not true," she said. "People involved with rescues come back and forth to drop off animals. And there's the couple who live here, the Burtons."

"Nobody but my brother would connect the Dylan who lives in Denver with the Dylan who occasionally shows up at RSQ." He rose from the table and stalked into the front room. "This is the place I come to escape."

"Escape from what?"

He shook his head. "My mind gets overloaded. I'm sure you know what I mean. A psychiatrist told me it happens to smart people."

His life wasn't deeply stressful or problematic. He and his family were in good health. He liked working at TST Security. But there were times when it felt like the world was too much. There was too much noise, constant noise, overwhelming bursts of colors and activity, more than the inside of a kaleidoscope. Sometimes, he wanted to stick his nose into the sand to block the multitude of smells.

"Everybody needs an escape," she said in a soft, husky tone.

"What do you do?"

She glided her fingers down the front of his shirt. "I like to get so deeply involved in a project that the rest of the world fades away."

"Like redecorating your house," he said, "and ending up with more bathrooms than bedrooms on one small floor."

"I like getting lost in an opera. Or reading a great book from cover to cover."

Her words were innocent, but her hands were signaling a different story. She tangled her fingers in his hair, pulled his face closer to hers and kissed him.

This marked the second time that she'd initiated contact. He wanted to be the aggressor but not too aggressive or too demanding. There should be an easier protocol for physical contact, clear indications of when a kiss was enough.

The answer to that question: Never.

A kiss was a just start.

He supported her back as he glided his hands over her breasts, teasing the dusky nipple between his fingertips and cupping the fullness. The smoothness of her flesh enticed him; she was too silky to be real. She made small, feral noises in her throat as he prolonged their kiss.

"Yikes." She jumped and looked down.

Fat, orange Taffy meowed and rubbed against Jayne's legs again. A small black-and-tan goat poked his nose through the door.

"Jealous?" Jayne asked.

"Are you asking me or the cat?"

"Show me the second bedroom."

He led the way down a short corridor that went to the bathroom. He removed a small, framed photo on the wall beside the door to the rear bedroom. Revealed behind the photo was a keypad. He felt sheepish about his secret keypad lock. An escape from sensory overload was an adult explanation for this extreme solitude. The locked bedroom seemed more like a teenager's secret hideout.

He punched the code into the pad, waited for the click, twisted the handle and opened the door for her.

If his life had been a movie, this was the time for dramatic chords to swell. Jayne was entering his world. There was much about her that he liked. She had natural charm and sensuality. When it came to intelligence, she ranked among the smartest people he'd ever known. He liked her decisiveness, her wit, her strength and her kindness toward her patients. In many ways, she seemed to be the perfect woman for him.

They were a good fit when it came to sex, too. If their kisses and brief caresses were a preview of coming attractions, he couldn't wait for the feature presentation.

She sauntered through the room, passing the long table at the front where an array of computers and electronics were scattered.

Technically, this was a bedroom because there was a single bed pushed up against the wall. But the rest of the large space was devoted to shelves in the closet that held equipment and supplies, more tables and a two-person gaming area where he tested his products.

She studied the photos on a bulletin board. "From

the Mars rover," she said. "And a desert. And this looks like the bottom of the ocean."

"I was creating a habitat." He wished she'd turn around and look at him. It was hard to know what she was thinking when he was staring at her shoulder blades. "I design computer games."

She focused on a piece of equipment attached to the ceiling. "What's this?"

He pulled it down. "A periscope."

"You have a periscope in a mountain cabin?"

"So I can watch the flying lizards." He adjusted the scope so she could see through it. "Take a peek."

"If I actually see flying lizards with this," she warned, "I'm going to freak out."

When she put her eyes to the scope, he guided her fingers to the dials. "You can zoom in or out or make the image sharper with these."

She played with the focus and turned the scope in different directions. He stood behind her with his hands on her tiny waist. "What do you see?"

"Amazing perspective," she murmured. "The far-away cars on a distant road seem to be the same size as the leaves on a bush."

"I like watching the weather. I can almost see the wind."

When she stepped back from the scope, she noticed a rectangular box on a table in the corner. "Oh, my God, Dylan, you have a 3-D printer."

Her excitement popped and sizzled like fireworks as she scampered across the floor to the machine and caressed it. She might have thought the periscope and drawings were somewhat interesting, but the 3-D printer lit a fire inside her. In a flash, she turned into a woman who could communicate with him on a creative level. He believed they could build perfect fantasies together.

Chapter Eleven

"I want brains," Jayne said, her voice fluttering with excitement. "I want to make models of brains. I've been dying to get my hands on a 3-D printer."

"We could do that," he said.

When she spun around and faced Dylan, she knew that she was grinning, because the bruise on her jaw hurt. She wasn't totally euphoric, but a stream of endorphins had lifted her mood. Building brains sounded like fun. And when was the last time she'd done something just for the fun of it?

"They could be transparent." She'd seen many varieties of brain models and modeling. Some showed the nerve endings. Others indicated blood flow. Others were artistic replicas of the swirling folds of the cerebrum and the chambered cerebellum. "I've got a lot of ideas."

"That's all you need."

"I can't wait." Playfully she grasped each of his arms and gave him a shake. "What have you done to me, Dylan?"

"Me?"

"It must be you. You're the one responsible for the way I'm feeling. I want to have fun."

"Everybody likes fun."

"Not me." Her grin became a chuckle. "And I never talk about my feelings."

Could there have been something else that caused her limbic system to blast into orbit? She considered the events of the past few days: an attack at her house, a strange meeting with her dad, a successful operation and an attempted abduction. The good outcome from Dr. Cameron's procedure was cause for celebration, of course, but she was goofy and giggly. "I'm a neurosurgeon, not the sort of person who gets excited about making models on a printing machine."

And, yet, she was giddy.

Taffy sashayed into the room, leaped onto a table by the door, struck a pose and glared at them. Maybe these animals had lightened her mood. Seeing a cat certainly wasn't uncommon, but the combination of cat, camel and ferrets might have affected her. She wondered if it was okay for the camel to be untended for this long. "Should we check on Loretta?"

"She's good. Even if she wanders off, the property is fenced." He made a square box with his fingers. "She's contained, like in here."

Contained? She looked at all four walls, noticing a great many photos and shelves and a sheet of water sliding down a flat slab of granite. "There are no windows in this room."

"It's supposed to keep the animals out and the dust down," he said. "Plus the ambient light is good for staring at screens for hours."

"And you've got the periscope," she teased, "which seems appropriate for a secret hideout."

He winced. "You picked up on that vibe, huh?"

"I did."

"You're not buying my mature 'sensory overload' bit?"

"Oh, I believe that, too. You're complex and interesting, but you're also a guy who likes his toys. Men enjoy playing with gadgetry and vehicles."

"What about women?" he asked. "What about you?"

"I like grown-up games." She walked her fingers up his chest and over his chin to his mouth. "I like games that involve lips."

"We're in agreement," he said. "Should we take this discussion to the other bedroom? It's more comfortable."

"Not yet. I want lunch."

A second cat—this one was white with black splotches or vice versa—joined Taffy on the table and whapped a computer screen with an all-black tail.

"Hey, you." Dylan picked up the cat. "Jayne, would you grab Taffy?"

"Why?"

"When the cats get in here, they mess up my equipment. That's why I usually keep this room locked."

She noticed two other cat faces in the doorway. "How many cats do you have?"

"Many."

She snuggled Taffy into her arms, and the cat climbed so his head was nestled under her chin. She could hear him purring against her collarbone as she strolled toward the door. Growing up, she'd never had pets. When her dad lived at the ranch in Texas, there'd been livestock but they were mostly for eating.

In the hallway outside his secret room, Dylan locked the door. Over his shoulder, he said, "I notified your father to let him know you're in a safe place. And I told Eloise to cancel your appointments for the rest of the week."

"Wednesday, Thursday, Friday, that's too long." She didn't like to take time off. Her schedule was tight. "I should go back by Friday."

"It's not up to me," he said. "As long as Koslov is on the loose, you need to stay here."

Her fleecy pink clouds of euphoria were showing their dark underbellies. She didn't want problems. She needed to have her happy mood back. "I can compromise. I'll work via phone conference and email."

"We'll figure out a way for you to stay in touch, but the timing will be limited. If you're connected to a phone signal, Koslov can trace the call and pinpoint your location."

"Is he tech savvy enough to do that?" she asked.

"He's not, but Tank Sherman is." Dylan unceremoniously dropped the black-and-white cat, which dashed across the floor and vaulted onto the windowsill. "Koslov used the kid before to breach your security system and might use him again to track your cell phone."

"How do we get around that?"

"Third party," Dylan said. "You call my brother at the TST Security offices, where the phones are encrypted and untraceable, and then Sean relays the message."

How could she possibly work that way? Passing messages from one person to the next sounded like an annoying children's game. There had to be an alternative.

She turned on her heel and went into her bedroom to change out of her pajamas. Jayne was pleased to find her clothing neatly tucked in dresser drawers and hanging in the closet.

If an emergency arose and she needed to get back to work, they'd have to find a way to get her back to the hospital, and ditto for her phone calls. Jayne was in charge here. She was footing the bill for a bodyguard, and his job was to make sure she didn't get attacked on his watch. He didn't get to make the rules about where she stayed and who she talked to.

Though it was September in the mountains, she'd been plenty warm enough in her pajamas. She threw on a pair of jeans, red-and-blue sneakers and a comfortably faded red hoodie over a white zip-up tank top. In the bathroom, she yanked up her hair and checked out the bruise on her face.

When she'd told Dylan she wasn't someone who went chasing after fun and good times, she hadn't been lying. At one time, Jayne had thought she was the only person in her age bracket who didn't play online games. It wasn't a conscious choice—there just wasn't time when she was busy with her studies. *Pathetic?* Some people might think so.

Some people, like her father or one of the idiot women he married, would hover over her and demand that she partake in some sort of "fun" event. Because Dad had insisted, Jayne had gone to her senior prom, never mind that she was a thirteen-year-old senior in high school.

Outside on the porch, she felt the warmth of a Colorado blue-sky day beaming down on her. She stretched and rotated her shoulders, noticing a few aches and twinges from getting banged around in yesterday's escape. The flat of her hand rested on her belly. The last time she'd eaten was the tuna sandwich from Mrs. Cameron. "I'm starving."

"Betty always has something on the burner."

The breeze smelled fresh and clean even though she saw a plume of smoke from the sprawling, two-

story cedar lodge beyond the forest and down an as-
phalt road. Much closer, at the foot of the cabin's porch
stairs, Loretta sat without moving. Her long lashes were
at half-mast, and she looked bored. A brown goat was
curled up beside her with his head resting against her
side.

"Who's Loretta's little friend?" she asked.

"That's Romeo. He has four fat nannies to frolic
around with, and he's in love with the camel." He approached Loretta. "Do you want to ride or should I?"

Though she wasn't sure this counted as fun, she'd
never taken a ride on a camel before. "Is there a trick
to it?"

"If you know how to ride a horse, you can do this.
Loretta was trained to obey the same commands."

"I'll ride."

He shooed away the goat and took her hand as she
approached the woolly Bactrian camel. "It's best to
mount while she's sitting. Just climb onto the saddle
between the humps and hang on. After she stands up,
I'll adjust the stirrups."

Jayne mounted without any major problem. But
when Loretta stood in a seesaw motion with back legs
first, then the front, balance was an issue. She nearly
slipped off into Dylan's arms. Scrambling and grabbing the humps and trying to hold on with her knees,
she got herself upright in the saddle again.

After he shortened the stirrups, she took the reins
in hand. "Okay, Loretta, let's move."

The camel shook her head from one side to the other,
opened her mouth and made a flat, ugly noise.

Jayne leaned forward to pat Loretta's long neck.
"It's okay, girl. Take your time. You can go whenever
you want."

"Don't tell her that," he said. "This is a stubborn lady. She likes to stand around."

"She doesn't understand what we're saying," Jayne said, chastising herself. *What's happening to me? Am I talking to a camel, really?* "Just go."

He took the harness and started walking Loretta along the road toward the house. Her gait was wobbly but the experience was not significantly more uncomfortable than riding on horseback. Jayne could get accustomed to travel by camel.

"Why is Loretta at RSQ?" she asked. "Is she ill?"

"The guy who owned her had a plan to raise camels, but he only could afford three, and it got too expensive to care for them."

"Why raise camels?"

"For the wool," he said, "like llamas. Also, camels give milk. Betty made cheese from Loretta's milk, and it wasn't horrible. I guess there are nomadic tribes who live on camel milk."

By any stretch of her imagination, this was a bizarre conversation. She looked down at his wide shoulders as he walked in front of her, leading Loretta. When she noticed the gun on his hip, she remembered that this visit to RSQ wasn't all about fun and games. This was a safe house. She was as much a victim as these animals, maybe even more so because she wasn't being neglected. Koslov was hunting Jayne.

"What will happen to Loretta?"

"A zoo in Montana took the other two camels. We'll find a spot for her."

Romeo the goat trotted along beside them. When the female goats got close, he actually lowered his head and took a run at them. "Romeo's mean," she said. "Where did the goats come from?"

"A petting zoo that went belly-up."

As they neared the house, an older woman with a long, silver braid rushed out the door. She gestured for them to hurry.

Dylan broke into a jog and so did Loretta. The two of them moved in a neat, synchronized motion. By contrast, Jayne jostled wildly between the humps. This saddle was a high seat. If she fell from here, it was going to hurt.

"Let me off," she said.

She swung her leg over the hump and slid down the saddle. Dylan caught her. Gently, he set her on the dirt beside the camel.

The silver-haired woman from the house jogged up close to them, dusted off her palms on her jeans and stuck out her hand. "I'm Betty Burton. Dylan tells me that you're a doctor."

"Yes," Jayne gasped.

"I don't suppose you've ever worked with animals."

Jayne introduced herself and returned the firm grip. "I haven't got vet experience, but maybe I can help. What's the problem?"

"Over there in the barn, we've got a giraffe going into labor."

Another first in Jayne's life. She hoped it would be the last time she played midwife to a giraffe.

Chapter Twelve

Dylan hustled Jayne toward the barn. Her neurosurgery skills wouldn't be much use with a pregnant giraffe, but she knew the basics of doctoring and blood didn't scare her.

When RSQ had agreed to take Bibi, short for Big Bertha, the interior of the barn had to be reconfigured. They'd kept the horse stalls along one wall. On the opposite wall, they'd shuffled some of the smaller pens and moved the goats outside to their own enclosure. In the center, at the apex of the barn, a large area was marked off with tall chain-link fences. That was where Bibi was kept. Her food was set out on the second story of the barn where the hay was stored in bales. All she needed to do was stretch her long neck and chomp. Outdoors would have been better, but she was just too big and too fast if she decided to make a run for it.

Betty's husband, Tom, greeted them at the double-wide barn doors with his cell phone in hand. He gladly passed it to Dylan. "It's the vet."

"Hey, Doc, I've got a woman here who's an MD. Her name is Jayne. Why don't you talk to her?"

He passed the cell phone to Jayne and asked Tom, "How do you know she's ready?"

"Same way as with a human. Her water broke." The old cowboy jabbed his thumb toward a messy corner of her indoor pen. "I wasn't sure what to do next. So I called the vet in Buena Vista."

"Will she get here in time for the birth?"

He shrugged and rubbed his hand along his clean-shaven jawline. "Beats me."

A man of few words, Tom Burton didn't demand much attention. Quietly and efficiently, he managed RSQ Ranch and took care of the animals. His wife handled the people part of the business. Dylan considered himself lucky to have hooked up with the Burtons.

While talking to the vet, Jayne was clearly in her element. She wrapped up the conversation with a promise to contact the vet after the birth. Calmly, she approached the pen. "This doesn't sound difficult at all."

"Most species of giraffe reproduce well in captivity," he said.

Dylan eased open the gate and stepped inside the pen with Jayne at his side. "Did the vet tell you anything we're supposed to do?"

"She said labor seldom lasts for more than a couple of hours and mostly consists of pacing and groaning. No trouble at all."

He didn't believe for one minute that delivering the calf would be easy. The vet tended to oversimplify. "When the time comes, will Bibi lie down?"

"Not usually."

Jayne stood very still while Bibi lowered her long neck and brought their faces close together. Jayne reached up and stroked the giraffe's cheek. Gazing into each other's eyes, they seemed to have a sweet and empathetic connection. Dylan took his phone from his pocket and framed a picture of Jayne's dark curls and Bibi's white face with the dark spots on her neck. The charm didn't last for long. Bibi stuck out her long, dark purple tongue and coiled it around Jayne's wrist.

To her credit, Jayne didn't shriek. "Not expecting that," she said. "It's a little gross."

Bibi raised her head and returned to her pacing. He wished the pen was bigger, but the vet had told him it wasn't good for her to have too much room.

"Look!" Jayne pointed.

The scrawny calf's legs were sticking out. Bibi paused to lick around the edges and went back to her pacing.

"You didn't answer me," he said. "If she doesn't lie down to give birth, what does she do?"

"She spreads her back legs and gives a push and splat—the calf comes out." She illustrated by stretching her legs apart and gesturing. "These are big babies, over six feet tall and over a hundred and twenty pounds. The umbilical cord snaps when the calf falls, and the bump is enough to get breathing started. All in all, it's quite efficient. Bibi will groom her calf, and the little one should get up and walk within a few minutes."

He saw the legs hanging from Bibi's rear. It didn't look at all normal. "That's a long fall to the ground."

"And that's where you come in," she said brightly. "Someone needs to catch the baby. At least, break the fall."

Somehow, this had gone from "no problem" to him standing under the back end of a giraffe waiting to catch a 120-pound baby. He might have argued but doubted it would do any good. Dylan was the tallest and the biggest among them.

He heard Tom Burton chuckle and shot him a glare. "You think this is funny?"

"Indeed, I do, and I'm planning to take pictures."

He entered the chain-link enclosure with Bibi and glanced over at his audience. There was Jayne, of course, and Tom. And a collection of barn cats, ferrets and goats. Several lop-eared bunnies stood at the edge of their large pen wiggling their noses. The cats formed two groups. Four of them perched in a row on a hay bale watching Bibi. Several others nudged Tom and meowed for food.

Jayne reached down and petted a fluffy gray cat that purred as loudly as a motorboat and wouldn't stop rubbing against her legs.

"You're a pushy one," Jayne said. "And it won't do you any good to kiss up. I don't have food."

Dylan hooked his fingers in the chain link and stared at her. "Did I just hear you talking to that cat?"

"Oh, my God, I'm turning into one of those people."

"Kindhearted animal people," he said. "Card-carrying members of PETA."

"Okay, animal lover." She pointed to the giraffe. "Here comes the head."

The head and long neck joined the legs. A gooey-looking placenta peeled back from the baby's face. Dylan saw the eyelashes flutter as Bibi took a stance. It was time.

"Go," Jayne urged him.

"She seems to be doing a good job on her own."

"This isn't like the wild where she could find a soft spot to have her baby. The floor is a concrete slab. She needs you."

He moved into position and held out his arms. Bibi

swatted at him with her tail, and he batted it away. He tried to squat under the giraffe's back legs.

When Bibi let out a moan and shifted her weight, the baby swung back and forth. More leg appeared. More neck. In a spurt, a long strange-looking creature slithered out.

Dylan managed to break the fall. He landed on the floor with a lapful of giraffe calf.

He scooted away from the calf. Bibi took over, licking her baby clean.

Breathing through his mouth, Dylan watched mama and calf. The gangly, adorable baby batted long eyelashes and nuzzled close to Bibi. Though he hadn't done anything but catch, he was proud of the role he'd played. How many Colorado cowboys could say they'd birthed a giraffe?

Chapter Thirteen

Urging her to hurry, Dylan led Jayne down the hallway in the big cedar house to an office with an L-shaped wooden desk that was part computer station and partly for writing. A row of black file cabinets lined the walls that weren't holding floor-to-ceiling shelves of well-worn books. The black plastic telephone on the desk looked like a piece of technology from years gone by that was being devoured by more modern equipment. He gestured toward the handset. "It's for you."

"My dad?"

He lowered his voice. "I called my brother at the TST office and you-know-who was there. He's insistent about talking to you."

Reluctantly, Jayne slid into the swivel chair behind the desk and picked up. "Hello, Dad."

"Where did you disappear to? I thought I was taking you back to Texas with me."

It was typical for him to make up a scenario that he hadn't discussed with her. She was utterly certain that she'd never given any indication that she'd return with him to Dallas. "I need to stay in Denver. It's where I work, where I live."

"I've had a chance to look at that little fixer-upper

house you bought. It's not as much of a mess as I thought."

"Thanks, Dad." Her father didn't make concessions lightly. Every other time he'd referred to her house, it was the "dump" or the "hovel." Saying it wasn't a total mess counted as a compliment from him. Buttering her up? He must want something really bad.

"I could stay at the house with you until this is over," he said in a reasonable tone. "I could bring in some contractors and finish up some of the repair work."

As if they'd ever worked together on a project without being at each other's throats? He was dangling a carrot, and she wanted to know why. "What do you want, Dad?"

"Tell me where you are?"

"In the mountains."

"Where, exactly, in the mountains?"

She repeated a version of what Dylan had said about hideouts. "A safe house isn't very safe if other people know where it's located."

"At least, give me a phone number."

"I'm not sure how this works." She looked across the home office to Dylan, who was leaning against the doorjamb. "Can we put this call on speaker?"

He extended his long arm and pressed a button on the computer attached to the phone. "Hello, sir. Can you hear me?"

"Loud and clear."

Her dad didn't sound happy about talking to Dylan, probably because he thought he could convince her to do what he wanted if no one else interfered. When was he going to learn that she made her own decisions and was stubborn as hell?

"Dylan," she said as she swiveled toward him, "can explain the telephone situation to you. Okay, Dad?"

"First I've got a bone to pick. Dylan, you gave me a burner phone and told me I could use it to contact you."

"Yes, sir," Dylan said. "And I'd appreciate if you keep that cell phone with you in case we need to make contact."

Her father's voice went loud. "Doesn't work, the damned cell phone doesn't work. The only place I can call is the TST Security office."

"Which is how you reached us this morning," Jayne pointed out. "Please continue, Dylan."

"As I'm sure you are aware," he said, "cell phone signals and technology are linked to GPS and can be tracked. Records for landlines are also accessible. If you had a phone number for Jayne and called it, anyone monitoring your phone could locate her."

"Of course, I know that. Everybody knows that."

"I've developed an ironclad firewall to protect the cyber-interconnections between the phone at the TST Security office—the one you're talking on—and my phone at the safe house. The signal bounces all around the globe before it's relayed. If a third party gets close, our words shred into binary code."

"Our government could use technology like that."

"Yes, sir, they already use it."

Her father's voice took on a huffy tone. "Are you saying that *our* government uses *your* technology?"

"I'd never be allowed to say that."

She studied him as he sat on the edge of the desk and delivered his explanation. Which variation of Dylan was this? He was dressed like a cowboy in jeans and a plaid cotton shirt with the sleeves rolled up. But his tone and his mannerisms seemed more like the professor. And his words were as confident as a business mogul and had resulted in a sly put-down of her dad, which Jayne, of course, cherished.

Her mind was still digesting the information she'd learned from Betty about Dylan being a child genius. His field of interest was far different from hers, and he'd already hinted that he didn't do well in school… maybe because his parents were schoolteachers? And she sensed the loneliness inside him, similar to her experiences.

"Jayne, what do you say?" her father asked. "Come back to Denver and we'll stay at your house. I'll hire more bodyguards. If Koslov dares to show his ugly face, we'll grab him."

Dylan shook his head. On a legal pad, he wrote, "Using you as bait."

Aloud, she said, "That sounds like you're setting a trap for Martin Viktor Koslov, and using me to lure him in."

"I'd never do anything to hurt my girl," he said.

"Excuse me." The smooth, lightly accented baritone of Javier Flores interrupted. "I would be honored if you both stayed with me until the danger had passed."

Dylan's head shaking became emphatic. In huge letters on the legal pad, he wrote, "NO!"

Flores continued, "I already have top-notch security and a full-time contingent of bodyguards."

"Why do you need so much protection?" she asked.

"My father made enemies when he established our family business. Even a legitimate entrepreneur such as myself runs into conflicts with the likes of Diego Romero. In the past, I have been targeted."

"What about your wife and kids?"

"Ex-wife," he corrected. "And I have not been blessed with children of my own."

The fact that he hadn't settled down and started the next generation of Flores offspring made her think he might be younger than she'd presumed. "I couldn't impose. The search for Koslov might take weeks, and it doesn't seem right for me to move into your house."

"I'd appreciate the opportunity to learn more about you," he said. "And you wouldn't be alone at my house. Your father would be a chaperone."

"It almost sounds like you're thinking of this as a date."

"And if I am…"

His hints drifted on waves of sensuality. Since her dad wasn't objecting, she figured that Dad approved of Flores as a suitor. Many times, he'd told her how he wished she'd find a man, settle down and do her doctoring part-time.

"I'll consider both offers," she said. "Today and tonight, I'm staying right where I am. I'll talk to you tomorrow. Goodbye, Señor Flores."

"Please," he said, "you must call me Javi."

Short for Javier, it was a very breathy name. "Very well, Javi, goodbye. Same to you, Dad."

"Before you leave the TST office," Dylan said, "it might be wise to set up a calling schedule. We'll make sure we're close to the phone at the right time."

As soon as the connection was severed, he came around the end of the desk and blocked her way so she was trapped in the swivel chair.

"Here's why," he said, "it's a bad idea to stay with Javi. He has enemies in Venezuela. He even mentioned Diego Romero who we know is connected to Koslov. Before you even consider the possibility of staying at his mansion full of bodyguards, who might be disloyal to Javi and working for Romero, let me do a full background check on him to make sure he's one of the good guys."

She recognized the rush of words and the nervous tension. "You're jealous."

"Of him?" He pulled a face. "I don't care one way or another about Javi. I'm just doing my job, guarding your safety."

She stood behind the desk, reached out and pushed lightly against his chest. "I haven't decided what I'll be doing or where I'll be staying." She gave another little push, and he stepped back. "Rest assured that it will be my decision. I call the shots when it comes to my life."

She pushed again. This time he didn't move back. He caught her hand and held it. "I have something to ask of you."

His voice was low and compelling. When she looked up into his warm gray eyes, she felt warmer and somehow safer. "Go ahead, ask."

"Don't put yourself in danger." He squeezed her hand. "I never want to see you hurt again."

With the many distractions of RSQ and the birth of the giraffe calf, her ordeal had faded from her mind. It seemed like a very long time ago that she had been drugged and captured by Koslov. Her hand rose to touch the swollen bruise on her cheek—her injuries could have been so much worse.

Dylan was right to remind her. She wasn't here on vacation. This wasn't playtime.

She promised him, "I'll be careful."

AFTER HIS CALL to Detective Cisneros, Dylan decided to spend the rest of the day with Jayne, mostly outdoors because the crisp September weather was idyllic and shouldn't be wasted. He found an old pair of glasses to replace the contact lenses that had been lost when he was being the giraffe's midwife. He had more contacts, but he preferred the glasses. From the way Jayne looked at him, he could tell she liked the glasses, too.

Gauging how she felt about him wasn't easy. Most of the time, she seemed to lump him in with everybody else who had given her a hard time. Occasionally, he really made her laugh. Or growl like a tigress. Once or twice, he'd looked at her and felt the heat. There was chemistry between them, but how much? He wanted to take a little stroll down that path.

As her bodyguard, he knew it was unprofessional to make a move on the woman who hired him. It wasn't as though they were on a date. He didn't even know if she'd agree to go out with him, and she must have told him a hundred times that she was the one who called the shots. She was the boss, and he needed to get a grip.

After lunch, they rounded up a couple of horses from the corral and went for an easygoing walk. Following a narrow creek, they rode into the wide Arkansas River Valley.

Jayne leaned forward in her saddle and patted her chestnut horse. "Why would anyone want to get rid of this fine mare? She's got plenty of spark left in her."

"You've got a good eye," he said. "That pretty lady is an American quarter horse, only five years old, and she's partly trained for rodeo. Her family ran into financial problems and left three horses with us until they get back on their feet."

"I'm not sure that's a good idea. Are you letting these people take advantage of you?"

"That's not how I like to think about it. I'm just

lending a nice family a hand. Someday, I might have to sell these ponies. But not right now. For now, RSQ is like their foster home."

At the base of the hill was a half acre of aspen trees with their round leaves turned bright yellow. He directed her along a path that led across the sloping hillside and into the forest. Their horses picked their way through the white trunks. With aspen leaves shimmering around her dark hair, Jayne looked like a golden goddess.

Back at the barn, they took care of their horses and then visited the enclosure to admire the calf. Wobbling around on its long legs, the six-foot-tall baby was adorable.

Tom Burton joined them. "The vet stopped by. She checked out Bibi and baby. Both are fine."

"Did you show her?" Dylan asked. "Did you show the photos you took on your phone?"

"She particularly liked the picture of you sprawled on your bottom." He chuckled under his breath. "You might have a future as an ob-gyn."

"Yeah, yeah, did you tell her the calf's name?"

"She liked that, too."

"What name?" Jayne asked. "What did you call her?"

"The giraffe calf is named in your honor."

"Jayne?" She wrinkled her nose. "It's an okay name for a person, but for a giraffe?"

He agreed, but he'd wanted to do something that would forever link her to the event of the baby's birth. "I used your last name. The baby is Shack, short for Shackleford, and reminiscent of a very tall former basketball star, Shaquille O'Neal."

"I like having a giraffe namesake. Thanks, Dylan."

She went up on her toes and gave him a peck on the cheek—a completely unsexy kiss.

After petting Shack and Bibi, they left the barn and hiked up the rise to his hideaway cabin. He kept the door locked, and the furry reasons for barricading the door were sitting on the porch, positioning their long, feline bodies to get maximum sun exposure. As soon as he opened the door, the cats shoved their way inside, followed by three ferrets with perky eyes.

As soon as Jayne sat in a rocking chair near the fireplace, a white cat with black spots, named Checkers, was on her lap. Jayne glided her hand over the pristine fur. "How does she keep herself so clean?"

"Constant tongue bath." In another time and in a different circumstance, that phrase might have had a more satisfying implication. He stretched out on the heavy leather sofa. "I've been meaning to ask. You say that you don't care for animals, but when I was in your house in Denver, I saw stuffed animals. Three cats with white fur."

"Maybe I wanted a cat when I was a little girl. I don't remember." While she talked, she continued to stroke Checkers. "I don't dislike animals. I just don't have time for pets."

He sensed a cover-up; there was more to that story than she was letting on, but he couldn't force her to trust him. And he had a bigger problem related to keeping her safe.

She was safe at RSQ Ranch. And she hadn't been grumbling about needing to rush back to town. He wanted to maintain the status quo, but Detective Cisneros had another idea.

Their best lead was the Tank Sherman. It was confirmed that Koslov had used Tank to bypass the alarm system at Jayne's house. Because Tank had dropped out of sight, it was likely that Koslov was after the hacker. These flimsy threads of logic were enough to make Cisneros believe that Tank had information that might lead to Koslov.

The problem was, Tank refused to meet with anyone but Dylan. An inconvenient demand but Dylan understood. Turning himself over to the authorities would probably land Tank in jail for a variety of cybercrimes and hacking. That was why he insisted on a face-to-face with Dylan.

But he couldn't leave Jayne here without a bodyguard while he had espressos with Tank. Would she be satisfied with his brother as a stand-in? Sean was better qualified to protect her. He had FBI training.

But would she agree to a change in plans? She liked to think she was running the show.

Dylan had considered giving Tank the directions to RSQ Ranch and having him come here. But he didn't want the hacker to know the location of his secret hideout. If Tank settled in, he'd never leave.

Somehow, Dylan had to make contact.

Chapter Fourteen

She and Dylan shared an early dinner with the Burtons, who were a charming couple, well-traveled, interesting and smart. As they talked and laughed, Jayne found herself unwinding. Her joints loosened, and her tension eased. Instead of zapping signals from one nerve synapse to another, her body electricity went on low current.

It had been a long time since she'd talked to anyone who wasn't a professional contact, either a doctor or a patient. High stress was part of her life, and escape was nearly impossible when she didn't have many friends outside work and no regular boyfriend.

Her gaze lingered on Dylan. What would it be like to come home from work and find him waiting? As soon as that question popped into her head, she realized how different she was from the little girl her dad had raised. Peter the Great would tell her that it wasn't a man's job to sit home waiting for her. It was supposed to be the other way around.

She doubted that Dylan worried about any of those old-fashioned gender stereotypes. He leaned forward, elbows on the dinner table, as he excitedly described a new fly reel he might buy for his next fishing trip.

She didn't understand half of what he was saying, but his enthusiasm made her grin.

Pushing his glasses up on his nose, he turned to her and said, "You'd like fly fishing. It requires skill and finesse."

"Don't you just bait the hook and drop it in the water?"

"Bite your tongue, woman."

This led to an involved discussion of casting, complete with physical acting out. Then he went into the philosophical, psychological battle between man and trout. This version of Dylan was nerd-like in his blind excitement and professorial in his explanation. And where was the seductive cowboy? Fishing wasn't something she generally associated with sex, but she liked the way Dylan moved his hips when he pretended to be casting onto still waters.

Later, they hiked back to the cabin, followed by the three female goats and a border collie that seemed to think he was herding their little group. "It's still early," he said.

The sun had gone behind the mountains, but it wasn't yet dark. "It's the changing time of day, when the tools are put away and goblins come out to play."

"Poetry?"

"My nanny used to tell me that every night."

"That's a little creepy," he said. "Were you brought up in an abandoned insane asylum?"

"It gets worse. Nanny would make a scary face when she said 'goblins.' Not that I was scared. I tried to stay awake and catch the monsters lurking in the shadows. I never did."

"Until the night before last," he said.

"When Koslov broke into my house."

The goats had slowed their pace, and the black-and-white dog nudged their backsides and gave a low bark. Jayne shook her head, and the evening breeze combed through her long hair.

"Maybe your nanny was right," Dylan said. "There really are goblins."

"Only in your fantasy games. Real life is harder to score. In our first encounter, I would be counted as the winner. On the second attempt, Koslov came close to successfully abducting me."

"And I wish we had learned more from that."

"Such as?"

"More." Whatever information he'd gleaned in his conversations with Cisneros and Agent Woody, Dylan wasn't sharing with her. He looked down at her. "Are you tired?"

"Not at all."

"I could teach you how to play one of my cyber-fantasy games. The scoring is real clear. You might even like it."

"Not tonight." She was feeling relaxed and wanted to enhance that mood. "I think I'll pamper myself. I never have time to follow a grooming schedule while I'm working. And your brother was thorough in packing things from my house."

"That's a surprise. Sean's kind of a slob."

"Well, he brought my organic shampoo and conditioner, a skin-rejuvenating formula for the bath and several other lotions and potions. He even picked up my aromatherapy candle."

Opening the cabin door proved difficult. The goats tromped up onto the porch as if expecting to be offered a nightcap. The Border collie knew this wasn't the right place for goats and started barking loudly to get them to move.

The cats weren't happy. Fangs bared. Backs went up. Claws came out.

When Dylan finally got the door open, he reached inside and turned on the porch light. The animal action froze. Then the very clever collie shoved one of the goats toward the stair. In a few seconds, all was back to normal.

Dylan held the door for her. "If you change your mind or want some company, I'll be in the computer room."

"Thanks."

She watched him saunter across the front room and disappear into his secret hideout. Computer games—no matter how brilliant and creative—weren't much of an enticement for her. If he'd suggested a different activity, something more sensual in nature, or if he'd pulled her into his arms and kissed her mouth, she would have been happy to stay up with him.

It was only half-past seven o'clock when she sank into the steaming hot bathtub. Her aromatherapy candle smelled like lavender, which was recommended for stress relief.

While she was soaking, she applied a facial masque to tighten her pores and tidied up her fingernails and cuticles. She never did manicures, didn't like the flash of an unusual color in the operating room. But she went wild with her feet and toenails. At the moment, her polish was intense purple.

Indulging herself was fun, but she'd get bored if she went through these rituals more frequently. Jayne enjoyed bright, pretty, feminine things—like her wild underwear and bras. But getting dressed from head to toe in fashion seemed like a lot of work when all she really needed was to toss on a pair of scrubs.

After drying and brushing her hair, she dressed in a soft, comfortable nightie. It was white cotton with delicate embroidered pink roses at the ballerina neckline, and her robe matched. She caught a glimpse of herself in the mirror over the dresser in her room. With her hair washed and brushed shiny and smooth and her virtuous white gown, she looked as innocent as a virgin. Underneath, she was wearing fire-engine-red panties with black lace. Not that anybody would know.

Jayne wished she could enjoy the best indulgence, which was having someone else appreciate her tight pores and tell her she was beautiful as he caressed her shaved legs. She imagined the appreciative expression on Dylan's face when he looked at her sexy panties. Her tongue ran across her lips, remembering how he tasted. Her nose wiggled, recalling his musky, masculine scent.

If she gave him the slightest hint, he'd be all over her. And she had the feeling that another of Dylan's mysterious talents would emerge when his clothes came off. Would he be a good lover? Did she dare to find out?

Seducing him wouldn't be fair. But it wasn't as though she was making any sort of promise about a relationship. Dylan was a big boy. He could make his own decision.

Stretched out under the blankets, she wiggled to find a comfortable spot. The RSQ Ranch bedsheets weren't as luxurious as the linens at her house, but the fabric was crisp and clean. The top blanket was a quilt with mostly blues and greens that looked homemade and had an interlinking ring design.

She felt a thud near the foot of the bed. Though her bedroom door was mostly closed, she'd had to leave a space so Dylan would hear if she called out in the night. For the cats, the open door was an invitation to party time. There was another thud…and another… and the big gray cat with the loud purr marched up to the pillow and lay down facing her.

She watched him for a moment. As soon as she closed her eyes, the cat batted a wisp of hair off her cheek.

"Hey." She raised a finger to warn him. "It's after nine o'clock. Not too early to be in bed."

The cat doesn't care, she told herself, *because he's a cat and doesn't live by clocks. And doesn't know what I'm saying, anyway.*

Determined to sleep, she rolled onto her side and attempted to sink more deeply into her relaxation. *Meditation might work.* As she tried to clear her mind, she was distracted by the sound of a creaking floorboard. Just across the hall, Dylan must be moving around, maybe peering through his periscope. Instead of releasing tension, her muscles clenched.

Maybe a glass of merlot would help.

She swung her legs out of the bed and slipped her feet into her scuffed moccasins. Then she threw on her robe and went across the hall.

As soon as she entered, Dylan looked up from his computer screen. "I thought I heard you moving around."

"Same here."

Simultaneously, they knew what they'd heard. "Cats!"

He stepped out from behind his computer, picked

up the orange cat with one hand and his beer with the other. "Can I get you a drink?"

"Merlot?" she asked.

"You're in luck. I've got some in the fridge."

When he left the room, she closed the door behind herself and followed him to the kitchen, where she perched on a chair by the table. Outside, she could hear the wind whipping the branches of pine trees, but this little cabin was warm and cozy and beginning to feel like home.

"You strike me as a beer drinker," she said. "But there's a bottle of red wine in the kitchen."

"It's there for you. I noticed what you drank and asked Betty to pick up a bottle when she stocked the cabin."

"Thanks."

"My pleasure." He opened the dark wine bottle with a corkscrew and poured a healthy dose into a stemmed wineglass. "Do you have a favorite brand?"

"I'm not a connoisseur," she readily admitted as she took a sip. "This tastes fine to me. A glass of wine at bedtime is a bit of a bad habit. Not that I do it every night."

He sat next to her and clinked his beer bottle with her wineglass. "Do you have insomnia?"

"Not really." Her occasional sleeplessness didn't rise to the level of a disorder. "When I'm especially worried, I have trouble falling to sleep. I first noticed it during my residency, when I'd been working double shifts on a rotation that included emergency medicine. I could never work in an ER."

"I understand."

"I was terrified about making a mistake and caus-ing harm to a patient. I'd stagger home exhausted, fall into bed and be unable to sleep. Then I did something really stupid."

Her voice caught in her throat. She'd never confided this story to another person. She was too ashamed. Would he judge her?

She watched his reaction as she said, "I took drugs."

His gaze stayed level and calm. "Did it help?"

"At first, it did. I hooked up with another resident who had the same problem. We wrote prescriptions for each other for sleeping pills, and they were wonderful…a little *too* wonderful."

She remembered those first few nights of perfect sleep. In the morning, she'd leap from the bed, alert and ready to take on the challenges of the day. "At first, I woke up refreshed. Since I was getting such great sleep, I figured that I didn't need more than five hours. My friend, the other resident, found another drug that would wake us up."

Though she and her friend denied their addiction, the roller coaster ups and downs got out of hand. "It didn't take long for us to get into trouble. We were haggard, unable to concentrate, abusing the dosage on the pills. But we told ourselves that we needed to do this. One of the senior nurses figured out what we were doing and threatened to report us."

"You could have lost your career," he said.

"I was terrified. I quit cold turkey. A month later, I found a middle-ground solution with the occasional merlot before bed. Only one glass. It seems civilized."

"And you're a very civilized lady."

She took a sip of her merlot, enjoying the tangy flavor on her tongue and feeling just the tiniest bit intoxicated. "How did we get started on this topic? I'm sure you don't care to know about all my bad habits, not that an addiction to prescription pills can be brushed off as a habit."

"Could have been a serious issue," he said. "You were wise enough to know when to stop."

"I'm lucky. My brain chemistry isn't set for addiction."

A lazy smile touched his lips. As he slouched in the chair, his posture was the epitome of *casual*. He reached up and tucked a piece of his long hair behind his ear. "Do you believe that all our behavior is programmed into our brains?"

"A big question." People had started religions and ended cultures trying to find answers to questions like this. "I don't think we're programmed, but I know that certain behaviors are genetic, similar to physical illnesses."

"I lean the other way," he said. "I think behavior comes from balancing the extremes. It's a matter of personal choice, like Aristotle's golden mean."

She winced. "I wish you hadn't said that. Because now I'll have to prove you wrong, and I'll feel bad."

"You think you know all the answers?"

"Well, I know more than an ancient Greek who'd never seen a laser scalpel, much less an MRI."

He took a swig of beer and gestured for her to get started. "Bring it on, Jayne."

She launched into a long explanation of neurochemical reactions and how dopamine affected behavior. "In experiments, I've stimulated a certain part of the brain and watched the subject break into tears, literally."

"But we're people," he said, "not computers. There's a whole lot about us that can't be explained. Your taste of addictive behavior wasn't about neurochemistry."

"It doesn't exactly fit with your golden mean, either. Would you say that my merlot is a balance between being a pill popper and a teetotaler?"

"I'm guessing that most of your behavior is finding a balance between your work and the rest of your life. You started taking sleeping pills so you could function on the job, and you quit for the same reason. I don't think there's a single spot on the brain that pinpoints your ambition, devotion and love for your work."

She was floored. People very seldom bested her in a rational discussion. "Good guess, cowboy."

"Thanks."

She watched him over the rim of her wineglass and gave him a few seconds to revel in his victory. "Now it's my turn to do a minianalysis on you."

"Take your best shot."

"In the few days I've known you," she said, "you've switched identities several times. You've been a computer nerd, a macho bodyguard, a philanthropist and a cowboy."

"Don't forget giraffe midwife," he said.

"You, my friend, are easily distracted. The opposite extreme is intense concentration that borders on obsession. When a subject finally grabs your interest, you study it until you're an expert."

He nodded, conceding the point. With his thumb and forefinger, he rubbed his jaw. He hadn't taken the time to shave this morning, and stubble covered his chin. "Right now," he said, "right this very minute, I have another problem of extremes. You could help me solve it."

"Go ahead."

He rose from the table and stretched his right fist

in one direction. "Over here is my professionalism. You've hired me to do a job, and I intend to do it well."

"I should hope so."

"On the left—" he held his left fist in the opposite direction "—I'm drawn to you in an unprofessional way."

A shiver of awareness slithered down her spine. Jayne liked where this was going. She also stood. "Tell me more."

"Are you wearing those red panties under that pretty white gown?"

"I am." She took her last sip of merlot and set the glass on the table. "What do you want to do about it?"

"If I bring these two opposing forces together, they might explode."

He put his two fists together and popped them apart. With one hand, he held the back of her skull. The other arm reached around her waist and pulled her toward him.

They kissed.

Chapter Fifteen

Jayne surrendered herself entirely to their kiss. His attention was all consuming, urgent, demanding her full response. She knew this kiss was nothing more than a normal physical process, but there was no room in her mind for biology. Instead of cataloging her response in terms of glands and limbic systems and secretions of hormones, she abandoned logic. Her mind went blank, happily. And she was floating on soft, billowing clouds.

The gentle pressure of his lips became harder, his embrace grew more intense and his tongue probed. From the first moment they'd met, this attraction had been building. This moment was inevitable. Her ears rang with amazing harmonies. His lean, hard body molded to hers, and she felt tingles of pleasure leaping from synapse to synapse.

Before she had recovered the ability to think coherently, Dylan scooped her off her feet. Her arms wrapped around his neck, and she snuggled against his muscled chest as he carried her to the bedroom, lowered her onto her bed and slid under the blankets beside her.

Lit only by edges of moonlight around the window shades and the glow from the front room, the room was dark. She could barely see his face, though his lips were only inches away from hers. He reached to turn on the bedside lamp, and she stopped him.

"The lamp is too bright."

"But I want to see those red panties."

"There's a candle in the bathroom."

"Atmosphere," he said. "I like it."

His departure from the bedroom gave her a chance to catch her breath. She wanted sex with him. There was no question in her mind about that. But she didn't want either of them to be hurt. Somehow, she needed to hold back, to stay in control.

She felt behind her head for the pillow and got a fistful of cat, instead. A hiss and a swat and the cat settled back, exactly where it had been before. One thing she was learning about cats: They knew what they wanted and wouldn't quit until they got it.

Some people might say the same thing about her. She craned her neck. *Hurry, Dylan.* If he gave her too much time to consider, she might change her mind. And that would be a shame. Or would it?

Maybe she was making a mistake. Jayne wasn't sophisticated when it came to sex. She was a klutz. She'd read all the studies about neuro-stimulation and sexual fulfillment. She enjoyed sex and achieved orgasm about 50 percent of the time. But she didn't crave sex, didn't need it.

Deciding to surprise him, she slipped out of her robe and nightie. Under the covers, she wore her sexy red panties and nothing else. Turning to the left and the right, she tried to find a sexy pose.

He returned with three candles that he placed strategically around the room. All were in containers, presumably to protect from cat attacks since the felines explored each candle he lit. The flickering light warmed the knotty pine walls and gleamed on the brass bed frame.

In this rugged cabin, the ambience reminded her of the Old West, and Dylan looked the part of a rugged cowboy in his jeans and long-sleeved shirt and vest, not to mention the gun he wore on his hip. He sat on the edge of the bed and took off his boots.

Somewhere between the bathroom and the bedroom, he'd removed his glasses, and she wondered how well he could see without corrective frames. "Are you wearing your contacts?"

"No. Is there something you wanted me to see?"

In a deliberately slow, languorous movement, she peeled back the blankets. A horrible thought crept into her mind. *What if she looked silly?*

No need to wonder. He gasped, and he gaped. His gaze stuck on her panties, and she felt like a regular femme fatale seductress. The hunger in his eyes was worth the price of her fancy lingerie.

She purred, "Do you like them?"

With his index finger, he tilted her chin up. Then he leaned down to taste her lips. In a low, husky voice, he whispered, "They're even better than I imagined."

He drew a line down the center of her body from the hollow of her throat to her sternum, passing between her breasts and ending below her belly button. It felt as though he was claiming her for his own, planting his flag.

His head lowered to the spot where his finger had stopped. He tugged at the lacy waistband of her panties with his teeth, and then he kissed lower. He spread her thighs.

Tremors of excitement shuddered through her as

he fondled, licked and caressed. Her back arched. She clenched her fists on the sheets. Her toes curled. Through clenched teeth, she said, "Oh, my God, I knew you'd be good at this."

When he sat up on the bed, he left his hand resting at her crotch as though he couldn't bear to part with that precious part of her. "I'm just getting started, Jayne."

In a moment, he'd unbuttoned his shirt and taken it off. Not an ounce of flab, his chest and abs were taut and sculpted. His jeans followed.

They were equally naked. She had her silky red panties. He had black jersey briefs.

He pounced. Shifting gears from slow and sensual, Dylan upgraded his passion to forceful, possessive and wild. His large hands pinned her wrists over her head on the baby-blue sheets while he covered her with nibbles and kisses, alternating hard and soft, fast and slow.

Straddling her thighs, his arousal was pressed hard and hot against her, and she wanted him. She yanked her hands from his grasp, and her fingers skittered down his torso with occasional pauses to feel the taut muscles and sprinkle of springy brown hair, darker than his sun-streaked ponytail. Her thumbs hooked in his briefs, yanking them down. At the same time, she struggled with her panties. *Why wouldn't these bits of clothing come off?* She needed to have him inside her. *Why was she so clumsy?*

Dylan took charge, calmly undressing her and then slipping out of his briefs. He glided his hand along her torso. "You're beautiful, Jayne, strong and beautiful."

"You're not bad yourself, and I'm an expert. Doctors see a lot of naked bodies, and yours is fine." She swallowed with a gulp. *Why would she say such a thing?*

"I mean, I'm not comparing you to a cadaver or an ill person. It's just that…"

"I understand."

She was glad when he covered her mouth with kisses, preventing her from making any other dopey comments. He held her close with their legs entwined. His fingers were doing wonderful, exciting things to the tight buds of her nipples, and the sensations rushing through her were electric. But she couldn't wait. Her patience was gone.

Rolling across the bed, she was on top of him. Her fingers tangled in his long hair, and she held him so he couldn't move his head while she kissed him hard.

"I want you," she growled.

"Condom in the drawer of the bedside table."

She lunged for the drawer, upsetting the orange cat in her rush to find the condom. And when she finally had it, she tore the package open with her teeth. One of the ferrets jumped up beside her, grabbed the package and dashed away. Condom police? In seconds, she had Dylan sheathed.

"That was fast," he said.

"I'm a doctor."

"Okay, Doc, what comes next?"

"Foreplay is over. I want you," she said. "Right now."

He didn't need a second invitation. His long legs tangled with hers. He separated her thighs and entered her, slowly at first and then faster and harder. At the moment when she thought she was about to explode, he'd pull almost all the way out and slowly start building the tension again.

It became a dance. She'd never felt so graceful in

bed. They were meant to be together. They fit so perfectly.

Finally, he led her, floating and swirling, all the way to a killer climax. Her world shattered, and diamonds rained down from the skies. All her life, she'd scoffed at flowery, romantic descriptions of sex, but now she felt like every gushing word was true. She flopped onto her tummy and exhaled a giant sigh. "Best sex ever."

He laughed and smacked her bottom. "One for the record books."

She buried her face in the pillow. "I didn't mean to say that out loud."

Though her eyes were closed, she no longer wanted to go to sleep. Her sexual experience—limited as it was—had taught her that it took at least two or three attempts before she reached orgasm. She and Dylan had set the standard high, and she couldn't imagine how it could get better…but if it could, she wanted to try. *Was it possible to die from pleasure?* As a neurosurgeon, she didn't want to contemplate that possibility. There were far too many kinky scenarios.

He lifted the hair off the back of her neck and nibbled her earlobe. "More wine?"

"A half glass of wine and a full glass of water."

"Feeling a need to hydrate?" he asked.

"Always good after vigorous exercise."

Naked, Dylan had left the bed and walked to the bedroom door when he turned and looked back at her. The blankets were in total disarray. Still lying on her belly, she hadn't bothered to cover herself. The candlelight cast golden shadows on her creamy white torso and shoulders, which were a marked contrasts to her shining dark curls. Her slender waist flared at the hips into a fine, round ass.

He took a mental photograph of her on the bed. The caption would be: Best Sex Ever.

He hustled through the living room to the kitchen. The lights were still on. After he took the wine bottle from the fridge, a beer for himself and a couple of waters, he turned off the lights. He usually left the curtains and blinds open—there was no need to protect from the prying eyes of strangers. No one knew their precise location, except for his brother.

He and Sean were very different people. Sean was six years older than Dylan and was definitely the alpha dog at TST Security. When he had been with the FBI, Sean had not only followed the rules but trusted them. It had been a shock when he quit.

Sean hadn't approved of bringing Jayne up here. Actually, he'd favored turning her over to the FBI, which was something Dylan refused to do. The feds had to work within guidelines, as did Detective Cisneros. Dylan, as a private security specialist, had more leeway. If he could contact Tank Sherman—who seemed like their only real link to Koslov—Dylan wouldn't have to arrest the little hacker.

Every spare minute since they'd got here, he'd been on his computer, actually on several different machines, trying to locate Tank. Slipping and sliding through the disgusting filth on the dark web, he'd learned that Tank had left town. But he hadn't gone far. He'd thrown up a marker for Dylan.

"Wanna talk," it read. And then the visual signpost faded out on the computer screen. Dylan hadn't found it again.

Hell, yes, I want to talk. Frustrated, Dylan groped for a lead to finding Tank. The kid must have information that would help find Koslov or, better yet, figure out who Koslov was working for. Most likely, it was Diego Romero—the aging cartel leader reputed to be Koslov's father. But maybe not.

Back in the bedroom, he handed her the wineglass. She was sitting up on the bed with the pillows fluffed up behind her. She had the sheet pulled up to her armpits and a goofy grin plastered across her face, but she was still sexy.

She raised her glass in a toast. "Here's to you. You're the very best bodyguard I've ever had."

He saluted her with his beer bottle and took a swig. "I don't think your dad would approve of my methods."

"Have you spoken to him?"

"Once this morning with you. And one more time before dinner."

Her dad also wanted him to come into town and set up a meeting with Tank Sherman. Peter the Great, working with Agent Woody, was prepared to offer Tank a good deal of cash if he'd betray Koslov. Dylan had tried to explain that money wouldn't do Tank any good if he was dead, but Peter wouldn't change his mind. Dylan might as well be shouting at a fence post. "He wants you back in Texas."

"Not interested, Dallas isn't my home."

"He wants to protect you." He shook his head. "I'm not sure why I'm trying to give you your father's viewpoint. I guess it's because I understand how he's feeling."

"Do you agree with him?"

"Like your dad, I think you need protection. But that's why you hired me."

"It's been a long time," she said, "since I was a baby bird being pushed out of the nest. I can take care of myself. Without any help from Dad."

From outside the house, the rhythms of the night shifted. The predator birds—hawks and owls—screeched as they swooped across the sky. The leaves rustled. The cats mewed. Horses stomped their feet and snorted. From the barn, the camel and two giraffes shifted in their stalls.

The atmosphere was different.

Someone was outside the cabin, walking fast, coming closer.

Chapter Sixteen

Dylan flicked the light switch and blew out the candles on the bedside table. Still naked, he picked up his gun, moved to the window and peeked through the blinds. A man strode up the gravel path to the cabin, not bothering to disguise his approach. He wore a black leather jacket.

"Sean," Dylan muttered.

"Your brother?"

"Maybe he's bringing good news."

"That's not how it works," Jayne said as she flailed across the bed, looking for her nightie and her wispy red panties. "Good news can always wait until morning. Bad news comes at night."

"What time is it, anyway?" He squinted at the clock.

"Almost eleven," she said. "Time for bad news."

Sean stomped up the stairs and across the porch to the door. He knocked hard and called out. No doubt he wanted to make sure they had time to get dressed if they were doing anything. For a moment, Dylan was tempted to leave his clothes off, just to irritate his brother. Not a good plan. Late-night bad news probably wasn't the best time to play games.

"Dylan," Sean yelled. "Open up."

He unlocked the front door for his brother. Two cats dashed in. "What is it?"

"I need to talk to you, both of you." Sean marched through the cabin and into the kitchen. "Have you got any food up here?"

"Half a cherry pie in the fridge."

Dylan never left anything on the counter. If the cats didn't get it, the ferrets would. It was only a matter of time before the beasts found a way to open the refrigerator.

Jayne emerged from the bedroom. Her puffy lips and flushed cheeks made a clear statement. Tying her robe over her nightie, she looked like a woman who had recently exercised her passions.

Pushing a wing of hair off her face, she asked, "Is everything all right? My patient, Dr. Cameron, isn't having problems, is he?"

"I gave our office number to the hospital in case they need to contact you, and nobody has called."

"Is Koslov in custody?"

Sean shook his head. "Cisneros isn't making much headway. After that messed-up traffic jam in the hospital parking structure, the DPD kind of look like fools. On the other hand, there is progress being made by Agent Woody and the feds."

"Sounds like a band," Dylan said. "Here they are, ladies and gents, welcome them to the stage, it's Agent Woody and the Feds."

Jayne gave a polite giggle. His brother didn't bother.

"Anyway," Sean said. "Woody got a computer contact from that Tank Sherman kid, informing him that Martin Viktor Koslov was looking for Jayne."

"Is that how he phrased it? Looking for me?" she asked. "Did he say why?"

"I don't think so," Sean said.

Dylan sensed something deeper buried underneath her question, something she knew. In the parking structure when Koslov had her in his grasp, they must have talked. "Did Koslov say something to you?"

"When?"

"In the parking structure." He hated to remind her of those harrowing moments.

"I don't remember. I was drugged out of my mind, and I'd been slapped hard." Her posture stiffened as she slid into her doctor persona. "The blow to my face was nowhere near memory centers and, therefore, wouldn't affect my ability to recall. But the drugs might be problematic."

"You're the expert on memory," he said. "What can we do to bring back your recollections of that time with Koslov?"

Her lips pinched together. He had the feeling that she didn't like being the subject of possible experimentation. Did she think he was going to saw off the top of her head and peek inside?

She cleared her throat. "I think he asked my medical opinion."

"That makes no sense," Sean said.

"I'm aware of that," she snapped.

"But it's consistent," Dylan said. "The first thing you said when I got you away from Koslov was, 'I am a doctor.'"

"Why would a kidnapper care?" Sean asked as he sliced a piece of cherry pie and slid it onto a paper plate.

"I don't know," she said.

She gave a little flounce as she sank into a chair at the round wooden table. Dylan saw ripe sensuality in every movement she made. If Sean hadn't been here, he'd tell her. He'd show her how beautiful she was. All he wanted was to be alone with her tonight, to be naked, snuggled under blankets in the bedroom.

He glared at his brother. "Why did you come here?"

"Because I'm sick of all these people calling and dropping by the office. They're driving me crazy."

"Tell them to get lost."

"I don't want to turn away potential business," Sean said. "I want this mess cleaned up."

Dylan repeated the words he'd heard Sean say dozens of time. "Even though it's not a bodyguard's job to solve the crime?"

"Even though," He took a fork from the drawer. "The only way to find Koslov is through the Sherman kid."

"I've lost track of him." He'd tried dozens of links and programs, searching for a sign or signature that looked like Tank Sherman's work. Nothing. "To tell you the truth, I'm glad he's off the grid. Tank's a kid, no match for Koslov."

Sean went into the fridge and took out the milk carton. "Want some?"

"A glass of milk goes with pie," Dylan said. "I want both."

"Me, too," Jayne piped up. "I suppose one of the people popping in and out of your office is my father."

"Him and his buddy Javier," Sean said. "I gave them a project to investigate this afternoon. Find Diego Romero."

Her blue eyes flashed. "I thought Romero was really old and never left Venezuela."

"Maybe." Sean poured three glasses of milk. "But if Romero wants something from your father, maybe your dad can negotiate his way out of the kidnapping and move straight to settlement, thereby ending the threat to you."

Dylan cut and served the pie. "You still haven't told me why you're here."

"Yeah, yeah, I want you to look at this."

Sean reached into the pocket of his leather jacket. He pulled out a scrap of paper and handed it to Dylan.

"Numbers," Dylan said as he took a seat at the table.

"Dots and dashes and more numbers," Sean said. "I got a call on our supersecure line. You didn't give that phone number to Tank, did you?"

"Definitely not."

"Well, he somehow got it. He wasn't on the phone. It was a female voice. She recited the numbers and dots twice, told me that you'd understand and hung up."

Without knowing the context of the numbers, it took him a moment to grasp what kind of message Tank was sending. "These are GPS coordinates."

"I guessed as much."

"If I'm not mistaken, this location isn't far from Buena Vista." Though certain that Tank didn't know how to find RSQ Ranch, Dylan might have let slip a mention of something in this area that alerted the kid. "And there's another code."

While they ate their pie and drank their milk, he stared at the markings on the paper and reviewed the code protocols he was familiar with. It was a long list; he'd plotted out a computer game using established codes and two spin-off games from the first one.

In deep concentration, Dylan was aware of his brother and Jayne talking and he tasted the pie and he felt one of the cats rubbing against his leg under the table. But he wasn't really present. In his mind, he was scanning an endless warehouse of information, rifling through files, digging for the information that would fit Tank's code.

"Got it!"

He slapped the flat of his hand on the table so hard that the cat at his feet leaped up, bonked its head on the table, screeched and ran away.

Sean jumped back in his chair. "And that's why you can't trust cats. They're always doing something freaky."

"That wasn't odd behavior." Jayne reached out and summoned the black-and-white cat named Checkers. As the cat curled up on her lap, Jayne explained. "A startle response is an acceptable way of protecting oneself. You might react the same way to the sound of gunfire."

Before they got into an argument, Dylan stood. "Would you like to hear what the code says?"

They both gave him their attention. Since they really didn't care about how the code was used, he didn't bother explaining his process. "The GPS is going to take us into Buena Vista, somewhere near the Arkansas River. The words that I could translate are 'Key-Yak-Two.'"

Sean shook his head. "What the…?"

"I'm guessing there's a kayak shop. And Tank is hiding on the second floor."

"Question," Sean said. "Why would Tank come so close to RSQ Ranch if he doesn't know it's here?"

"I might have mentioned Buena Vista a couple of times, which would cause him to zoom in on the area." The hacker kid would love to find the hideout where Dylan created his software. "Oh yeah, and I used photos of the Collegiate Peaks—Mount Princeton and Mount Yale—for the background in a game."

Still holding the cat, Jayne bounced to her feet. "It sounds like you found him. Let's go."

"Whoa, there," Sean said. "You're not going anywhere."

Her jaw stuck out. "I most certainly am."

Dylan weighed the alternatives. If she stayed here, she was unguarded. If she went with them, there could be danger. But she had both Sean and himself to keep her safe.

Jayne and Sean batted the question back and forth until she firmly announced, "I refuse to stay here by myself."

Sean looked at Dylan. "A little help, please."

"I'm on her side," he said. "All in all, I think she's safer with us than alone."

"Thank you, Dylan." She pivoted and went into the bedroom. "I'll be changed in a minute."

As soon as she left the room, Sean punched his shoulder. "That's for taking her side over mine."

"You know I'm right." Dylan liked to imagine that RSQ Ranch was completely invisible, but that wasn't exactly true. With recent advances in surveillance technology, nowhere was truly safe. Too easily, Koslov could locate this place. And Jayne would be at his mercy.

"We could be walking into an ambush," Sean said. "You and I can usually kick ass, but we're talking about an assassin from the Romero drug cartel."

"Not looking for a fight," Dylan said. "We approach with caution. At the first sign of trouble, we call for backup. The local sheriff's name is Swanson. We'll alert him before we get there."

Dylan went to the front closet, unlocked a hidden panel and took out a green army duffel bag loaded with guns and ammo. Since buying RSQ, he'd given up hunting. It didn't seem right to be rescuing camels and chasing down elk. But he'd kept his rifles and miscellaneous firepower.

Sean raised an eyebrow. "That's a hell of a defense."

"Just being prepared. We'll take two vehicles."

Sean reached into a pocket. "Earbuds so we can communicate."

"I'll get a pair for Jayne."

He strode across the floor and went into his bedroom/workroom where a couple of screens were devoted to his efforts to locate Tank. On one screen, a driver's license photo of Tank was displayed. His face was narrow. Though mostly clean shaven, his pointy chin sprouted a pathetic attempt at a goatee.

Jayne came into the room. "That's Tank? He looks like a teenager."

"He's twenty-six, only two years younger than me."

"And can barely sprout a beard—he's just a kid." She went up on tiptoe and whispered in his ear. "You're definitely a full-grown man."

"Do me a favor," he whispered back.

"Anything."

"Don't let my brother hear you say that. He'll never let me forget it."

She grinned and stepped back. "I won't embarrass you."

Her nearness fired enough electricity to power the whole valley and beyond. He wished they hadn't been so abruptly interrupted after sex. There was so much more he wanted to give her and to take from her.

Chapter Seventeen

The physical awareness of fear, including the adrenaline surge, tightness of breath, tense muscles and urge to scream, became more and more familiar to Jayne. As she sat in the passenger seat of Dylan's SUV, she felt a tic at the corner of her eye. That was new. The cherry pie she'd just eaten did a tango in her belly.

If they ran into an assault from the bad guys, there was nothing she could do to stop them. She didn't know how to shoot and had virtually no skills in hand-to-hand combat. A knife was actually the best weapon for her—she knew the location of important arteries and could slash them in an instant. Or could she? In her Hippocratic Oath, she'd promised not to hurt other people, and she couldn't imagine committing murder, even in self-defense.

But when Dylan had wanted to go after Tank, she couldn't stay behind and wait for him. She had to be at his side. She inhaled and exhaled slowly, determined to stay calm.

In Dylan's SUV, they drove from the shelter of the narrow canyon where RSQ Ranch was located. The first time they'd been on this road, Jayne had been sleeping hard, recovering from the drugs, so the surroundings were new to her. She tried not to focus on the shadows where scary things could be lurking. When the headlights emerged from the dark forest, they were on a high mesa above the Arkansas River Valley. Lit by moonlight, the vista was broad and open. No danger could be hiding here.

She hadn't been to the mountains all summer, and she marveled—as she always did—at the scope of towering rocks and thick forest. Above it all, a pale half-moon arced high in the star-spattered heavens. She concentrated on the beauty. *Forget the fear.* A vast swath of land spread below them in an untamed valley enclosed by rugged hills. Since it was the middle of the night, there were few house lights.

"I should come to the mountains more often," she said.

"Now you have a reason," he said.

"What do you mean?"

"You're not the type of person who takes an aimless trip to the mountains. You need a destination. That can be RSQ."

"Would I be your guest?"

"You'd be my guest in my cabin…" His voice took on a husky, seductive tone. "You'd stay in my bed."

"I'd like that."

"I can't promise we'd be naming giraffe babies after you every time you showed, but there's usually something interesting going on. You're welcome to visit when I'm not here, too. There's plenty of room. And Betty can do with the company. She likes you."

"I like her, too." Her gaze focused on him. His profile, illuminated by the dashboard lights, was strong but not perfect. His nose had a crook that meant it had probably been broken and badly reset. His jaw was too square, but his laid-back smile kept his features from appearing sharp.

Generally, she preferred men who were neatly dressed and groomed, but there was something about Dylan's scruffy appearance that made her want to tear his clothes off. Naked, he was amazing. As she thought of Dylan lying in bed, her fears began to fade away. Dylan the porn star? Another identity?

He was good at disguises but had always been straightforward with her. He had a face she could trust, and that was saying a lot. His brother, Sean? Not so much.

Dylan glanced toward her. "Are you putting me under a microscope?"

"Why would I do that?"

"A brain experiment?" His shoulders rose and fell in a shrug. "I don't know why, but you were staring."

"I wanted to make a tangible memory of you, a mental picture I could summon whenever I want to see you."

"Or you could call me."

"Sure."

That was what he said right now, but she knew better than to count on a "call me." More likely, when this was over, they'd go back to Denver, live their separate lives and never see each other again.

"You don't believe we'll stay in touch," he said. "You think you're going to have the best sex ever, then turn your back and walk away."

Was he a mind reader? "Were you thinking the same thing?"

"Hell, no."

"Are we bickering?" she asked.

"Maybe. I don't know."

Bickering was better than sitting there like a frozen lump of fear. "I think we are."

She figured that he was familiar with this winding road because he was driving fast. He went faster. His fingers tensed on the steering wheel.

"I'll keep it simple." He pushed his glasses up on his nose. "I like you, Jayne. We have a lot in common. You're smart and fun to be around. Among a hundred other positive attributes, you're great in bed. No way am I turning my back on you."

That was what he said now while his memory was still fresh. Only a short while ago, they'd been in bed together. The scent of their passion still clung to her nostrils. She could still taste him on her lips. Would he remember her next week? In a year, would he even recall her name?

She tried to explain. "I'm not dumping you or anything like that. But there's a good chance that we'll say goodbye when I don't need a bodyguard. It's just the way things are. We both have busy lives and no time for a relationship."

"Instead of starting with the rejection you seem to think is inevitable, start with something good. You like me. I know you do."

"No lack of ego on your part." She was teasing, but she appreciated his confidence. The way she felt about neurosurgery was much the same. She loved her work and knew she was brilliant. "You've probably had success with women."

"Not great success."

She found that hard to believe. "Come on, Dylan. Tell the truth."

"I'm almost thirty and not married. Not a winning scorecard," he said. "My parents are getting real frustrated with me and Sean. He was married once, but she turned out to be a wildcat."

"Divorced?"

"A total reboot." He waved his hand as though wiping an invisible blackboard. "Forget I said that. Sean's love life isn't a good example. I just don't want you to think I'm looking for a bride. You probably hear enough from your dad about getting hitched."

"I made a deal with my dad a long time ago. He doesn't push me about my lack of a mate or spouse if I don't get mad at him about his many marriages." She couldn't stop herself from adding, "He had his one great love in this lifetime. That was my mom. He'll never find another like her."

He reached across the console and picked up her hand. The warmth of his skin felt delicious. He gave a squeeze. "That's why you forgive your dad for not understanding you and being demanding. He lost his soul mate and was badly hurt."

"Yes," she said quietly.

"The same applies to you. You lost your mother. That's a deep wound."

And she'd been to enough psychotherapists to hear dozens of theories about how that loss had affected her. Had she chosen a career in medicine because her mother was a biochemist? Was she trying to be a surrogate for her father? Did she run from relationships with men because she feared love?

"Complicated," she said as she mentally slammed the door on those painful theories.

"I prefer complexity. I could spend a long time trying to figure you out."

"You make it sound like that would be fun."

"It would be."

This conversation was taking an odd twist. They were talking about the future and the past all at once. On the plus side, she wasn't scared anymore. "Betty Burton told me that you spent a lot of time alone when you were a kid."

"I still do," he said. "And I'm going out on a limb and guessing that you were a loner kid, too."

"Making friends was hard while I was skipping from one grade to the next. I was always around people who were older. I dated guys who were older."

"That must have been a treat for your dad."

She cringed inside, acknowledging that on the occasions when her dad paid attention to what she was doing, he didn't approve. And, sometimes, his judgments were on-target.

When she'd been sixteen years old and preparing to graduate premed from Stanford, she'd thought that she was madly in love with a drama student in his senior year. He was twenty…and gorgeous…and the biggest narcissist she'd ever known. His ego was the size of the Dumbo balloon in the Thanksgiving parade, but all she saw was the glitter in his eyes, the blinding white glare of his teeth and the mahogany-tanned ridges of his six-pack abs.

She'd gone after him with laser-focused determination, studying fashion magazines as though they were medical texts. She'd colored her dark brown hair with sexy platinum streaks, learned how to do a "smoky eye" makeup and bought a bra that transformed her A-cups into plump, healthy C's.

In the back of his Lexus, she'd given him her virginity. The sex was pathetic, messy and totally unsatisfying, even though she'd studied sex, too. Deciding it must be her fault because he was so gorgeous, she'd tried again and again.

Finally, in an act of sheer desperation, she offered to drop out of medical school and move to New York with him. That was when the best thing ever happened—he broke up with her.

"I didn't do well," she said, "with relationships when I was growing up. What about you?"

"I was a typical computer geek. I'd get buried in my calculations. Every spare minute, I was on my computer."

"Skinny?"

"No tan, no muscles, thick glasses."

"And lonely," she said.

"So true."

"That's the curse of being really smart. The other kids ostracized me and, to be quite honest, I didn't blame them. I was totally caught up in my studies."

"I was never sad," he said.

"Me neither. My isolation came because nobody else could understand what I was doing, and that stung. But I wasn't depressed."

"When did you find people who could understand you?"

"In med school," she said. "For the first time in my life, I wasn't always the smartest kid in the room."

"My wake-up came during my first year in high

school when I had a monster growth spurt. I was still a nerd, but a very tall nerd that coaches wanted to get into sports. I liked the stats and symmetry of team games, but they weren't for me. I started biking and running. And I found that those exercises were a good way to shut out the rest of the world and think. I've done Ride The Rockies twice."

"The bicycle race out of Grand Junction? Isn't that four hundred miles or something?"

"The last time I did it, a couple of years ago, the route was 465 miles and 40,537 vertical feet."

"Well, that's one thing we don't have in common," she said. If he was looking for a riding partner, he needed to search elsewhere. "I've always been a klutz."

He gallantly said nothing, but she knew he'd noticed. Wherever she went, there were spills and stumbles. That was why their passion had been so incredible for her. Every kiss, every caress felt choreographed, completely right in every way.

He drove around the edges of Buena Vista, which were less quaint than the downtown area where there were several diners, lodges, motels and hotels. In the spring, there were lots of tourists. This area was renowned for white-water rafting. Along the Arkansas were several small businesses, all of them dark and seemingly deserted.

She pointed to a sign. "Kayaks. It's an A-frame. That means there are two stories."

"I see it," Dylan said.

Her fear came rushing back, but it wasn't overwhelming. She could handle it. "Why aren't we stopping?"

"Sean and I agreed that we should treat this approach as if there's danger. For all I know, Tank is working for Koslov. Or the computer communications were sent by Koslov."

"Not the message with the code," she said. "Koslov isn't that clever. If he forced Tank to send it, Tank would have embedded something to warn you."

They went silent. Her ears rang with each beat of her pulse. Tension coiled her gut. He drove about a mile and made a right turn away from the river and into a lightly forested area where he parked and killed the lights. Sean drove in behind them. They got out of their cars and met in the middle.

The chill wind made her glad that she'd worn her dark green parka with the fake fur around the hood. Though there was no one in sight, they spoke in low voices.

"We'll drive closer in one of the cars," Sean said. "We park near the river. The noise from the rapids will cover our approach. I'll go first and tell you when to follow."

"Got it," Dylan said.

Sean popped the trunk on his car, took out bullet-proof vests and handed them around. "It's going to be big on you, Jayne. I don't have anything smaller."

She fastened the vest over her parka and clothes. Not only was it too big, but the stiff edges felt like she was packaged up inside an iron shoe box.

Dylan passed out the earbuds and told her, "This device is active and transmitting. Turn it on like this and off like that. Tuck it into your ear, and I can hear you up to three hundred yards away. Don't say anything unless you sight danger. Stick with me."

None of the instructions sounded particularly difficult, and she hoped she wouldn't somehow make a mistake. Her adrenaline was already pumping. Her pulse accelerated as she climbed into the back of Sean's car with Dylan beside her. Both men were armed with semiautomatic rifles and handguns.

She asked, "Should I have a weapon?"

"No." They spoke with one voice. The sound of their actual voices mixed with the voices inside the earbud, and they sounded like four refusals instead of just two.

"What if," she said, "someone comes after me?"

"Stay close to me," Dylan said.

"And if you get injured?"

"I won't."

This moment was a test of just how much she trusted him. They'd already gone through a trial by fire at the hospital when Koslov had grabbed her and Dylan had pursued without hesitation. This was different. Dylan was literally risking his life to protect her.

Sean nudged his car along the edge of the road. The headlights were off. He parked and disabled the overhead interior car light before they opened the door and climbed out.

The rushing sound of the river masked the little noises they made as they crept through the forest. Sean went first. She followed him. And Dylan brought up the rear.

Staying on a path that followed the shoreline, they went through the backyard of a private home that was far from the river and close to the road. Very few people occupied the land closest to the water. Nearly every spring, the runoff from the high mountains sloshed over the river's edge. Flooding was a real possibility.

They crept along a narrow dirt track past pines and

rocks and shrubs. Inside her parka and bulletproof vest, she started to sweat. Though she'd stumbled a couple of times, she hadn't fallen flat on her face.

The flimsy A-frame had a sign suspended from the peak of the letter *A*—KAYAK. The rest of the space on the road side of the building had signage listing brand names for kayaks, as well as rates for lessons, rentals and purchases.

More significantly for them was a sign on the glass window in the door. Dylan pointed to it. Wi-Fi was available inside. The owner of the kayak shack might be cyberpals with Tank.

Sweat prickled under her armpits and along her hairline. She clustered in a tight threesome with the two brothers who seemed to communicate without words. Sean had peered inside through the filthy glass window in the door. He lowered his hand and tried the door handle. It turned easily.

When they entered, moving quietly but not silently, Sean went to the single winding flight of stairs near the front entrance. The lower floor was packed with displays of kayaks, associated equipment and clothes. A trophy was mounted on the back wall near the cash register.

She stuck like Velcro to Dylan as he crossed the display room to the counter. Behind the counter was a door. He opened it slowly. This room had no windows. He took a Maglite from his jacket pocket and turned it on. The bright beam crisscrossed the messy back office where invoices and unopened mail spewed across a desk that also had a neat stack of personal checks in the corner. Was this shack a front for something else? Or just an example of sloppy business practice?

She heard her name being called from upstairs and moved to respond.

Dylan caught her arm. "I go first."

"That was your brother's voice." Surely, he trusted Sean.

She heard Sean in her earbud. "Come quick, Jayne."

Together, she and Dylan raced to the staircase at the front of the shop. Dylan went first. At the top of the staircase, he aimed his Maglite beam at hazy forms of sofas and chairs and desks in the semidarkness of a slanted second floor with only one window.

Sean squatted on the floor over the heaving body of a scrawny, shirtless young man whose face was bloody. Spatters of blood marked his torso and arms. He gulped down air in violent gasps. Convulsions caused the jungle of tattoos on his arms and chest to writhe.

Panic gripped Jayne's gut. A drug overdose? Where was the blood coming from? She recoiled, feeling like a turtle shrinking back inside her bulletproof shell. It had been a long time since her training rotation in the emergency room. She wanted to run away, but that wasn't an option. *I am a doctor.*

She pushed Sean out of the way and knelt on the floor beside the young man whose body jerked convulsively.

Accurate diagnosis would be difficult. First, she treated the symptoms, clearing the area so he wouldn't hurt himself as he convulsed. "Can we turn on the light in here?"

Through the earbud, she heard Dylan and Sean discuss the dangers of turning on a light. Since there was only the one window, they decided it was okay. In the dim glow of a bare lightbulb near the center of the room, the second-floor apartment was dull and dingy, as though every surface was covered with a layer of dust. She dragged over a cushion from the beat-up sofa. "Dylan, bring me a blanket and a damp washcloth."

She checked the tattooed body, neck and face as best she could while he was shuddering and lashing out. There didn't appear to be any severe lacerations. Nothing like a gunshot or knife wound. Most of the blood seemed to come from his nose.

When Dylan returned with the blanket and cloth, she touched the forehead of the tattooed young man. He was feverish. "This is Tank, right?"

"Yes."

"Does he have a medical condition that you're aware of? Is he epileptic? Does he take drugs?"

"I don't know his medical history. We're not buddies, don't hang out together. If he does drugs, it's probably only pot."

"Then, we have a problem." Immediately, she corrected herself. "Another problem. I'm guessing that Tank is having an overdose from an amphetamine-based stimulant."

"And if he didn't take it himself, somebody gave it to him." Dylan caught on quickly. "Somebody else was here with him."

And it wasn't someone she wanted to meet.

Chapter Eighteen

Dylan knew just enough about drugs to understand that they weren't for him. He didn't think Tank was into the drug scene, but if he was, his drug of choice would be an amphetamine, an upper, speed.

He called to his brother, who had taken a position at the top of the staircase. "We got a problem."

"I heard," Sean said. "I've been in touch with Sheriff Swanson. His deputies are coming, and he's got an ambulance on the way."

"We're not far from the hospital in Buena Vista. They'll be here in a couple of minutes."

"I don't get it," Sean said. "If Koslov was here and gave your buddy Tank drugs, why did he leave? This A-frame is a neat setup for an ambush."

It didn't make sense. Koslov was famous for not leaving witnesses behind. Why had he given Tank drugs? Why hadn't he launched an ambush? Why were any of them still alive?

"He doesn't want us dead," Dylan said. "He wants Jayne. And he wants her in good shape. He's not going to come after us."

"Well, in case he changes his mind and we get into

a shoot-out, I want you down here with me by the stair-case. It's the only access to the second floor."

Glancing over his shoulder, Dylan saw that Tank's seizure was slowing down. Jayne had turned him on his side and elevated his head and shoulders. Through the earbud, Dylan heard her talking to Tank, asking his name, asking if he knew where he was.

"Is he saying anything?" Dylan asked.

"He's unresponsive," she said. "I hope the ambulance gets here before he crashes."

"Stay with him."

Dylan had the strong feeling that the only reason Tank was still alive was to pass on a message. Koslov had used the hacker as bait to lure them to this place, and his ploy had been successful. They were here. Why didn't Koslov attack?

It would have been simple for a sharpshooter to lie in wait, to kill Sean and Dylan and to grab Jayne. While Dylan listened to his brother talking to the 911 dispatcher and explaining that there was a potential danger in approaching the kayak shack, he rolled the scenario around in his mind. Why did Koslov hold back?

For one thing, Koslov didn't know who would show up at the shack. If Dylan had more time and had been more plugged in to the investigation in Denver, he might have sent Cisneros and kept Jayne safely tucked away at RSQ. Koslov wouldn't make an assault on a bunch of cops for no reason. He wanted Jayne.

And he didn't want her injured. That had to be the reason he hadn't opened fire when he and Sean had shown up with the prize Koslov had been seeking. He couldn't risk taking a shot at them and hurting Jayne. Why was it so important to keep from harming her?

Drug cartels weren't usually so considerate of the people they kidnapped. If they weren't deliberately cruel, they treated their captives with calculated disregard for their comfort. No food. No water. Captives would be held in wretched surroundings. He hated to imagine what would happen to a woman as beautiful as Jayne if her care and safety was left to the discretion of Koslov and his men.

Through the earbud, he heard Jayne soothing Tank as he tried to speak.

"Doc…tor. Jayne. Help. Me. Doc…tor."

"That's right," she murmured. "I'm Jayne, and I'm a doctor. And you need to relax as much as you can."

"Water," he said.

"The ambulance is going to be here in a moment. You can have water then."

Dylan gazed back toward them. Jayne stroked Tank's forehead with the damp washcloth, cooling his fever. At the same time, she had him wrapped in a blanket. He wasn't going to question her methods, but he wondered if she'd spent too much time poking at brains to remember basic first aid.

"You're shivering," she said. "Are you cold?"

"Cold, Doctor, cold."

Dylan heard the wail of the ambulance and wondered if Koslov was hearing it, too. The assassin wouldn't attack the local sheriff or the ambulance staff. There was no point, and shooting an officer would bring down the full force of Colorado law enforcement upon them. So much speculation—Dylan wished he had more answers.

When Sean went downstairs to let the crew into the

building, he moved to the center of the room and leaned over Jayne. "He hasn't said anything."

"He's cold and wants some water." She looked up at him. "Since the ambulance was close, I didn't want to give him anything to drink that his body might reject."

"You mean, he'd puke."

"Yes. I have no idea what kind of drug is invading his system. I looked around here and searched his pockets, couldn't find anything."

"Koslov drugged him," Dylan said.

"Like he did with me."

"You guessed it." He tucked the edge of the blanket around the shivering form of Tank Sherman. "Why are you dabbing his forehead to cool him down and covering him at the same time?"

"The blanket is for shock. The washcloth is for fever. Patience is the main caregiving procedure now. Until they know what he overdosed on, treatment is problematic. I don't want to make things worse for him."

When it came to medicine, she knew what she was doing. His job was to keep her safe.

JAYNE RODE IN the back of the ambulance with Tank and Dylan. It was too crowded, but she felt responsible for the skinny, tattooed hacker, and Dylan refused to leave her side. She couldn't fault his behavior—staying with her was what a bodyguard was supposed to do. And she'd miss him if he left. To be totally honest, she felt very comfortable around the macho version of Dylan, probably because there was still a lot of nerd in him. With one hand, he held a semiautomatic pistol. With the other, he pushed his glasses up on his nose.

At the Buena Vista hospital, she conferred with the

other docs, scrubbed up and joined them in the OR where Tank was on an IV and a breathing apparatus. The drug he'd been given had damaged his heart. Immediate bypass surgery was required.

Her greatest concern was, of course, his brain. Even a moment without blood circulation to the brain could cause irreparable damage. In the operating room, she observed with her gloved hands clenched behind her back so she wouldn't be tempted to interfere while Tank was hooked up to the cerebral-function monitor, a device to measure brain electricity. The neurologist at this small hospital was competent, someone she'd worked with before.

Through the observation window for the OR, she watched Dylan standing guard and remembered the last time they were in a hospital. Dylan wasn't moving. Sean came over to talk to him, and they stood with their heads together, no doubt discussing where her next safe house would be.

She wished they could go back to RSQ Ranch. As soon as that thought occurred, she recognized the irony. Her interest in the animal kingdom was minimal. As a child, she'd never really had a pet and wasn't interested in animals. But she would miss seeing the baby giraffe grow and riding Loretta the camel. There were horses in the RSQ corral that she hadn't met. And her fingers were itching to stroke the soft fur of Checkers the cat.

But that hideout was no longer a secret. Dylan knew the sheriff and his deputies, and they'd put together that he was both the owner of the RSQ Ranch and a bodyguard. If they returned, they might be bringing trouble with them, and she couldn't bear the thought that any of the animals might be hurt because of her.

She'd go wherever Dylan told her to go because she needed him to keep her safe. There were a hundred other reasons she wanted to be with him, starting with a desire to feel his lips pressed against hers.

The neurologist stepped up beside her in the OR and asked, "Is there anything we should be doing for this young man? In terms of his neural functions?"

"Not until after he's stabilized," she said quietly. "I'm sure there will be swelling of the brain and probably concussion. Before we loaded him in the ambulance, he was having a seizure, banging his head on the floor."

"Can I contact you later?"

"Certainly," she said. She didn't approve of Tank's lifestyle, using his intelligence to work on the outer fringes of what was legal and what wasn't. But she would never deny her expertise to anyone who needed help.

Since there was nothing she could do in the OR, she glanced toward the window where Dylan stood watching her. Though he wasn't carrying a weapon, he radiated protective strength and courage. If anybody got too close to her, her man would attack.

She patted the arm of the neurologist. "It was nice to meet you, Doctor."

"Same to you," he said. "Did you get the message?"

"What message?"

"The Sherman kid mumbled it several times, said the word message repeatedly. It was something about doctors and Martin."

Every other thought was wiped from her brain. She had a clean slate. She grasped his arm, "Come with me."

"If I take off my gown and mask, I'll have to scrub again and put on new stuff to go back into the OR."

As she pulled him into the hallway, she didn't care how many times he had to change clothes. She yanked down her own mask, then his. "This is very important. Tell me exactly what Sherman said, word for word."

"He repeated several variations on 'Dr. Jayne. Message. Jayne is a doctor.'"

She remembered when Koslov was holding her at the parking structure in the medical complex. His words were unclear, but she'd told him that as a doctor, she was obligated to come to the aid of anyone who needed her help. She would turn no one away.

Still clinging to his arm, she stared into the eyes of the neurologist. "What else did he say? Tell me as much as you can recall."

Dylan had come up behind her. "What is it, Jayne? What's wrong?"

"Hush," she said to him, keeping her focus on the neurologist. "Go on, Doctor, please."

"Help Martin. Martin needs you." He gestured helplessly. "And there was another name. Diego. That was it. Diego needs your help."

She released her grip on his arm and stepped backward until she was leaning against the wall. "Thank you."

Everything made sense to her now. She closed her eyes and inhaled a deep breath. From the very start when he'd broken into her house, Koslov had made it clear that he didn't want to hurt her. No matter what happened, she would not be harmed.

He needed her skill as a doctor. He wanted her to operate on his father, Diego Romero, an elderly man who had probably had a stroke.

She looked up at Dylan and said, "This was never about a kidnapping. It wasn't about my father. Martin Koslov was coming after me."

Chapter Nineteen

Dylan couldn't believe they'd been so blind. And he wasn't the only one. The professionals, like Cisneros and Agent Woody, had wasted their time tracking down connections to her rich, powerful father. They were so sure that it was a case of kidnapping, and they were so dead wrong.

"Can we get a diagnosis for Diego Romero?" he asked."

"We need proof that he's incapacitated."

"His doctor won't say anything."

"Why not?"

"I wouldn't," she said. "Information about patients is privileged. Plus, Romero is a powerful man, the leader of a cartel. If he was weakened, he wouldn't want his enemies to know."

Her reasoning was on track. If the old man was suffering the aftereffects of a stroke and had lost his memory, criminals from other cartels would take advantage. Not to mention, law enforcement moving in. The Romero organization would be picked apart.

Why did Martin Viktor Koslov want Jayne to bring back Romero's memory? Secrets, the old man had secrets. He'd run the cartel for over thirty years, knew who could be trusted and where the stash was hidden. Koslov—who was probably the old man's bastard son—might see these secrets as his inheritance. He needed Jayne and her groundbreaking neurosurgery to open Romero's memory.

He wrapped an arm around her shoulder. "You're safe now."

"How do you figure?"

"We get word to Koslov that you refuse to operate." He guided her through a set of double doors and down a corridor. "He won't have any reason to come after you."

"Who says I refuse to operate?"

"Believe me, Jayne. You don't want to help this man. He's violent, cruel, evil, altogether a bad guy." He started walking her down the corridor. "Nothing good can come from operating on the old man."

"Where are we going?"

He hadn't really come up with his next plan. Returning to the shelter didn't seem wise. Koslov might be clever enough to follow them. The thought of a cartel assassin at large in his gentle sanctuary horrified Dylan.

He and Sean had talked about returning to the hotel in Denver, but he wanted to stay close, to find out if there was anything more he could do for Tank. Dylan knew it wasn't his fault that Tank had gotten himself hooked up with Koslov, but he still felt responsible. In terms of chronological age, Tank was an adult. But he acted like a kid.

He glanced over at the beautiful woman who strode down the hallway beside him. "I need to take you somewhere safe."

"Too bad we can't stay here," she said with a grin. "I mean, the place is full of beds."

"Was that a joke? Are you being funny?"

"Giving it a shot."

He considered it a good sign that she was able to smile after all the threats to her. Discovering Koslov's true agenda was sort of a relief.

He came to a quick halt and pulled her close. Her pliant, slender body molded against his. Through the layers of shirts and jackets, he felt her firm breasts crush against his chest. His hand slid down the curve of her back.

His lips joined with hers for a hard, hot kiss. Her natural fragrance mingled with the leftover smell of the river outside the kayak shack and the hospital and the metallic scent of blood. Life experiences crowded around them and deepened their connection.

Jayne was more to him than a client or a woman who needed his help. She was becoming central to his life, and he wanted her always beside him. She balanced him. If she weren't here, he'd go spinning wildly of control.

The double doors behind them whooshed open. A loud, angry voice demanded, "What the hell are you doing, Jayne?"

Her father. Well, of course. Dylan separated himself from her. They'd been so tightly joined that pulling apart felt like tearing Velcro.

"Hi, Dad," she said. "And you, too, Javi. Would you like to hear what we've figured out?"

"Let me go first," said Peter the Great. "Dylan Timmons, you're fired."

"You can't do that," she said. "He works for me, not you."

"I'm not firing him because of this." He gestured toward the two of them standing close. "I get it. You're an attractive young woman, and men have a hard time keeping their hands off you."

She drew herself up. Her posture was ramrod straight. "Thanks, Dad, for the charming description."

Peter the Great was not cowed by her sarcasm. He thrust out his barrel chest. His resonant voice dropped an octave; he sounded like Darth Vader without the wheezing. "Dylan and his brother, Sean, took you into a dangerous situation. It was an irresponsible act. You could have been killed."

"I was never in danger," she said coolly. "We were able to rescue Sherman, and he had valuable information for the police."

"You can tell Agent Woodward when he gets here. After he takes a statement from Dylan and his brother, they will be dismissed. You will go with Woodward into protective custody, WitSec."

"Do you even care about solving this?" she demanded.

"I care about you." He jabbed the air between them with a forefinger. "I care about your safety."

"What about the truth? Do you care about the truth?"

"Of course, I do."

"Then listen to me," she said. "We all thought the attack by Koslov was about you. Peter the Great Shackleford is so important that a cartel sent an assassin to abduct his helpless daughter to make him change his mind about some kind of business dealing."

"And I'm sorry," he said. "How many times do you have to hear it, Jayne?"

"Never again." Her blue eyes went icy cold. "I never needed to hear it in the first place. Koslov was after a world-renowned neurosurgeon to operate on his father. He was after me."

Dylan heard a strange note of triumph in her statement. He doubted that she often got to tell her father that she was more prized and more important than he was. Being the target of a murderous Venezuelan cartel wasn't the sort of success to brag about, but it was something.

Agent Woody saved them from further awkwardness when he shoved through the doors. Another agent, also dressed in suit and necktie, accompanied him.

Both Jayne and her father went toward Woody. Both were talking without pause. Both gestured dramatically as they stated their opinions about what should happen next. Neither hesitated in telling Special agent Woody exactly what the FBI needed to do.

The father-daughter resemblance was inescapable. The Shacklefords were a hard-driving family, and Dylan was pleased to see that Jayne was winning the battle for Woody's attention. The other agent was listening only to her and nodding like an FBI bobblehead.

When she mentioned Diego Romero's need for the neurosurgery that only she could provide, Dylan saw Woody's eyes light up. The agent held up his hand for silence. He spoke to Jayne. "Are you saying that Diego Romero is in the United States? That he's nearby?"

"I don't know," she said. "It's unlikely that a sick, old man like Romero would travel. It'd be easier to kidnap me and take me to Venezuela."

"If there's a chance that Romero is here," Woody said, "I need to take advantage of it. I need to coordinate with other agencies."

"Think about it," Dylan said. "Not only does he need Jayne to perform the surgery, but he also needs all that specialized equipment. You saw the operating theater. You know what it's like."

"What do you think, Doctor?" He turned back to Jayne. "Would most hospitals have the necessary equipment?"

"It's hard to say. MRIs and CT scanners are pretty much standard, but my work requires extremely delicate electro-imaging equipment. And how would Koslov gain access? I seriously doubt that a dangerous assassin can waltz into a hospital and commandeer an operating room."

"Right," her father said. "So, we can assume that Koslov plans to kidnap Jayne and take her to Venezuela where she can operate."

Peter the Great seemed proud of himself for drawing this conclusion. Dylan almost hated shooting it down. "Except for one thing."

"What's that?" her father turned on him.

"Koslov could have already purchased the equipment he needs. He could have created an operating room in a house or a hotel room or a clinic. Diego Romero could be there, under a nurse's care, waiting."

Peter Shackleford blustered, "How would he know what to get?"

"My work isn't secretive," Jayne explained. "I've done a lot to publicize my procedures. I want other neurosurgeons to adopt and improve upon my methods."

Her motives were simple and pure as opposed to the

devilish complexities of Koslov and the Romero cartel. Jayne worked for the greater good. Sure, she was gratified when her skill and talent was recognized, but she hadn't become a neurosurgeon for the acclaim.

She didn't deserve to be stuck in the middle of this mess. She wasn't safe, and it was up to him to take her away from the hospital and get her to somewhere safe. He hooked his arm through hers. "We're going now. My brother has a car by the emergency entrance."

"Sorry." Woody blocked their way. "I have more questions for all of you, including your brother."

"Jayne needs to be in a safe house."

"Agreed," Woody said. "This won't take long."

As Woody and his partner whisked Jayne down the hall and away from the rest of them, Dylan caught her gaze. He pointed to his ear where he wore the tiny, near invisible earbud. Did she still have hers?

She touched her ear and nodded. She'd be able to hear him.

Chapter Twenty

Though accompanied by the feds, Jayne managed to apologize to the staff at Buena Vista hospital half-a-dozen times for disrupting their ER, OR and admissions area. Sheriff Swanson and two of his deputies herded the various groups from one room to the next until Jayne and the two FBI agents were settled in the social worker's office in the admissions area.

A nameplate on the messy desk identified Grace McHenry, and Jayne had a feeling that Grace wasn't going to be happy about the way Agent Woody took over her office and scooped her papers out of the way.

"I don't think you should move those," she said.

"This is chaos. I have to move something." He turned on a small recorder, stated his name and hers and their location and the time. It was all very official, and she stayed on point as she described how they had learned about Tank and his whereabouts, then left their safe house.

"Where is it?" Woody asked. "I need a location on the safe house."

"I don't feel right about telling you." She didn't want Woody and the feds charging through RSQ Ranch, disturbing the cats, goats and camels. "You'll have to ask Dylan."

"Continue," he said.

As best she could, she explained what had happened when they got to the kayak shack. She probably shouldn't have left the vehicle. But if she hadn't, Tank might not have made it.

"That's when Dylan should have called," he said. "I should have been part of that bust at the kayak shack."

"Dylan didn't want it to be a bust and neither did I. Tank was helping us voluntarily. It doesn't seem right for him to be arrested for that."

"He won't be," Woody said. "He'll be arrested for hacking into an NSA database last month."

"If he survives," she said darkly. While she had been apologizing to the Buena Vista staff, she'd gotten an update on Tank's condition. After his surgery, which had gone well, Tank was in an induced coma. Tomorrow, they would wake him.

"He'll be fine."

"I'm hiring an attorney for him," she said. "You can't ask questions until the attorney is in place."

"You haven't been a whole lot of help, Doctor."

"Nor have you," she said. "May I ask a question?"

"Go ahead."

"If I operate on Diego Romero and make it possible for him to regain his memory, am I breaking any laws?"

"Why the hell would you want to do that?"

"I'm a doctor," she said. "It's my job to cure my patients, not to judge them. If Koslov had come to me and asked for my assistance, I might have gone along with his plan."

The door to Grace McHenry's office crashed open. Dylan stood facing them. His tone was serious. "You can't operate. Don't even think about it."

"Why not?"

"Diego Romero isn't like anyone you've ever met. He doesn't operate by the same standards of right and wrong. Don't make me run through the whole litany of terrible things he's done. Help me, Woody."

"What are you doing in here?" Woody stood behind the desk. "Were you eavesdropping?"

Dylan removed his earbud. "Jayne has one of these. It transmits both ways."

Jayne touched her ear. "My receiver is turned off. I couldn't hear him, but he heard me."

"Obviously."

She stood and faced Dylan. "You see the differences in Diego Romero. I see the similarities. His heart pumps the same way yours does…or mine. His brain is constructed the same way."

"If he were dead, the world would be a better place."

"That's not your call," she said. "As a doctor, I don't get to decide who lives and who dies. It's my job to patch people up and send them on their way."

Dylan came toward her. Totally disregarding Agent Woody, he embraced her. "I agree with you in theory, Jayne. I really do, but I don't want anything bad to happen to you. Romero doesn't leave witnesses. He'll kill you."

"Not if I save his life," she said.

"He won't care. As soon as you're done with him, you're a dead woman."

The smooth, handsome Javier Flores rushed through the door. Her dad was right behind him.

Javier said, "We must go. Koslov has been sighted at the hospital."

Her father grasped her wrist, attempting to literally drag her away from Dylan. "Seriously," he growled, "we're all in danger."

"Stop it." Woody waved his arms. "Everyone settle down."

Then she heard the echo of gunfire from down the hall.

Dylan couldn't tell where the shots were coming from. There was a lot of firepower at the Buena Vista hospital, including Sheriff Swanson and his deputies and the federal agents and his brother, Sean. Their presence didn't seem to deter the assault from Koslov and his men.

He would have liked to grab Jayne's hand and run for cover, but they encountered resistance at every turn. The sheriff's men directed them toward a supposedly safe exit. Her father clung to her. The two of them had a lot to clean up, but that conversation was more suited to a psychotherapist's office than a gun battle in a hospital.

Through his earbud, Dylan heard his brother's voice. "Don't come to the ER entrance. Koslov and his men are coming in through these doors."

Their "supposedly safe exit" had been compromised. He separated Jayne from the others and guided her into the OR and recovery unit, which was now deserted. For the moment, they were alone.

"There's something I need to tell you," he said.

He didn't lift his gaze, didn't look into her eyes, and he realized that he was scared about how she'd respond. Ironic! They faced real-life bullets, the kind that can kill, and he was afraid of what she'd say to him, how she could hurt him.

"What is it, Dylan?"

"I quit."

She stopped dead in her tracks. "You picked a real bad time to tell me you're not going to be my body-guard."

"Not what I meant." He pivoted to face her. "I quit because I don't want to work for you. We need to be equals…as much as we can be."

"I haven't been treating you like an employee," she huffed. "I don't sleep with my employees."

"Not what I meant…again."

The pop-pop-pop of gunfire became clearer. It seemed like the shooters were just outside the recovery unit. And they were looking for her. Jayne was the object of their search.

He had to get her to safety. Adrenaline flooded his brain and gave him clarity. He grasped her hand and gave a light tug. As they went forward, he spoke in a calm voice.

"Equals," he said, "in terms of what we both bring to the table. We both have money. We're both successful. The sex is good."

"Yes, the sex is very good."

He admitted, "I'm fairly sure that you're smarter than I am, but that can't be helped."

Determining their route purely by instinct, he went left at one corner, then right at the next. Much of their time together had been spent chasing through corridors and staircases. He was beginning to feel like a rat in a maze or one of those cartoon characters in early video games that hopped from one area to another.

He'd spent hours playing those games. Given all that time, he ought to be better at this.

She stopped to catch her breath and looked up at him. "I can't believe we're having a relationship discussion right now."

"This might be the perfect time." Most guys, like him, believed that gunfire made appropriate background noise for a talk about their relationship.

"Well, you're right. You and I are very well matched."

"Live with me, Jayne. At my house in Denver."

"Until the danger is over?"

"I was thinking of something more permanent."

It was too soon to make this kind of commitment. But in a flash of adrenaline-fueled intelligence, he saw himself standing beside her with two small children—their children—playing in the yard. They were such a perfect fit.

"We agree on one thing," she said. "I don't want you to be my bodyguard." She twisted her head, looking toward the door. "I want you out of the bodyguard business, entirely."

"What? Why?"

She gestured angrily in the direction of the gunfire. "Danger, I don't want you to be in danger."

"What about my brother? What about Mason? I can't just leave TST Security in the lurch."

"They're big boys. They can take care of themselves. You don't need this job. You've already made a fortune with your computer games and designs. That's where your real interest lies."

She had a point, but there was no way he'd abandon his brother and his best friend. He could work something out, figure a way around her demand. *A demand?* Where did she get off making demands on him?

A loud burst of gunfire outside the door alerted him. They needed to change position. Exiting through the other door into this area, they charged down a narrow corridor that ended at a door. Other doors along the way were closed.

He jiggled the handle; it was locked. The sign outside the door indicated that this was an entrance to the pharmacy. Dylan picked the lock and they slipped into the darkened room, carefully walking past shelves stocked with all manner of bottles and containers. The front wall of the pharmacy was reinforced windows from the waist to ceiling with the blinds drawn. At the far left was a windowed door with a wide counter for picking up prescriptions.

He peered over the edge of the counter and lifted the blind so he could see. He was looking into the main entrance lobby and waiting area.

They ducked beneath the counter. In the shadows, he could see only a faint outline of her face and her long hair. He pushed his glasses up on his nose. "Will you move in with me, Jayne?"

"I have a house, and I'm only halfway through renovations."

"You'll like my place. I have a home gym, a couple of offices, outdoor barbecue..." He stopped himself before he got into square footage and number of bathrooms. He sounded like a real estate agent. "This isn't about where we live. Only that we're together."

Her fingers clenched around his. "Are you asking me to marry you?"

He'd been trying to avoid using that specific term. "Not really… This is more about living together."

"Oh, Dylan, I don't know. I can't say."

"If you want to be together, we can work out the details."

"Details first," she said. "I won't let you railroad me. I still have a lot I want to do in my career."

"I won't stop you. I'm proud of you."

He heard a disturbance in the area outside the pharmacy window. Peeking over the ledge, he saw several people dressed in scrubs racing across the lobby. Evacuation was under way.

Moments later, he saw two men in camouflage fatigues. Their boots pounded on the smooth vinyl flooring. They were jogging in formation. How many were there? Had Koslov recruited an army?

Through his earbud, he communicated with Sean. "We need an exit strategy."

His brother replied immediately, "I got separated from the vehicle. I suggest you try to get a ride with somebody else."

"Got it," Dylan said.

She gave him a puzzled look. "What?"

"I was talking to my brother on the earbud."

She reached for her own ear. "I don't know how you keep those things straight with me in one ear and your brother in the other."

When she started to remove her earbud, he stopped her. "Keep it in. Might come in handy to be able to hear you when you're three hundred yards away."

"Why? I have it turned off."

"But I can still hear you, and I like being inside your ear." He cupped her chin, leaned forward and kissed her. After all they'd been through tonight, she still smelled good, and her lips were as soft as rose petals.

He separated from her and sat with his back against the door under the counter. "My timing sucks."

"Yeah, it kind of does."

He frowned. "By the by, there's no way in hell I'd quit my job just because you tell me to."

"And I refuse to leave my house until I'm ready." A tiny smile lifted the corner of her mouth. "It's always going to be like this between us. We've both got busy lives, full lives with very little extra time."

He heard someone approaching and peeked over the window ledge. "It's your dad and Javier. I'm going to call them over."

"Why?" She groaned. "I don't want to go with them."

"Sean can't get to our SUV. Your dad might be your best way out of here."

"Let me stay with you."

"Too dangerous." He stood, pulled up the blinds that had been covering the window and rapped on the glass. When he had Javier's attention, he got the lock on the door unfastened.

Javier caught hold of Jayne's upper arm. "Come with us. We have a vehicle."

That was all Dylan needed to hear. He stepped back into the shadows and watched as she was pulled away from him.

She turned back toward him. "I'll talk to you later."

"Count on it."

Chapter Twenty-One

Held between her father and Javier Flores, Jayne ran for the exit. She wished that Dylan was here. Without him, she felt unprotected. Had Javier checked to make sure none of Koslov's army were waiting for them in the lobby? Was he armed? She knew her dad had a pistol in his pocket. Years ago, he'd gotten a "concealed carry" permit.

They ran down a short sidewalk and jumped into a vehicle. Javi and her father got in back. She was in the passenger seat. The driver had his jacket collar turned up and wore his baseball cap low on his forehead.

Not much of a disguise. She recognized him. "Koslov."

Panic flared behind her eyelids. Her nervous systems went on high alert. Her brain told her to leap from the moving vehicle and run to safety. But she was paralyzed, every muscle clenched.

She turned and looked into the backseat. Her father had passed out and slumped unconscious against the door. Javier Flores had a gun aimed in her direction.

"What did you do to him?"

"I administered an injection to make him sleep," Javi said. "I have no intention of harming your father though he has profited greatly from dealings with my family. It's just business. I've taken my share from him."

She'd thought it was odd for him to be tagging along throughout their cat-and-mouse game, running here and running there. A bulwark of anger rose up and blocked her fear and the panicky feelings of helplessness. Javier Flores had betrayed her father and led him into the hands of his enemies. "What are you after?"

"I want you to perform your miracle surgery and bring back the memory of Diego Romero."

"Why?"

"Somewhere in those lost memories are people and places and numbers for bank accounts that are important to certain members of my family."

If she hadn't been so furious, she would have laughed. Among the details the old man had forgotten were the pieces needed to access the ill-gotten gains of Javier's family…locations of safe-deposit boxes, account numbers, portfolio information. It would serve Javier right if the old man never recalled that particular data.

Turning in the seat, she stared through the windshield. She knew who was really in charge here—the man driving the car. "You finally have me, Koslov. What do you want me to do?"

"I don't want to hurt you," he said in his oddly accented voice. "I could have killed you and your boyfriend several times, but I didn't. I could have killed the hacker, Sherman. But that didn't happen. All I ask of you is to heal my father."

"Diego Romero is your father?"

"Yes, and my mother was Elena Petrovski, an exotic Russian beauty. I am named Koslov after an uncle."

A strange way to talk about his mother, but she guessed Koslov had a lot of psychotic, weird problems when it came to family and relationships. "Your accent," she said. "Is it partly Russian?"

"My mother's influence. Her photograph, taken in the nightclub where she worked, still makes my father smile. After his stroke, he lost memory of almost everything else. I want you to operate on him."

"You asked me this before," she said, half-remembering their conversation in the parking structure.

"And you agreed to operate. You said that you are a doctor, and doctors are obligated to help whenever they can. You will cure him."

She wasn't sure what would happen, but she was afraid that Dylan had called it correctly when he'd said that Koslov would kill her—and now her father, too—when he no longer had a use for her.

"I'll do my best," she said.

At TEN MINUTES past three o'clock in the morning, the conference room in the Buena Vista sheriff's office was filled with law-enforcement personnel: cops, feds and deputies. Dylan had taken a position near a table at the rear exit where a forty-two-cup stainless-steel coffeemaker belched steam and squirted a dark, slightly filmy liquid into disposable cups. He stared toward the front of the room, where Jayne's father leaned his elbows on a podium.

Peter the Great looked like hell. He'd aged twenty years in twenty minutes. The collar on his shirt was open. His necktie hung loose. His suit was rumpled, and his perfectly trimmed hair stood out in messy clumps. His eyes looked like he hadn't slept in weeks. According to Sheriff Swanson, Peter had stumbled onto a porch at the north end of town and hammered at the door until the family inside responded. They called the police and a patrol car picked him up.

Swanson introduced him and asked for questions.

One of the officers called out, "You were in the vehicle with Koslov. Did he say where he was going?"

"I was drugged," Shackleford said wearily. "I don't remember much."

"Who is Javier Flores?"

"I thought he was my friend. I knew him and his family because we're all involved in the Venezuelan oil business." His mouth tensed as he fought back tears. "I'm not a hundred percent sure, but I think Javi gave me an injection in the thigh. Everything went blank."

Sheriff Swanson added, "We are operating under the theory that Javier Flores is working with Koslov."

"They have my daughter." Shackleford's voice cracked. "The only thing I can tell you that might be useful is that she agreed to do neurosurgery on Diego Romero. The operation takes five hours. That's all the time we have to find her."

"Unless Koslov has already taken her out of town," the sheriff said as he took the podium and gestured for Peter to sit. "The airports, including private facilities for small planes, were immediately shut down."

Dylan hoped they'd acted in time. If Jayne was in the air, on her way to Caracas, there wasn't much he could do to find her. The sheriff and his men had verified that the local hospitals and clinics were not being used for the surgery on Romero. Highway surveillance cameras had been activated.

In three hours, it would be dawn. That was when Agent Woody and the feds could start helicopter sweeps of the area. Dylan figured the overhead surveillance would be their best chance. Koslov must have set up a clinic in a house or cabin. But how would he know that they'd be in this area? Koslov didn't know about RSQ Ranch. Why would he establish his operating theater nearby?

Sean nudged his shoulder. "Let's get out of here before somebody gives us a time-wasting assignment."

"The way I figure," Dylan said, "Koslov assembled the operating room in a motorhome or in the rear of a semitrailer. That way, he wasn't tied to a location."

"You need coffee," his brother said. "Real coffee, not this swill."

"I need Jayne. How could I have let her go?"

"You got played, little brother. It happens. Even to geniuses like you and Jayne. That Javier guy probably had Jayne's dad running all over the hospital, looking for her. When they found her, you did what you thought was best."

Dylan hated being wrong. He went into an adjoining room to check on the network of computer surveillance that was searching for any sign of Jayne, such as using a credit card or a phone. A deputy and a fed were assigned to that job. Both were competent. They weren't Tank, but they'd do okay.

Sean gave him a shove. "We're going. Now."

"But what if…"

"Leave this end of the search to the sheriff and

Woody. They're bureaucrats. They know how to do this stuff."

"You're right." Pacing up and down these corridors was making him crazy.

IN THE CAR, Sean drove. He headed back toward Denver, which was the opposite direction of most of the other searchers. The night began to thin. Stars faded, and the half-moon disappeared.

"When you interrogated that guy," Dylan said, "how could you be sure he was telling the truth?"

Woody had taken advantage of Sean's FBI training in profiling and questioning suspects. He used Sean to interview one of Koslov's men who had been injured and hadn't escaped with the others.

Without bragging, Sean said, "I'm pretty good at interrogation. And I only had one thing I needed to find out—if they were going to take Jayne on a plane."

"How did you get him to talk?"

"He's a paid mercenary and doesn't have any grand ideals he's hanging on to. I didn't hurt him. Torture isn't my style. But I didn't give him the pain meds, either. And I might have hinted about how he was going to lose his leg if I didn't let the doctor see him."

"Sounds like the way you'd question me when we were kids."

"Natural talent," his brother said. "Anyway, this guy babbled and doubled back and made a lot of mistakes. Taking her away on an airplane wasn't part of the plan. I guarantee that the old man—Diego Romero himself—is here in Colorado."

"Waiting for Jayne."

The search for a decent cup of coffee led them to

one of the more expensive lodges in town. Sean drove down a winding road, then another, then another. He tried to find areas with wide overlooks where they could stop and scan the valley.

The sun was up, and the minutes were ticking down. Dylan figured they only had an hour and a half before she'd be done with the surgery.

Sean asked, "Are you in love with her?"

"I'm afraid so." He scanned the landscape outside the windows, using the binoculars when something looked promising. "I asked her to move in with me. She said no."

"Are you going to let that stop you?"

"Hell, no."

He would get her back. He had to bring her back to him. And he would never let her go. They rounded another curve and… Dylan heard a crackle in his ear. The bud was coming to life. He glanced at Sean. "Did you hear that?"

"Jayne must have figured out how to turn it on."

"I think it's been on all the time. We were too far away to pick up the signal. Transmissions in the mountains are tricky."

But the bud was transmitting now.

Chapter Twenty-Two

The thread of sound connecting them gave Dylan fresh hope. He hadn't given up on finding them, but the odds had been stacked against them. He'd never let her go again. Whatever it took, they would be together.

He heard Jayne clearly as she said, "I'll close his skull. In about an hour, I should know if the operation was a success."

The next voice was that of Javier Flores. "Can he talk now? Can he answer questions?"

Jane spoke up. "I have to ask you to step away from the enclosed area. Your clothes aren't sanitized."

A weak voice spoke a stream of Spanish that Dylan knew was peppered with profanity. He murmured, "That must be the old man."

"One question," Javier said, "just one question. I need to know the name of the bank with the safe-deposit box. That's where this old dog stashed the codes to accounts filled with my family's money."

That explained why Javier was so involved in retrieving Romero's memories.

He heard Jayne speaking in Spanish, asking Romero if he had anything he wanted to say to Javier. There was a mumble, then Jayne translated. "He says you should go to the devil."

He wished that she could give them a clue as to where she was. He heard the beeping and buzzing of the many machines in the background and remembered her doing this surgery in Denver.

Another voice intruded, "Get away from my father, Flores."

It was Koslov.

Sean drove to the left at a fork in the road. "Talk to her, Dylan. Maybe she can hear you."

That obvious thought hadn't even occurred to him. He'd been so thrilled to hear her voice that his brain had disconnected. "Jayne," he whispered, "it's Dylan. If you can hear me, say morning."

Her response was immediate. "Wonder what the weather will be like this morning?"

He asked, "Where are you?"

"You know, Koslov, I still can't help but marvel at what you've done here. You turned this ugly white motor home into a traveling neurosurgery center. Will you leave it here for me? I could help so many people with this."

"When will you be finished?" Koslov asked.

"Like I said, in about an hour I'll be able to tell if the operation was a success."

There were rustling noises, and he imagined her taking off her sterile gown and gloves.

Sean pulled onto the gravelly shoulder of the two-lane mountain road. Their SUV was at a high point. Sean took the binoculars, climbed out of the car and scanned the rocky ridges and thick forests below. He pointed. "Can you see it? A white-and-gold motor home with the sun glaring off the side?"

"Jayne," Dylan said, "we're going to get you out of there. Be ready. I'm signing off for a few minutes, but don't worry. I'll be back."

He adjusted his earbud so he could hear her but she couldn't hear him, and he motioned for his brother to do the same. For a long moment, they stood side by side in front of the SUV, squinting into the rising sun at the faraway reflection off the motor home where Jayne was being held.

"We found her," Sean said.

"Damn right, we did."

Dylan let go with a wild cheer, Sean did the same, and they threw their arms around each other. Everything was going to be all right.

Sean broke contact. "Koslov had an army when he came through the hospital. We need to find them, and arrange for backup."

"There's only one thing I'm worried about," Dylan said. "How do I get Jayne out of that tin can? As long as she's trapped in there with Koslov, Javi and the old man, she's in danger."

"You'll figure it out," his brother said. "It's a matter of mechanics, plays right into your talents."

He was right. Dylan had been training all his life for a moment like this when he had to figure out how to steal the princess from the trolls in their fortress.

He remembered all the machines in Jayne's operating theater. Likewise, the motor home OR needed a power source, a generator and something to regulate the temperature and humidity. That plain-looking motor home had been customized. There had to be a way for Dylan to break in and rescue Jayne.

Rushing back to the car, he issued instructions. "Take me as close to the motor home as you can without being seen. Then you go back and coordinate everything with the backup."

"What are you going to do?"

"Protect Jayne."

THE INTERIOR OF the motor home was surprisingly spacious. There was room for Jayne and all of her neurosurgery equipment at the rear. In the center section, there was a bed where Romero was resting and recovering. A small table and chairs were arranged near the steering wheel. The windows were completely blanked out. No one could see in or out. If she'd been afflicted with claustrophobia, she never would have been able to function in this space.

But she'd performed well, better than she'd expected. In the usual course of a long operation like this, she took breaks when other docs and specialists were checking and referencing MRIs and other material. Today's surgery was nonstop except for one pause when she'd insisted on stretching and hydrating. She would have liked a walk, but Koslov wouldn't let her leave the motor home; she feared she would never see daylight again.

Sitting at the table with Javi opposite her and Koslov behind him, she tried to lift her teacup. No use. Her fingers were trembling too much.

"Something wrong?" Javi asked. He turned his arm so he could see the face of his gold wristwatch. "We have thirty-nine minutes to go."

Not if Dylan could rescue her first. "Then what?" she asked. "If the operation is a success, what happens to me?"

"I can't exactly set you free," Javi said. "I might be able to talk my way out of the situation, claiming I was captured by Koslov and Romero. You are, unfortunately, an eye witness."

"I won't say anything," she said. "I promise."

"There's no need to beg for your life," he said with a sneer. "My decision is already made."

Koslov cleared his throat. "I make the decisions. Not you."

A slight twitch at the corner of Javi's eye betrayed his fear of the assassin. Koslov was the alpha wolf; he didn't need to say much or make threats. Danger oozed from him. If she hoped for any sort of concession, he was the one she ought to negotiate with.

"I saved your father," she said. "That must count for something."

Javi corrected her. "His life wasn't in danger."

"But his memory was lost," she said. "My surgery helped him. What do you think, Koslov?"

"You're a strange woman."

"Maybe you could donate all this equipment to me and my hospital," she suggested. "Or arrange for me to travel to Venezuela to consult with neurosurgeons there."

Javi held up his fancy gold watch. "Twenty-two minutes left."

Hurry, Dylan, hurry. She didn't know how long she could stall. She assumed that he and Sean had gone to get backup. Koslov had several other men, but she didn't know where they were. They could be surrounding the motor home or could be sleeping. In the meantime, her life was measured by the tick-tick-tick of the second hand on Javi's fancy watch.

"I could be your father's nurse," she offered.

"You're overqualified."

Great! She'd finally found a man who appreciated

her skills, and he was getting ready to kill her. "I'll do whatever you want."

Koslov rose and walked toward her. When he placed his hand on her shoulder, she fought the urge to flinch. He leaned close to her ear. In his strangely accented voice, he said, "I promise you a fast death. You won't feel a thing."

All the fear she'd been holding in check gushed through her. Her heart shattered. Her bones melted. If she hadn't heard a crackle in her ear, she would have come completely undone.

Abruptly, she stood. Jayne didn't want to take a chance on having Koslov hear a sound from the earbud.

"Jayne." Dylan's voice was a whisper. "Go to the back of the motor home. As far back as you can go on the driver's side."

She snapped her fingers as though remembering a detail. "There are a few readouts I need to check. Then I'll do the final tests on your father."

"I'm impressed," Javi said, "with how professional you are. You're showing no fear."

"Maybe I can't believe you're going to hurt me after I did such a good job," she said. "Maybe I think there's still something good and ethical in you."

"Really?"

Not at all, not a bit. She truly believed that these three men were evil. Dylan had warned her from the start. "Maybe."

As she passed through the middle section, Diego Romero gave her a weak smile. Koslov followed her. He eyed her suspiciously.

When she reached the back of the motor home, she picked up a readout of neuromuscular activity and followed the center line with her finger. "Here I am," she said so Dylan would know. "Back in the corner with my readouts."

Koslov stopped at the edge of the back section. "What are you doing?"

"I wanted to make a quick check on the interface between the neural olfactory and the limbic systems." She tossed out a few more terms that she hoped he didn't understand.

In her ear, Dylan said, "When I tell you, I want you to duck down."

Javi stepped up behind Koslov, watching and listening. He glanced down at the old man in the bed. In Spanish, he asked the location of the safe-deposit box for the funds of the Flores family.

Without hesitation, Romero said, *"Banco Federal Caracas."*

Javi laughed as he took his gun from the side holster under his jacket. "I'm done. Don't have to stick around."

Quick as a rattlesnake, Koslov whipped out his Glock and fired one bullet into the center of Javi's forehead. A mist of blood and matter surrounded Javi's skull before his legs crumpled.

"Duck!"

The lights in the motor home went out.

Darkness covered her. Jayne sank into a crouch.

Before she had a chance to react, she felt Dylan's hands on her arms. Though she couldn't see, she knew it was him. She recognized his touch and his scent as he dragged her backward. The machine that had been against the wall was gone and they were sliding into a luggage compartment, packed tightly with a generator and air-conditioning equipment.

When the lights in her house had been cut, she'd

been terrified. This was different. This time, she blessed the darkness that would help her escape.

When Dylan flipped open the door to the compartment, the morning sunlight blinded her. She staggered to her feet.

He grasped her hand. "Run."

As they dashed through the tall grasses toward the forest, she heard gunfire. She saw Koslov's men taking aim and firing at the sheriff, the deputies, the police and others. And she imagined bullets whizzing past them, barely missing. When she and Dylan hit the forest, he pulled her into the shelter of the trees and embraced her.

"You're safe now," he said. "I've got you."

Though not aware of crying, her cheeks were damp. And she was tired, so tired that she felt limp. "I can't stand up, can't stand."

"No problem." He lowered them to the ground, leaned his back against a rock and held her.

"This feels like heaven," she said. "How did you figure out how to get me?"

"I'm the guy," he said. "I can fix any security system and that goes double for motor homes rigged to generators."

"That's right. When we first met, you promised a repair job at my house."

"If you're still planning to live there."

She gazed into his warm gray eyes. "My house or yours. Wherever we stay, I want to be together."

"Living together," he said.

"Isn't that what people do when they're in love?"

"I love you, Jayne."

A few moments ago, she'd expected to be dead. And now…he loved her. And she felt the same way about him. She snuggled closer in his arms, aware that the battle had gone quiet.

She exhaled a sigh. "I guess we should report in and let people know we're okay."

He helped her stand and offered his arm for her to lean on. She gestured him away, not wanting to show that she couldn't support herself.

Dylan's brother came toward them. After he gave her a hug, he reported, "Only a few injuries on our side. Koslov and his men are in custody, several are injured. Javier Flores is dead."

"What about Romero?" she asked.

"He's in good shape, and he's a regular chatterbox. The FBI is all over him."

She recognized a voice and turned toward it. "Dad?"

He held his arms open. "I have a lot to apologize for."

"Yes." Damn right he had a lot to be sorry for, starting with firing Dylan and ending with turning her over to Koslov. She wrapped her arms around him. It was better not to dwell in the past. "Let's start fresh."

"You've got it, sweetheart."

She looked her father in the eye. "Dylan and I are moving in together."

Peter the Great swallowed hard. "Do you love him?"

"So very, very much."

"You've got my blessing."

She slipped back into Dylan's waiting arms. This was all the shelter she would ever need.

* * * * *

MILLS & BOON®

INTRIGUE
Romantic Suspense

A SEDUCTIVE COMBINATION OF DANGER AND DESIRE

A sneak peek at next month's titles...

In stores from 15th December 2016:

- **Riding Shotgun** – Joanna Wayne *and*
  Stone Cold Texas Ranger – Nicole Helm
- **One Tough Texan** – Barb Han *and*
  Battle Tested – Janie Crouch
- **Turquoise Guardian** – Jenna Kernan *and*
  San Antonio Secret – Robin Perini

Romantic Suspense

- **Undercover in Conard County** – Rachel Lee
- **Dr. Do-or-Die** – Lara Lacombe

1216/46

MILLS & BOON®

Why shop at millsandboon.co.uk?

Each year, thousands of romance readers find their perfect read at millsandboon.co.uk. That's because we're passionate about bringing you the very best romantic fiction. Here are some of the advantages of shopping at www.millsandboon.co.uk:

* **Get new books first**—you'll be able to buy your favourite books one month before they hit the shops

* **Get exclusive discounts**—you'll also be able to buy our specially created monthly collections, with up to 50% off the RRP

* **Find your favourite authors**—latest news, interviews and new releases for all your favourite authors and series on our website, plus ideas for what to try next

* **Join in**—once you've bought your favourite books, don't forget to register with us to rate, review and join in the discussions

Visit **www.millsandboon.co.uk**
for all this and more today!